An Awakening of Fates

An Awakening of Fates

The Awakening: Book One

Nicole Sessions

This is a work of fiction. All characters, locations, and events are creations of the author. Any similarities to real events, locations, or people, living or dead are entirely coincidental and unintentional. AI was not used to create any part of this book. As such, no part of this book may be used in any manner for the purposes of training or enhancing AI.

Cover art by Hannarchy Studios

Map by Manolis Karavidas

Editing by ImmyGrace

ISBN-13: 979-8-9957194-0-3 (paperback)

ISBN-13: 979-8-9957194-1-0 (ebook)

Dedication

To you. You are the strength that someone else looks up to. Even when you feel your weakest, someone else sees the incredible strength you possess to put one foot in front of another. Always remember you are a strong, badass bitch, and one day you will conquer everything.

To me. Because I am a strong, badass bitch and this is me conquering my insecurities. This is me telling everyone who ever said I wasn't good enough, that they can shove it. Because I love me and I am enough

Content Warning:

This book contains references to domestic violence which is told in flashbacks. The descriptions are not detailed but they are there. If you or someone you know is a victim of domestic violence, please know you are not alone. There are resources available to you and you can get free.

The National Domestic Violence hotline is 1-800-799-7233.

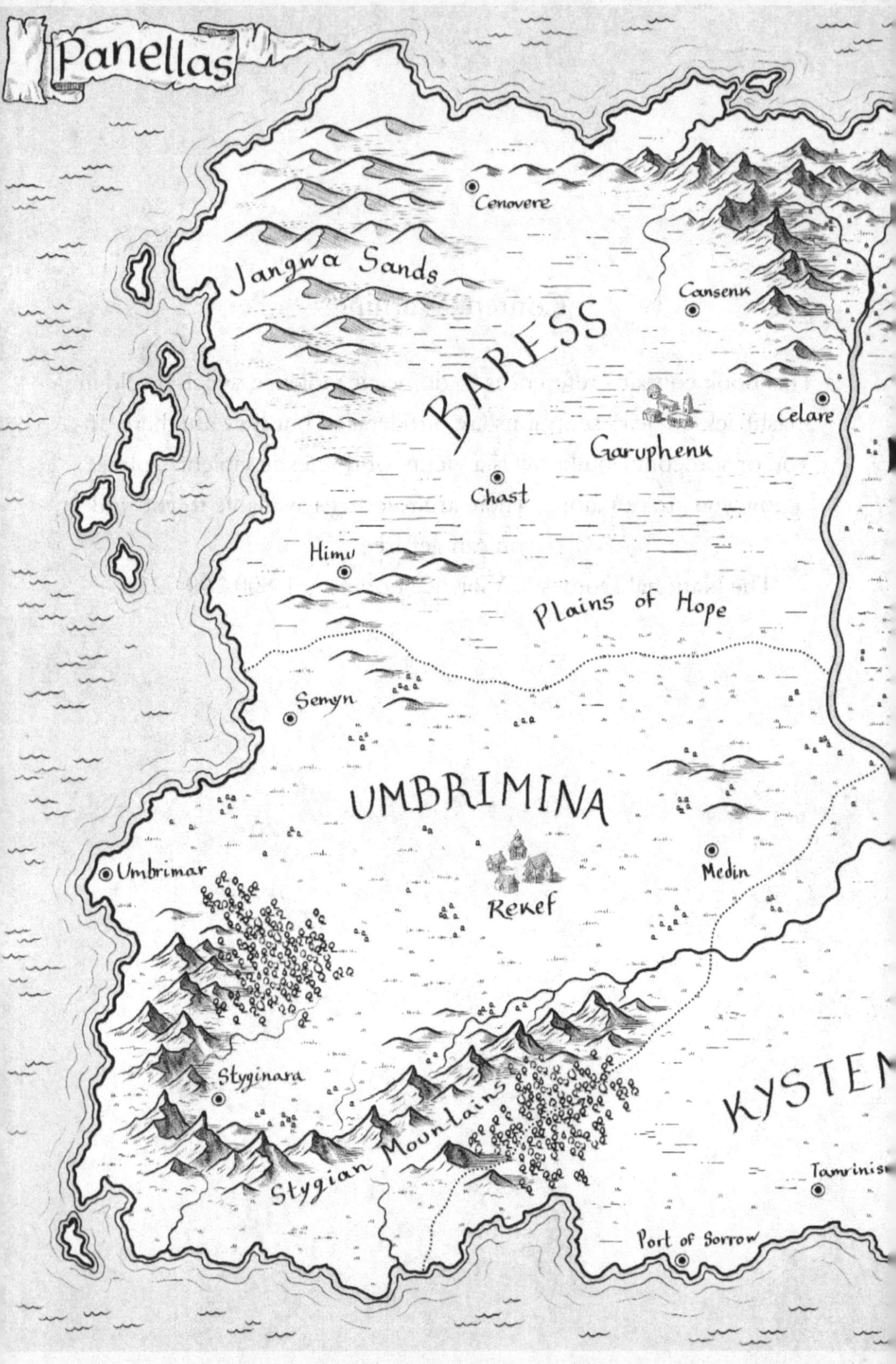

Panellas
Cenovere
Jangwa Sands
Cansenn
BARESS
Celare
Garuphenn
Chast
Himu
Plains of Hope
Semyn
UMBRIMINA
Umbrimar
Medin
Rekef
Styginara
Stygian Mountains
KYSTEN
Port of Sorrow

Cliffs of Tenega
Urek
Forest of Umor
Hist
SAMAITH
Darrow River
Nuwender
Lenoris
Falmor
Sandameer
NUWEN
Colchen
Valley of Mist
Jessin
Alis
SAETORIS
Jarm
Pepolas
Ulet
Satollis Mountains
Dawarin Pass
Otthon
Forest of Alm
Illus
Keneven
FENSHEGUS
Koosh
Calestenea River
NVAR
Tanabaa
Kystenvarian Marshes

Guide to the Gods

Astrid: Goddess of Passion, Patron of Fenshegus

Bas: God of Life and Death, Patron of Kystenvar,

Leighis: Goddess of Healing, Patron of Samaith

Sofiya: Goddess of Wisdom, Patron of Nuwen

Neart: God of Strength, Patron of Baress

Polemas: God of War, Patron of Saetoris

Moro: God of Jubilation, Patron of Umbrimina

Chapter One

The rhythmic thump-thump-thump of punches hitting padded leather fills the air, a heavy bass line beneath the general din of the palace gym. Seriously, did everyone in the palace decide to work out at the exact same time? It feels like we've been here for ages, long enough that I no longer notice the funk of stale sweat coating the air. My usual routine is taking forever, thanks to the crowds, and my patience is officially wearing thin. Soon, I remind myself. Just finish this set, and then it's dagger time.

Lost in my internal whine-fest, I barely register Tilde stepping up to the heavy bag I'm holding. Wham! Her punch lands with such force that the bag jolts, and I have to take a quick step back to keep my balance. Okay, hint taken, pity party over. I look at Tilde and see a devious fire in her eyes.

"Okay, time for a break," I exclaim, maybe a little too enthusiastically. "My arms need a serious time out before you completely kick the shit out of me."

Tilde laughs, smirking at me knowingly, "What? I thought you were paying attention."

"Bitch." I scoff, and Mina snickers, already heading toward the benches. We all grab a spot and gulp down some water.

"Admit it, Mae, it could be worse. At least the view's decent today," Mina purrs.

She's right. The Maise Palace gym is huge. Enormous, gleaming mirrors line two walls, reflecting the organized chaos of exercise machines and enough free weights to sink a small ship. Thick training mats cover the other half, and rows of weapon racks and the punching bags we'd just abandoned line the back wall. A line of sturdy benches runs down the middle, which is where we have just staked our claim. The gym isn't in the palace proper, but attached to the barracks next to it. No way would this many fae be granted access otherwise.

The gym hosts many high fae, males and females, who push their limits on equipment or spar intensely. A few common fae are also taking advantage of the facilities. Some, like us, are taking breaks, but ultimately, it's a feast for the eyes, whatever someone's preference. Only those who've just started still have all their clothes on. By now, most males have stripped off their shirts, and let's just say the sheer amount of toned, sweaty skin on display is… appreciated. Most of the females have also removed their shirts and are clad only in sports bras and workout pants. My friends and I are no exception to this, but we're a common enough sight in this gym that it's only the fresh faces that bother with the subtle, or not-so-subtle, glances.

As I take a long swig of water, I notice Mina scan the room. She looks like she's about to break a diet and can't decide which dessert she wants to devour first. I snort a little laugh and shake my head. With her long hair, skin like polished porcelain, and those big, round, sky-blue eyes, Mina never struggles with catching a male's eye. Add in her killer curves, the kind I sometimes fantasize about having, and most males are goners once she sets her eyes on them.

I have never been so lucky. I know I'm far from ugly, but damn if she doesn't make me jealous sometimes. I love my copper hair, the way it has just the right amount of natural waves. I love my green eyes. On a good day, I can even appreciate my own curves. But today isn't a good day. Today is the kind of day when I'm acutely aware that I'm too short and too "young." Today, I look in the mirror and only see the freckles on my nose that make me look younger, and my boobs, which are just a pain in the ass to bind down during training. Seriously, what is wrong with me? I'm upset about freckles and having big boobs. Ugh, even I recognize I'm being whiny. All this pre-Council stress is getting to me. This gym session was supposed to relieve stress, not add to it.

I've known Mina for what seems like my whole life. One of my earliest clear memories is the day we met. There was this girl, probably my age, but with all the confidence of someone much older. She'd just walked right up to me, stuck out her hand, and introduced herself. "Hi, I'm Aphilomina. I can already tell we'll be best friends, so you absolutely have to call me Mina." I shyly extended my hand and shook hers, completely thrown by her forwardness. I'm still in awe of Mina's confidence, but honestly, she's earned every bit.

Tilde stands next to us, toweling off some sweat. She's definitely drawing her fair share of admiring glances, too. Like Mina and me, Tilde is from Fenshegus, blessed—or cursed, depending on who you ask—with the fair skin and lighter hair common in our kingdom. Unlike my copper tones or Mina's honey blonde, Tilde's hair is a gorgeous shade of strawberry blonde, braided down her back today. She's tall and lean, with toned muscles and legs for days. Tilde, unlike Mina and me, also possesses skin that doesn't turn the color of a tomato when she works out.

Thwack! The sharp sound makes all three of us turn our heads toward the mats, and sly smiles form on our faces. Two mats over, Prince Calian of Nuwen has just sent another male sprawling onto his back, and they are now grappling. Both shirtless, skin gleaming with sweat, every muscle defined, we all take a moment to appreciate it. A small sigh escapes from either Mina's or Tilde's lips. I can't tell which, but honestly, it could have come from any of us. Calian is everything you'd expect from a Nuwen high fae: golden tan skin and sun-streaked hair. Although he's on the shorter side for a high fae male, maybe six feet even, his muscles are toned and tight, and wow, is he attractive. A scar runs from the corner of his left eyebrow to his jawline, which somehow doesn't detract from his looks at all; it just adds an air of mystery. I wonder how he got it. I make a mental note to put Tilde on the case. She has a knack for uncovering secrets.

The other male is equally beautiful, with sapphire eyes and a body that rivals Calian's in terms of pure eye candy. I don't recognize him, but with so many fae in town for the Council of Pan, that isn't exactly surprising.

"Ugh," I groan before I can help myself, hoping no one heard me.

"And what, pray tell, was that for?" Tilde inquires, raising a brow.

I look at both of my friends and mutter, "The Council of Pan is in two days."

"I'm sorry, what? Tilde, could you understand what Mae was saying?" Mina calls out rather loudly, immediately garnering the attention of those closest to us.

"Nope, I mean, I think she said, 'the trout is a can in a maze,' but I have absolutely no idea what she meant by that."

"Oh, shut up," I retort, then louder this time, I say, "The Council of Pan is in two days."

"Oh, we know that," Tilde responds, completely unfazed. "But what we don't know is why you're acting like the sky is falling. This happens every year. Fenshegus just happens to be hosting it this time. I've been working extra with the palace and city guards to make sure we outshine everyone else."

"Yeah, and we get to see Prince Darius again." Mina brightens. "You know, Tilde and I missed the last Council, so it's been ages since we've seen him. Aren't you excited to see our friends from the other courts? Hear all the juicy gossip and scandals?"

"You know I am, Mina," I say, but a little whine escapes, "but I have to participate this year." I can't help the dramatic sigh that follows. "Uncle Emeric's insisting, yet he hasn't given me any training for whatever I'm supposed to do. Hello? It's me! I'm practically guaranteed to say the wrong thing and embarrass the entire kingdom. I just… I really don't want to let anyone down."

Every year, the rulers from each of the seven kingdoms on the Continent gather, along with a bevy of advisers and sometimes the next in line. The whole thing will last for a solid week, filled with endless meetings—some as a massive group, others in smaller, more focused sessions—to hash out disputes, reaffirm old treaties, discuss the needs of individual realms, update trade agreements, and solidify alliances. The evenings will be a blur of formal balls, stuffy dinners, and other mind-numbingly dull events I have absolutely zero interest in. I know it's part of my duties, but it's for sure the part I'm dreading the most.

This is my first year as an actual participant, not just an observer, as I have been in all the previous Councils I've attended. I have been begging Uncle Emeric to help me learn what exactly I'll need to do in my specific role. Teach me any key functions I'll have and tutor me on what actually goes on in the meeting. I've never attended the meetings, and no one has really been forthcoming about what actually happens. All Uncle Emeric has done is go over the calendar and tell me to just sit back and watch. Which, of course, does nothing to alleviate any of my stress.

"Plus," I add with a grimace, "I saw on the official guest list that Felicity will be there, and I just can't with her."

Mina makes a face as if she'd just tasted something sour, while Tilde actually shudders. "Yeah, not looking forward to that. But I am looking forward to putting my… particular skills to good use." Tilde whispers with a wink.

"You mean flirting for secrets?" I retort.

Mina leans in close. "Flirting? So that's what the kids call it these days? I thought it was called being easy, but —"

Mina is cut off as Tilde launches her half-empty water bottle at her. Mina shrieks, ducking just in time to avoid a direct hit.

"Hey! My way of spying just happens to be more enjoyable," Tilde defends. "And trust me, I will do whatever dirty work is needed to get the job done."

I laugh at the two of them, and then all three of us turn our attention back to the mats as Calian effectively ends his sparring match with another resounding thump. He looks up at us, amusement sparkling in his eyes.

"Are you here to work out, Princess, or just to admire my stunningly good looks and perfect form?" he calls out, offering a hand to help his opponent up.

"We were just about to spar, actually," I reply, motioning to the mat next to theirs. Calian's sparring partner hops up, thanking him, then takes off.

We walk over, and Calian grins, that charming, slightly crooked smile of his. "Princess Maevery. Lady Aphilomina. Lady Tildewynn." Calian bows to each of us in turn.

"Mina, please, I prefer Mina." She curtsies, looking graceful even in workout gear.

"Prince Calian," Tilde says, her gaze assessing him with an intensity that could melt steel, "haven't I told you not to call me a lady?"

I shake my head; she hadn't risen through the army ranks as quickly as she had by being soft. She has faced down and eliminated her fair share of threats, both high and common fae, for the sake of Fenshegus, not to mention many other nasty creatures. She isn't one to be messed with, and there's no one I'd rather have fighting by my side. She's a certified badass and has earned that title a hundred times over. Honestly, I'm a little scared of her myself sometimes, which makes me even more grateful that she's one of my closest friends, instead of an enemy.

We agree to dispense with titles, seeing as how we've all known each other for ages, when a scream rips through the air from across the gym. Whipping our heads around, a male I've seen a few times but don't know his name, is on the floor, clutching his knee. The lower half of his leg is bent at a weird angle, and I can see white bone sticking out through the torn skin. Blood pours out, forming a dark, spreading pool beneath him. Oh Gods, that is gross.

"My leg! You broke my fucking leg! What the fuck. You fucking broke my leg!" he screams, his face contorted in agony.

"Yeah, heard you the first time," his opponent drawls, completely unconcerned. "Sorry, didn't realize you were such a fragile little bitch." He steps back, and when I get a clear look at him, my mind goes momentarily blank.

Oh. My. Gods. He's without a doubt the sexiest male I have ever seen. He has to be at least a foot taller than me, with dark hair that falls in loose curls around his head. The top is slightly longer than the sides, framing his face in a way that makes me want to reach out and run my fingers through it. His skin is a deep golden tan that highlights every muscle in his body. I could spend a considerable amount of time tracing the lines of his physique with my tongue. His thighs are thick and powerful, with each muscle so ripped that I can see them flexing through his workout pants. He turns to grab a towel from his friend, and my gaze strays to the muscles that line his abs, and oh, fuck. A deep V-line disappears into the waistband of his pants, and just from looking at him, I can tell he's… substantial.

"Like what you see, Red?"

I snap my eyes back up to his, and for a dizzying moment, I get lost in the hazel depths of his gaze. His face is even more gorgeous than his body, all sharp angles and intense eyes. But then I register what he just said.

"Excuse me?" I demand, and Mina instinctively steps slightly in front next to Tilde, a silent warning. His friend notices and smirks, clearly checking one of them out, but I'm too pissed to notice which one.

"I said, like what you see, Red?" He enunciates each word slowly, as if I'm particularly dense.

"Oh, I heard you. I was just giving you a chance to correct yourself." My tone is acidic.

He saunters toward me, stopping just short, towering over my much smaller frame. Tilde and Mina are both ready to eviscerate him if he so much as breathes on me wrong. Not that I can't take care of myself, but it's good to know they always have my back.

"Oh, there was nothing to correct," he says, his eyes sweeping over me in blatant appraisal. "But I must say I do like what I see. Such a sexy, sassy little thing you are."

That's it, I've had it.

"Oh really, you think I'm sexy?" I purr, tilting my head and batting my eyelashes in what I hope is an overly dramatic, mocking way.

He bites his lip, his eyes raking over my body again, this time with a more blatant hunger. "Oh yeah, I think we could have a lot of fun together while I'm here."

"Is that so?" I lean into him, just a fraction, my voice low.

"Absolu–" The rest of the word is cut off as he suddenly doubles over, collapsing to the floor with a strangled groan, clutching his groin. Tilde and Mina erupt into laughter while Calian chuckles, though his expression holds a touch more sympathy. His friend, however, lets out the loudest, most unrestrained laugh of all, tears leaking from his eyes.

I lean close to the fallen male, my voice deceptively sweet. "If you ever talk to me, or any female in my presence, like that again, it won't just be my knee that will get intimately acquainted with a certain part of your anatomy. It will be my dagger."

"Bitch," he groans from the floor as Mina, Tilde, and I turn and walk out of the gym. This guy just completely killed my mood for sparring. Now I just need to get to the practice field and let my daggers fly.

As we walk by, I notice the healers are already tending to the injured male and someone else has used their power to clean up the gruesome pool of blood. Laughter continues as we step out into the hallway, and I'm pretty sure I hear Calian say, "You so had that coming."

Chapter Two

A red haze clouds my vision as anger roils through me, so intense that I wouldn't be surprised if the lingering sweat on my skin sizzles. I don't walk; I storm through the corridor that connects the gym to the practice fields, Mina and Tilde glued to my heels.

"Have I told you lately how much I love it when you go full-on bitch?" Tilde sings the words, her steps bouncing with glee.

"I mean, technically, she probably shouldn't have done that," Mina says, ever the voice of reason. "It wasn't exactly the most diplomatic move. Although," she quickly adds, "the female and the friend in me wholeheartedly approve."

Good old Mina. Her parents were my parents' closest advisers, and she can't help but follow in their meticulously sensible footsteps. Without her, I would've gotten into so much more trouble over the years. Then again, without me, she would've had a significantly less… eventful life.

"I get that I maybe overreacted a little," I huff, still fuming, "but seriously, fuck that male. Why in the name of all the gods does he think he can talk to me like that? Or to any female, for that matter? It's like they're all strutting around with this invisible rulebook that says if you've got a penis, you may automatically disrespect anyone who doesn't."

Tilde places a hand on my shoulder, stopping me just before we reach the heavy oak door that leads to the practice field. "Mae," she says, her usual playful tone softening with genuine concern, "you know I'm the first in line to kick anyone's ass, especially some arrogant male who can't see past his own ego." She takes a deep breath, and I know there's a but coming. "But… I can't help feeling like there's more to your anger than just what happened in the gym. What's going on? You know you can tell us anything."

Mina nods, her sky-blue eyes filled with sympathy. Ugh, seriously, I have the absolute best friends. I'm not sure which of the many gods I should thank for them. I need to figure it out, though, because they're due a seriously big offering. Maybe even a brand-new temple.

"I just…" I cut myself off, take a big breath, and glance around the vacant stone corridor. Part of me just wants to make sure no one is close enough to hear my royal meltdown, but mostly I just need a damn moment to collect myself. "I just feel like I'm standing at the edge of a cliff right now, and any wrong step is going to send me plummeting." My shoulders slump, and everything I've been desperately trying to keep buried starts spilling out, a river I can't seem to dam.

"Uncle Emeric hasn't prepared me at all for the upcoming Council. He keeps promising he will, but it starts in two days! Not one lesson on what my actual role will be. Not even a conversation about what will be expected of me. I know I have some things I have to do, but he hasn't gone over anything. I'm doubting myself. It feels as if he doesn't think I can do this." My words tumble out faster now, and my feet move on their own, pacing a frantic rhythm.

"I'm turning twenty-five in a few months. I'll have reached my legal majority. My coronation is supposed to be soon after that, and still, nothing. He keeps saying everything is under control, and once the Council wraps up, we'll sit down and start in earnest. His excuse is that he doesn't want to overwhelm me. I get that. I so get that. And I'm so thankful for him doing the amazing job he's done as regent. But..."

I pause again, my throat seizing up, and I have to swallow hard a few times to get it to work. Unbidden tears prick my eyes, and I fight like hell to keep them from falling.

"It's been nine years, almost to the exact day Mom and Dad died. Nine years of feeling like I'm adrift in a sea, tossed and turned by every wave, barely able to keep my head above water. Nine years where every time I think I've finally found my footing, another wave slams into me, knocking me off whatever piece of flotsam I've clung to. Nine years of trying to figure out who I am without them, and trying to figure out what I need to be for Fenshegus. Nine years of missing them every single godsdamned day. Of wanting to tell them when I've accomplished something, or just wanting a fucking hug from them on a day when everything feels like it's falling apart."

I take a shaky breath, trying to slow my runaway mouth as I wipe at the tears that have gone rogue and are now tracing wet paths down my cheeks. "I miss them so fucking much, and I'm terrified of letting them down. I can't do that. I just can't. What if I screw up and embarrass their memory? What if I screw up and embarrass Fenshegus? How the hell am I supposed to do this? I wasn't supposed to be queen this early. I was supposed to have hundreds of years with them."

I look away, trying—and mostly succeeding—to compose myself. I hate this. I hate feeling like I'm letting anyone down. Letting my country down isn't even a possibility I'm allowed to consider. I'm the next Queen of Fenshegus. My family has ruled Fenshegus since the very beginning. It's been drilled into my head since I was a kid that letting down Fenshegus is akin to torturing baby animals. But the idea of letting down my parents, or at least their memory? The mere thought of it guts me, cutting right down to my soul. My parents were the absolute best, the best parents in the entire damn world. Plus, they ruled Fenshegus for almost five hundred years, and everyone loved them. How am I supposed to live up to that? How do I make them proud?

Sofiya, seriously, help a girl out. I need to borrow some of that wisdom you're supposedly hoarding. I all but beg the goddess of wisdom. My head is hanging low when I feel a gentle hand on my shoulder. I look up and see Mina and Tilde looking at me solemnly. Mina removes her hand and gently brushes away a tear that's caressing her cheek.

"You will never let your parents down, Mae. And gods know, Bas is probably tired of hearing how proud they are of you," she says with a kind smile, dipping down so that her face is level with mine. "He's probably ruing the day he ever let them into the Land of the Blessed."

I give a slight chuckle, and the knot in my chest loosens, just a bit. I truly look at her face and see the determination and honest-to-goodness truth shining out of her eyes.

"I've got you," she adds, her gaze steady. "I've been studying all this for ages, as you well know. I've always taken my role as your future adviser incredibly seriously. While I can't officially be named until after your coronation, my parents have been preparing me. I've been devouring every piece of information there is to know about the different countries, their needs, and the assets they possess that we can use to our advantage. Mom has even been sharing her insights on the best way to navigate interpersonal relationships with their respective leaders."

My eyes widen slightly, and even though I probably shouldn't be, I'm a little shocked. Mina has always loved learning, soaking up any and every bit of knowledge, but she's such a stickler for the rules that it never occurred to me to ask her about this. As the next in line, I'm not technically allowed to have any political advisers until I officially become queen. Since my uncle is the king regent until then, he's the only one with an advisory Council. I mean, I've never really understood that particular rule, but until I'm queen, I can't exactly change it.

"We all have our final wardrobe fittings tomorrow, and I was planning on going over everything with you then," she says. "I know for a fact that you know more than you think you do, and I'll prove it to you, I swear."

"I'll even make a wager with you," Tilde chimes in, and I turn my head to look at her. "And you know damn well that I don't make wagers I can't win." A subtle, confident smile plays on her lips, and I feel the crushing weight on my shoulders lighten. Seriously, these two are amazing. They've somehow taken this massive weight that's been building up to an epic explosion and turned it into something I actually feel like I can handle.

I take my first real breath in what feels like weeks, the world not quite so heavy for a moment, and manage to squeak out, "What's the wager?"

They both grin, a look that says, mission accomplished, for now.

"I haven't decided yet," comes Tilde's careful reply. "Let me stew on it overnight. I can't decide if I want it to be fun, serious, or deliciously devious." That wicked gleam in her eyes definitely leans toward the devious end of the spectrum. I'm so screwed if I lose this.

"I'm so glad I'm not wagering with you this time. Last time I did, I was still blushing a week later," Mina exclaims, her face flushing a faint pink even now as she opens the heavy wooden door. "No more tears. Let's go throw some knives and pretend every single target is that arrogant jerk from the gym."

As we step out into the bright sunlight, she extends her hand to the plant beside the doorway. In a move so graceful I can only watch, completely spellbound, a vibrant green vine reaches out, twining around her fingers as if it's greeting an old friend. A flower bud forms in her palm, slowly, gracefully unfurling its delicate petals to reveal a perfect, creamy white peony.

It was about a year after my parents died that Mina's powers kicked in. All fae have common magic, but real power, the kind the gods hand out, is a high fae thing. It's different for everyone and usually shows up sometime in their teens. Since Mina's affinity for plants emerged, she's been making these peonies just for me.

Peonies were my mom's and my favorite flower. After my parents died, she crept into my room and turned it into a veritable forest of peonies. Peonies were everywhere. Hanging from my lights, the posts of my bed, and my dressing table. Absolutely everywhere. It seemed like thousands of the delicate blooms graced the room. I had no idea how she hadn't completely drained herself creating so many.

I cried when I saw them, being reminded once again of my mom and the quiet joy we used to share. Mina had wiped my tears, pulled me into a tight hug, and then told me, in no uncertain terms, to stop it. She'd explained that every single peony represented a moment in time when my mom would have been proud of me, would have kissed me, hugged me.

Instead of feeling sad when I saw a peony, I was to think of it as a message from my mom, reminding me of her love. Reminding me that they would want me to embrace life, to have fun, to make mistakes, and to live every single day proud to be their daughter.

She gently tucks the freshly bloomed peony behind my ear as Tilde nudges my shoulder with a reassuring grin. I look at the two incredible friends I've been blessed with, offering Mina a small, grateful nod. It's a silent acknowledgment of that day so long ago, and also a thank you. A thank you for reminding me that I'm their daughter, and I'm going to be okay.

"Let's go throw some fucking knives already. I don't know why you two are being so damn morose. Sheesh," I say with a newfound surge of determination, turning and striding with purpose toward the practice field.

Chapter Three

Before we even round the final corner, a distinct sound reaches our ears: a staccato thwump, thwump, thwump of metal hitting wood. Tension continues to ease its grip as the familiar sound washes over me. Rounding the corner, the practice field bursts into view. It's an explosion of sights and sounds, instantly reminding me of some of the happiest times in my life. As I scan the field from left to right, I notice that the various paddocks and training areas are teeming with horses and riders, diligently practicing mounted attacks, defensive maneuvers, and thunderous charges. With every hoof fall, puffs of dirt fly up from the trampled field that, as of a week ago, used to be grass. It looks rather cramped, and many of the more dominant steeds are making their displeasure at having to share their space with so many unfamiliar horses quite clear to their riders. A small smile touches my lips as I spot Mionnan, my own stubborn horse, unceremoniously dumping a poor groom when he tries to steer him past another stallion on the way to the stables.

"Mionnan's in a mood, I see," I jump slightly, turning to find Iskra standing right behind me.

"Gods, Isk! Don't sneak up on me like that!" My hand flies to my chest, where my heart is hammering. "Aren't you supposed to be getting ready to leave for Sabaid?"

Iskra rolls her eyes and brushes me off with a dismissive flick of her wrist. "You know I don't even leave until after the Council, right?"

"You know I worry. You're my baby sister. I have to protect you. What am I supposed to do without you?"

In just a fortnight, Iskra will be on her way to Sabaid Military Academy. Military service is a mandatory requirement for every able-bodied citizen of Fenshegus, starting at the age they're legally considered an adult. That varies depending on what type of fae, but for high fae like us, it's eighteen. Before their official service begins, however, all citizens must attend a military school to learn the fundamental skills and receive proper training. Once they graduate, they complete their required two years of service. After their service is complete, they'll repeat this training and two years of service every seventy-five years until they are no longer able-bodied. Some choose to remain in the military, like Tilde, while others, like Mina, opt to return to civilian life. Being a royal doesn't grant any exemptions from this requirement, and so, just as I did after turning eighteen, Iskra will begin her schooling when the new semester starts.

"I'm sure you'll do fine." She winks.

I can't help but worry for my sweet sister. We're so close in age, only six years apart, which is practically unheard of for fae. Typically, fae have difficulty conceiving, and often decades will pass between children. Our own parents hadn't even had children until they were over seven hundred years old, then suddenly two daughters just six years apart. A small twinge of sadness pierces my heart as I remember my mother had been pregnant when she died, but I forcefully push the grief aside. It doesn't serve me in this moment, and I've shed enough tears for one day.

Taking a good look at Iskra, I marvel at how someone living amid the often-cynical atmosphere of the court can remain so genuinely good. Iskra is short, like me—although the little brat is a few inches taller—but that is where the similarities end. Her hair is so light blonde it's almost white, and her eyes are the deep, rich blue of only the finest sapphires. Her fair skin never seems to burn in the sun the way mine does, and she has a lean, athletic build.

But it isn't just in looks where we differ. She can't help but see the good in all fae and finds the positive in almost every situation. She believes learning is the most important thing in the world. She even helps to run a school for all the fae children in the castle, so they can learn to read and write.

It's one of the few things she has talked to me about changing when I become queen. One of only two things, in fact. The first is for me to make all schooling free for all fae, high and common, rich or poor, so everyone can learn. Currently, schooling is only free for the first six years. After that, if a fae can't afford it, their schooling is done. Honestly, in a kingdom renowned for artistic endeavors and scientific advancements, I have no idea why this isn't already a fundamental right.

The other is for permission to become an acolyte of Sofiya at her temple in Nuwen. I haven't told her yet, but I've already been working on the first, and once she gets closer to graduating from the academy, I'll arrange a meeting with one of Sofiya's priests or priestesses to discuss that path with her.

"Wait," I start, frowning slightly. "Why are you even here? I thought your sword lessons were earlier?" My question seems to pull her back from her own thoughts, and her smile widens.

"Well, a little birdy told me you had to deal with a not-so-nice male in the gym and then may or may not have had a teeny tiny moment of weakness on your way here. I came to bring you your happy daggers."

"Her happy what?" Tilde questions, brows furrowing in utter confusion.

"Her happy daggers. They're the daggers Dad had made for her for her thirteenth birthday." She holds them out, and I do indeed smile a little. When I received these from Dad, they were too big, the hilts too thick, the weight too much for my smaller hands. Now, they feel like an extension of myself, a part of me.

"Ah, those. Yeah, that is a good name for them." Tilde nods, then asks, "How exactly did a little birdy tell you what happened inside?"

"Well, actually," Isk answers like birds talking is the most normal thing in the world—and honestly, for her, it kind of is—"Sam, the robin," she clarifies for Mina and Tilde, "heard it from Stuart, the rabbit. Stuart saw you make the peony, Mina, and asked Mary, a mouse that has a den in the walls by that door, if she knew what was going on. Mary said she was gathering fluff for her next nest when she saw it happen. Stuart then told Sam so he could tell me to bring you the happy daggers."

Isk stills and then jumps as if something poked her. "Oh, that reminds me, Stuart saw Uncle Emeric talking to someone that he said didn't look trustworthy. He thinks it was Queen Penelope of

Saetoris, but couldn't be sure. He said it looked like it was an intimate conversation, so he didn't want to pry."

"Gods, you're adorable, Iskra." Tilde shakes her head in genuine wonder.

When Isk was three, her power manifested, surprising everyone. Like my mother and her mother before her, Isk can speak to animals. It was first noticed when the nurse saw mice bringing her raspberries from the kitchen garden. No one was allowed to touch Cook's precious berries without her say-so. Isk had just been told no, they were for a special dessert the next night, but she wouldn't have it. She had to have the raspberries now. When my mom had gently interrogated the mice, they squeaked that the little princess had gone outside and sweet-talked a friendly bird into finding someone who could sneak the forbidden fruit to her.

That night, both Isk and I had gotten the royal lecture about never asking the animals to do something for us that we ourselves could not do. I know for a fact that Isk has bent that rule pretty much every week since then, but honestly, sometimes rules are just meant to be broken. Especially if it means getting dessert even when you're grounded.

"Okay, enough chit-chat. Time to make some targets regret their existence." I turn and walk away from the horse paddocks, heading over to the targets designated for daggers and other small arms. The girls trail after me, and Iskra gives them the lowdown on some more juicy gossip Sam the robin apparently spilled. Gods, animals gossip more than anyone else. I roll my eyes but can't help a small smile as I sheathe the daggers Isk brought me.

When we get to the throwing area, we each grab our favorite weapon of choice. In Fenshegus, most fae start learning how to use weapons before they're even five. Usually, it starts with wooden versions of whatever their parents were best at. Then, as they get older, it's blunted steel, and finally, around ten or so, they get the sharp steel. If a family's got the coin or knows someone willing to teach, kids will often pick up a secondary weapon too. Isk and I had the best tutors and could basically choose whatever we wanted. I'm proficient with most blades, but daggers and stars are by far my favorite. Arrows though? Total disaster. I don't get it, and even my weapons master threw his hands up in defeat years ago. Oh well, can't be good at everything, right? Isk took to weapons like she takes to everything else, but hand her a sword, and it's like the rest of the world just fades away.

Watching Isk with her sword is like that time Mom snuck me into the Council of Pan dances. I was ten, and Fenshegus was hosting again. One of the evening entertainments my parents had arranged was this troupe of incredible dancers. I was too young to go, but Mom spirited me through the servants' quarters. Her in her fancy gown and heels, me in my nightdress and robe, both of us giggling like we were pulling the biggest prank ever on all the rulers of Panellas, not just the court of Fenshegus. She took me to a secret passageway that had a hidden screen where the servants could watch the performances if they wanted. When the dancers took the stage and started to move, I swear I stopped breathing. Everything else just vanished. All I could hear was the music; all I could see was the story the dancers were telling me with their bodies. It was as if they were dancing just for me. Sharing their story just for me. Time melted away, and I couldn't look away until the very end, when the entire theater erupted into the loudest applause I'd ever heard.

Watching Isk wield her sword is just like that. It's like the sword is an extension of her body, her soul. They move as one; her movements are both powerful and effortless. I've seen grown-ass high fae males and females stop mid-spar to just watch the mesmerizing dance that is Isk with her sword. It's one of the few things that keeps me from completely freaking out about her going to Sabaid. I know she can handle herself if she ever gets into trouble.

We take our places at four separate targets. Mina's got her daggers out today, Tilde's picked a few throwing axes, I've got my "happy" daggers ready, and Isk's chosen her throwing stars. Each of us is poised, ready to show the world that we're all a little badass.

Tilde turns to look at us, a wicked glint in her eyes. Oh, shit, I know that look. "Whoever does the worst has to buy the first round for the whole tavern tonight."

"Seriously, Tilde? What the actual fuck? You know throwing weapons isn't my strong suit," Mina complains, a definite whine creeping into her voice.

"Hey, you know what they say about payback?" Tilde retorts, her smile widening.

"That you two share a name?" I hear Mina mutter under her breath, and then the blades are flying.

After about thirty minutes, Mina is indeed declared the loser. To be fair, she'd have easily turned an enemy into a fae pincushion with her throws. It's just that the three of us are ridiculously good at this. Now hand her a bow, or even better, a crossbow, and Tilde wouldn't have dared suggest this wager. No one, and I mean no one, can beat Mina with arrows.

We start cleaning up our area and then head back through the just-blooming gardens toward the palace. The large, cream stone palace rises proudly in the center of the city. It sits on a gentle hill, a guardian watching over its charges. The palace has one central wing, the end of which is capped by wings of equal size and grandeur. I've lived here my whole life, and still, the majesty of Maise Palace can overwhelm me. Luckily, Mina and Tilde have rooms in the same wing as Isk and me. We enter through the central wing and head toward our wing, making plans to meet up after dinner to go to our favorite tavern. As we enter the long hall that leads to our rooms, I throw my arm around Mina and rest my head against her. I hand her my peony, which has somehow stayed perfectly intact, and pull her to a stop.

I lower my voice, making sure I'm barely above a whisper, "Thank you. You have no idea how much your friendship means to me. How much you mean to me."

"Oh, but I do," she replies, "because you mean just as much to me." She leans her head down to mine as she continues, "You're the sister I never had and always wanted. The day I met you, I knew it was the beginning of something special." She pauses, worrying her lip as if she's debating whether to continue. "I've never told you this, but when I visited the oracle before we went to Sabaid, he told me something about you."

She hesitates again, and I can practically feel the weight of whatever she's holding back. "He said... he said that you and I would be there for each other for the rest of our lives. That our happiness was intertwined. That when you fell, I was to pick you up. And when I fell, you were to pick me up. That you and I were two sides of the same coin. I mean, I thought he was a total quack because, well, duh. Anyone who knows us could've figured that out. But then he said something that... hit me." She takes a shallow breath. "He told me that soon, before your twenty-fifth birthday, you would be tested in ways that would push you close to breaking. That someone would hurt you in a way that could never be imagined. And when that time came... I was to let it happen."

I gasp, and she continues sadly. "I asked him how I could ever let this happen, and he said if I didn't, you'd… never know happiness. You're only a few months away from your birthday, and time's running out." She shakes her head, her voice barely audible. "I don't know what it will be. He refused to tell me. Told me I wasn't supposed to say anything to you about this until now. I think." She pauses, as if she's trying to piece it together. "I think he wanted me to warn you that something was coming so that when the time came, you would have this insight. He told me that when I finally did tell you about this, I was supposed to tell you to remember to listen to your heart. That your heart would give you strength."

"Wow. Okay. Thanks." Seriously? I have no freaking clue what to do with this bombshell other than overthink it until my brain melts.

"Ugh. I'm sorry. I can see the gears grinding in your head, and shoot." She groans, hanging her head. "I shouldn't have said anything about it yet."

"No," I give a weak laugh. "Yeah, you probably should've waited, but it's fine. Honestly, I promise. I'm actually glad you told me." I give her a quick hug and then try for a smile. "Don't tell

Tilde, but I'm buying the first round at the tavern. I'll tell Merl to play along, but send me the bill. No complaining. You guys are basically my therapists, so just consider it me paying today's bill."

She shakes her head, but a smile breaks through. "I love you, Mae."

We part ways, heading to our respective rooms to get ready for the night out, footsteps silent on the green and silver carpet. Two more nights, and then the Council of Pan opens, and I'll be center stage for all of Panellas to see and judge. Awesome. Just freaking awesome.

Chapter Four

Sunlight drifts through the sheer curtains around my bed, a soft invitation to wake. One of my few guilty pleasures is the luxury of easing into consciousness, that slow slide from sleep to full wakefulness. I stretch languidly, sinking deeper into the ridiculously comfortable mattress. When I finally open my eyes, a dull throb behind my temples makes me squeeze them shut again. Ugh. Why did I let Tilde talk me into that last round? Or three?

"Still abed, milady?" A voice, way too chipper and way too loud for this early hour, slices through my fuzzy thoughts. Saori, my ever-efficient maid, flits around my room, tidying and preparing for the day ahead—which, apparently, includes me actually getting out of bed. As she lays out my dressing gown, the softest silk imaginable, she rattles off my schedule. "You and the girls have your final fittings for the Council wardrobe in about two hours."

I groan softly but push myself up, shrugging on the dressing gown and shuffling toward the bathroom, listening to the rest of my schedule.

"You have a bit of a break after that, and then your lessons this afternoon." Lessons that are currently battling it out in my brain between 'total dread,' and 'actually kind of looking forward to it.'

"Which lessons specifically, Saori?" I ask, my voice tinged with a healthy dose of dread. "Please tell me it's just the stabby-stabby kind? I'll even suffer through comportment lessons if I have to." I give her my best pleading eyes.

"Don't look at me like that," Saori says, her tone firm, but her eyes softening. "I'm just the messenger, milady. I don't get to play schedule-master." She heads over to my wardrobe and pulls out a simple day dress, the soft green of brand-new leaves. Shit. She knows I adore this dress and that color. This can only mean the news is going to suck.

"Which lessons?" I whine, all pretense of royal dignity out the window.

"Well, all your bloodshed lessons, obviously." She shoots me a devious little grin, then turns to help me into the dress, deftly doing up the back.

Once the last button is fastened, she spins me around and nudges me to sit at my vanity. Saori starts braiding my hair in some complicated pattern, humming softly as she weaves my copper strands. Saori's been my maid since I left the nursery. She's one of my most loyal champions, stepping into a sort of maternal role after Mom died, just when I needed it most. After she finishes taming my unruly hair, she places her hands on my shoulders, leaning down so our faces are reflected side-by-side in the mirror. Her gently aging face next to my youthful one. Her honey-blonde hair contrasts with my copper. Her warm brown eyes against my bright green ones. We couldn't look more different, and yet, she feels more like family than many of my actual family.

Saori's soft, brown eyes are sparkling with pure mischief as she whispers, "Oh, and the dancing lessons, of course." And just like that, she's all business again, bustling around, tidying the room.

"What!" I scoff, whirling around to face her. I jump to my feet and stalk over to her. "But…" I stammer. "But I hate dancing. Why do I still have to take those lessons? I'm proficient enough." Gods, I sound like such a whiny brat.

"Listen up, Your Highness," her voice is stern, meeting mine head-on. "You're a princess of Fenshegus." She starts toward me, her gaze intense. "You're the next Queen of Fenshegus." Now her long finger is pointing at me, almost poking me in the chest, but not quite. "You're a Roighail. And Roighails aren't just 'proficient,' by the gods. Roighails excel." Oh shit, she's coming out swinging. "I swore to your mother on the day I became your maid that I would do everything in my power and ability to help you grow into the female, into the queen you're destined to be."

"I know that," I admit, cringing a little at how I sound, "but you know I hate dancing. I have to concentrate so hard not to completely screw it up, and then I can't even enjoy myself. I'm such a disaster at it if I don't."

An exasperated sigh puffs out of her. "I know, sweetie, I know." She pulls me into a hug. Her arms are like a second home, always there when I need them. "But you also know that the Council of Pan always has a ball to kick things off and another to wrap it up. The opening ball is tonight. You can't wiggle out of that one." I can hear the sympathy in her voice as he rubs my back gently, "You'll be expected to dance with representatives from all the other six kingdoms. The extra practice will at least give you a tiny bit more confidence, right? Besides," she whispers, "I'm just a maid. I don't get to decide what you're allowed to do or what you have to do."

"Saori, you've never been just a maid." I insist, squeezing her tightly. "You're practically my aunt. I can't even imagine my life without you in my corner."

As she presses a quick kiss to the top of my head, a firm knock-knock comes from the door.

"Come in," we both call out, breaking apart.

A slender male strolls in, balancing a tray laden with a steaming pot of tea and my usual tonics. "Ah, Your Highness. You look absolutely fetching in that dress," Lukavo says, and I can practically hear the charming smile in his voice.

Lukavo's worked in the palace for about seven years. Officially, he's one of my footmen, but he moonlights, helping the court healer cart around all the delightful tonics and medicinal concoctions. He's got dreams of becoming a full-fledged healer himself, so he spends a chunk of his day shadowing the head healer. Ambitious, I'll give him that.

I watch as he carefully sets my tray down on the low table in the sitting room, then wanders over to inspect the goods. "All right, spill it. What's the potion of the day?" I eye the familiar teapot and, yep, there it is—my monthly dose of 'no unexpected royal additions' tonic. Gotta love court life.

"Ah, well, there might have been some chatter in the servants' quarters about a certain group of young ladies who had a wildly entertaining night, Your Highness," Lukavo drawls, trying, and failing, to suppress a grin.

"I have absolutely no idea what you're implying," I say, going for my best haughty princess impression.

"Hmph," Saori mutters, pointedly ignoring both of us as she finishes laying out my clothes for the day.

"Well, tell that to the guard at the gate. He just happened to see four"—Lukavo's eyes meet mine with playful accusation—"four stunningly gorgeous ladies of the court stumble through his post last night." I wince internally, bracing myself for the inevitable. "Said he distinctly heard two of them belting out some seriously off-key… and rather bawdy tavern song." Another pointed look skewers my pathetic attempt at innocence.

"Don't look at me. I'm physically incapable of singing off-key," I retort, feigning outrage.

A full-blown smile finally breaks across Lukavo's face. "Well, he mentioned that those two were being… assisted by one, shall we say, generously proportioned lady, and one rather vertically challenged one. Said the four of them were barely able to walk straight on their way back in." He raises an eyebrow, a sly challenge in his eyes.

"Now, I'll not tolerate any slanderous rumors being spread about my charge," Saori interjects, her voice sharp enough to cut. She glares at Lukavo. "You will tell me the name of this… guard," she practically spits the word, "so I can deal with him!"

"Relax, Sai," Lukavo says, his voice soothing. "It was Gerelle. He gave me the heads-up privately so I could whip up a particularly potent hangover cure for those four mysterious ladies." Ah, that explains the weirdly colored tonic. "He suggested they might be in… considerable need of it this morning."

"Ah, Gerelle. That son of mine is a good one." With a nod of her head, Saori makes her way to the door. "I'll have to make him something special for keeping an eye out for you ladies."

"Thanks, Lukavo," I say, my gratitude genuine. This headache-vanquishing tonic is a freaking lifesaver.

Saori holds the door open, and they disappear, leaving me alone with my thoughts for approximately two seconds. I down the two tonics and the tea in record time. Right, time to go see if I can pull a disappearing act before this torture they call a "dancing lesson" begins.

It isn't until I'm practically out the door for our final fittings with Iskra, Tilde, and Mina that I finally track down Uncle Emeric. He's holed up in the library, poring over what look like ancient law books. The countless tomes filling the towering shelves, standing watch behind him, I tap softly on the elm door, and he whips his head up, snapping a book shut as if he's hiding something scandalous.

"Ah, Maevery," he says, his voice all warm and fuzzy, a smile crinkling the corners of his eyes. "What brings you here, my dear? Shouldn't you be off to the dressmaker's soon?"

My reply is out before I can overthink it, a little too timid even for my liking. "I was just about to leave, but… I had a question." I look at him, crossing my fingers internally that I've caught him in a halfway decent mood.

"Well, what can I help you with?" His warm tone actually gives me a sliver of hope. "I'm busy with last-minute preparations, but I can always make time for you."

Before my brain can stage a full-blown retreat, I blurt it out. "I was hoping… could I maybe skip my dance lesson this afternoon? And maybe… possibly… skip some of the dancing at the ball?"

His eyes are questioning, but soft. "I thought you loved dancing?"

"I love watching dancing. I get all twisted up with nerves when I have to actually do it." My head drops a little, even though I know I shouldn't feel this embarrassed. "And I have to concentrate so hard on not tripping over my own feet that I can never actually enjoy it."

"Ah," he breathes out, understanding dawning in his expression. He pauses for a beat, and I can practically see the wheels turning as he figures out how to let me down gently. The light from the windows cast dancing shadows on his face. "I'm so sorry, Maevery, but I can't. As we're hosting the Council this year, you absolutely have to play the role of hostess," he explains, his tone apologetic. "That means I'm obligated to dance with the female dignitaries, and you with the males. If we weren't the host country, I would let you out of attending the ball if you wanted to." His sad eyes meet mine. "I'm sorry. I truly am."

I nod, trying to make it look like it's no big deal. It was a long shot anyway, so I'm not exactly heartbroken. "It's totally fine. Thanks, though. I should probably head out."

I turn to leave, and his voice stops me. "I really am sorry. Have a good day, take a nice nap, and then enjoy the ball. You're only young once, Princess, and soon, when you're queen, you might actually miss these days."

I smile and nod, knowing he's probably right. The thought of being queen is both exciting and terrifying. Maybe a nap would be a good idea.

I stand on the dais in the dressmaker's shop, staring at my reflection as if the female in the mirror is some stranger.

"Porvi," I exclaim. "You're wondrous." I can't stop turning this way and that, checking out every angle of this dress. "I can't believe how gorgeous this dress is!"

A faint blush appears on Porvi's green skin. "It's nothing, Your Highness. Just wait until you see the next one."

Porvi snips the last thread, a small, satisfied smile on her lips. She knows she's nailed it. Porvi has been the main dressmaker for my family for, like, three centuries, and she creates the most insane, beautiful clothing. Porvi is an Anthousai, a plant nymph. With her long, spindly arms, a body like a swaying willow, vines, and little blossoms woven through her hair, and that soft green skin, she's incredibly beautiful. Mom and I always figured that being an Anthousai is what gave her such an edge in creating these incredible outfits. Her magic is tied to what the land gives us. The cloth, the thread, and the ribbons listen to her magic. She can mold them exactly how she envisions them. I've never seen anything like it and am eternally grateful for her genius.

The dress itself is this killer emerald green. One of Fenshegus's official colors, and one of my favorites. The skirt is full and flows out gently from my hips, all these gorgeous layers of fabric. You can't tell when I'm standing still, but there's a slit hidden in all those yards of material that goes all the way up my leg. I love it; it's a little sexy and lets me move freely. The capped sleeves that hang just off my shoulders are made of the most delicate silk lace, and as I examine them, I notice something.

"Are those peonies?" I ask.

Porvi nods, smiling, and glances over at Mina.

"So, Mae," Mina asks, a smirk spreading across her face as if she's been in on this the whole time. "If Porvi wanted to get her hands on the most exquisite lace, where would she have to go?"

"Nuwen," I reply automatically. "Everyone knows Nuwen makes the best lace."

My eyes continue to examine the dress, scanning the low-cut bodice. It's not so low that anything's going to pop out, thank the gods, but any lower and it would definitely be indecent. Intricate designs woven with tiny glass beads cover the bodice. They're so small they all blend, looking more like actual gold thread.

"Are these beads the ones that Darius sent?" I throw the question out to no one in particular.

Tilde is quick to answer, "Why would you think that?"

"Well, the last time we talked, he was telling me about a visit to one of the glass-blowing masters in Baress." My fingers skim the patterns on the dress. The feel of the hard beads blending with the soft fabric is something I find fascinating. "He was describing beads exactly like this, said they were famous for them, and promised he'd send me some."

I look up and see all of them grinning at me as if they know something I don't.

"What?"

Iskra smiles all sneaky-like. "Well, we knew you'd be a bundle of nerves, so we came up with a plan…" Iskra trails off, looking at the other females.

"We decided to ask Porvi to stitch in something from each of the kingdoms into your dress," Tilde continues, picking up where Iskra left off.

"That way, when you worry you don't know enough tonight," Iskra rushes to finish, "you can just look at your dress and be reminded."

Porvi smiles. "A wearable cheat sheet, Your Highness."

"Oh my gods," I say, totally stunned. Tears are definitely threatening to make an appearance now. "You're the best."

Mina smiles and, with a challenging tone, says, "Let's see how well you know your kingdoms." My smile falters, but she continues on. "You and I, and well, everyone here, know you know the rulers. You've practically been brought up with them." I roll my eyes because, yeah, royal life, and she continues, "So, for your ridiculously amazing dress, we focused on what each country is famous for. That way, if you get stuck for something to say, you've got a built-in conversation starter."

I eye the gown skeptically. "Okay, but all I'm seeing right now is a lot of fancy beads and lace?"

"Try finding something from Saetoris," Iskra pipes up, all excited.

"Um..." I stare at my reflection, thinking hard. My hands land on my hips, fingers caressing the fabric. "Okay, I think I remember that Saetoris is all about cotton and Tinuvar," I finally say. "But this doesn't feel like cotton, and the only metal I can feel is the boning in the corset." I pause for a second, then it clicks. Turning to Porvi, I ask, "Porvi, did you... Did you make my boning out of Tinuvar?"

"I did, Your Highness." She beams, a clear pride in her work. "And the fabric is cotton from Saetoris. I wove it specially, so it has that extra bit of shine and softness."

She continues, her fingers gently adjusting a fold of the skirt. "And that pattern you keep fiddling with? That's very specific to one of the courts."

I look down at the intricate, yet somehow soft and romantic design again. "Kystenvar?" I guess, looking at Mina for confirmation. "They're the other big art kingdom, right? So I'm guessing this is one of the official fancy patterns they have?"

Mina's face lights up, practically glowing with pride. "Spot on! It's called the Kystenvarian Love Knot." She takes a breath, her expression softening. "It's a traditional knot given between bonded mates in Kystenvar. Since your parents were... well, you know, bonded mates... I thought it was appropriate."

"Okay, try Samaith!" Iskra demands gleefully.

I peer at the dress again, my gaze landing on the sheer, gossamer overlay on the skirt. "Wait a minute… are those tiny tropical flowers embroidered there?"

"They are indeed!" Mina claps her hands together excitedly. "They're actually some of the flowers from medicinal plants that only grow in Samaith."

"That just leaves Umbrimina," Tilde says, a ridiculously bright smile on her face.

I scrunch up my brows, totally drawing a blank. "Umbrimina… okay, they're all about their fierce warriors. But I'm not seeing anything on this dress that screams 'battle-ready.'"

A laugh escapes Tilde, and Porvi hands me a box. When I flip open the lid, I find a pair of stunningly crafted green leather thigh sheaths; the leather is soft and clearly high-quality. Embossed along the length are delicate peonies, and they're honestly the most beautiful weapon sheaths I've ever seen.

"It's for your happy daggers," Iskra says, a smile evident in her voice. I look up at her, and she continues. "You're from Fenshegus. We like weapons here. Might as well have them handy." I smile, but she isn't done yet. "Just, please don't stab anyone at the party?"

I laugh and pull her into a quick hug. I feel as though the God of Jubilation is here with me. Moro knows how happy I'm right now.

"There's just one last thing." Tilde hands me a small box, and I tilt my head. When I open it, I swear my words have abandoned me. Tears threaten to spill, and Iskra squeezes my hand. Laid out on a bed of black velvet is one of my mother's favorite necklaces. The one her own mother gave her to commemorate her first official Council of Pan. The necklace is three elegant strands of pearls, each the color of fresh cream, the pearls gradually increasing as they descend. In the very center, the strands connect to an exquisite starburst. Tiny diamonds and warm citrines cover its surface, glittering beautifully.

But being a Fenshegus noble isn't just about pretty jewelry. This isn't just a necklace; it's a secret, a tradition passed down through the female line. The only ones alive who know about this are right here in this room, and my grandmother, Willi. The star has a special, almost invisible clasp. When pressed just right, the back silently falls away, revealing the throwing star it truly is. Beautiful and deadly. Just like every fae female should be.

Chapter Six

Breathe. Just breathe. You've got this. I remind myself, trying to suck in as much air as possible in this dress. My feet beat a staccato rhythm on the marble as I pace. My hands keep wandering up to my necklace, fidgeting while I wait for Uncle Emeric so we can finally make our grand entrance into the ballroom. As the hosts, we can't exactly waltz in fashionably late. I'm scanning the paintings lining the walls of the hall. Trying to draw strength from both my ancestors and the other fae looking down on us from the paintings.

"Stop it," Iskra hisses, but her voice is soft. "You look absolutely stunning, and you're going to nail this."

I glance at Iskra and try to give her a smile that screams, "I've totally got this." She looks gorgeous in her own green dress. It's a softer, lighter shade that actually makes my own dress pop, and it looks striking with her strawberry-blonde hair. Her gown is more modest but still totally elegant and somehow a little sensual. Her ears and throat sparkle with fire opals that are so bright they look like little flames licking her skin when the light catches them.

"How do you do it, Isk?" I ask, a slight wobble in my voice.

"Do what?" she asks, genuinely confused.

"Stay so calm and positive."

Her lips lift, and a soft chuckle escapes them. "It's pretty simple, really." Her smile widens. "I'd rather go through life with love and happiness. Choosing to see the best in fae—or at least trying to find something good—makes that happen." She grabs my hand gently. "And for the love of the gods, stop fidgeting. You're going to be great!"

"She's right, you know," Tilde adds from behind us as she steps off the stairs that lead into the hall.

The cream runner renders her footsteps silent as she descends. She's in her dress uniform since she's on duty tonight. The all-black uniform actually looks pretty sharp, but it's definitely made for kicking ass first and looking good second. What looks like a skirt is actually wide-leg pants, so if things go south, she can still run and fight. As head of my personal guard, she's stuck with me until I decide to call it a night. Which, if I have my way, will be approximately five minutes after we make our grand entrance.

Footsteps echo closer, and we turn to see Uncle Emeric strolling toward us. Two stiff-backed footmen trail behind him, each lugging a heavy-looking wooden box emblazoned with the royal crest. His platinum blonde hair is slicked back, and he's wearing an expertly tailored tuxedo. A swath of emerald green fabric cuts diagonally across his chest, and the ornate livery collar that screams "I'm in charge" takes center stage.

"Forgive me for cutting it close," Uncle Emeric says, waving away his tardiness with a practiced flick of his wrist. "I simply thought a night like tonight required… something special."

He waves the two footmen closer. Standing in front of Iskra, he gently lifts her smaller tiara from her hair. "Little one, for a night like tonight, you deserve something far more dazzling."

He opens the lid of the box on the right and pulls out a stunning tiara. It's way more exquisite than the one she was wearing. Braided gold wraps around three huge fire opals, with diamonds sparkling in between.

A soft gasp escapes Iskra's lips, and her hand flies up to cover her mouth. Uncle Emeric carefully places the piece of art on her head.

"This belonged to my mother," he says, checking to make sure it's sitting comfortably and hasn't messed up her perfectly styled hair. "It was one of her favorites, and I find it entirely fitting that it's now yours."

"Oh my. Thank you so, so much." Her voice is a little shaky, as if she's trying not to cry.

Uncle Emeric turns to me and gently takes my own simple tiara off my head.

"My dear. In just a few months, you'll be queen," he says, turning to lift the lid off the remaining box. "The time for tiaras is over." Carefully, reverently, he places the crown on my head. My breath hitches, and I have to fight back a sudden wave of emotion. It's Mom's crown, the one she only ever wore for the Council of Pan. Simple, yet still elegant, and utterly breathtaking.

"Where did you even get this?" I whisper, my voice thick. "I thought it was on the ship with them when it sank?"

"It was supposed to be," he replies, grabbing both my hand and Iskra's as he looks between us. "The wagon with your parents' jewels and some of their things broke a wheel on the way to the ship. The decision was to send it on the next ship rather than making everyone late."

He pauses before continuing on. "I probably should've given you two everything before now, but I wanted to save it for a time when you would really want them to be with you." He gives a small, sad smile. "I know my brother would be bursting with pride for both of you. Your mother, too."

The three of us fall into a hug, a silent acknowledgment of everything that's not being said. I'm trying my best not to lose it, and mostly succeeding, when a polite cough breaks the moment. That's our cue. Time for the royal parade. I know it sounds silly, but with Mom's crown settled on my head, I feel like she's watching out for me from somewhere. We turn and face the grand ballroom doors. Each door is easily fourteen feet high. Intricate carvings cover the doors, but the part I've always liked best was the inlay in the center of each door. Ebony, lime, and ironwood make up a swirling pattern of entwined vines, with the native flowers of Fenshegus in the openings. Another clearing of a throat has me straightening my spine and taking my place.

Uncle Emeric and I walk side-by-side, followed by Iskra, and then Tilde and the other guards bringing up the rear. I plaster on my most regal smile and take the first step forward, onto the next act in the never-ending play that is my life. Hoping the audience can't see the nervous wreck hiding beneath the perfectly poised princess.

*My gods, I'm so over thi*s. We have been standing in this receiving line for over an hour, and I desperately need some champagne. Uncle Emeric promised Iskra and me that we only have to receive the next group, then we're free to actually enjoy the night.

"Your Royal Highnesses, please welcome King Tavarik and Queen Kalimina of Kystenvar!" the major domo announces. His voice somehow echoes through the hall, despite the swarm of fae and the tapestries that line the walls. I automatically begin to curtsy, but Queen Kalimina takes my hand, stopping me before I can finish the motion.

"Absolutely none of that," she gently but quietly admonishes, her voice low enough that only I can hear. She glances over to see her husband still engrossed in conversation with Uncle Emeric, then turns back to me. "You're a queen in your own right. You don't curtsey to anyone."

Instantly, I like her, and I make a mental note to seek her out later; she may be an unexpected ally. She's stunning, dressed in the traditional Kystenvarian colors of rich gold and deep black, and her smile is warm. We exchange pleasantries about the journey and the weather, just small talk for a few minutes, before King Tavarik finally makes his presence known.

"Your Highness," he grates out, and something about the way he speaks makes my skin crawl, though I can't pinpoint why. I mean, he and Uncle Emeric are great friends, so how bad can he actually be? "I'm grateful for your lovely welcome to your kingdom and city. I look forward to working with you next week."

He looks around. "Our son Conaill is around here somewhere," he continues. "Probably trying to see which female he can beguile tonight." He laughs as though what he said is anywhere close to appropriate. "I know you're eager to get to the party yourself, so we won't keep you. Just save a dance for me later, won't you?" He winks, a lecherous gesture that makes my stomach churn, before turning back to Uncle Emeric.

"Of course, Your Majesty," I somehow manage to get out, forcing a polite smile before quickly excusing myself with Iskra. Thank the gods that's over. "Come on, Isk," I whisper, grabbing her hand. "I need a drink. A large one."

Laughing, she squeezes my hand, and we weave our way through the glittering crowd. I'm looking to get lost in the throng and enjoy this last night before I have to really, truly act like a queen.

Moro must be looking out for me right now because I'm shocked at how much I'm actually enjoying myself. I've been dreading this night for what seems like forever, and yet the God of Jubilation seems to have seriously come through for me. I've even managed to avoid dancing so far, but I know my time is coming. Luckily, Darius found us and has been regaling us with tales from his travels.

I sometimes envy Darius. His older brother, Prince Becket, is next in line for the throne, which allows Darius to chase whatever passions he wants. Not that he wouldn't be a great king—he really does love his kingdom and would be a good king—but his brother just fits the role better.

I tap Darius on the shoulder, giving him a little nudge to lean down. "I need you," I whisper in his ear.

His eyes fly to mine, a wicked gleam sparking beneath the surface. "Oh, really?" The words are spoken rakishly. "I thought you would never ask."

A blush kisses the apples of my cheeks, and I gently swat his arm. "Oh, gods! Not like that, you cad!" Okay, fine, I've definitely thought about it. Darius is extremely handsome. He's got dark brown eyes, black hair that always looks perfectly styled, and his skin is simply flawless, with a deep, chestnut tone. Add in his height, and that he's clearly no stranger to the gym, and it's no wonder that so many females *and* males are practically throwing themselves at him. But he's also one of my dearest friends, and I refuse to do anything that might mess up that friendship.

I quickly compose myself and explain. "I have to dance tonight," I say, the words practically rancid in my mouth. "You know how much I hate that, but with you, I don't have to worry about judgment."

"That, and I'll make you look good." He smiles down at me, then smoothly brings the back of my hand to his lips for a kiss. "I've got you, just let me know when."

"When!" I blurt out, relief flooding through me. Darius gives me a quizzical look, as if he didn't mean *right this second.* "I just saw Uncle Emeric motion for me…"

"Well then, lead the way, fair princess." He offers an exaggerated bow, his eyes twinkling, and takes my hand.

We head over to my uncle, trying to look only a little hurried.

As we approach, Uncle Emeric beams. "Ah, there she is." He holds his hand out to me, and I take it, stepping up onto the small raised platform he's standing on. Turning to Darius, his smile appears just the littlest bit forced. He says, "Prince Darius! How are you finding our capital?"

Darius bows deeply, his voice completely sincere. "I find it exquisite, Your Highness."

That seems to placate Uncle Emeric for a moment, and he turns to me. "Now, I know you don't like it, and I've done all I can to help alleviate your requirements," he says, a subtle warning in his tone. *Yup, called it.* It's time to quite literally face the music and dance. "But it's time to dance, Maevery."

I quickly play the only card I have. "I figured as much, and Prince Darius has graciously agreed to escort me during the next dance."

"Nonsense," Uncle Emeric dismisses the idea instantly. "I've been talking with King Tavarik, and he agrees." Oh gods. Please don't make me dance with *him*. "You're the future queen. Your partner should be next in line, too. Tavarik just left to retrieve his son." I let out a breath I didn't realize I was holding, thankful I don't have to dance with King Tavarik himself. "Ah, there they are now."

I turn, and my relief instantly vanishes, replaced by a fresh wave of disbelief and revulsion. You have *got* to be kidding me. King Tavarik has reached us, and the male standing next to him, with that infuriatingly confident smirk, is the very same jerk from the gym.

"There you are, my dear." King Tavarik smiles broadly at me. He must have had his fair share of champagne already, because his face is quite ruddy. He turns to the male next to him and, with a booming voice that echoes a little too loudly in the ballroom, announces, "This is my son, Conaill. Conaill, Princess Maevery. You two will dance the next waltz." His tone leaves no room for me to decline.

"Of course, Your Majesty," I say, dipping my head just enough to convey modesty. Ugh, I absolutely hate this dutiful facade I have to wear in public. If I had my way, I wouldn't be dancing at all, especially not with some random, arrogant prince.

"Well, hello, Princess." Conaill's eyes flare with a mix of surprise and anger. Guess he's still feeling a bit sore about his... incident. Oh well, not my problem.

The musicians finish a lively tune, and the familiar, elegant opening notes of a waltz drift through the ballroom. "I believe that's our cue, Red." His hand is outstretched, clearly waiting for mine.

I place my hand in his, trying not to show how much I'd rather be anywhere else, and we make our way to the dance floor. As we settle into position, I lean in just a fraction, barely moving my lips, and quietly hiss, "I thought I made myself very clear about what I think of that name?"

A soft, infuriatingly confident chuckle rumbles from his chest. "Oh, I remember. But, damn, you're sexy when you're pissed." He winks, a mischievous glint in his hazel eyes, and then his hand settles on the small of my back, and his other clasps mine.

I can feel the surprising heat of his palm, even through the lace and satin. The pressure is insistent, firm, and his touch sends a jolt of pure electricity sparking through my body. Where his hand rests, I practically hum, a strange vibration coiling deep inside me. I've never experienced anything remotely like this before, and honestly, I can't decide if I love it or absolutely hate it. How can he, the arrogant jerk, make me feel... this?

He must feel it too, because his eyes flash to mine, confusion swirling in those shockingly beautiful hazel depths. Before I can even respond, the music swells, and Conaill leads me into the first steps. His presence is commanding, his movements flawless, and he guides me in a dance that feels less like a waltz and more like a sensual battle.

I don't think; I just dance. This low hum of power between us grows stronger with every step. I'm not even conscious of my own movements; all I know is that we're gliding across the polished floor. The other couples have faded into nothing more than swirling swaths of brilliant colors and black. I can't hear the music anymore; instead, I feel it. As he twirls me, he pulls me closer, our bodies skimming against each other. My breasts barely brush his coat, and my nipples immediately pebble at the sensation. We lock eyes, lost in each other's gaze, and I literally can't look away. I don't understand it. I definitely don't like this arrogant male, and yet my body is undeniably drawn to him. I haven't thought of the steps once. Right now, I feel like our movements are pure instinct.

I don't even realize the music has stopped. We just keep holding onto each other for another beat, both of us totally frozen, like the entire world outside us has just disappeared. Someone bumps into us, jarring us, and our eyes finally break apart. I quickly look away, totally embarrassed by my reaction. What the actual fuck *was* that?

He seems to snap out of whatever magic was holding us a lot faster than I do. "Thanks for the dance, Red." His voice is deep and... sensual. Ugh. He leans in close, his breath a whispering caress on my ear. "If that's how you dance, I can't wait to get you beneath me."

I gasp, a sharp intake of breath as he just walks away, leaving my anger rising to a boil. As gracefully as I can, I storm straight to where Iskra, Darius, and Mina are snagging glasses of champagne off a fancy tray. Tilde is stoically drinking water until she's off duty.

"I need to get out of here," I practically snarl, draining my glass in one huge gulp. "Now." I stalk off, not even caring who's following. If I don't leave this stupid ballroom right this second, I swear I'm going back there and ditching my very proper princess persona to punch a certain prince right in his smug face.

Chapter Seven

The Lusty Lord is, as ever, absolutely packed with fae, all of them probably trying to escape whatever drama is currently plaguing their lives. I honestly love this tavern and the quirky mix who call it their second home. A relic of years past, the outside is timber with lime-washed plaster between the beams. Bright splotches of color break up the dark wood paneling of the interior in the form of paintings. White linen curtains frame the windows, brightening the room even more. Tonight, the pub's lit dimly with twinkling fae lights, giving off a cozy glow. Scared tables and comfortable booths fill the space, offering plenty of seating. Shadowy corners invite those wanting to disappear, contrasting the subtly lit spots for those who actually want to, you know, see each other.

The moment we step inside, a hush falls over the normally boisterous pub. It feels like every single eye in the place swivels to our little group. I don't blame them, honestly. I'd stare too. None of us bothered to change out of our fancy clothes; we simply ditched the jewels before leaving the palace. As we make our way through the pub, talking gradually resumes until it is as if we had never arrived.

"Your Highnesses!" a jovial voice booms from behind the bar. I turn and see Merl, the tavern's owner, a mountain of a male, already stationed there. "Your usual room is open if you wish, Your Highnesses." With a bow, he spins away to deal with a thirsty patron who's practically drooling for a drink.

"You all go along." I shoo them with a flick of my wrist. "I'll be in shortly; I just need to pass Merl a quick message."

Iskra looks confused, but an understanding Darius quickly ushers her away. Mina nods, following after them, leaving a very vigilant Tilde by my side.

"You can go, you know," I tell her, even though I know perfectly well she won't budge. "I'm safe here."

Tilde snorts. "Yeah, that's not happening," she says, arms crossed over her chest. "You know I *am* one of your guards. And a friend."

I can't help but smile, and we make our way to the bar, positioning ourselves casually under the second light to the left. Merl glances our way and gives a subtle nod. Anyone looking would simply assume that he's acknowledging us, waiting for service. In reality, we only stand here when there's information to be passed.

"Two more boats will be needed with full provisions," I say under my breath when Merl finally approaches us. Tilde shifts, facing the bustling crowd, making sure no one gets too close.

"I'll see it done," Merl ever so quietly responds as he expertly pulls pints for our group. As he sets down the last glass, he adds, "The last wanted to pass along thanks to you for the supplies."

Tilde snatches the tray, and I give a quick nod before we make our way to our usual private side room. Merl is one of my connections in helping those who can't help themselves. It's imperative that no one discovers what I'm doing. Now, I need to figure out how to get the additional supplies he needs.

For the past few years, common fae have been mysteriously losing their magic. One night, they go to bed, and when they wake up, their magic is gone. No one seems to know what's causing it. Even the scientists in the lab where I volunteer when I have free time can't explain it.

As more cases surfaced, all of them affecting only common fae, laws were enacted to "protect" our citizens. Restrictive laws that stripped the affected individuals of their rights. They called it "quarantining," but in reality, they ripped the affected individuals away from their loved ones and threw them into a quarantine zone. Once a fae went into quarantine, they were never heard from again. I'm absolutely disgusted by everyone involved in making and enforcing this law.

As future queen, I couldn't let this be the fate of my subjects. Not when they needed help and care, not being punished for something devastatingly out of their control. So I created the Order of Auxilium, allowing for a network of like-minded fae. Together, we help those affected flee with their families to safe zones. We provide them with supplies and help them get settled into their new lives. Technically, I was breaking a ton of laws doing this, but there's no way I could just sit back and do nothing.

Worrying my lip, my mind engaged in the Order, and I don't notice the extra fae in the room at first. When I finally do, a scowl immediately crosses my face.

"Well, hello there, Red," comes a dark, seductive drawl. Conaill is sprawled in our private room, along with the Calian and that mountain of a male who was in the gym earlier.

"Who invited you?" I clip out, deliberately taking a seat on the opposite side of the room.

"Well, that isn't very nice, Your Highness," he remarks, the corner of his mouth lifting in a smug half-smile.

"Good, I wasn't trying to be," I retort, my tone acerbic.

Looking uneasy, Darius pipes up, "Yeah, that was me." He holds his hands up in a gesture of surrender. "Unintentionally," he rushes to add. "I invited Calian on our way out, and I guess he extended the invitation."

Taking a large swallow of ale, I wave him off. I'll figure it out. I always do. At this point, I should be an actress, considering how much I have to hide who I really am. I notice Tilde's glare directed at our interlopers and smirk into my glass.

Iskra, being Iskra, smiles at Conaill and the other male. "Hi, I'm Princess Iskra of Fenshegus, but you can skip the whole princess part."

The stranger stands and bows in a maneuver so graceful I wouldn't have thought possible, given his sheer size. "Your Highness, may I introduce myself?" He picks up her hand, placing a chaste kiss across her knuckles. A blush creeps across her face, and she suddenly turns shy. "My name is Madok Cebrail of Umbrimina, and this is Prince Conaill of Kystenvar."

Hellos echo around the room, people exchange names, and people pass out pints. Merl enters with pints for the party crashers and refills ours. When his power came into being, Moro must have known he'd own a tavern. Merl is able to manipulate and command any liquid. If Merl is in a good mood, and you leave a big enough tip, he can refill any glass if only a drop remains.

"By Moro!" Madok shouts. "That is one of the best powers. To always have your ale full? A dream come true." Madok looks at Merl as if he hung the moon.

"I don't know if it's a dream come true." Merl laughs. "But it does help with my bottom line."

We all raise a glass to him in thanks as he turns to leave. An awkward silence descends, and I busy myself by taking a long drink.

Calian breaks the silence, asking, "Who's up for a drinking game?"

We all agree, and the options narrow down to two. We decide to combine them: it's either a statement where those who have done it drink, or they can request a truth from someone. If you don't want to answer the truth, you have to drink instead.

"Calian, it was your idea, so you go first." Mina insists kindly.

"Hmm…" He looks around the room. "Group question: Drink if you have ever…" He pauses for effect. "Used your position to get out of trouble."

We all groan, and everyone but Mina and Madok drinks.

"Wait a minute." Tilde turns on Iskra. "*You* have? But you're, like, so pure and sweet?"

Iskra scoffs. "I may be sweet, but I'm not a goody-two-shoes. That's Mina." She looks pointedly at Mina, who shrugs good-naturedly, and we all laugh. "Wait, how are you shocked about *me* but not him?" Her hand flings out, and we all swing our heads to Madok. "He has to be lying." Realizing how that sounds, a blush creeping up her neck, she rushes to add, "I'm so sorry, I mean no offense, but… you just look the type."

Madok laughs, shaking his head. "Absolutely, and no offense taken, darling." He winks at her, a charming, easy gesture. "I don't have a position. I can't use what I don't have to get me out of trouble. But you're right," his smile widens, showing off perfectly straight white teeth. "If I did have one, I totally would."

The tension in the room loosens, and we do a few more rounds of group questions. No one is brave enough to choose a "truth" yet.

A strangely studious look graces Conaill's face as he stares at Iskra. My need to protect her flares, and I glare at him. "Iskra," he says, and her head snaps to his, "group question or truth?"

"Hmm," she hums out, her finger tapping against her lip in contemplation. "I think I'll do a truth." She lowers her hand to her lap, where the tavern's resident cat, Teachdaire, a beautiful orange tabby with whom she clearly has a special bond, has been resting. "But first, I shall get us refills."

The males rush to stand up, eager to get the refills themselves, but Iskra stalls them with a gentle hand. "Gentlemales, no need to do anything." She gently taps Teachdaire, and the males, somewhat reluctantly, retake their seats. "Daire," she coos to the orange tabby, "would you please be a dear and let Merl know we need refills? And maybe some snacks?"

Teachdaire rises, stretching in the way only cats can manage, and with a quick, soft nuzzle to Iskra's cheek, he trots off toward the bar. The males, clearly baffled by what they've just witnessed, stare openly at Iskra. Calian's mouth actually falls open before he shakes his head, as if waking from a trance, and remembers to snap it shut.

"Now wait a godsdamn minute," he finally gets out. "What was that?"

"I can talk to animals." Iskra shrugs, turning to Conaill. "Now, what was the truth you wanted to ask me?"

He takes a minute as if processing what he just saw. I mean, being an animal speaker is very rare, but it runs in our family. To us, it's normal.

"Well then," Conaill clears his throat. "What is it with you and orange?" He notices her quizzical look and continues. "I've been here a few days, and every time I've seen you, you have something orange on."

"Oh, that," she dismisses. "It's my favorite color."

"Okay," he says, clearly not satisfied. "But why? I mean, that's like the least liked color."

Merl chooses that moment to enter, laden down with a tray piled high with frothing ales and ciders. Another server follows close behind, carrying a tray filled with meats, cheeses, fresh breads, and fruits. Teachdaire saunters in last, hopping gracefully back onto Iskra's lap. After distributing everything, Merl nods to us. "Just tell Daire if you have a need for anything else," he says, and with that, he leaves.

Reaching out to grab her cider, Iskra looks to Conaill, answering his other question. "I love it because it reminds me of fire." Lost looks stare at her from all sides, and she chuckles in amusement.

"Fire is one of the most giving things out there." More confused looks are exchanged among the group, but Iskra just smiles, unbothered, and continues on. "I think that many of the gods would've had a hand in its creation. Astrid, the Goddess of Passion, would use it for warming the hearts of lovers. Obviously, Bas, as the God of Life and Death, would use it for most of his dealings, either through killing or removing the bodies of those killed. When water or tools need to be sterilized for healing, Leighis would partake of its cleansing nature." Raising her cider to her lips, she takes a large drink, a twinkle in her eye. "And as the God of Jubilation, Moro uses its flames to roast the barley for ale, and in the process of making and distilling alcohol."

Loud laughs erupt at this, Madok's loudest of all. "I'll drink, and pray, to that!" Lifting his glass, he toasts, "Moro, may you ever bless us with the libations you so wondrously create through fire."

"To Moro," we cry in unison, all taking a drink.

"But it's more than that," Iskra continues, her voice softening. "Orange reminds me of the fire that warms a family's hearth. Turning even the simplest structure into a welcoming respite from the cold." Her eyes soften further, clearly envisioning the scene. "Fire turns simple ingredients into a meal. A meal that is shared between family and friends. Creating bonds, nourishing the body, maybe even sparking happy memories of loved ones who've passed." She pauses, as if caught in a memory herself. "With everything fire can do, how can I not love the color that reminds me of it?"

We all sit in contemplation for a few seconds before Darius interrupts our thoughts, "Well, fuck, that was deep." We all laugh, and Tilde good-naturedly throws a piece of bread at him.

Snatching the bread out of the air, he pops it into his mouth. "I have an idea." Looking around the table and taking a sip of his drink, he announces, "Let's ask a question and all of us have to answer it. Whoever doesn't want to answer, drinks."

We nod in agreement, and it's decided that, in honor of Iskra, we all share our favorite color.

Mina and I share a love for green, while Darius and Conaill both agree that blue is the best. Shocking all the males, Tilde reveals that pink is her favorite color.

"Pink," Calian asks incredulously. "But that is a color for females."

If looks could kill, Calian would be dead many times over. "Are you suggesting I'm anything other?" Tilde asks, her voice dangerously calm.

Shaking his head, he quickly explains, "You just look like black would be your favorite. You practically scream death and pain. Not frills and lace."

"Oh, sweetie," she drawls in what I like to think of as her 'bedroom spy voice.' The one that entrances males, making them think of tangled sheets and smooth skin. While they're lost in thought, she strikes, getting them to spill their secrets, just hoping to get a glimpse of hers. "You'll *never* get to see my lace. And I assure you, I really, really do love lace, and little bits of nothing frills." She winks and takes a drink.

Mina and I look at each other, laughter erupting. Calian looks like he *very* much wants to see just that. "Anyway," I interject, changing the subject, "What's everyone scared of? I'll go first. I'm terrified of soggy things."

"*Seriously*?" Conaill scoffs, a disbelieving laugh escaping him. "That isn't a real thing to be scared of. Like you see wet bread and break out in a sweat?"

"Gods, you're an ass. It's called an irrational fear for a reason." I glare, my voice sharp. "And no, I'm not scared of wet bread. More like touching something slimy and squishy, or walking along by a stream and stepping into soggy, trapping ground." I retort, "I'm sure you're scared of something equally odd."

"I'll have you know I'm scared of snakes," he says, crossing his arms with a huff. "A perfectly normal fear, thank you very much."

I roll my eyes and turn away from him. Madok, it turns out, is scared of flying insects. In a similar vein, Mina is scared of spiders, and Tilde is just scared of all bugs — "the creepy crawly kind," as she puts it. Calian can't stand heights, and small, enclosed spaces do Darius in. Iskra is the last to go, sharing that she isn't scared of anything at all.

Mina, her brow furrowed in genuine confusion, implores, "How can you not be scared of anything?"

"Simple," Iskra replies with a thoughtful pause. "Everything is here for a reason, so no need to be scared of it." She shrugs. "I mean, I guess I'm scared of wraiths and crin; but, then again, I think everyone is."

Everyone shudders, and the game continues, the questions growing more ridiculous and daring as the night wears on. When the night is over, we all stumble back to the palace, our laughter echoing a little too loudly in the quiet halls. We part ways when we reach the paths that lead to our different quarters. As I go to tackle the grand staircase that will take me to my rooms, I'm stopped by Conaill's voice.

"Goodnight, Red." Humor drips from his words. "I hope you don't find anything soggy in your bed." I glare, about to respond, when he adds, "You could always join me in mine." A lascivious gleam twinkles in his eyes. "I promise, the only thing you'll feel in my bed will be hard."

"I can assure you, I would rather sleep with a vampyr." I turn and start my ascent up the stairs.

His deep laugh follows me. "Trust me, Red. If you were in my bed, you wouldn't be sleeping."

Refusing to turn around, I continue up the stairs and produce a very unprincess-like gesture over my shoulder. Laughter is my only answer, adding to my anger. Gods, I can't stand this male and his arrogance

Chapter Eight

Sitting to the right of Uncle Emeric, I discreetly scan the opulent meeting room. The Council of Pan is about to begin, and today, thankfully, I'm merely an observer. I send a quick prayer of thanks to the gods for that small mercy. Lukavo's miraculous tonic has me feeling almost completely myself after last night's adventure. Mentally, I prepare myself, drawing on my experiences of the Council and everything my many tutors, and especially Mina, have drilled into me.

The Council of Pan first started after the Great War, six hundred years ago. Ever since then, the leaders of each of the seven kingdoms have met for one week every year. The meeting location rotates annually, ensuring each kingdom hosts once every seven years. Since I'm set to become queen next year and will be Fenshegus's official representative, I desperately need to soak up every single detail I can this time around.

This upcoming week is going to be a blur of endless meetings and tense negotiations. Trade agreements will extend or dissolve, alliances will forge and strengthen, all theoretically ensuring peace continues for another year across Panellas. Well, at least, that's the *hope*. So far, it's actually worked, holding strong since the Council's inception.

Six hundred years ago, King Harrend of Saetoris tried to conquer all the other kingdoms. Enslaving those they defeated and killing those who stood in their way. Saetoris even made alliances with wraiths and vampyrs, offering them free rein to feed on the opposing armies as long as they left the Saetorian forces untouched. Traditionally, the rulers of Saetoris have always detested the lesser fae, even enslaving those who couldn't hide. It never made sense to me why they would ally with such evils, given their hatred for lesser fae. Yet, with the monstrous advantage that the alliance provided, they conquered Nuwen and even made significant headway into Baress.

My grandfather, King Oren the Second, banded together with Kystenvar and Umbrimina to fight this abhorrent spread of hatred and evil. They were joined by the Dochais. The Dochais were the bringers of hope and the only creatures capable of killing a wraith without Tinuvar blades. Honestly, without them, there would've been no way to deal with the evil hordes allied with Saetoris.

Eventually, the armies of those three kingdoms and the Dochais met King Harrend in a pitched battle near the city of Chast. The Battle of Chast is one that every child in Panellas knows the story of. My grandfather faced King Harrend, sword to sword. That day, my grandfather was victorious, severing the head of King Harrend, ending the war, and setting things right, restoring peace and justice as much as possible. Unfortunately, that day was the last day anyone saw the Dochais. It was as if they used up all of themselves, fighting the evil that plagued our continent.

I shake my head, trying to clear away those dark thoughts. Instead, I focus on the evenings. They promise varied entertainment and supposedly friendly competitions. All of which I'm actually pretty eager to see.

Looking outside the window, I can just see a vast ocean of multicolored tents that have sprung up overnight. Council meetings and gatherings take place in the Talla Tionail, a grand building built specifically for these occasions. Its exterior matches that of the palace just next door. When not in use, the Talla Tionail holds conferences, debates, fairs, and exhibitions. Next to the Talla Tionail is a sprawling, wide-open field, usually reserved for various events throughout the year. This week, it's transformed into a seemingly endless market.

And oh, my gods, what a market it is. It's an absolute smorgasbord, an explosion of everything Panellas offers. Vendors have journeyed from all seven kingdoms, their stalls crammed with wares designed to showcase their homelands' finest. Stalls laden with exotic delicacies and unique foods, found only in their native lands, already fill the air with aromas tempting taste buds and lightening purses. Even from this distance, my nose twitches, catching hints of sweet spices and roasting meats, making my stomach rumble loudly enough to be heard in the next room. My mouth waters at the thought of sampling it all, a welcome distraction from the looming meetings. I just need this meeting to be *over* so I can sample the stalls.

Motion across the room draws my attention. King Tavarik enters, boisterous as always. He's practically a walking roar. Trailing just behind him, Conaill strides in, a distinct swagger in his hips, and I watch, annoyed, as he winks at a serving girl who's carefully balancing a tray of tea and coffee. She blushes and lowers her head, attempting to continue about her work. Gods, why must he be so sexy and yet so awful?

King Tavarik ambles toward his seat, his corpulent mass testing the limits of the sturdy chair. Whoever subtly provided him that armless chair deserves a massive raise. Conaill settles into the seat on his father's right, and he points to the serving girl. They both leer at her, and my stomach turns. *Fucking gross.*

I turn my head and realize that we're only missing the rulers of Samaith. As if my thoughts summoned them, King Caderyn and Queen Rayna enter the hall. Caderyn nods to me as he takes his seat, eliciting a smile. He was my mom's cousin, and I know he misses her terribly.

Soon, all the necessary papers are in order, and it's time to start. "I would like to take a minute and thank all of you," Uncle Emeric begins, his voice carrying clearly across the room, "for your timely arrival and to welcome you to the official start of the Council of Pan."

A chorus of agreements sounds, and just like that, my first Council of Pan is officially underway. The first few hours are mind-numbing and unremitting. The Council discussed treaties needing updates, but it did not enact any changes. Instead, plans are made to speak about them in specific, smaller meetings throughout the week.

Ceaseless bickering about trade agreements follows, and honestly, it's exhausting. I know that these are important, but there *has* to be a better way than this. Or at least a more streamlined way, right?

Lunch is brought in and, to my supreme disappointment, we continue to work through it. The dishes are quickly cleared, and sadly, there are still a few more hours of this torture left. My body is starting to ache from sitting in this chair for so long. Surreptitiously, I try to stretch, wiggling a bit to alleviate some of the ache. My efforts haven't gone unnoticed, because across the room, Conaill is staring at me, a smirk on his face and a knowing glint in his eyes.

This is by far the longest day I have been told, and I can't even express how relieved I am about that fact. Throughout it all, my gaze keeps straying to Conaill. What *is* it about him that causes this weird pull? The few things he's actually said today have been condescending in the extreme. And a few of the times I glanced his way, he was openly staring at me. Hunger emanates from his eyes, and I can't understand it. One time, he even winked at me before turning away, as if he hadn't just done something outrageous.

Shaking my head, I try to force my focus back to the incredibly dull matter at hand. Darius's father, Emperor Callen of Baress, clears his throat, drawing everyone's attention. With what seems like slight hesitation, he begins. "I think it's now time we speak of something very troubling." He pauses, looking each of the rulers in the eye in turn. "We in Baress have been receiving word of a very concerning issue. An issue that I fear is affecting all of us, and one we are overlooking."

Emperor Callen pointedly looks to Queen Penelope of Saetoris and King Tavarik. "Common fae have made it known to us, and others, that power is leaving them." Contemplating his words, he continues, "Not leaving them, but being *stolen* from them. They can feel it being leeched from them, unable to stop it." A loud, troubled exhale leaves his lips; his face is a picture of worry. "I fear that if we can't stop it, soon all fae will be left without magic."

Sitting next to her husband, the queen of Nuwen lets out a slight gasp, her hand flying to her mouth. "Father," she directs her question to Emperor Callen, "has this issue affected the high fae in Baress?" She quickly continues, "I only ask, as we too have heard about this in Nuwen. So far, we have not heard of high fae being afflicted."

King Jara, her husband, grasps her hand tenderly. "We had hoped to discuss this matter here this week as well," he states. Nuwen's king looks around, noticing nods coming from most of the rulers. "I have had our finest healers look into the matter, and they can't find the cause," he reveals.

A collective startle ripples across the room. My mind reels in shock and denial. *How is that the case?* Nuwen is renowned for its healers. Fae from all over the continent, even beyond the sea, journey there to attend their university. If they can't find a cure, this is seriously bad news.

It's also incredibly bad for the Order. All the work I've put into motion to ensure that those affected, and those in danger of being affected, would be safe may not be enough. We thought that it was an illness. We thought we could find a cure and return their power, at least to those we were able to get to safety. We had even sent an operative to Nuwen to look into this, and he was actually supposed to report back this week.

I hated going behind Uncle Emeric's back, but I had no other choice. When I brought up my concerns, he seemed to think I was blowing this out of proportion. But I'm going to be queen in a matter of months, and I don't want my subjects to go through this. Every time I try to do something, my efforts keep getting beaten back. Lately, we've even helped those in Saetoris affected, and those scared of being affected, seek refuge in our kingdom. Which, to be perfectly honest, goes against our treaty with them. I'll just add it to the ever-growing list of laws I've been breaking.

A deep, "Not as of yet," draws my attention back to the tense room. Again, Callen is looking between Queen Penelope and King Tavarik, almost glaring. Both of them are brazenly looking back at Callen, with small smiles on their lips.

"Well, then, there you have it." Conaill smirks. "If it isn't affecting *us*, then why should we care?" He dismisses the entire issue, immediately drawing my ire. "Let them figure it out," he adds, and Tavarik chuckles from beside him. That's it. I lose it.

"What's wrong with you?" The words rip from my throat, and heads snap in my direction. *Shit, I said that out loud.* Blood rushes to my face, hot and stinging.

"Please excuse my niece," Uncle Emeric urges, a forced chuckle rumbling in his chest as he tries to smooth over my outburst. "It's been a long day. I think between that and it being her first Council, she's a bit overwhelmed." His tone is placating.

"Tsk, tsk." Conaill actually has the *nerve* to wag his finger in my direction. "That wasn't very proper of you, Princess."

Oh, hell no. My jaw clenches so hard that my teeth ache. No way am I letting that slide, not from *him*. I may be a princess now, but I'll soon be queen. And they'd better learn right now not to disrespect me.

"No," I say firmly. "I really would like to know what's wrong with him." My arm sweeps around the room, encompassing not just Conaill, but every single ruler and adviser present. "What's wrong with anyone here who could just write this off?" My voice rings with disbelief.

"My dear, it may be distressing, but what can we do?" Queen Penelope states matter-of-factly. "There is nothing, so we must move on. If we are lucky enough, maybe they will disappear one day, just like those other non-magic things. What were they called again?" She taps a perfectly manicured finger to her chin, feigning a thoughtful expression.

"Humans, I believe," King Tavarik grates out, repulsion evident.

"I refuse to accept that," I declare, my voice gaining strength with every word. "I refuse to accept that we would abandon our own! Even if they're not high fae, how can any good ruler let this happen and do nothing?" My voice weakens. "How can we not help? Not try to find a cure?" My voice lowers almost to a whisper by the end of my outburst. "How can we not help those affected? Support them and their families if there's no way to fix it?" I glare at them, silently daring anyone to contradict me.

King Ewan of Umbrimina nods his head in agreement, a grim line set on his lips. "I, too, find this troubling." He turns his gaze to Queen Penelope, looking her straight in the eyes. "Just as I find it troubling that knowledge has reached me which shows that, once again, common fae in Saetoris are a rare sight. And those that are seen show no sign of the magic that used to bless them."

With her words deadly calm and cold as ice, Queen Penelope retorts, "Just what exactly are you insinuating, Ewan?"

"Why, nothing, of course," he replies smoothly. "I just find that rather…" He pauses, clearly searching for a word that won't ignite another war. "Shall we say, *coincidental* that it's Saetoris's common fae that seem to suffer the worst, while their high fae act as if nothing is happening. It strikes me as very reminiscent of six hundred years ago."

And just like that, all hell breaks loose. The room erupts into shouts, accusations, and angry murmurs. Everyone is talking over each other, their carefully maintained composure shattering. The fragile peace, the meticulous hours we've spent in this room solidifying our continent, seem to hang by a single, fraying thread. Uncle Emeric pounds his fist on the table, a booming sound that brings the chaos back to some semblance of order.

"I insist we close today's meeting and speak again with fresh minds tomorrow." Uncle Emeric declares, his voice still a bit strained. Nods of agreement spread throughout the room, though many eyes still burn with agitation, clearly not ready to let go of the anger. "Tonight we have many amusing entertainments planned, and hopefully that will help to dispel any lingering enmity." I highly doubt that, but I keep my mouth shut.

Agreements sound, and we all take our exits. I practically race out, as quickly as I'm able, storming toward the palace to change out of these ridiculous, restricting clothes. Tilde straightens upon seeing me, instantly knowing I'm upset. "Who are we throwing knives at now?" She questions, turning to fall into stride with me, her voice already eager.

"Oh, I don't know," I huff, anger still boiling hot inside me. "Just every entitled, bigoted fae there is in this entire damn palace."

"So I take it we're dressing functionally, so we can drink afterward."

"Abso-fucking-lutely," I say, bursting into my room and ripping at the fastenings of my gown. Knives and alcohol are very much needed right now. Just definitely not at the same time. I might be fuming, but even I know that combining the two is a spectacularly bad idea.

Chapter Nine

The *clink* and *thud* of glasses hitting the worn wooden bar echoes around us. *Gods, that needs to be my last one.* "No more, Merl, please, I beg you," I plead to him, my words a little slurred and my tongue feeling thick in my mouth.

"Not my call." A laugh escapes his mouth. "It's you ladies who keep demanding them."

"Well"—*hic*—"my royal command"—*hic*—"is that that was"—*hic*—"the last one." *Hic.*

Mina nods vigorously beside me, her eyes just as glazed as mine. We both swing our gaze to Tilde, who, impossibly, still looks perfectly composed, not even a hair out of place.

"Fine, be that way, babies." Tilde slaps her hand twice on the bar, the sharp *crack* cutting through the tavern's hum. She winks at Merl. "Merl, one more shot."

Twin groans pour from Mina and me. Chuckling, Merl pulls a different, unlabeled bottle from beneath the bar, pouring three shots. Tilting my head like a confused puppy, I stare at the orange liquid in my glass. It's thick as cream and is so brilliantly orange, I know Iskra would absolutely adore it.

Looking over, I notice Mina's head is a mirror image of mine, tilted in exactly the same way. The realization hits us simultaneously, and we both burst into loud, unrestrained laughter, the sound drawing curious glances from patrons nearby.

"Well, it must be a miracle, boys. Turns out Red *does* know how to have fun." The drawl is unmistakably Conaill's.

Whipping my head around, a terrible idea that sends the room spinning wildly, I spot him. He's lounging at a table against the far wall, Madok and Calian flanking him. "I guess you did win," he adds, an evil smile stretching across his lips. He casually reaches into his pocket and, with a flourish, hands Madok money. "I plan on making you pay that money back to me one day, princess."

Giving him and his table a very un-princess-like gesture over my shoulder, I turn back to the bar, my cheeks burning. Laughter follows me, and, gods, why does his laughter have to be so sexy?

"Okay, last shot," I say, glaring at Tilde, my voice firm despite my giddiness. "Seriously."

She crosses her heart, and we raise our glasses. "To not always being proper." Tilde offers up as a toast. Mina looks slightly disgusted at this toast, a shudder passing through her, but we repeat it anyway and slam our shots back. The liquid coats my tongue, thick and sweet with the surprising, bright taste of oranges, quickly followed by a rich, creamy warmth. *Wow, that's delicious!*

A strange tingling sensation spreads through me. It's oddly invigorating, chasing away the last vestiges of my tipsy haze. My gaze snaps between Tilde and Merl, both of whom are now sharing a knowing, conspiratorial grin.

"Merl," I say tentatively, my voice a little breathless as I try to pinpoint the source of this sudden clarity. "What was that shot?"

"That shot?" he asks, his movements unhurried as he gathers our empty glasses and wipes down the counter. "That shot is a secret." He winks, a flash of mischief in his eyes, before turning his back to us, clearly dismissing the topic.

"Nope, that won't do!" My drunken state has almost instantly been rectified, leaving me feeling as if I have only had one drink all night. "I need to know what that was."

"Agreed," Mina says, shaking her head. "I was very worried we wouldn't be able to attend the concert tonight and *that*"—she points to the used glass in the sink — "is a gods darn miracle."

Tilde gives a soft chuckle, finally putting us out of our misery. "Charion, one of the centaurs we"— she pauses, lowering her voice and looking around, she continues — "helped, if you will, taught the healing arts in Saetoris."

"Had him *working* here for a bit," Merl picks up, "taught me how to make that. Helps out quite a bit when patrons get unruly." He gives us a pointed look, which is immediately ruined by his smile, and we can't help but giggle. "Wasn't the only thing he taught me, either; he's still teaching. Sent me a letter, actually. Started up a school of sorts there, teaching and healing to those willing to learn."

A smile breaks across my face as I remember Charion, that sweet centaur. His wife's magic was stolen, and he fled with her. So hearing he's doing well now warms something deep inside me. The boisterous laughter from a nearby table suddenly cuts through my happy thoughts; their raucous shouts are just as loud as ours were moments ago. My smile, however, takes a sharp, devious turn as a new, mischievous thought flits across my mind.

"Oh no," Mina says with a groan, "I know that smile, Mae, and I most assuredly will not like what you're about to do."

"Oh, I think you will." I turn to Merl, my voice dripping with honey. "Merl, you wouldn't happen to be able to camouflage that miraculous potion of yours now, would you?"

Catching my drift instantly, Merl's eyes light up, and he pulls out a wide assortment of bottles and glasses from beneath the bar, their glass clinking softly. "You know what, Princess, I think I just might be able to."

"If I didn't already love you, I would for sure now." I breathe. Tilde bumps into me with her hip, having caught on to my plan. "You know I love it when you scheme." We both turn to Mina, knowing this will only work if she's in on it.

"I knew I wouldn't like this," she says softly, a sigh escaping her. But the resigned tone and faint twitch of her lips tell me all I need to know. We have her.

A few minutes later, Mina, tray in hand, is striding confidently toward Conaill and his friends. She sets her tray on their table; she passes out her drinks.

"To what do we owe this honor, my dear sweet 'Lo?" A deep, resonant timber flows from Madok; his eyes glued to Mina.

"Please don't call me that. I like Mina," she gently corrects him. "I just thought we got off to a rocky start, and I want to make amends."

Tilde and I are at the door by now, muscles tensed, ready to make our escape the instant the plan unfolds. How we're keeping our faces straight, not giving away everything with our barely suppressed giggles, I have no idea.

"I would like to make a toast, please," Mina announces, her voice carrying a feigned innocence. She raises her glass, one that holds a very different, carefully concocted drink, and looks plaintively around at the unsuspecting males. "I was hoping we could drink to new friendships."

"That sounds like a great idea to me!" Calian responds, a slight, happy slur already present in his voice.

"Prince Conaill," Mina says in her sweetest voice, making the name sound almost endearing, "please do me the honor?"

"Of course, my dear." Conaill raises his glass even higher. "To new friendships!"

All four of them eagerly down their drinks, the liquid disappearing in quick gulps. Mina gives them a huge smile.

"'Lo darling, why don't you sit with us? You seem to be the sweetest of the bunch." Madok pats his lap with a heavy hand.

"Um," Mina murmurs, her expression an adorable mix of attempted propriety and barely concealed fury. "While that does sound…"—a tiny pause, her gaze darting away as if considering the offer — "...tempting, we really must get back to get ready for tonight." Without waiting for a single response, she turns sharply on her heel, the swish of her skirt a whisper of defiance, and the three of us practically bolt for the door.

We position ourselves just out of sight, pressed against the cool stone wall next to an open window. The faint murmur of the tavern still reaches us, a muffled hum of conversation and clinking glasses. Merl had warned us the special concoction would take a little longer to kick in, having been mixed into other drinks, so we had a few precious moments to make our escape.

Then, a sudden shout, unmistakable, rips through the quiet night air. "What the fuck?" It's Madok's voice, laced with anger. "What the hell did she give us?!"

Tilde claps a hand over her mouth, her shoulders shaking. We run toward the palace, our steps light and quick. It's everything we can do to get around the corner before we finally burst into uncontrollable, triumphant laughter.

Chapter Ten

A smile graces my lips upon seeing Conaill's glare the next morning. Today, we're set to talk again about the disappearing magic and what we could, and should, do. I knew it was going to be a stressful day, and the memory of ruining his buzz last night will help me get through it.

Striding toward me, Conaill's look is dangerous. He has already planned out his payback, and it won't be pretty for me. He comes around to my back, pushing his body so close that only a whisper of breath remains between us.

Leaning his considerable height down, he brings his face just behind mine. His breath, a caress on my neck, sends chills down my body, heat pooling deep within.

"I don't know how you did that last night," Conaill quietly says, "but I intend to pay you back. And I intend to have fun while I do." He takes a deep breath along my neck. It's as if he's scenting me, and it takes everything in me to hold still and not shudder.

"Watch your back, Red." With that, he straightens up, taking his place.

I'm so screwed. Why did that feel so good? Why was that threat the first thing in ages that affected my body so? But also, what in the name of all the gods does he have planned?

Giving my body a little shake, I turn my mind to the task at hand. How can we figure out what's causing the common fae to stop losing their power, and how can we stop it? But also, which kingdom leaders can I look to for allies in my fight to end this?

We won't start for a few more minutes, and most are still talking. Clearly, no one is excited to start the day. Uncle Emeric is in deep conversation with Queen Penelope of Saetoris as King Tavarik makes his way over to them. *Ugh*, how can he stand to be near those two?

Tavarik makes my skin crawl. Anytime I have been forced to share a room with him, it takes all my willpower not to recoil. He openly cheats on his wife, constantly belittling her. His eyes are always hungrily taking in any female in his presence, assessing them as if they were his next meal, and that the female in question should be grateful for it. Then, there's also his thinly veiled hatred of common fae. Which anyone with half a brain can see through. Conaill, it seems, didn't fall very far from that tree.

Penelope isn't much better. I feel as if her acid tongue flays anyone she dislikes. She's turned it into a veritable art form. The path to having a crown atop her head was particularly suspicious. I know that I'm not the first to think it either. She had three older brothers, all in line before her, all of whom somehow perished in the last war. One of whom never even set foot on a battleground. It's all speculation, but I would put good money on her having something to do with it.

A few minutes pass, and it's finally time for us to start the meeting. Much like yesterday, very little is actually accomplished. I want to scream at the inefficiency of everything. Tavarik and Penelope, as well as their attending dignitaries, are all in favor of doing nothing. No shock there. What's surprising, though, is that Uncle Emeric is in favor of reducing the movement of common fae, denying them the ability to cross either kingdom or even town borders anymore.

"I know we need to do something about this horrible sickness plaguing them. I feel that if we can stop them from moving around, it might keep the situation contained. Not letting it spread further," he argues.

A few heads nod, and unfortunately, he has support in the room. I don't like this option. In fact, I hate it. It was even confirmed yesterday that it isn't a sickness. Keeping them in place will only allow whatever is attacking them to continue to do so. Why do they not see that?

Mentally, I plan out how to get word to the others in the Order. I may be the head from which the idea of this Order sprang, but there are others like me in each kingdom, eager to help those in need. With this development reducing movement, it will make getting the common fae to safety that much trickier. For a moment, I'm lost in planning.

"Maevery." The sound of my name brings me back to the present, and I notice everyone looking at me. Conaill is even rolling his eyes at my lost attention.

"I'm so sorry, Uncle Emeric," I stammer out. "Are we truly closing all borders in Panellas to common fae?"

Uncle Emeric shakes his head. "No, my dear." I let loose a silent prayer of thanks. "Samaith and Baress have refused to close any borders. Nuwen and Umbrimina will only close borders to other kingdoms, not internally." Okay, some good news, but I fear for what I'm about to hear. "The rest of us will close all borders, internal and external."

"That is preposterous!" I all but shout. *Shit, I didn't mean to say that out loud.* The room stares at me. Those of Kystenvar and Saetoris are glaring at me.

"I'm so sorry, forgive me." I plead. "I only meant that if all borders are closed, how are we to conduct trade?" I try to cover my blunder, hoping that they buy my excuse.

My eyes travel over the room, landing on King Jara. "It's just…" I pause, swinging my head to Uncle Emeric. *Oh gods, please let this idea work.* "My coronation is only a few months away." I force emotion into my eyes, hoping disappointment can be seen there. Not for what I'm truly disappointed in, but what I'm about to say.

"I had hoped that I could have my coronation gown made from Nuwen silk and lace." I nod to King Jara and rush to continue, "Everyone knows that the Takac make the best lace. And those fae only live in Nuwen. If they can't travel, how can I get the material for my dress?"

Uncle Emeric's eyes soften, and I know that at least for him, I was able to deflect. Soft chuckles come from the more misogynistic in the room. Penelope's eyes roll so far back in her head I'm afraid they might get stuck. The queen of Nuwen looks positively confused, and Conaill's face shows visible disgust.

Patting my hand like I'm a skittish horse, Uncle Emeric reassures me. "My darling, no need to worry. We'll make sure that trade isn't impacted." Heads nod all around me, as if that is more important than the common fae losing their powers. "We will just havc to makc sure that a high fae is the one in charge of transportation."

My body relaxes. I'm sure to others it looks as though I'm simply happy my dress won't be without the lace I want. Really, it's that this still leaves the Order with a method to get much-needed supplies and messages across the realms. Especially if we can't help them flee anymore.

With this issue pushed to the back of most leaders' minds, we break for the day as a whole group. Meetings will still take place throughout the day, but only between those needing to meet, thank the gods.

"Maevery," Uncle Emeric calls out just as I'm about to flee, desperate to figure out my next step. "There's something I need to talk to you about. Would you be able to meet in the library after you eat lunch?" He looks up, and I see sadness in his eyes.

"Of course, what do you need?"

"Don't worry about it now." He waves me off. "Go enjoy your lunch. I'll see you in a little bit."

I nod, turning away and making my way out.

Entering the library, I take in the warmth that emanates from the room. It was my father's favorite room, and when I walk in, it's like getting a hug from him. Lunch passed in a blur, my mind constantly returning to what this could be about. Now that I'm about to find out, I don't know what to think.

"Let's sit." He gestures to the overstuffed chairs flanking the empty fireplace. "I'm afraid this isn't anything you'll want to hear standing."

Sitting, I face him. Now nervous for more than just the common fae. The last time he sat me down like this, it was to tell me my parents had died.

"What's wrong?" I resent the nervous tremor I hear in my voice.

"Nothing is wrong," Uncle Emeric rushes to reassure me. "Only…" He pauses, carefully choosing his words. "There's a… complication that has come to light." He grasps my hand, holding it firmly. "As you know, you'll be the youngest ruler Fenshegus has had in five thousand years, and you'll be a queen at that."

I nod my head. I have no idea why he's bringing that up, or why my being a queen matters. "What does that have to do with anything? Succession in Fenshegus doesn't take gender into account?" I'm utterly confused. If my furrowed brow is any indication, my face is surely screaming that fact.

"Yes, well," he continues, shifting on his seat. Something must be really wrong, as I have never seen him look so nervous. "As my counselors and I were going through everything in preparation for your coronation…" He pauses again. I really don't like how much he's stalling.

"Well, something completely unexpected was discovered." He takes a deep breath, hurrying to finish. "According to Fenshegus law, as you're a female, as it stands right now, you're unable to inherit the throne."

Excuse me? What the actual fuck did I just hear him say? "I'm sorry, what did you just say?" I grind out through my teeth, enunciating each word as carefully as I can. Completely flabbergasted at what I think he just said.

With a deep exhale, Uncle Emeric leans back and runs his hands over his face. "There is a way for you to still inherit." A sigh of relief rushes out. It's not like I longed to be queen my whole life, but it's what I was raised for. I could do so much good for my kingdom as queen. So much more than I could in any other role.

"We were unaware of this, shall I say, issue, as it never played a role in the other queens inheriting," he says.

"Go on," I say slowly, raising my eyebrow.

"Well, all the other queens were already married when it came time for them to inherit. So the law didn't apply." He looks at me as if this answers anything.

Yeah, I'm still confused. "And how does that matter? Why did they get a pass, and I don't?"

Oh gods. I think I know where this is going, and I just pray that I'm wrong.

"Please remember that this law was written in a different time," he assures.

No, gods no. Please don't say it.

He looks softly at me. "I tried to see if I could change the law, but as I'm only regent, I can't change inheritance laws."

"What's the law?" I breathe out.

"An unmarried female cannot be queen. To take your crown, you must marry." Breath rushing out as he finishes.

Shit, this is bad. I can work with bad, though.

I think of every way I can to make this work, finally settling on an idea. "Okay, so we'll put off the coronation, and you'll keep on being regent."

Uncle Emeric shakes his head. "I'm afraid it doesn't work like that. I already looked into that option. I can only go on as regent if you're unfit to take the throne in mind or body. As you're neither, I'll be unable to keep going in that role once you turn twenty-five."

"So that means…"

"If you can't become queen at twenty-five, then the throne will be passed to the next in line. Iskra would become the new queen."

"She'd hate that; it's the farthest thing from what she wants," I insist.

"Then, she'd have to abdicate, which leaves no other choice but for the crown to go to me." I tilt my head, looking at him intently. He notices and rushes out, "That is the furthest thing from what I want. What your parents wanted."

I nod. "So what do I do?"

"The only thing you can." His voice is resigned. "You must get married before your twenty-fifth birthday. In three months."

Well, shit.

Chapter Eleven

Thwack. Thwack. The rhythmic sound soothes me more than anything else has in the last few hours. Married, I have to get married. Picking up another dagger, I launch it at the target I brought into the gym. Technically, I'm not supposed to do this, but I don't really care.

"Who does he think you're going to marry?" Tilde asks, adding even more weight to her bar. "I mean, you turn twenty-five in three months. It isn't like you have a lot of time."

"I'm aware of that." My shoulders fall, hopelessness trying its best to creep in. "I know I could find a way around it if I only had more time."

A loud crash sounds from a group of males working out a bit away from us. As if my day couldn't get worse, Conaill and Madok clearly decided they had to work out at the same time as us. So far, they have left us alone, only glancing our way now and then. Well, if they have to be here, at least they provide a good view.

"Why are the sexy ones always jerks?" Mina whines. We agree and spare them another glance before moving on. "We will find a way. I'm certain of that."

I thank her, retrieving my daggers. The doors bang open as Darius and Iskra enter, looking around widely. When they spot us, they seem relieved and head over.

"Thank the gods I found you," Iskra says loudly. "Mary told me she thought you were headed this way. I think I found a solution to your problem."

Shushing her, I look around, noticing that Conaill and Madok have closed the distance between us. Glaring at them, Tilde waves her hand, throwing up a silencing shield before I say. "And what solution is that?"

"Me," Darius speaks up.

"Huh?" Tilde blurts. "How are you able to fix this?"

Rolling his eyes, he continues, "If you had let me finish"—he scowls at Tilde — "I would have said you marry me."

"Umm, Darius, how does that help me with the issue of me needing to marry? I don't want to get married. I was hoping to avoid that. Marrying you doesn't avoid that."

Mina tilts her head, clearly working through this "solution" in her head.

Iskra shakes her head, a smile on her face. "You marry Darius, get crowned, change the law, and then get divorced. Or annulled. Whichever you prefer."

"That would totally work." Mina smiles through her words. "I mean, neither are exactly common, but it could work. You'll be queen after all, and they can't take it away once you're crowned and have gotten rid of the law."

Sliding his hand up to rub the back of his neck, Darius looks slightly sheepish. "I mean, it wouldn't have to be me. I know we don't love each other, but we're friends, and we get along well. I'll even sign something that says I want nothing from you."

"Well, better you than any other male I know." My shoulder bumps him, and I smile. What I thought was an insurmountable peak has just turned into a small hill.

Iskra rushes on. "I mean, we will keep looking for a loophole, but there are much worse options out there if we can't find one."

I huff out an agreement, my eyes straying to Conaill's back. "Much worse options."

The rest of the week flies by. A myriad of meetings have been arranged occupying every morning. It seems that nothing is ever actually settled and that many of the rulers, King Tavarik and Queen Penelope in particular, speak simply to hear their own voice. I swear every time they speak, they say nothing. At least the current trade agreements for Fenshegus have been agreed upon for another year. At least I can count that as a win.

The afternoons are for entertainment and competitions, that were supposedly friendly but were anything but. Each day consists of one of each. Musicians, dancers, actors, and singers have lavished their attention and skills in Otthon. The Council pays for their services during the official events; however, should one just so happen to sneak out of the palace disguised as a commoner, these same industrious fae can be seen performing for the masses. Often with much more bawdy and humorous shows. The only thing they ask for in return are tips, whether that be a coin, a loaf of bread, or whatever that fae can easily spare.

Jousts, wrestling tournaments, and various other athletic activities have each kingdom's competitor pushing their bodies to new limits. Poets, song writers, and artists each showcase the talents the gods have bestowed on them. Scientists and engineers compete to prove that their kingdom has the brightest citizens. One thing remains constant though. Regardless of the competition, each participant hopes to bring pride to their kingdom.

All the excitement of the Council had brought in fae from all over Fenshegus. As much as I dislike the much of the pageantry, I love this aspect. Getting to know the citizens of my kingdom and learning from them is something I'll never tire of. Spending my free time with them also allows me to avoid too many interactions with Conaill. I mostly had to see him in meetings and formal entertainment. Nothing, though, forced us to work one-on-one, nor did it allow me to flat-out ignore him.

In between my crazy schedule, I somehow managed to find time for training, work in the laboratory where I am helping with research and handle Order business. Earlier today, I received a new message from Walthier, my main contact in Kystenvar. His letter helped to alleviate some of my stress. He assured me that arrangements for extra supplies as well as additional transportation for those fleeing had been made. He was also working on a location in Kystenvar where fae could hide out with increased security.

Every time I get a letter from Walthier my heart flutters and my brain grows more confused. What started as a basic exchange of letters to coordinate our efforts, became an effortless connection between two fae who only want to help the helpless. As each letter was sent, a little bit more of ourself was carved out and offered up for the other. It only took two months before our letters turned into a soul deep connection.

As soon as order business was conferred, we wrote endless words to each other. Sharing hopes and dreams, fears and triumphs, insecurities and small wins. I've found myself looking forward to these letters, and when I get one, it invariably becomes the best part of my day.

I'd just finished my reply when a knock on the door sounded. "Come in," I reply, hastily sealing my missive.

Saori sails through the door, a bevy of maids trailing behind her. Tonight is the last ball, and all my girls will be getting ready here.

"Ready for me to work my magic, milady?" Saori says with a wink.

"As I'll ever be," I reply. She knows that while I prefer my everyday look and training clothes, I love getting dressed up, on occasion. "While you're at it," my voice lowers, "I have the instructions for my next wardrobe in that envelope."

Saori nods in understanding before grabbing the letter and slipping it into a pocket. I hate putting her at risk, but she's a veritable genius at subterfuge and can get a message to anyone.

We set to work and are soon joined by the rest of my girls. The closing ball of the Council is bittersweet, as the end of the Council also marks when Iskra will leave to attend Sabaid.

"Mae, I think you should let loose and do something daring tonight," Mina announces out of the blue.

My head whirls to hers, mouth open like a fish's. "E-excuse me?" I stammer out.

"I agree," Iskra seconds. "Maybe find some handsome male to take into a dark corner." She winks.

"Isk!" I practically shout. "You should not be encouraging me to do that." Whirling to look at Mina, I see Tilde smothering a laugh. "And you, Mina. Miss prim and proper herself. You've never suggested anything like that."

"What?" she asks. Eyes wide, the picture of shocked innocence. "Look, you're getting married in less than three months. And yeah, Darius is great, but you don't love him." She grasps my hand. "You're beyond loyal, so while yes, that marriage will be in name only, you know you would not even let yourself look at another male, let alone do anything. So while you still can, take one night to enjoy life."

"You know, she has a point," Tilde adds. "Tonight's ball is a masquerade; after you take the potion, no one will even know it's you. You'd be able to do something just for you for once with no repercussions."

Biting my lip, I think seriously about their idea. It does have merit. A masking potion will be available to anyone who wants to participate tonight. So long as no one else sees me before I take it, I could have a night without all the responsibilities.

Saori pipes up just then, "You know it isn't my place to say anything, but…" She pauses to make sure the other maids aren't listening. "I think you should do it."

Gasps escape all of us, and she simply waves them off. "What? You know that the gods only allow the magic in the potion to work on the last day of the Council. Live a little." She winks and goes to lay out my dress.

"I'll think about it," I grumble to the delight of all my girls. They know damn well that means I'll do it.

I'm trying, and somewhat succeeding, not to pace in the antechamber off to the side. The small cream and mauve room makes me feel exceedingly anxious. As the potion doesn't work on clothing, I made sure no one saw me slip in here. Iskra and Mina are also with me, both of whom look stunning. Looking at Iskra hurts my heart a little. She looks so much like Mom tonight. How I wish she could see us all grown up.

"Got them!" Tilde exclaims, breaking me out of my momentary melancholy. She passes out the potions, and we raise them in a toast.

"To the best friends," I say.

"Screw that." Tilde rolls her eyes. "To handsome males and dark corners…"

We laugh and echo her sentiments, taking our potion like a shot. The potion works almost instantly; the visage of my friends changing before my eyes. The potion doesn't physically change us, only what others perceive. Things like height and body shape aren't affected, but oddly enough, voice is. We take turns speaking and laughing at our ridiculously sounding voices and accents. Normally, fae could do this all by glamouring. The advantage of this potion is that you don't have to concentrate to keep it, nor does it drain any of your power. Also, unlike a glamour, if someone were to touch you after taking the potion, all they would feel is the altered facade.

Both Mina and Tilde sound like Baressians, while Iskra is proudly Samaith. I myself have the unmistakable lilt of a Kystenvarian. Still laughing at our impressions, I catch sight of myself in a mirror.

For the first time since I found out I must marry, my eyes sparkle with happiness. My eyes are still green, but a softer shade. The red of my hair is replaced with black, as dark as a moonless night. The perfect match for my dress. The black fabric is shot through with gold that twinkles in the light. The overall effect evokes a starry night sky. With my back completely bare, this is by far the most daring dress I've ever worn. Even before the potion, I didn't recognize myself. I guess this truly is a night to be daring.

Chapter Twelve

This night is amazing! Tipping back my head, I drain another glass of champagne. I'm far from drunk, but the bubbles are for sure making me a little extra giddy. The upbeat music of the orchestra that plays on a raised dais only adds to the giddiness.

Scanning the ballroom, I see a group of handsome males standing together. One of the males shifts, and my mood sours slightly when I see Felicity standing with them. Of course, she wouldn't take the potion, as obsessed with herself as she is. I've been beyond blessed and have avoided her so far. But it seems like that is finally at an end.

I'm about to continue scanning when one of the males catches my eye. His eyes are devouring me, and a smile tips my lips. Screw Felicity, I need to meet this male. "I think I just found my bad decision for tonight."

The husky laugh coming from Mina is so unlike her natural laugh that I giggle. "Which one is he?" she asks in all seriousness. "Because I think I just found mine as well."

A very undignified snort leaves my mouth. She's looking at the same group of males, and I'm instantly jealous for some reason. "You better not be drooling at the one in green, because he's most assuredly mine." Continuing to assess him, my mind becomes more and more made up. I can practically feel the desire emanating from him. I'm so looking forward to making a few bad decisions tonight.

"Nope," she pops the p, her face a study in sensuality. "Mine is in the deep blue," she practically growls.

"Well then, now that that's settled, shall we make our introductions?" I grab two glasses of champagne from a passing tray, and we make our way over.

As we near the males, they stop talking, their eyes feasting on us. Striding up to the male in green, I portray a confidence I most assuredly do not feel. Mina's doing the same to her prey for the evening.

"Well, hello there, beautiful." He taps his glass against mine in greeting. "To what do we owe the pleasure of the company of the most beautiful female in the room?"

"We thought you males looked in need of something sweet," Mina responds, her normally reserved demeanor nowhere in sight. Her eyes are locked on the male in blue, his just as focused. "My friend and I figured we could be the candy on your arms."

Felicity looks ready to kill, and my smile only grows. Pissing her off is a guilty pleasure of mine. Normally, I wouldn't waste my energy, but she's just a horrible excuse for a female.

"Love," the blue male responds, "You most certainly are candy, but it's not my arm I want you on."

I almost choke on my champagne. Mina, though, is oddly entranced by that horrible line.

"Hmm." Her finger traces the lapels of his coat, and I can see he's utterly gone. "Well, the night is still young; maybe you'll get just what you want."

I turn to the male I've claimed, his eyes still riveted on me. "So, what do you say we have a little fun tonight?"

He smiles. "What did you have in mind, little one?"

"Not that." I laugh, "Not yet, at least. I want to have a different kind of fun first."

He laughs, and I realize we're no longer surrounded by his friends. No idea where Mina and her male went, but she's a grown female, she can do what she wants. Plus, I know she can take care of herself. The other two males have dragged Felicity away, and she's glaring daggers. Two birds, one stone. Sounds like a good night to me.

"Oh, trust me. I think we'd have fun doing that." He takes my hand, raising it to his lips. "But if my lady insists on other diversions first, then that is what she shall have. I do have a rule, though."

I raise my eyebrow, and he continues.

"No real names. We have to make up false ones. Give me a minute." He looks at me pensively before snapping his fingers. "Got it. For tonight, you shall be Melangell."

My disgust at the name is evident, and he quickly adds, "But, I'll call you Mel for short."

"Umm, yeah." I laugh. "That name is horrendous. For you, I'll go with Lugh."

"Lugh?"

"Yup, nice to meet you, Lugh."

He laughs, and we spend the next couple of hours laughing and making up silly games. Creating backstories for guests and imagining what they're talking about. We share random little facts about ourselves. True ones that mean nothing and yet let us see each other deeply. Nothing we share could be used by someone if they knew who I really was. But nothing I would willingly share with a stranger otherwise.

I feel safe with Lugh. Safer than I have been with anyone outside my core group. This is by far one of the best nights I have had in a long time.

"Well, Mel," he states rather seriously. "I think we must dance now. In fact, I insist on it."

I bite my lip. "Can I be honest with you?"

"Of course not." He winks.

I gently slap his chest. "I hate dancing. Like, truly hate it. I always trip and stumble and can't seem to get the flow right."

"That is utter nonsense." He grabs my hands, all but dragging me to the dance floor. "I'm a phenomenal dancer, I'll make you look good."

He pulls me in so close that only a breath separates our chests. His eyes lock on mine, and I instantly forget we're in the middle of a crowded ballroom. I forget that I'm not Mel and he isn't Lugh. That we only just met a few hours ago.

My left hand rests on his shoulder, my right cradled in his left. His solid arm comes around my back, his large hand finding its home on the small of my back. I gasp as the bare skin of his hand lands on mine, and we're both breathing faster.

With a slight groan, he pulls me closer, and the fragment of space is gone. Our chests touch, thighs against each other. With every breath, my nipples scrape against the fabric of my dress. The pressure on his chest is just what I need to send the feeling all the way to my core. I know he can feel how hard they are for him. Just as I can feel the evidence against my lower stomach that says he's just as into this as I am.

Looking into my eyes, suddenly serious for the first time tonight, his next words drain any remaining trepidation. "I've got you; I won't ever let you down."

The music starts, and we move. Our bodies flow perfectly in time with one another. The only time I have ever come close to dancing this well is with Conaill at the opening ball, and I refuse to think about him now. His powerful thighs guide mine, our movements sensual and seductive. The hand at my back is tracing ever lower, his fingers caressing the skin just under the edge of my fabric. The touch of a promise of what's coming.

The music changes, and neither of us notices. I'm so enraptured by how we move together, it feels as if time stills. I know that the potion will wear off soon, and I'm not ready to end this.

Pulling his face down, I whisper in his ear, "I think it's time we find somewhere a little more private."

Fire blazes behind his eyes, and he grabs my hand, practically dragging me off the dance floor. We find an alcove behind a fountain, and he leads me in. With a wave of his hand, the water rises to form a larger barrier before he freezes it, giving us more privacy.

A heartbeat later, I feel the cool wall of the stone on my exposed back. His mouth devours mine as if he's a dying male and my kiss is the only way to save him. Hands travel up my body, exploring as mine do the same with the muscled expanse of his. Gods, I wish I knew what face truly went with this body.

One hand grabs the back of my neck, angling me to deepen the kiss. My breasts are suddenly freed as his large palm kneads my soft flesh, fingers toying with my nipples.

Groans escape both our mouths, our breaths intermingling. With trembling hands, I start to unfasten his jacket and shirt. Finally, I feel his hard flesh against my bare skin.

"Gods, you're perfect," he moans, leaning down to take a nipple in his mouth. My head falls back, breath coming faster as I hold his head to my breast. He bites my nipple, causing the sting of pain to make me gasp, but only for a moment before his tongue soothes the bite.

Pulling his head back to my mouth, I reach my hand down between us, gripping him. *Gods, he's huge!* He groans as I tighten my grip for a moment before running my fingers up and down the length.

"I need you, Lugh," I breathe out as his hand snakes down my thigh, grabbing the fabric of my dress, pulling it up.

"No," he demands, "No names. I don't want to hear another male's name on your lips." He gives me a hungry kiss. "Not until I can hear you moan my real name. I insist."

"Done, just don't stop." I pant.

A small laugh rumbles out of him as I feel his fingers gently caress the skin next to my new sheath. "Vicious little thing, are you?"

"A female can't be too careful." I gasp, pulling his mouth to mine, desperate for him. His hand is now on my bare thigh, and my head falls back at the feeling.

Devouring my lips, our tongues dance to a music all our own, his hand moving higher on my thigh. His fingers are now playing with the edge of my panties. Breaking the kiss, he asks for permission with his eyes.

"Yes," I breathe. "Fuck yes."

With that, his hand slips under the fabric, fingers finding my slit.

"Gods, you're soaked." His fingers tease me. Sliding up and down, stopping just before my clit, and not entering me.

"More. Please, I need more." I grip his shoulders, and he complies, slipping a finger inside me. *Gods, that feels so good. So fucking good.* We're kissing again as his finger curls inside me. The edge just touching that spot inside makes my toes curl.

He adds another finger and brings his thumb to my clit. Heat builds in my body as he applies just the right amount of pressure to build me up. My hands shakily undo the buttons of his pants, and my hand slips inside, feeling nothing but velvet-soft skin covering a cock so hard it must be painful.

His fingers continue to work their magic as I pump him. Moisture is leaking from his tip. Adding in a slight twist of my wrist, I hear him curse against my lips.

I can feel the heat building, starting in my feet and working its way up my body. I need more. I have to have more, I'm so close, just a little more.

"Please," I beg. "Please, I want to come."

"Your wish is my command." Lips going to the space behind my ear, he increases his tempo. His thumb presses down just a little more, and I come apart. I come apart so hard I have to bite my lip to keep from screaming, my hand gripping him harder. I close my eyes as I hear him finish, too.

His head drops to my neck, and we stand there breathing together as our racing hearts slow. When I can think again, I hear Tilde from the other side trying to get my attention.

He must notice, too, and melts the ice while turning away to right his clothing. Tilde enters as I fix myself, a wicked twinkle in her eyes and a shit-eating grin on her face, her real face. Clearly, the potion has worn off. I feel my cheeks heat, but honestly, that may have been the best orgasm of my life, so I can't really feel all that embarrassed.

"Sorry to end the" — she pauses slightly — "party. But your uncle needs you."

I nod, and she leaves after helping me set myself to rights. Thank the gods for magic. I turn to Lugh to excuse myself, but he cuts me off.

"I have to say, I *loved* it when you begged me to make you come, Princess." He turns, and my eyes widen. Sticking the fingers that were just inside me in his mouth, he sucks them clean. His eyes close as a groan escapes from his lips. "Fuck, do you taste good, Red." With that, he winks and walks out.

What the fuck! What the actual fuck? Conaill is Lugh? I just let Conaill finger me in an alcove. Screw what I thought earlier, I'm so embarrassed, and I'm so going to regret this night.

Chapter Thirteen

Shock and fury course through me. Hurling up a silencing shield, I scream as loud as I can. A few breaths later, I leave the alcove and then make my way to Uncle Emeric. Thank the gods that Conaill didn't turn around while Tilde was there. I don't need anyone else to know about this.

The relief in Uncle Emeric's eyes is evident upon seeing me. "There you are, Maevery. I couldn't find you and thought you must have been hiding somewhere."

"Nowhere, I just needed a minute." It's true enough.

He gently takes my hand and places it on his arm, then turns and walks us to the dais. "Unfortunately, we'll need to announce your betrothal tonight." *What? Why?* I haven't even talked to him about the plan Iskra had.

Ignorant of my distress, he continues on, not even aware of my faltering steps. "I know it isn't what you want, but we have to announce a royal engagement to all the kingdoms, and this is the easiest way." When we reach the dais, he pats my hand as if I'm a child.

Facing the ballroom, he magically amplifies his voice, getting everyone's attention. Looking around frantically, I scan for allies and notice my girls in a huddle. The look of concern on their face isn't good.

Turning to my left, I spot Tavarik and Conaill off to the side of the dais. Conaill licks his lips, winking at me. My face flames as anger pours off me. *Get composed, you can't look like this in front of everyone.* Surreptitiously taking a few breaths, my attention returns to Uncle Emeric. It's then that I realize I have no idea what he has been saying.

"So it's with great enthusiasm that we call an end to a successful Council of Pan. With this Council, we hope to continue the tradition of peace that has been with us since the end of the Great War six hundred years ago." Uncle Emeric pauses for the polite applause of the crowd.

Holding his hand up to quiet the crowd once more, he continues on. "Nine years ago, we lost my brother, King Oren the Third, and his amazing wife, Queen Nissera." My heart clenches at the reminder. "Since then, I have tried to guide Princess Maevery and Princess Iskra as best as I can. I think their parents would have been proud of how they have grown and the females they are now."

Deep breaths, you can do this. Just don't cry. I look to Uncle Emeric as he glances down at me before proceeding. "So, while I wish her father were here to announce this instead, I'll do my best." *No, no, no. Please don't do it. Please.*

"Early today, another alliance was made between Fenshegus and another of our great kingdoms. I wish to announce to you the engagement of Princess Maevery to Prince Conaill of Kystenvar." I freeze; obviously, I misheard that. There's no way he just said I was to marry that pretentious asshole.

Movement catches my eye. King Tavarik and Queen Kalimina are leading Conaill to stand next to us. He looks just as shaken by this, but is clearly trying to cover it up.

"Smile, my dear," Uncle Emeric whispers, leaning down.

"I thought we were announcing I was going to be getting betrothed soon?" I say.

"My dear." His smile is permanent, words escaping through his teeth. "We will talk about this later."

Conaill has reached me, a smile plastered to his stupid face. Grasping my hand, I notice his is warm, while mine is cold and clammy. Turning to me, he says in a voice so low I almost don't hear him. "Smile, love, I was just informed it was a…" He pauses, his smile slipping into a grimace. "A love match."

"I'm sorry, what did you say?" I say, trying to calm myself.

Conaill ignores me, instead playing to the cheering crowd. He brings my hand to his lips as his eyes meet mine. The heat in them is back, and I can feel my body dampen in response. *Traitor.*

"I mean, I did *love* how you tasted. At least it seems like Astrid has blessed us in that department." Conaill winks again and returns to the crowd.

What a pig. I'll be damned by all the gods if he thinks he will be getting another taste of me anytime soon.

We're swarmed with well-wishers for the next hour. Tilde and Mina are by my side, acting as the pillars holding me up. Without them, I would be a crumpled mess on the floor. Finally able to excuse myself, I go in search of Uncle Emeric. To add to the shit pile that this night has devolved into, I'm informed that he has retired for the evening. Now I have to wait until tomorrow to speak with him.

Great, this is just freaking great. Can I not catch a break? My feet strike a determined staccato on the marble floor as I head to my room. I just want to go to sleep and forget this night ever happened.

"Maevery!" Conaill's voice echoes down the hallway. Refusing to stop, my pace increases. "Maevery!" he calls again, closer this time.

Before I know it, my elbow is grabbed, and I'm spun around. I react blindly, lashing out and attacking him. I get one shot in, right to his face, *gods, that felt good*, before he defends himself. We fight right here in the middle of the hallway. Any number of servants could see us and spread rumors, but that is the farthest thing from my mind right now. My dress hampers my movements, but I fight on.

"Maevery, fucking stop," Conaill says firmly. He's only defending himself and hasn't attacked once. *Gods that pisses me off.*

"Fight back!" I all but yell.

"No," he says, right in my face. He's finally able to get me off balance, and we go down. I'm under him, and my traitorous body sings in anticipation. I can feel every delicious inch of his body pressing against mine, and gods, do I want it. "Seriously, Maevery, I just want to talk."

"So talk," I demand, stilling. The fight suddenly leaves me. Sadness overtakes anything else I might have momentarily felt.

He doesn't get off me, but raises his chest so he can look at me better. His eyes are gentle as they examine mine, and I can't reconcile that with every other interaction we've had so far. Lugh, yes; Conaill, no. "Maevery, I didn't know about any of this until Emeric announced it. My father didn't tell me anything."

"I can't marry you." I hate the way my voice breaks, a single tear escaping my eyes. Gods, I hate that I cry when any strong emotion overtakes me. "We can't even stand each other."

"Trust me, I know." He rolls his eyes. "We will figure something out. It's not like I want to marry you either."

I glare. Ouch.

"I just wanted to say that I didn't know about this, but that I'll help us figure a way out. I guess we have lunch scheduled to go over everything tomorrow. We can plead our case then."

I nod, pushing at his shoulders. "Can you please let me up now?"

He smirks, "I don't know, Red. I like how you feel beneath me."

Breath rushes out of that beautifully dangerous mouth as I knee him in the balls. I push him off, and he falls to the side.

"Fuck, Red, you have to stop doing that." He wheezes.

"I don't know?" I say, standing over him. "If I do it enough, maybe I can injure you permanently. I'll be able to call off the wedding due to your inability to consummate."

His eyes burn with anger, his voice husky with pain. "Fuck that. Never going to happen."

I step over his body, as he's still clutching his favorite part, and escape to my room. Gods, I need to figure this out. And shit, does my body need to calm the hell down around him.

Chapter Fourteen

The next day, I'm wearing a path in the carpet of the dining room where I'm supposed to meet Uncle Emeric, Tavarik, and Conaill. I'm early, hoping to speak to Uncle Emeric alone. The snick of the door opening has me spinning on my heel.

King Tavarik waddles through the door, laughing at Uncle Emeric, who's close behind. Guess I won't be speaking to him alone.

"Ah, there's my future daughter-in-law!" Tavarik cries, reaching to pull me into a hug.

My whole body stiffens, revulsion written all over my face. My face has never learned how to stay silent. Yet somehow, Tavarik doesn't notice and instead smiles lecherously at me. "It's a shame Kalimina is still with us, Emerick. Or I'd have been able to take my son's place."

My face drains of blood. He must be joking. There's no way I would ever marry that odious male. The thought alone is enough to make me want to vomit.

"Now, now, Tavarik," Uncle Emeric chides. "You know you're way too old for her."

Tavarik chuckles and agrees reluctantly. Though that doesn't stop him from grabbing my butt when I turn to sit. I watch which seat he's using so I can put some distance between us. It's taking everything I have not to punch that vile male right in the throat. Or stab his hand to the table if he even thinks of touching me like that again.

Time crawls by while we wait for Conaill to appear. Uncle Emeric and Tavarik don't seem to notice and spend the time reliving past glory days, it seems. I'm about to ask if I can just speak to Uncle Emeric alone when Conaill bursts through the door.

"Sorry I'm late," he says, "I was in a card game and time got away from me."

They all laugh like this is completely understandable and wave him off. My eyes fixate on him, glaring with a contempt I hope he can feel.

"I'm not sure how it is in your kingdom," I say through clenched teeth. "But typically, it's not polite to be almost an hour late to a meeting. And, should someone be late, it should be for a good reason. Not just some silly card game."

"For your information, it wasn't just a silly card game as I was winning alliances with other kingdoms." He motions for a servant to fill up his wine glass even though it's barely after midday. "And furthermore, in Kystenvar, it's customary for females to be courteous. Not curmudgeons with a stick up their ass."

Did I really just hear him say that? "Excuse me? I'm sure I misheard you." I look at Uncle Emeric for support, but he's fully engrossed with whatever Tavarik is saying.

"Oh, I'm sure you heard me just fine," he retorts with an evil grin on his smug face.

"Uncle Emeric," my voice demands. "I absolutely refuse to marry this pitiful excuse for a male." Uncle Emeric's attention swings to me and he now looks uncomfortable. I don't know if he's uncomfortable because of what I just said, or what was said to me.

"Seriously, I refuse. There has to be another way," I insist.

"Please excuse Maevery." He quickly turns to Conaill and Tavarik. "You know how females get. This has all been a shock; everything will work out."

He tries to continue on, but is cut off by Conaill. "Yeah, I'm not really thrilled to marry her either. I always thought my future wife would be fun." Turning to his father, he says, "Father, you understand, help me out here."

"Sorry, my boy, I can't," is the only response Tavarik gives, gesturing to Uncle Emeric. "He'll explain everything."

"Yes, well…" Uncle Emeric is trying, and failing, to hide how uncomfortable he is. "The way the law is written, Maevery must marry someone of royal blood. Not even noble, the law specified royal. No idea why, really, but that was part of it."

"I'll marry Darius then," I blurt out. I swear I hear a low growl coming from Conaill, but when I look at him, it's gone. "I already spoke to him about this."

"Sorry. Another stipulation is that the male you marry must have family serving in one of the temples," Uncle Emeric adds.

Tavarik nods, "As your sister, Ahinoam is an acolyte of Astrid, which makes you the only eligible male on the Continent. Well, that or your brothers. But look on the bright side, maybe your sister can say special prayers for you. Beseeching the God of Passion might be fun for you." His brows waggle, and bile rises in my throat.

"Oh, I think Maevery is quite passionate. Why last night I—" He abruptly cuts off as I kick him hard under the table. Uncle Emeric and Tavarik turn, looking at him strangely. "Never mind."

Turning to me, sympathy flows out of Uncle Emeric's eyes. "I truly am sorry, my dear, but Conaill is the only one who meets the requirements in the short time we have. I'm sure once the two of you get to know each other better, you'll grow to develop some fondness."

"Say, that's not a bad idea," Tavarik says, stroking what I'm sure used to be a strong jaw a long time ago. "We'll have you two set off on a tour of Fenshegus and Kystenvar. A prenuptial visit, if you will, to your future realms. After all, when Conaill inherits, you'll join the two kingdoms into one."

"You know, Tavarik, that isn't a bad idea at all," Uncle Emeric says enthusiastically.

Two long, painful hours later, I'm in Iskra's room helping her pack. She leaves tomorrow for Sabaid, and gods, am I going to miss her. Helping her pack gives us some time together where we can just be sisters. The servants are beside themselves that we wanted to do it ourselves, but Iskra insisted, and I'm very glad she did.

"Oh, Mae, I'm so sorry I can't come with you." Iskra's voice is laced with regret and pain. She folds another uniform and places it in a trunk. She's almost done, and then we'll head to my room to finish packing my things.

"I know you do, but you have to go," I say, grasping her hand. "Besides, that's where Mom and Dad met. Didn't you always say you were excited to go so you could find a male for yourself away from all the…" I pause, thinking for a second. "What was it you called them?"

She laughs, and I knew reminding her would help. "Insipid, elitist jerkfaces."

"Yes, that." I laugh. "And don't forget, we both agreed they most likely wouldn't know what to do with a female if she tripped and fell into their beds."

We look at each other and burst into cathartic laughter. Sam lands on the windowsill and titters as if asking what's going on, but Iskra just laughs harder, inviting him in.

"I know the two I've been with haven't," she says. Her face turning instantly red at this admission.

"Iskra Moira Eulalia Roighail, are you telling me you've slept with two males and didn't tell me about it?" I demand, one eyebrow raised in surprise. "You need to tell me everything now."

"See, this is why I didn't tell you. I knew you would blow it out of proportion." Her blush has lessened but not gone away completely.

"Don't stall, spill." I insist.

"Ugh, fine. Well, there really isn't anything to tell, besides the fact that they were both very disappointing." Her face falls a little, and we both keep packing. "Well, the first was Laszo. We both agreed we were curious and wanted it to be with someone we trusted."

"That makes sense; you two have been friends forever," I say gently. "If it makes you feel better, I think everyone's first time isn't great. I know mine wasn't anything to write home about." I try to suppress a shudder at how awkward that was, actually.

"It wasn't just the first time that was bad with him. Like every time." She emphasizes, and I grin. "I kept thinking it would get better, but nope, it was so… blah. The other was Benedek."

"Ah, yes. Didn't you break up with him only like a month ago?" I pick up her poetry journal, placing it carefully on top of her things before shutting the chest.

"Yeah, that was him." She finishes packing up a few things, then closes the last chest with a sigh. "I mean, he was better, but that male couldn't take direction to save his life."

A laugh escapes, and I urge her to continue.

"Like, I would tell him 'to the right a little more,' and he'd go up! I had to place him exactly where I wanted." She blushes slightly but continues, "And, like, he wasn't very adventurous. I would ask him if he wanted to try things, and it was always shocking to him. Like, I shouldn't want that because I was a princess and princesses shouldn't like to be adventurous. It made me feel bad about myself, so I ended it with him." Her head tips down, sadness now surrounding her.

Sam flies over and lands on her shoulder, head gently laid on hers. Tipping her head up gently, I say, "There's absolutely nothing wrong with wanting to try new things and wanting to be adventurous. Life should be an adventure. In and out of bed. Never let anyone make you think otherwise."

She hugs me fiercely, causing Sam to fly off, startled. "Thank you, Mae, you have no idea how much I needed to hear that."

"I love you, Isk, you know you can always come to me with anything," I say.

"I love you too, Mae." Iskra tightens her hold and steps back.

I grin at her, saying, "Now, if you want to be really adventurous, talk to Tilde on your trip."

"Talk to me about what?" She steps through the door with Mina at her side. "You're all packed, by the way. I packed a few fun things for you, too. You know, just in case you want to mess with Conaill." She winks.

Mina cuts in before I can ask, "Don't worry, I supervised. I made sure you still have everything you need and not just Tilde's suggestions. You're all set to leave tomorrow for your 'get to know you trip,'" she says with air quotes.

"Thank you!" I smile at them, so happy they're in my life. They supervised my things getting packed so I could do this with Iskra as we leave at the same time tomorrow. She head to the east toward Sabaid, and I'll go to the south to show Conaill the kingdom. Mina's coming with me, but I made Tilde promise she'd watch after Iskra until she got to Sabaid. She bristled, saying her place was at my side as a guard. She relented only when I agreed to three extra guards while she was with Iskra.

"So, what does Iskra need to talk to me about?" Tilde grabs Iskra's sword, making sure it's sharp and that it's put in the pile being loaded in the carriage they will travel in, not the baggage wagon.

I look at Iskra and wink. "Oh, only the best spots to be corrupted in and how to be adventurous."

A devious smile erupts on Tilde's face as she clasps her hands. "Oh, little one, let me teach you my ways! I'm so excited about our journey."

"Tilde, no! Iskra is a princess. You shouldn't be corrupting her," Mina says.

"Yes, please corrupt me, Tilde." Iskra laughs.

"Umm, Mina, I'm a princess. You didn't seem to have a problem when you were with me, and we were up to all kinds of shenanigans at Sabaid?" I point out.

Shaking her head, Mina replies, "Don't remind me. You two always dragged me into it."

Tilde holds open the door, and we head out. "I seem to remember you always had fun on those adventures. In fact, if I remember correctly, you're the one who got us banned from that one pub."

Mina's flushing harder than ever while Iskra looks shocked. "Oh, I so have to hear this."

Mina's face springs up. "No, I forbid it. I'm invoking the code."

Damn, she has us on that. Our first year in Sabaid, we were placed in the same squad with four others. Squad Eighteen. The seven of us came up with the Code of Eighteen on a drunken night. Any one of us can invoke the code, and the others have to go with it. Sometimes it was invoked to get another member to join us on adventures; sometimes it was used to keep secrets safe. To us, the code was sacred.

"Fine, but I'm still giving her adventurous options." Tilde puts her arm in Iskra's, and they head down the stairs.

My hand is suddenly clenched, and Mina stops me. "You know Iskra will be okay. She's strong, and Tilde loves her like a little sister. She will get her there safely; she won't allow it otherwise."

"I know, but I still worry." I sigh, letting out some tension I've been holding onto. "Let's go enjoy our last night together for a while."

Chapter Fifteen

Cold fog envelops the courtyard the following morning. My whole body is a mess of nerves, dread, and trepidation, all of which are warring with each other. I feel like any moment I'm going to be sick, but I refuse to allow anyone to see that. After all, I have to appear happy that I'm about to set off with my newly betrothed. At least until we leave Maise Palace and Otthon behind.

Through the fog, I just make out Iskra standing with Mionnan, having what looks like an intense conversation. For the first time today, the corners of my mouth rise ever so slightly. *Gods, I'll miss her.* As I make my way toward them, Mionnan whinnies, nodding and bowing his head to Iskra. Her arms wrap around his thick neck, which he has brought down slightly for her.

"Thank you," Iskra whispers. My giant of a stallion gently rests his head against her back before walking off, taking his place in the traveling company. *Gods, sometimes he's such a softie.*

"What was that about?" My head tilts ever so slightly in question. Turning, she looks at me, and I can see tear stains on her beautiful face. *Shit, I can't do this.* Pulling her to me, I start to cry myself.

What feels like only a moment later, she's pulling back and wiping her cheeks. "That was between Mionnan and me. But if you must know, I made him promise something." Iskra wraps her arm through mine, leaning down slightly to rest her head on my shoulder. "And no, I'm not telling you what it was."

"Secrets don't make friends…" I murmur in her ear.

"But friends make secrets." She bumps my hip, and we both laugh. "Speaking of secrets, are you ever going to tell me what it is you're doing with certain… individuals?" Her eyebrow is arched. "Certain individuals who require you, Tilde, and Mina to make random trips around Otthon and require lots of secret letters."

I freeze, going unnaturally still. After a few breaths, my body and mind start working again. "I don't know what you're talking about." There's no way in hell that I'm letting her get involved in the Order. I know she'd love to help, but I have to protect her. At least for now. "And even if I did, I surely wouldn't be able to explain or confirm anything until after you've completed Sabaid *and* your mandatory service time."

"Ugh, I knew you'd say that," Iskra whines but drops it, thank the gods. We've reached her carriage, and the time has finally come to say goodbye. I'm not ready for her to go. But I don't really have a choice. "I'm going to miss you so much, Mae. I hate that I can't be there for you during this trip."

Her love for me is evident in her hug. Her arms are holding me up, just as I know mine are doing the same for her. Tears flow in unbidden rivulets down both our cheeks. Leave it to Iskra to be thinking of anyone other than herself.

"I love you, Isk. I wish you could be with me too, but now it's your time. You need to figure out who you are and have your own adventures. I'll be right here when you're done, waiting to hear every little detail." I lean slightly back, noticing that everyone is here and they're just waiting on us.

"You're the most important thing to me, Isk, and I'd love nothing more than to have you at my side. But that isn't the way it will be, it seems." Kissing her cheek, I step back. "You better write, I want to hear about everything. Especially all the fun, juicy adventures Tilde helps you plan on your way. I have to live vicariously through you now. Remember, I'm to be a proper queen," I say, a false air of importance coating every word.

Iskra giggles, and I know I've succeeded in lightening both of our hearts. "I know, I'll send you messages through my birds. I know they'll only give you the message, no one else. Otherwise, there's no way I could share all the scandals I have planned." She winks, and I swat at her. "I do hate that I can't attend your wedding. It's stupid that an exception can't be made." She pouts.

"Me too, but you know it doesn't work that way." I pull her into my arms one last time. "Be safe, Isk. I love you more than you could know. It's only six months, and then you'll be able to have visitors. It'll be sooner than you know. But I refuse to say goodbye, so I'll just say see you soon."

Hugging me back, she whispers, "I love you. You're the best sister ever. See you soon." Stepping back, each of us heads to our separate carriages. "Maevery!" she yells across the courtyard. "Keep Mionnan with you whenever you can. And trust him in everything, please." Seeing the worry in her eyes. I nod.

With that, she steps into her carriage, and she's whisked away. The next time I'll see her will be at her graduation, and she won't just be my sister. She'll be an officer in my army. An officer whom I'll have to send into combat if the need should ever arise. *Polemas*, I send a quick prayer to the God of War, *please don't make me have to do that.*

I watch until her carriage leaves the gates, then turn to mine. Taking a deep breath, I put on my proverbial big girl panties, making my way to the carriage that will start my journey into the next part of my life.

Conaill's waiting for me, a bored expression gracing his too handsome face. His thick, muscular legs are spread, taking up the vast majority of the carriage space. There's nowhere for me to sit without touching some part of my body to his. *Soon*, I remind myself. Soon we'll leave Otthon behind, and I can exit this cage, riding Mionnan instead.

"Do you mind?" I say acerbically, gesturing to his sprawled legs? "You haven't left a lot of room for me."

"Not at all, Red." His tone is casual and bored, obviously not looking forward to this trip either. Patting his lap, he says, "You can always sit right here." My eyes narrow at the lascivious smile now gracing his face. "I wouldn't mind having my hands on your body again. In fact, it's the only thing about this marriage I'm looking forward to."

With a roll of my eyes, I climb into the carriage, forcing his legs to move, giving me at least some room. "It'll be a cold day in hell before I let you get your grubby hands on my body again," I spit out, fury shining in my eyes.

"We'll see," he retorts smoothly, opening the windows.

Exiting the palace gates, I take in everything I can. The cacophony of sights and sounds is so familiar, it warms my heart. I love this city that surrounds my home. I love my kingdom. So much that I'll marry this odious male to help protect it.

We wind our way through a warren of streets, making slow progress. Excited children run alongside. Their little legs pump until they can no longer keep up, and they fall behind. The sight brings out a genuine smile, and the weight on me presses down a little less. Loud laughter comes from the left and startles me. Looking, I see Conaill's head hanging out of the window, making all sorts of weird, comical faces, much to the delight of the children. I don't know how to process what I'm seeing. This is so at odds with what I've experienced with him, and it reminds me of something that 'Lugh' would do.

I watch him for a minute more before looking out my side again. I wave back to those wishing us well, and I'm gladdened by the overall show of support. Once more, I remind myself that they're worth everything I'm doing. Both this farce of a marriage and the Order.

The crowd of well-wishers and those eager to see our procession dwindles the closer we get to the countryside. By the time we're fully on country roads, I don't have it in me to pretend anymore. I'm ready to just sink against the seat and try to puzzle everything out in peace. One downside of being out of the city is the dust we're now kicking up. Closing the window, I notice Conaill has as well, leaving the two of us trapped in here.

Blissful silence keeps me company for the next hour. I've spent the time planning what I can get done for the Order on this trip, and now I'm at a stopping point. Putting my work away, I reach underneath my seat for a book to read. Unfortunately, I can't quite reach them with how I'm sitting.

"I'm really sorry to ask." I pause, glancing at Conaill. He's looking up from his book, eyes screaming annoyance. "But, do you think you could hand me the book under this bench? I can't reach it from this side."

Sighing loud enough to be heard outside, he places a finger in his book to mark his place, leans over, and grabs the book. Glimpsing the title of the book, he snorts and huffs out, "You've got to be kidding me?"

I grab it and see what he's laughing at. *How to Comport Yourself as a Lady of Kystenvar- The Complete Guide of Kystenvarian Etiquette For Discerning Ladies Looking to Enter Court Life.* "What's this?" I stammer out.

"The book under your seat?" Conaill says incredulously. "I mean, it's not really my kind of reading material, but if it floats your boat, knock yourself out."

"But..." I stutter, flabbergasted. "This isn't the book that was supposed to be here. I've never even seen this book before." Seriously, I left out a spicy new romance from one of my favorite authors. Tilde had just read it and said it made even her blush. For a book to make Tilde blush, it must be extremely spicy, and I was very much looking forward to it.

"Uh-huh. Sure, whatever you need to tell yourself." A small chuckle escapes his lips. "If that's the case, then someone clearly thinks you need to be more *ladylike.* Probably my father."

"I'm *not* reading this," I say churlishly. "I'm a princess. I already know how to act like a lady."

"Fine, whatever." He opens up his book again, but stops short. "What book were you expecting?"

A blush creeps across my skin. I swear the gods cursed me with this fair skin. "None of your business."

"Ah, so it was one of *those* novels." He wags his eyebrows, and his voice is light. "Please tell me more. I would love to hear what you… enjoy reading about."

"Again, it's none of your business." Gods, it's hot in here.

"On the contrary. As your soon-to-be husband and provider of your conjugal pleasures, I think it is my, and only my, business to know exactly what you like and fantasize about."

I narrow my eyes at him until suddenly I have an idea. "Maybe I should let you read it. You might just learn from it. Pick up some tips that might help you be more… effective."

He's on me in a second, caging my body between strong arms as he leans over me, pressing me completely into the seat. The heat of his body burns through our many layers of clothing and the breath of space left between us.

"Red, you know godsdamn well that I'm effective." He closes even more of that infinitesimal space separating us, and his scent fills me with desire. Warm leather and vanilla flood my senses, and my traitorous body can't get enough.

Gods, why does he smell so damn good? His smell alone lights a fire in me. The burn is tantalizing, and warmth pools low inside me. His nostrils flare, and I know he can sense just how turned on I am. My breasts rise and fall as my breathing deepens. Each breath causes the tips to just caress his hard chest. Leaning closer, his lips skim the shell of my ear, and it takes all my effort to suppress the shudder tearing through my body. He breathes in deeply, and I swear I hear a groan escape him.

"But I'm nothing if not an eager student. And I'm *always* willing to learn new tricks so I can be more effective over and over and over again." His lips brush that one spot, just behind my ear, trailing down my neck slightly. "You won't be able to stand Red when I'm done showing you just how effective I can truly be."

He takes one more deep breath, reveling in the smell of arousal pouring from me. "But," he says, falling back into his seat, "you did say it would be a cold day in hell before you willingly let me touch you again. So, I guess you'll never know." Crossing his leg on his knee, he turns his attention back to his book. "Let me know if you ever feel like changing your mind about that."

Chapter Sixteen

What the hell just happened? It takes a few moments to get myself under control. Looking under my lashes, I try to observe Conaill, searching for evidence that he was just as affected as I was. He shifts slightly, and my lips tip up ever so slightly. *There it is.* It's faint, but I can pick out the distinct smell of arousal mixed with the warm leather and vanilla filling my nose once again. Glancing down, I see he's sporting a large bulge that was most assuredly not there earlier, and my smile widens.

Directing my attention back to the book in my lap, I see a paper just sticking out of the top. Curiosity piqued, I open the book, and a letter falls out.

Mae,

Please don't be mad, but I think you and Conaill need to get to know each other. So, that said, I hid all your books, your snacks, your happy daggers, and a few other choice things. You only get them back when you're able to tell me something about Conaill. And I'll know if you're lying because I'll confirm it with Madok. Tilde talked to him about it, and he agreed rather quickly. Come to think of it, he seemed almost gleeful about it. Anyway, at each stop on our journey, you can share what you learned.

Should either of you lie, you don't get anything back, so don't even think of telling him something false. I know the plan is to divorce him once you've fixed this law. I'm still working on that, trust me, but I think if you're able to forge some peace and get to know him, then maybe the interim won't be so bad? To help, I have included a list of things to ask each other and things to do together.

Mina

My head falls back against the seat, and I let out an audible groan of frustration. *Seriously Mina.* I just wanted to escape into a good book, and now I can't even do that.

"I see you found your letter." Conaill's looking at me now, a folded sheet of paper held up between two fingers.

"She wrote you one, too?" Disbelief is evident through my tone.

"Nope." He sighs. "This gem is from Madok, the traitor. And in addition to our individual property they hid, he has informed me that all alcohol has been removed and put under the care of someone called 'Saori.' Oh, and the inns along the way have received instructions that they are not allowed to serve alcohol unless Madok or Aphilomina orders it."

"You have got to be joking!" I snatch the letter he's holding out. Everything is right there, including the bit about no alcohol. "Now we can't even get drunk to make this bearable?"

"Yup." Resignation drips from him. "Come to think of it. I may be more upset about that than Madok hiding all my clean underwear."

"I'm sorry, what?" I laugh.

"That bastard hid all my clean underwear, along with my socks, swords, books, and money. So I can't purchase any more."

"That is utterly diabolical." Huffing out a breath, I look for the list Mina has given me. "Well, we're about an hour and a half from a lunch stop; should we try to tackle some of this?"

"Might as well. Start with the first?" He holds up his list. I nod, and he starts to read. "It says we each have a different list, and for me to get my stuff back, both of us have to answer my questions or do my activities. And likewise for yours." He stops for a minute before continuing on, "When did they find time to do this? And why is it so complicated?"

"Your guess would be as good as mine. Go ahead, what's your first question? We'll go back and forth."

"Okay." He looks down, confirming the question, and then asks, "If you weren't in line for the throne, what would you want to be?"

A smile comes to my lips. Thank the gods it's an easy one. "A scientist. What about you?"

"I would love to be a historian and archeologist." A lopsided smile appears, and it makes his face even more handsome, if possible. "It also says we have to say why. So, when I was little, my Grandpa Otenyo would read to me from this giant history book. Stories from all the kingdoms, even those from across the sea. He told me that it's in history that we find our future. He also told me stories of hidden treasure, so naturally I wanted to dig it up and claim it as mine."

"Naturally, of course." I chuckle, and for the briefest of moments, I forget the animosity between us. "So in Fenshegus, science and art are both revered. I'm not in the least artistic, so I never liked those classes, but science…" I pause for a beat. "Science sings to me. It can explain everything. Bring reason to the unreasonable. But more than that, I really just like learning new things." I realize that I'm smiling for the first time in a while.

"And the idea of being the first to discover or invent something, just… I don't know, it seems amazing. Like Sofiya is sharing a little of her wisdom with just you, and for that moment in time, until that discovery is shared." I pause, noticing Conaill still has that small, lopsided smile on his face. "It's like a secret between just the two of you, and she has entrusted you to spread that knowledge. I don't know, I just, I love it."

"I can tell," he says softly, and we fall silent for a time. I'm thinking about what we shared. We went from contempt to sharing something very personal. I'm not sure how it happened, but I'm not mad about it right now.

I ask Conaill to share one of the stories he liked the most, which he does, readily. He tells me all about the origin of the Great Rite in Baress, where his grandfather's family was from. His deep voice reveals both his love for his grandfather and the story he shares.

Time moves faster than either of us realizes, and it isn't long before the carriage has rolled to a stop. The door is yanked open, and Madok's head is thrust into the carriage.

"Ah, I don't see any blood." He smirks, stepping back. "I'll take that as a win." Holding his hand out, I escape the carriage and step into the yard of a smaller tavern. "Come on, Con, let's get some food. Maybe take a look at the scenery." Madok winks, and I can see that the scenery he's talking about consists of a few beautiful female patrons. *Ugh.*

Laughing, Conaill responds, "Sounds like a plan to me." And the two of them head out.

"I'm sorry, Mae," Mina says, sadness tinging her voice. "They're so gross, and now you have to marry him."

"Hey, remember, it's just temporary." I look at her. "Now, I want my book back and some food." The glare I'm leveling at her does nothing. She just wraps her arm around mine, and we head in.

Lunch passes quickly, and soon it's time to get on the road again. Both Conaill and I passed the first part, it seems, and I earned back a bit of the chocolate I'd brought. Without a book, I refuse to be cooped up in the carriage any longer, making my way to Mionnan instead.

"Hey, handsome," I say, stroking his nose. "You mind if I ride for a while?" He whinnies and nuzzles my chest, indicating his enthusiasm.

Soon, the party is mounted and ready to set forth. Pushing past other riders, Mionnan heads straight for a group of males near the front. As he draws closer, I see that it's Darius, Madok, and, of course, Conaill. I try to redirect him, but Mionnan won't be dissuaded and heads straight for Conaill.

"Mionnan, no. We don't like him." I whisper, hoping the males won't hear. Much to my dismay, Mionnan picks up speed and nudges in right next to Conaill.

Conaill leans over and pats him on the neck. "Hey there, Mionnan. You know you aren't supposed to like me, right?"

Mionnan, the traitor, tosses his head as if laughing. Darius and Madok chuckle as well, and I glare at them. Choosing to ignore this, I lean over, directing my attention to Darius.

"How long are you traveling with us?" I ask, hoping he's staying for a while. Not only is he good company, but it would be nice to have him as a buffer as well.

"Only to Keneven, I'm afraid. From there I'll take a boat up the Cale to Baress," he says. "I have to check in at home, and then I'm off again to play with plants."

I smile at this. "That makes sense." The Calestenea, or Cale, runs the entire length of Panellas, separating east and west. It's wide and easily navigable, allowing for swift travel through the center of the continent. "Doing anything fun with your plants?"

A huge grin erupts on his face, indicating the love he has for plants and their many uses. "I am actually. I've been looking at new medicinal uses for plants. Well, that and poisons." He winks.

At the mention of poisons, Madok whips his head around, intrigue clear on his face. "Find anything fun?"

With this simple inquiry, Darius's whole face lights up, and he starts talking. We spend the next hour or so learning about what plants can help or harm. Soon, we reach a stream, and we stop to water the horses and take care of our own needs.

I'm just looking around when I notice Conaill. *What's he doing?* He's carrying a basket and looks like he's sneaking away, and my interest is piqued. As quietly as I can, I follow until he stops. We're far enough away from the group that we can't be seen, but close enough to hear should I scream.

A bird call sounds, and Conaill returns it. Clearly a signal. But for whom? A trio of fauns emerges from behind trees and bushes, answering my silent question almost immediately. The tallest faun steps forward, his hooves making no sound. He's only a few feet tall, with shaggy brown fur that matches the golden tan of his upper body. Close behind him, a female fawn tentatively steps forward, holding the hand of a tiny faun child. Clearly, no more than a few years old.

"Prince Conaill," the male says, bowing, then takes the basket from Conaill's outstretched hand. "Thank you. I don't know what we would do without you. This will help us out tremendously."

"No thanks needed, Livius." Conaill tips his head toward the basket. "I included a little present in there for Felix, too." At the mention of his name, the little faun perks his head up, a smile brightening his face. "I've been told there will be another group coming through in three days. Will that be a problem?"

"No, my prince. Aelia and I'll be able to lead them on to the next stage." The female nods in agreement, then turns away with the little one. Blending back into the forest as if they were never there. "As always, we are here to help." He, too, turns away, returning to the forest.

"Spying, are we, Red?" Conaill turns around, staring right at me. I obviously need Tilde to tutor me in espionage.

"I've asked you to stop calling me that." I grind out, trying to change the subject. "What was that? Who are they and what did you give them?"

"That," he says dryly, "is none of your concern. Go back to the carriage and talk about dresses or something with Aphilomina." He starts walking, and I grab his wrist.

As soon as our skin touches, an electrical current runs up my arm. He tenses, and I know he feels it too. "Seriously, what was that?"

"Go back to the carriage, Red. I'm not saying it again," he cuts out.

"No, I want to know. It looked like you were helping them. Who is the other group?" I insist.

Conaill looks skyward, lets out a frustrated groan, then takes a step toward me. Without a word, he bends down, throwing me over his shoulder. "I told you I wasn't saying it again. Now, I'm taking care of it myself." He starts off toward the carriage, and I put my hands on his lower back, pushing up as best I can.

"What the actual fuck! Put me down now. I can walk by myself, and how dare you?" I demand. To emphasize my point, I ball my fist and hit his back. A sharp crack sounds a moment before my butt hurts. "Did you just spank me?"

"Sure did, Red, and I'll spank you again if you don't stop acting like a petulant child. Next time, though, I'll put you over my knee and spank your bare ass. Who knows, you might even enjoy it. Moro and Astrid know I would," he says.

My face is beet red, and my body warms at the idea of that. *What the hell?* Why am I finding the idea of him spanking me such a turn-on? The shock has worn off, and I notice that his hand is still on me.

"Take your hand off my butt right now!" I demand.

"No. I quite like it there, actually. Too bad you're wearing so many clothes." I can hear the smile in his voice, and I narrow my eyes. Not that he can see.

Soon, I'm set down in front of the carriage door, my face flaming in embarrassment. Mina and Madok stroll toward us, but otherwise, everyone else is making themselves busy elsewhere.

"We talked about it, and we both agreed," Mina starts, Madok nodding next to her. "Since it looks like you were fighting, we took back what you earned earlier."

My mouth drops open. Conaill glares daggers at Madok, who simply looks at us with a stupid smile on his face. He steers us into the carriage, "You two go in there and learn more about each other." The door shuts, and he pokes his head through the window. "Or, you can always kiss and make up." With a wink, he turns away, leaving us.

We sit glaring at each other. Neither is willing to be the first to speak. *Damn, this is going to be a long afternoon.*

Chapter Seventeen

The next few hours crawl by, my mind a busy factory specializing in over-analysis. I can't figure out Conaill. What was he doing? Why doesn't he show that side to anyone? Does he always do things like this, or is it more periodic? My mind wanders, constantly replaying everything until Conaill's voice finally breaks the silence.

"So, we should be stopping for the evening in about an hour, I think." Pausing, he pulls out his list. "As much as I have enjoyed your riveting company this afternoon, I would really enjoy having some of my things back."

I nod in agreement. "So, what's next on your list?"

Glancing down, he says, "What's your favorite sweet treat? I'll go first." He purses his lip for a moment before saying, "Raspberry cheesecake with fresh raspberry sauce. What about you?"

"Salted caramel chocolates. Easy." I sigh, pulling out my own list. "What's something unusual you get easily annoyed by and why?" I direct a pointed look at him, eliciting a chuckle. "Since I'm sure I can't just say you, I'm going with roses."

"Roses?" he deadpans. "Why roses? I mean, aren't they supposed to be romantic? Romance annoys you?"

"As I was about to explain," I say through clenched teeth. "I get annoyed by roses because they're lazy." I want to smack that incredulous look off his face. He looks as if he's about to say something, so I hold up a hand to forestall him.

"There are so many more flowers someone could give instead that are more personal or have deeper meanings. If a male wants to say 'I love you' or rather 'I lust after you,' they immediately reach for roses. It's generic with no thought put into it."

Rolling his eyes, he responds with, "Got it. Well, for me, it would be clothing." Seeing my scoff at his response, he clarifies, "I don't mean wearing clothing, although I wouldn't mind if we weren't wearing any right now." His pointed look is full of heat, and now I'm even more annoyed. "I just think fashion and all the trappings that go with it are so… unnecessary. I really hate having to take so long to get ready for formal events. And going to the tailor. It would just be so much easier without all the needless fuss."

"Well, then we must agree to disagree, as I love fashion," I say, turning my gaze back out to the window.

The dimming light outside is a clear signal that night will soon be here. Lanterns flare with fae lights conjured up by Conaill, casting the interior in a warm glow. Soon we're at our first stop of many through Fenshegus and Kystenvar. The entire journey will last about a month and a half. The first part is a tour of the western portion of Fenshegus. We'll then cross the Calestenea at Keneven, Fenshegus's largest river port.

From there, we'll spend time exploring Kystenvar to familiarize ourselves with the kingdom and its citizens. Finally, ending at the Temple of Astrid back in Fenshegus to bless the marriage. At that point, we'll part ways until just before the wedding. Gods, I wish Iskra could be with me for that.

I'm dragged from my thoughts as the carriage rumbles to a stop at the inn. Time to put on a show for the fae of this village. Plastering a smile on my face as the door opens, I descend the few steps to the ground. A smaller, but pristine inn sits before us. White stone walls rising two stories are interspersed with dark wooden beams. The windows are filled with welcoming light, each with a blooming flowerbox.

"Welcome to the Quiet Knight, your majesties. My name is Elliot, and this is my inn." The innkeeper bows low as Conaill gently pulls my arm through his. "If there's anything you require, please don't hesitate to let me know. I'm at your service." Turning slightly, not giving us his back, he holds out his arm, gesturing for us to head inside. "The wagon carrying your supplies arrived not long before you, and your room has been prepared."

I stop short at this, noting that Conaill has stiffened beside me. "Room? Surely you mean rooms?" I question.

"Sorry, Your Majesty. We only have one room available that is suitable for your needs." He stammers slightly, "Your maid and valet said that would be fine. All the other rooms are multi-person bunks with shared bathrooms. We figured you would want the private bathing chamber, and as you're to be married in a few months, they deemed it appropriate."

Conaill rolls his eyes, and I barely keep my face a picture of serenity. "I'm sure it will be fine. I thank you for your hospitality."

We spend the next few minutes getting acquainted with the layout of the inn and its facilities. Soon, Greer, Elliot's wife and the inn's cook, informs us that dinner is ready. It's a simple meal of stew and warm bread, but it is so delicious that I'm almost over the whole *one-room* thing. I'm ready to fall asleep at the table when Mina notices. She makes our excuses, and I follow after her.

She draws my bath while quizzing me about what I learned. Adding in some jasmine oil, she helps me into the bath and washes my hair for me.

"Now don't get used to this. I'm only doing it because I feel bad that I took your things," she says while brushing my hair, somehow portraying both sadness and determination.

"Bad enough to give everything back?" I test out.

A tug on my hair and her giggle tells me she doesn't feel *that* bad. "Absolutely not. But, you did earn back a book today."

"Thank Moro." The God of Jubilation sure hasn't been on my side lately. "I was worried about getting through tomorrow. Do you have any idea how boring it is traveling without a book or even a friend with me?" My gaze fixed on hers.

"Nope, I have all my books." The smile on her face is wide and teasing; her eyes sparkling with mischief as they meet my glare.

I'm tucked under the covers of this surprisingly comfortable bed when there's a knock at the door. Before I can answer, Conaill's head peeks in. "Ah, good, you're finished." Stepping in fully, his hands fly to the buttons on his shirt.

"And just what do you think you're doing?" I demand.

Turning his back to me, he continues to undress. "Well, this is my room for tonight, isn't it? And I would very much like to be clean." The powerful muscles of his back ripple with every movement, and gods, is that a sight. Sitting on the bed, he removes his boots and socks, then pads to the bath.

"You can't bathe in here. I'm in here," I cry out in alarm.

With a deft flick of the wrist, Conaill fills the porcelain tub, much faster than any spout could. Warm steam drifts languidly from the basin; no need to wait for it to heat. *Gods, that's handy.* "Why not? You may not have seen me naked yet, but it isn't like you haven't had your hands all over me."

With that, he drops his pants, and his perfect, muscular ass is all I can focus on. That is, until he sinks into the tub, turning to face me with a smirk. Fire blazes across my cheeks, and I quickly turn to my other side.

The sound of water sloshing against his golden body plagues my ears. I imagine the cloth skimming over skin as he scrubs the day away from him. *Astrid, what I wouldn't give to be that cloth right now. Wait, no, Mae. He's a jerk, no, you don't want to be that cloth.*

Before long, I hear him stand up, followed by water as it pours over his skin. Soon, the bed dips as he slides in.

Nope, not happening. He can't sleep here. "Excuse me?" I ask incredulously. "Just what do you think you're doing?"

"Going to bed." He uses common magic to turn off the lights in the room and lock the door.

"Not in here. Go find somewhere else," Comes my tart reply.

"No. You heard Elliot. Everywhere else is full, even the bunks now." I can feel him shifting around behind me.

"That's your problem. Sleep on the floor if you have to, but you aren't sleeping in this bed," I say.

"The fuck I'm not, Maevery." His voice is commanding and deep. *Damn, that shouldn't be as sexy as it is.* "That floor is hard, and this bed is comfortable."

"Conaill," I say, making him jerk suddenly. I realize that it's the first time I've called him by his name. I have to admit, I do like the feel of it coming out of my mouth. "You can't sleep with me. I don't want to have sex with you."

"Maevery, seriously, I just want to sleep. It has been a really long day, and I'm exhausted. You're not the only one getting the short end of the stick in this situation." He pauses, "Seriously, I'm exhausted. I just want to sleep."

"Fine," I concede. "But if you try anything, you will regret it."

"Trust me, I will not fuck you for the first time like this. You'll beg for it before I take you."

A gasp escapes me, and before I can respond, he pulls up the covers. He falls almost instantly asleep, the lucky ass.

Great, just great. Now I'll be dreaming of just that.

My body is on fire, my back pressed against an exquisitely muscled chest. Tender hands hold me close, lips brushing along my neck. I can feel the desire of the male behind me, his thick length hard and pressing between my legs.

My hand stretches behind my head, fingers spearing through his hair. A moan slips past my lips just as I hear a quiet, "Yes." My eyes fly open. It's Conaill's chest that's pressed against me, and damn, he is larger than I remember. His hard body is perfectly molded to mine. *What the hell, Astrid?* I bemoan the God of Passion.

My elbow flies back, hitting Conaill right in the stomach as I scramble out of bed.

"What was that for?" Conaill barely wheezes out. He's curled over his stomach, doubtless surprised by my attack. "You didn't need to hit me to wake me up."

"You were pressing yourself against me and feeling me up." Indignation is rampant in my tone. "And for gods' sake, control yourself," I add, gesturing to his groin.

"It's morning, Red. I *was* sleeping before you woke me up. It's not like I can help it," he says, getting to his feet and heading to the bathroom. Just before he shuts the door to the toilet, I hear him add, "Besides, I'd have to be dead not to rise to attention if I'm pressed against that ass of yours."

Once again, my face floods with heat, and I'm surprised steam isn't coming off me. I quickly gather my clothes, heading to the bathroom. At this point, I don't care if I have to share, as long as I can get out of here.

Chapter Eighteen

Mionnan shuffles under me impatiently, plainly not happy waiting. In my haste to escape my room and subsequently the inn, I found myself ready to depart before anyone else. Fortunately, this allowed me to tend to some order business. It also allowed me to saddle Mionnan myself, something I don't get to do as often as I like.

"It's okay, my handsome one. We'll get going soon." I stroke his neck as I lean over my saddle. "I promise I'll give you some sugar cubes later if you're patient."

If I didn't know better, I'd swear I had the same gift as Iskra. Mionnan's whole temperament changes, eager to earn those sugar cubes. A small chuckle comes from my left, and I startle. Mina's shaking her head. She's never approved of me bribing Mionnan, but if it works, I don't see what's wrong with it.

Soon, saddled horses fill the yard, jockeying for space between the ready carriages. Mionnan whinnies again before moving of his own accord. I think he's trying to distance himself from the madness that is the inn yard, but of course, I can't be so lucky. Directly in our path are Conaill and Madok, mounting their horses and murmuring.

I'm trying to turn Mionnan, not that he really does anything he doesn't want to do, when we're caught.

"I wondered where you ran off to, Red." The shit-eating grin on Conaill's face only stokes my irritation.

Deciding to chime in, Madok adds, "Yeah, Princess Maevery. Were you avoiding us this morning?" A glint twinkles in his eye that I don't like.

"No, I'm just eager to get to our next stop," I reply shortly, still trying, and failing, to urge Mionnan to leave.

"You didn't like this inn?" Madok seems concerned. I'm about to take pity on him when he says, "Was it the bed that wasn't to your liking? Too… *hard* for you?"

Oh, hell no. He didn't just say that. The emphasis he put on the word *hard,* making it clear that Conaill let him in on this morning. I'm about to respond when Mionnan rears, squealing a warning. Turning, I see Lukavo approaching with a mug and my tonics. *Shit,* I forgot to take it this morning.

"Shh, it's okay, Mionnan." I try to calm him. "It's just Lukavo, you know him." Mionnan won't settle, though, so I dismount. I refuse to let Lukavo get hurt because of my mistake.

"Sorry about that. Not sure what's gotten into him," I say, reaching for the cup.

His eyes never leaving Mionnan, Lukavo replies, "It's fine, Your Highness. I noticed you hadn't taken your tonics today and wanted to make sure you got them before we left."

I throw back the tonics like a shot and drink my tea as fast as I can without burning my mouth. Remounting as soon as I'm finished, I urge Mionnan into a fast walk, eager to leave this morning behind.

Those of us traveling on horses are the first to leave, thank the gods. I wouldn't relish choking on the dust kicked up by carriages all morning.

Just a short distance from the inn lies the city of Orom, our first official city visit of the trip. Orom may be one of the larger cities between Otthon and Keneven, but we're able to traverse its streets with relative ease.

Urging the horses to a stop in front of an imposing, yet elegant building, we dismount and hand them off to a groom. I can't help the smile that breaks across my face as I stare up at the sign proclaiming where we are. The Orom Institute of Science and Technology is one of the largest research facilities in Fenshegus. It also happens to be home to a few scientists who are instrumental in the Order.

The airy atrium welcomes visitors in, eager to share the knowledge within. The gentle, singing sound of water greets my ears. The culprit is a massive marble fountain, the centerpiece of this grand space. Sofiya stands tall on one side with Astrid, the patron Goddess of Fenshegus, her mirror on the other. It's a reminder that knowledge and passion go together. For without passion, knowledge cannot be truly found. Without knowledge, passion cannot be understood.

Glancing past the fountain, I spot Dr. Ervin Tudos waiting patiently for us. His presence is austere and formidable, completely at odds with his warm personality once you get to know him.

"Dr. Tudos!" I call, hurrying excitedly across the hall. "It's been so long. How have you been?"

Dr. Tudos bows to both me and Conaill, who I see has come to my side. "Your Royal Highnesses, welcome to my little home away from home. Princess Maevery, everything has been great. I wanted to thank you in person for the extra supplies and funding for our lab."

Great, he received the last shipment. We easily developed this code when he joined the Order. The crown is always funding research facilities, so no one bats an eye when we speak of supplying and funding any research facility.

"If you would follow me this way." He gestures to a hallway to the right. "I would love to show you what we're working on."

The love Dr. Tudos has for both the research going on here and for this facility is evident. His enthusiasm is contagious, and it isn't long before I'm completely engrossed. I've asked so many questions, and Dr. Tudos has answered each of them thoroughly. Surprisingly, Madok has even gotten engrossed in the visit. Dr. Tudos is equally curious about the research I am helping out with in Otthon, which makes me enjoy the visit even more. I could easily spend all day here, but unfortunately, our time has come to an end.

"Thank you so much, Dr. Tudos," Conaill says in all seriousness. "I've been truly delighted to learn about the research going on here. When I get home, I'm going to see if there's any room in the budget to invest in future projects."

Practically bouncing on his feet, Dr. Tudos can't contain his joy. "Thank you so much, Your Highness. That would mean so much to us."

With goodbyes completed, we collect the horses and find a place to eat. Regrettably, lunch isn't as enjoyable as spending time at the research institute. But it isn't as bad as I thought it would be, so maybe there is hope for the rest of the day.

Happy to be out of the bustle of the city, Mionnan's steps are light, and he can't help but prance a little. I'm thinking back to the research Dr. Tudos is doing when I'm startled by a presence suddenly next to me.

Conaill's caught up, and both his mare and Mionnan seem thrilled by this. Mionnan seems to have developed a crush on her, one that seems to be returned.

We walk in silence for a while until Conaill clears his throat. Evidently wanting to talk about something.

"So… our horses seem to get along better than us," he states.

I'm sorry, what?

"That can't be what you wanted to talk to me about." I glance at him, my incredulity written on my face.

"It's not. I wanted to call a truce." He pauses for a beat. "Aphilomina reminded me that whether we like it or not, we're getting married in a few months. I'd rather not spend that time hating each other."

"I agree that would be for the best." Grabbing the water that hangs from my pommel, I take a long drink, using the time to collect my thoughts. "I don't know how to go about this. Everything I know about you, everything I've heard about you, is something that…" I pause again, huffing out a breath. "Shall I say, it doesn't paint you in the best light. Or is something that goes against everything I stand for."

Turning to face Conaill, his head hangs low. "Maevery. All I can say is that not everything is what it looks like."

I nod my head. "I'm willing to try. I agree with what you said, and I too would like to not hate my husband."

Reaching into his pocket, he produces the list of questions we were given yesterday. Shrugging, he holds it up between two fingers. "Might as well get some of our things back."

"You don't like not having your underwear?" I ask.

"It makes riding rather uncomfortable," he grumbles.

The next few hours pass quickly, and surprisingly, I'm actually enjoying myself. He now knows my favorite animal is a fox; my love of shoes may be classified as unhealthy; and daggers are my favorite weapon, while bows are my least. In return, he let me know that otters take the top spot for him. He actually loves reading, preferring non-fiction, and swords are where his strength lies. We've each shared our favorite joke and what our least favorite food is.

By the time we've reached the inn for the night, I must say that I'm not completely loathing Conaill. At least not at this moment. We've checked off many of the questions, and I'm *so* looking forward to getting my things back. Just thinking of the possibility of wine with dinner makes me smile.

"I'm proud of you, Mae," Mina says from her seat next to me at dinner. "But you still need to do some more work before you get the alcohol back. Maybe check off some activities." She chooses this moment to grab her glass of wine and take a long swallow.

"Bitch," I mummer under my breath.

"What was that?" She leans over, cupping her ear as if she's trying to hear better.

"Ugh, fine," I groan. I mean, would I love some wine? Yes. But do I really need it? No. Plus, if I'm honest with myself, it probably isn't a good idea to mix alcohol with Conaill. Not if the last time I'd been drinking around him is any indication. Granted, I didn't know it was him at the time. But still.

Between Mina on my left and Darius on my right, conversation flows, and soon dinner is over. I'm almost ready to head to bed when a presence looms behind me.

"Move," Conaill growls, actually growls. The sound acts as kindling, igniting a flicker of arousal. *Damn hormones.*

Mid-conversation, Darius and I stop, whipping our heads around. Conaill stares daggers at Darius, whose face has paled as much as his rich chestnut tone will allow.

"Excuse me?" I demand. His commanding tone may have turned me on, not that I'll admit it, but he can't speak to Darius that way. To anyone, really.

"Move, Darius. You're sitting next to *my* fiancé, and I want to sit here." His eyes never leave Darius's, and I'll admit, I'm slightly worried for him.

"Hey, no worries." Darius raises his hands in supplication. "I was just about to get up and get to know her a little better." He points to the beautiful server who waited on us tonight. Getting up quickly, he whispers, "Good luck." I swear Conaill growls in reply.

"Um, what was that?" I demand.

Taking Darius's seat, he looks at me innocently. "What? I wanted to speak with you, and he was in the way."

"That doesn't give you the right to be rude," I hiss. Guess we're back to ass-hat Conaill.

Huffing out a sigh, he rolls his eyes at me. "Anyway, I wanted to see if you would be willing to ride with me in the carriage tomorrow?"

My eyebrow rises, my face showing the *what in all the gods' name* thoughts that are flying around my mind.

Clearing his throat, he continues, "We have activities on our lists. I was thinking we could do some of them in the carriage tomorrow."

Okay, so yeah, that makes sense. "I guess, at least for the morning. Now, if that's all, I'm going to bed. See you in the morning."

I've just left the table when Conaill grabs my hand. My skin tingles where his connects with mine, sending a spark shooting through my arm. When I turn, he says, "You wouldn't have to wait until morning if you let me come to bed with you." Heat and desire pour from him, and for the barest sliver of a heartbeat, I think about it.

But then I remember that only a minute ago he acted like a complete ass. Ripping my hand from him, I storm away in as dignified a manner as possible. All the while, the sexy rumble of his laugh fills my ears.

The scent floods my system before I'm even in my room. It's the sickly, sweet odor of too many flowers. And not just any flower, but roses. My pace slows, and I stop in front of my door. I push open the door with all the enthusiasm of a convict on the way to the gallows, and my jaw drops open.

Red roses are everywhere. Roses cover every imaginable surface. *Damn it, Conaill.* I snarl out my irritation and stomp to the window. Throwing open the window with way more force than necessary, I wince when the glass rattles. I'm blindly throwing all the roses out the window when I spot it.

Perched like a present in the middle of my pillow is a note. Curiosity has to wait. I need to get rid of the roses before I can read it. The smell is overwhelming me right now. When I'm finally done, I attack the letter.

My Dearest Red,

One as beautiful as you deserves all the roses in the world. Please accept these as a token of the sincere affection I hold for you.

Your Future Husband

P.S. Just because I said we should have a truce and try to get to know one another doesn't mean we can't have a little fun while we're at it…

Just as I'm finished reading, Mina pops her head in. "I see you got your gift." She smiles and walks in.

"You were in on this!" I blurt, trying and failing to keep my voice down.

"Of course I was, Mae. Who do you think made all the roses?" She winks.

"Why, you little traitor!" I gasp. "That's it. Tilde is now my favorite. You've been downgraded to at least six."

"There's no way I'm not in your top five, and you damn well know it." She sits beside me on the bed, folding one leg beneath her. "Plus, I liked it."

I start to protest, but I'm stalled when she holds up a hand. "Ah, ah, ah. Let me explain. His wanting to prank you with a room full of the flower you hate the most means he was paying attention. If it were just him trying to be nice, I never would have helped. But as a prank, he clearly put some thought into it."

"Fine," I say, resigned. "But it's still annoying."

"I know, Mae, but think of our revenge." I look at her and see the mischievous smile on her face.

My grin widens, and we both start laughing. Mina may be as rule-following as they come, but when it comes to pranks, she's downright diabolical.

We establish a routine over the next week and a half. In the mornings, Conaill and I use the carriage; in the afternoons, we ride. It's been surprisingly non-combative in the carriage, and I'm honestly shocked it's gone so well.

The morning after the rose incident, I chose to pretend that it never happened. Conaill clearly wanted me to bring it up, but ignoring it was much more satisfying. Plus, Mina and I decided on my revenge, and now I just have to wait until the time is right.

I must say the tasks that Mina and Madok have assigned have been interesting. So far, we've drawn a representation of the other without drawing a portrait of them (Madok's requirement). Played our favorite card games with each other. Had to write non-rude (Mina's requirement) poems about a part of each other. I wrote about Conaill's legs taking up the carriage space while he wrote an 'ode' to my breasts.

While the tasks and questions are odd and varied, at least I've gotten back all of my books. Well, all except the extra spicy one Tilde gave me. Mina said she had to finish it first, the traitor.

Chapter Nineteen

After what seemed like endless travel, we're rewarded with two days of rest upon reaching Keneven. The way everything worked out had us celebrating the spring equinox here, thus affording an extra day of rest. The spring equinox is one of only five major holidays celebrated throughout Panellas. The others are the fall equinox, the summer and winter solstice, and the end of the Great War.

In honor of the spring equinox, Keneven traditionally holds one of the largest fairs in Fenshegus. I'm looking forward to being able to spend a day just exploring and shopping. Spending time among the everyday citizens. Of course, not being cooped up in a carriage or with a sore ass from riding for hours is also a perk. This trip has also severely limited my ability to organize the Order and get those in need to safety. I plan to make that a priority today.

Saori helps me get ready this morning faster than I would've thought possible. Both of us are eager to get to the fair.

"Oh, milady," Saori titters. "I'm so excited to get away from that baggage train. Those maids they sent only want to talk about the males, and the males only want to speak of inappropriate matters." Her head shakes with disapproval, and one corner of my mouth tips.

We're scarfing down a quick breakfast in the dining room when Mina and Lukavo join us. They too eat with stunning speed, and we all set off. For the next hour, we wander and weave through stalls and shops. Two guards are trailing us like hopeful puppies, taking in as much of the festival as they can while also protecting us. We're not purchasing anything yet, but we are making mental notes of where the good deals are. Eventually, Lukavo reluctantly informs us he will be unable to accompany us the rest of the morning, as he's been tasked with retrieving something for Uncle Emeric. It's only after we assure him that we're fine and armed that he feels better about leaving us.

Lukavo's departure actually allows us the opportunity to take care of some of the business we couldn't get done with him around. The focus shifts to getting medicinals, tonics, clothing, and other odds and ends purchased and shipped to various Order members. Nothing ever goes to the same place; otherwise, it would be too easy to track. From there, the items are sent out to others and are then put together into packages for common fae who have been affected.

After deciding that we've tackled enough for the morning, we finally break for lunch at the Sneaky Drake. I absolutely love this pub. A slate roof tops yellow sandstone bricks that always make the pub seem cheerful to me. Long before Dad was born, a drake was added to the roof, curving around the chimney, just poking its head out. Thus the name.

It's become tradition now that every few decades, or when the pub changes owners, a new drake is added. Each hiding somewhere, hoping to sneak up on a patron. Dad took me here when I was little, and we were visiting for another spring equinox fair. Ever since, I makc it a point to stop at this pub when I'm here. Plus, the owner is part of the Order. Two birds, one stone.

"Hey, Segi," I call out to the male behind the bar. "Where is Zsofia?"

"Mom couldn't make it today. Got really sick this past week, and I told her she needed to rest," he says while drying a glass. *Shit.* I was supposed to talk with her. Almost as if he can read my mind, he says, "She said you can stop by the house if you need anything." With a wink, he leaves to attend to the new arrivals at the end of the bar.

With a sigh, Mina says, "Well, that complicates things. How are we going to meet with Zsofia and still make our other appointments today?"

"We don't." Saori retorts, draining her glass in resignation.

I worry my lip for a minute, trying to figure out what we can skip. Each of our appointments has been specifically made for Order business. "I'll go to see her, and you two keep the other appointments," I say reluctantly. There's nothing else for it. Two sets of wide eyes meet mine before narrowing.

Holding up a hand before they can say anything, I continue, "We have to get this done. I'm the only one who can meet with Zsofia, and some of the other appointments can only be done by either a servant or a lady." I nod to each of them. "Both of you are needed for the appointments to be successful. Zsofia only lives about fifteen minutes from here. I'll go and meet her, then meet back up with you. Plus, I have my daggers."

After much consideration, they reluctantly agree. It helps that I'm dressed simply today and much less likely to get recognized. One guard comes with me, while the other will watch over Mina and Saori. We part ways, and soon I'm on my way to Zsofia's. I only feel slightly guilty that I didn't tell them that Zsofia actually lives in the forest, not the city proper. Although it does only take fifteen minutes to get there, at least if you have a horse…

With a determined stride, I weave through the city streets. My feet are eating up the ground beneath. Soon, the shops stop, and it isn't long after that the houses become sparse and the towering trees more pervasive. Suddenly, my guard doubles over, grabbing his stomach and moaning in pain.

"Humphrey!" I call. "What's wrong?"

"I'm sorry, Your Highness." He doubles over in pain, grunting again. "I'm not sure." He wrenches to the side and brings up what looks like everything he ate today.

I gently rub my hand over his back while he continues heaving until he's finally done.

"Humphrey, you need to go back to the inn," I say softly.

He shakes his head vehemently. "I can't, Your Highness. I can't leave you alone." He turns his head, retching again.

"That's it. I'm ordering you to go," I command. He looks like he's about to argue when he's sick again. "Humphrey, you are a great guard, but you can't protect me in this condition. Please, go back to the inn."

After a little arguing and a lot of retching, he finally agrees and sets off back to the inn. Now that my guard is gone, I walk as quickly as I can without drawing attention to myself. Only a few minutes later, I'm entering the forest, and am almost to Zsofia's. The quiet walk has allowed my brain to do what it does best: overthink. My mind keeps examining the riddle that is the two different Conaills. Both are struggling for domination. The first, I've been calling ass-hat Conaill. He's the one I knew of before this trip. The entitled one. The one who doesn't give two shits about common fae losing their powers. The one who's rude and demeaning to me. He's crass and vulgar.

But then, the other Conaill, the charming Conaill, his existence surprised me. And he's been coming out swinging. When it's just the two of us, or when it's just Madok or Mina with him, it's like he's a completely different person. I've seen him help those less fortunate. He plays with children in the villages we pass through. Gives food and money to the starving and the sick. He meets with satyrs in the forest to give much-needed supplies. He enjoys teasing and coaxing smiles out of those around him, myself included.

I'm rooting for charming Conaill to be the real one. The male behind the mask. Charming Conaill, beyond all explanation, has become almost like a friend over the last few days. He's someone I could, just maybe, be proud to have on my arm. But what if that's really just a ruse? What if he knows I'm watching and is just trying to pull the wool over my eyes?

These thoughts carry my feet until I notice the sky darkening. For the first time in a while, I actually notice my surroundings. I'm still on the right path, but the forest has grown thicker, and the sun struggles to reach the ground. Just like the new shoot of a plant, struggling forth, peaking its way to the sky, desperate for the smallest glimpse of sunlight. Ancient oaks dominate this forest, and the canopy is dense with branches and twigs cloaked in new leaves just starting their journey.

Shaking my head, I push this debate aside for another time and continue to walk. I'm rounding a curve when I notice a little girl crying on a moss-covered rock. A towering oak stands sentinel at her back, blocking out the warmth of the sun. Her simple smock dress is rumpled and dirty. Her light brown hair is barely held in check by what used to be braided pigtails. She's either had a very long morning playing, or she's been by herself for a while.

As I walk toward her, a twig snaps underfoot, and she flinches. Holding my hands up, I approach slowly. "Don't worry. I won't hurt you. I just want to see if you need anything."

She shakes her head rapidly, wiping a tear from her plump cheek. Crouching down so I'm level with her eyes, I ask, "Are you sure?"

She nods.

"Are you lost?"

Another nod.

"Do your parents live in the forest?"

Another nod.

"Well, that settles that," I say, holding out my hand to her. Let's continue on until you recognize the surrounding houses. We can always ask a neighbor if they know where you live."

A small grin tips the corners of her lips, and we start on our way. Worst-case scenario, I'll ask Zsofia. As the owner of one of the most popular pubs in Keneven, she knows pretty much everything about everyone.

She refuses to talk, but I fill the silence for us as we traverse the dim forest path. I tell her about our journey so far and about Mina and Tilde. I'm about to tell her about Iskra when I notice her hand now grips mine harder. Harder than it should be for a child her size. Small pinpricks of pain erupt on my skin where her fingertips dig into my skin.

Looking down, I see it for the first time. The blood instantly drains from my face. We've hit a rare break in the canopy, allowing a sunny patch, revealing her true self. Her fingernails are gone; in their place, black claws are just breaking through the first few layers of my skin.

"Gods, you talk too fucking much," she complains in a voice that is way too mature for the age she looks.

Chapter Twenty

I know what I'll find when I lift my head, but nothing prepares me for the actual sight. Bloodshot eyes and obsidian veins paint her pale ivory skin. Skin that was only just minutes ago smooth and fresh, fair but full of life. *Vampyr*, my mind supplies the name. I've read about them, but I've never actually seen one. Her eerie smile reminds me of a shark's, full of sharp teeth and gray gums.

Yanking on my wrist, she pulls me toward her with surprising strength. But now it's her turn to widen her eyes as I reflexively put my dagger between us, stopping her teeth from breaching my skin with only a hair's breadth of space between them. Thank the gods, I never leave home without daggers. It just so happens that these are also my happy daggers.

A guttural cry bellows out of her mouth. One so wild that I feel it all the way to my soul. She bites down on my dagger, blood flowing from her mouth where it's cutting her, black blood dribbling onto my arm. She moves her body directly in front of mine and flings her head, sending my dagger flying. *Shit, I needed that one.*

Switching my remaining dagger to my right hand, I use a few precious seconds to plan. I go on the offensive and lunge, my dagger just missing her neck, instead only nicking her. But it's not enough. She may be significantly smaller than me, but she's considerably stronger. I risk the second it takes for me to look around and assess my surroundings.

I realize that if I keep running straight along the path, it's only about a two-minute hard run to Zsofia's house. I'm sure I can make it, but then I'm leading a vampyr straight to her. *Fuck it, not an option.* Oaks surround the clearing, boxing me in. She lunges toward me, arms outstretched. I step to the side, pushing her arms out of the way, grabbing one in the process. Using her momentum, I force her to spin, then kick the back of her knee as she rounds me. She collapses to the ground, and I fall onto her, using my weight to hold her down and push my knee into her back. As quickly as I can, I swipe my last dagger twice, cutting the tendons at the back of her hamstrings. She won't be able to walk, let alone run, with that injury. And there's no way I'm giving her the time to heal.

A bloodcurdling scream erupts from her. It's quickly cut off when I stab her through the heart and then remove her head, one of only two ways to kill a vampyr. I don't even have a moment to catch my breath when a cacophony of roars fills my ears, echoing off the surrounding trees. My head snaps up, and a scene straight from hell surrounds me. Everywhere I look, I see vampyrs. *Polmas, help me.* Eight vampyrs completely surround me, cutting off all chance of escape. *Shit, shit, shit.*

"What did you do to my daughter?" thunders the tallest male. *Fuck me.* He's easily seven feet tall, and based on the glow coming from his eyes, very, very old.

Time slows as they all rush me, and I know that this is it. There's no way I'm getting out of this alive. *Bas*, I implore the God of Life and Death, *if you have decided it's my time, at least let me take out as many of these bastards as I can first.*

He's clearly listening, and I'm able to dodge one and get on the outside of the group. They skid to a halt, adjusting their positions so they all face me. There's no way I can outrun them. I'm fast, but nowhere near as fast as a vampyr. *Fuck, Isk! Please lend her your strength to go on without me.* I throw one last prayer up, hoping the God of Strength is listening.

Shrill cries assault my ears as a female lunges, and I'm not fast enough. Blood streams down my face from her claws, but at least my dagger sliced her forearm. There are just too many of them. There's no way out of this. Suddenly, a savage cry pierces the air. Without warning, every last one of them flies from me as if yanked by a cord.

I stumble, and strong arms steady me, as warm leather and vanilla fill the air. Turning my head ever so slightly, Conaill comes into view. His lips are peeled back, exposing his teeth in a snarl, eyes feral and focused on the vampyrs. With a flick of his wrist, my other dagger lifts from the ground, flying into my hand.

"If you can, I just need you to cut them," he says before launching himself at the vampyrs that are almost back to us.

I nod, and then, with a dagger in each hand, I take on the one furthest to the left. Holding my right dagger against my arm, I step into him. For once, I thank the gods for my smaller stature, as it allows me to get in so close he can't effectively attack. Blocking across my body, I push him away, but not before slicing his back.

My momentum carries me forward, and I spin. The movement sets me up perfectly, and I drop into a crouch at the end of my spin, my left dagger sinking into the gut of another. A second later, I see a vampyr about to attack Conaill from behind. *Fuck. That.* Without another thought, I throw my dagger, hitting the vampyr in the arm and pinning him to a tree.

"Thanks, Red," Conaill calls out, not even looking my way.

I yell out when a monstrous weight hits me in the back. All the air leaves my body as I'm slammed into the ground, my remaining dagger flying off. I'm completely frozen. All I can do is gasp for the air I so desperately need. The weight on my back is too much, though, and even when my lungs do start to work, I can't get more than a trickle in.

Hot, rancid breath touches the back of my ear, and saliva drips onto my cheek. "You killed my daughter, bitch."

Reaching out my arm, I try to grab onto something I can use as a weapon. There's nothing, though, and I still can't breathe. My vision dims, but I don't stop fighting. I refuse to die this way.

Acid climbs its way up my throat as his nose runs up my neck. *Oh gods, he's scenting me.* I try to swallow down the need to vomit when there…

Right there. The edge of a rock teeters against my fingertips. Using every ounce of strength I can, I stretch farther than I thought possible. But it's no use. My fingers can't stretch far enough.

"You killed my daughter, and now I'm going to kill you."

Reaching out one final time, I push the tendons in my arm to stretch to the breaking point. Bas must have heard my plea, though, and this time I'm able to grab the rock. Before I can do anything, he flips me onto my back, pinning my arms with his.

Air, sweet, glorious air fills my lungs, and for one tiny second, I feel hope. But then he smells me again. A shudder racks me at the bloodlust in his eyes.

"You smell so good." Running his tongue up my neck, he groans. "It would be a shame to let all that glorious blood go to waste."

He yanks my head to the side, and white, hot pain explodes through me. I'm frozen for a moment before realizing he had to release my arms to do that. Fighting through the pain, I slam the rock into his head with every bit of strength I have left. I've startled him enough to break his hold on my neck. I do it again and again. This time, he falls back.

Conaill's war cry fills my ears as the vampyr is picked up on a stream of air and slammed back into a tree. Impaled on a broken branch.

Manic laughter escapes from the vampyr's bloody mouth. A mouth covered in my blood. "You don't even know."

Conaill helps me up, his eyes glued to the vampyr as it continues to laugh. "To think all this time, and you didn't even know."

"Know what?" I demand, my hand going to my throat, trying to direct my limited healing abilities there.

"Let me live, and I'll tell you," he counters.

"Tell her, and I won't kill you slowly," Conaill growls. "You're dead no matter what."

A light breeze brushes the hair against my neck, and the scent of my blood must hit the vampyr because he goes absolutely feral. Ripping himself off the tree, he launches toward me.

Just before he reaches me, he freezes. What little color he has drains from his skin, and he looks down, taking a staggering step back. *What the hell?* My eyes grow wide as I take in everything. Blood pours from the wound in his stomach. So much blood that his skin is now ashen. His body is sinking into itself.

"I told you you were going to die," Conaill says calmly, his hand raised slightly. *Holy shit,* Conaill is desiccating him. Conaill can't just command water; he can command all liquids. "All you had to do was tell her what you meant, and I would've cut off your head. Nice and quick." He shakes his head at the gasping vampyr.

"But… you had to try to attack her again. No one, and I mean no one, hurts what's mine. So now, when all your blood is gone, I'm going to bury you. I'm going to bury you and all your friends. And then I'm going to get a friend of mine. She's going to grow a tree over each and every one of you." He breaks eye contact with the vampyr for the first time since he started draining his blood. Turning slightly, he motions to the other vampyrs. The ones that I'm only just now realizing are all desiccated husks.

"Why trees? I'm so glad you asked. See, I'll have her grow the trees so that a root from each one is poised just above each of your hearts." He leans down to the vampyr that's now collapsed on the ground. "And then, I'm going to have her stop. We're going to leave, forget about you, and go on living. All the while you'll be stuck underground. Each year, the root will grow longer and longer. Piercing your heart little by little, until one day, it finally breaks through. Only then will you be released to death's embrace."

Conaill raises both hands, and all the vampyrs lift into the air. "Until I can bury you, though, I need to put you somewhere safe." The vampyrs fly into the trees out of the way for now. Another flick of his hand glamours the clearing where we fought and the vampyrs in the trees. Grabbing my hand, Conaill leads me away from this nightmare.

Chapter Twenty-One

The ragged sound of my breathing fills my ears; everything else has gone silent. Looking down, I realize Conaill has grabbed my hand and is dragging me away. The warm, callus-hardened skin of his hand in mine is all that's keeping my imminent breakdown at bay. The soft, comforting sensation of Conaill's thumb stroking the back of my hand finally breaks through the haze that's been trapping my brain. My face lifts to his, and it's only then that I realize he's just as affected.

We walk a short distance away, and I'm finally able to find my voice. "Conaill," I croak weakly before clearing my throat. "Conaill, are you okay?" I ask, my voice somewhat stronger.

Stopping suddenly, he twists me to face him. "Am I okay?" he asks, a touch of panic lacing the words. Still holding my hand, he pulls us off and away from the path before throwing up a sound shield. "Gods, Red. I thought I had lost you." He drops my hand as his are now too busy. He's running them up and down his face and through his hair, over and over. "Red, I heard that vampyr roar, and I ran. When I saw how many of them there were, I knew there wasn't much hope." He takes a deep breath and sighs. "And then I saw it was you." His voice catches before he pauses again.

Swallowing hard, he continues, "Red, there were so many, and she had you cornered. I was so scared. I saw you only had one dagger, and then she did this." Ever so gently, he cups my face in his large hand, his fingers lightly dancing over the claw marks on my cheek. "I lost it, and then when I saw he had you." I don't resist as he pulls me into his arms, and we cling to each other. We both need this comfort. He holds me so tightly I feel our heartbeats merge. He presses his lips to the top of my head before resting his cheek there.

"I didn't even see you go down." The words are rough, clogged with emotion. "I was so focused on the others, and when I looked up, he had his fangs in you. Gods, I just got you, and I almost lost you, Red." His hands lift, cradling my cheeks, and suddenly he's bending down, kissing me.

Full lips capture mine, teasing and playing. Tentatively, he licks the seam of my lips, asking for permission, and *Gods, yes, I need this.* My lips part, and instantly the dam between us breaks. Passion erupts, neither of us holding back. Our tongues, our bodies, they say what we can't or won't. I suck on his tongue, and he lets out a groan.

His hands skim down my body, squeezing my ass, before going to the backs of my thighs. He lifts me up, and I wrap my legs around his hips. Our cores are lined up, and I mewl at the feel of his swollen cock against me. Suddenly, a tree is pressing into my back, and I use it for leverage to grind my core against his length.

Breaking the kiss, my mouth moves to his neck. Kissing, sucking, and licking my way up and down. From the top of his collarbone to right behind his ear and back. "Maevery," he calls out, twitching against me.

My mouth is yanked back to his, where our tongues wage war, and we're both winning. He pulls my shirt out of my leather pants, then rips down my bra. Covering a breast with his large, warm palm, he squeezes gently before finding my nipple.

He thrusts against me as he pinches my nipple, and I cry out. The pain sends a bolt of pleasure to my core like they're connected. Then he's caressing the pain away with calloused fingers, and I want him to do it again. My hand reaches for him at the same time he undoes the button on my pants. I nod in silent permission, and he emits a small groan before capturing my lips again, biting the lower one before soothing it.

Just as his fingers reach me, he cries out, "Touch me, Maevery, please." Plunging his middle finger in, I cry out.

"I am," I moan.

"No," He kisses me deeply, as if our lives depend on it. "I want to feel your skin on mine."

Another finger plunges in, and I'm already on the edge. Tearing open his pants, my hand quickly finds him. *Gods, he's huge.* I can't even wrap my hand all the way around him.

"Please," I whimper, squeezing him as I explore his thick length. "Please, I need more."

"I've got you, Maevery." His thumb presses into my clit, and soon he's rubbing it just the way I like. Curling his fingers, he's able to stroke that secret spot inside me. His thumb moves, and now the edge of his nail is pressing into my clit as well. It's the additional sharp edge of sensation that does it, and my orgasm takes over.

I scream out my pleasure as my hand clamps down on him. "Conaill, please. I need you," I beg when I'm finally able to talk again.

"You have me." He pants, clearly on edge.

"No, Conaill," I moan as he starts stroking feather-light touches over my sensitive flesh again. "I need you inside me."

"Fuck," he roars. Taking his hand from me, he gently grasps my face, looking me straight in the eyes. "Are you sure?"

"Yes, Conaill, please. I promise. I *need* you inside me." I kiss him again before demanding, "Now!"

A possessive growl escapes his throat, and the next second, I'm on the ground, and we tear at each other's clothing. Using the shirts as a makeshift sheet, he stills above me.

"I take the pregnancy suppressant," he assures, kissing me again before looking me in the eyes. "Last chance."

"Me too," I say, pulling his face down to mine. "Now shut up and fuck me, Conaill."

A chuckle escapes his lips before our mouths collide. Rough hands lift one of my thighs, opening me to him more. Running the head of his cock up and down my opening, he teases me before pushing in an inch.

"Conaill," I groan. He's barely in, and I'm already stretching. He's so big. Surging forward again, he sinks in another inch. He hooks his arm under my thigh, my leg now resting on his upper arm. Another thrust and he sinks in more.

"Gods, Maevery, you're so fucking tight," he says through gritted teeth.

"Well, you're godsdamn huge," I moan out, and he chuckles again.

"You do know how to stroke my ego," he says, leaning down and kissing me quickly.

"If you don't start fucking me soon," I pant, "your hand's going to be the only thing stroking you."

"Your wish is my command, princess." He pulls out slightly and then, with a surge of his hips, he's seated to the hilt.

Groans tangle, and pleasure rises. Soon, he's fucking me with a singular purpose. His hips pump into me with deep, sure strokes. I hold myself tight against his chest, bringing my hips to his with every thrust. Our bodies dance to a rhythm only we know. One that's an instinct, somehow, each of us knows exactly what the other needs.

"I'm close," he moans through gritted teeth, reaching between us to rub my clit. "Come for me, baby."

"Conaill!" I erupt. The orgasm coursing through my body is stronger than any I've had before. My channel clamps around him, and he stiffens as he comes inside me. His head drops to mine, his weight braced on his forearms, and for a minute, we just breathe. I'm about to say something stupid, like we should do that again, when the sound of talking reaches my ears.

We freeze. Like a cloud has lifted, the realization of where we are hits me square in the face. *What did I just do?* How could I forget that we're out in the open, where anyone could walk by? *Is the sound shield still up?* I tap my ear, looking at Conaill with pleading eyes.

"It's still up," he says, kissing me lightly on the nose. "But we should probably get dressed as soon as we can. I can't keep the glamour up back there and glamour us as well."

"Crap," I say softly, causing Conaill to chuckle. "I can't glamour this big. I don't have that kind of power."

Conaill furrows his brow, a question clearly written on his face. I don't want to end this moment, though, so I put my finger to his lips, shushing him. We listen for a few more minutes until no more sounds can be heard. We get dressed as quickly as possible, and I'm just about to step onto the road when Conaill grabs my hand, entwining his fingers with mine. He gives the back of my hand a quick kiss before pulling me up on the road behind him.

"Come on. Your wounds haven't stopped bleeding, and I know someone who can help." Pulling my hand from his, I reach up to my now throbbing cheek, my hand coming away bloody.

"What? It should've healed by now. I'm trying, but I can't heal it." Then realization dawns on me. "That bitch had poison on her claws."

A mumbled, "Fuck," is all that Conaill says before picking up his pace. We walk for a few moments before he asks, "You said you didn't have the power to glamour us. What did you mean by that?"

Shit, I did say that. *Well, he's going to figure it out sooner or later.* "I only have common magic," I say softly, but the tensing of his body tells me he heard. "And what I do have is weak." My head hangs in shame. "Everyone in my family has always been extremely powerful, except me." I shrug. "The queen to be, with no power."

"I don't understand. Like, it just hasn't manifested yet or..." His voice trails off, and I can practically see how hard he's thinking.

Gods, this is embarrassing. Conaill is so powerful that he can command blood to leave a vampyr, then throw said vampyr *and* all his cronies into the trees. All without touching them.

"I've. We've…" I correct, "tried everything. Even though I should have at least some high power. But, nope, nothing."

He's quiet for a second, biting his lip as if deep in thought. "Well, like I said, I know someone who's good at healing; maybe she can think of something you haven't tried before."

"You know Zsofia?" I question. My brows furrow in confusion as we walk up to her house.

"You know Zsofia?" he parrots back. "I've known her for years. How do you know her?"

"She, ah…" *Shit*, what can I say without revealing anything? "She helps me out sometimes. I met her through the Sneaky Drake."

He seems to accept this and raises his hand to knock. Before he can do that, though, the door is flung open. Zsofia's worried face fills my vision as she throws her arms around me.

"Oh, thank the gods, Your Highness. I was worried something had happened," she says, stepping back. "I knew Segi would get the message to you, and you're never late." Stepping back to let us enter, she turns to Conaill, noticing him for the first time. Her head tilts in confusion, her eyes narrowed.

"What are you doing here early? Our meeting isn't for another hour, Walthier?"

Chapter Twenty-Two

I'm sorry. What did she just say? I freeze as I feel Conaill stiffen beside me. I must have heard her wrong. "I'm sorry, Zsofia, but what did you just call him?"

"That's Walthier." She gestures to him before turning and walking inside.

The tan skin of his face has lost most of its color, and his eyes are wide. "Let's get inside," he says quickly, shaking himself out of his stupor. "Please."

It's the please that does it, and I comply. I, too, wouldn't mind having a little more privacy for this. We go inside and are led to a comfortable living room. Zsofia leaves us to go get supplies, and I use this time to collect myself. My brain starts to work again, at least partly, and I ask, "Why does she call you Walthier?" Gods, I hate how squeaky my voice sounded.

"Listen, I…" he starts, but is interrupted by Zsofia's return.

"Oh, shush." She waves him off and then sits me on the couch and starts cleaning my wounds. "No need to lie to each other. You're both in the Order, after all. I'm shocked you hadn't met before, given your roles."

My mouth falls open, and it takes all my years of training to shut it again. When I look at Conaill, his face matches how I feel.

"I'm sorry, what do you mean by 'given our roles'?" Conaill asks.

Without stopping her ministrations, she responds, "You're the head of the Order in Kystenvar; she's Fenshegus's head."

Conaill's eyes are locked on mine, and I can see him trying to put things together, just as I am. Walthier and I have been working together for over a year now. He's been my main contact in Kystenvar the whole time. But the more I think, the more different pieces fall into place. During the Council, Walthier seemed to be completely updated on what was happening with surprising speed, as if he had been there. And he did tell me that everything is not always as it seems. In fact, if I think about who Conaill is when it's just the two of us, I could actually believe that they're the same person.

I sigh. "I think you may know me better as Flora."

He sinks into the chair across from us. "Are you saying that we've been communicating through letters for over a year now?" His head lifts, looking directly at me.

"It would appear so." I wince at whatever Zsofia is doing. "Damn, that stings."

"Enough jibber-jabber about all that. What in Bas made these wounds?" she inquires.

"That would be a vampyr," I say, and Zsofia drops her cloth.

"You were attacked by a vampyr? That's why you were late." She stands quickly, going to her medical chest on the side of the room.

Conaill corrects, "Eight attacked her. Well, nine if you count the child."

Zsofia goes still, turning around eerily, a tin clutched in her hand, she says shakily, "Nine vampires attacked you, at least one of which was old enough to have a born, not made, child. And you survived with only those scratches?"

"Not exactly," I say, my hand flying to my neck. "The sire vampyr, I guess you would call him, bit me. But Conaill was able to kill him." I look at him, grateful again that he was there. "Killed all but the one I did."

Zsofia appraises Conaill shrewdly, then nods and goes back to her cabinet. "Okay, I'm going to send something with you. Ah-ha!" She pulls out a vial of blood-red liquid. "Take a mouthful each day for a week. That'll make sure any venom is completely removed from your system."

Sitting next to me, she opens a tin of salve and applies it to my wounds. The sweet aroma of a meadow reaches me, and I'm instantly calmed. "I'm also going to send you with this. It's yarrow and horsetail bush. Put it on twice a day, and you'll heal well with no scars. Vampyr wounds are one of the few that our natural healing abilities struggle with." When she's finished, she hands me both the tin and the vial.

"Zsofia, I was hoping you could help with something else." Conaill looks at me, asking permission. I nod, and he continues. "Maevery hasn't manifested her powers, and she claims even her common magic is weak."

"What's this nonsense?" Her shock is evident, and embarrassment floods me again. "I was there the day the oracle made her prophecy."

My head flies up. "Excuse me? What prophecy?"

"Humph," she grumbles. "You don't remember?" I give her my best, *well, duh*, look, and she continues. "When your dad brought you to Keneven that first time, you ate lunch in my pub. Well, an oracle happened to be passing through. On its way to its new home, I guess. Anyway, he was in the pub too, and when he saw you, a prophecy came to him. Let me think…" She pauses, her lip between her teeth. "Ah, yes, that's it. He said you would be one of the most powerful rulers of Fenshegus."

"But I don't have any power. Not beyond common magic," I say.

"Well then, clearly you're being suppressed." She waves off and goes to her medicines again.

"What exactly do you mean by being suppressed?" Conaill asks. "Someone's power can't be suppressed."

"Pish-posh," she responds, grabbing a flask and bringing it to me. "It can, and she is."

"But, why wouldn't anyone have figured that out before now? Wouldn't we have heard of it before?" I say, hope edging my voice. If I've been suppressed, maybe she can figure out how to get my power to come back.

"Because as far as anyone knows, only prisoners have had their magic suppressed. But that requires a bespelled tattoo, and I'm assuming you don't have one of those." It's a statement, not a question, but I answer it anyway.

"No, no tattoos."

Conaill sits forward, elbows on his knees. "What do you mean as far as anyone knows?"

"There's another way to suppress magic, or rather, power. A very old way. It actually became illegal long before your grandfather, King Oren the Second, was born," Zsofia adds, turning to me. "They tried, and obviously failed, to remove all record of it. A potion can be made and administered to a fae that suppresses magic. As long as the fae keeps taking the potion, their magic will be suppressed."

"So, theoretically, all I need to do is stop taking the potion, and my power will awaken?"

"It's not as simple as that," she says sadly. "If a fae stops taking it suddenly, the power coming back can be overwhelming, and it can kill them."

"Fuck," Conaill hisses.

"Exactly." Zsofia puts her hand on my knee, "But I have a plan." She winks, then nods to the flask. "You're not to take any tonic or drink any unless it's made in front of you or you break the seal on it. You've got enough pregnancy suppressant there for about six months. That'll give you time to figure out who's doing this and still be able to have fun." She waggles her eyebrows, looking pointedly between Conaill and me.

Conaill's sexy as sin smirk is back, but my face is flaming with embarrassment. "Zsofia!" I chide.

"What?" she says as if she didn't just give us the go-ahead to screw as much as we wanted. Which, admittedly, is quite a bit now that I know how good he is. "I may be old, but my nose works just fine. I smelled it when you entered. Lust, arousal, *and* sex. It wasn't only the vampyrs that made you late, I bet." Somehow, my cheeks burn even hotter. "Plus, if I had that one" — she points to Conaill — "well, Astrid knows I'd spend a lot more time in bed." She actually winks at Conaill, and now his stupid, sexy face sports an absolutely huge shit-eating grin. *Ugh, he's going to be even more unbearable.*

Her eyes light up as if she just thought of something. "You're friends with Prince Darius, yes?"

"Yes," we say simultaneously.

"Good, if rumors are true, he's knowledgeable in herbs. The suppressant will contain an herb called thor thairis. He can teach you how to confirm if it's present in anything you're given," she says with authority.

We spend the next hour or so creating a plan and discussing the next steps for the Order. Zsofia also left me with some herbs I'm to make a tea out of for the next week. This will allow me to not die when my power awakens. We also decided that the only fae we can trust with us right now are Mina, Darius, and Madok. As I have to keep being dosed with the suppressant for it to work, not only do they have to be on our journey, but they would need to have some access to me continuously. Meaning everyone else is a suspect.

We walk back toward town in silence, both lost in thought. We're almost back to where the vampyrs attacked when Conaill breaks the silence.

"So, turns out you aren't just some spoiled princess. Kind of a shock you're leading the Order." My glare burns into him.

"I could say the same of you," I say, indignation evident in my tone, one eyebrow arched in silent judgment.

Holding his hands up in surrender, he continues. "Based on what you said at the Council, I figured you would want to help; I just didn't think you'd actively be leading anything."

"Well, I am," I huff, walking faster.

His long legs easily match my stride, and he grabs my hand to stop me. "Look, I'm glad you are. We can work together more easily now that we know who's in charge. Plus, with you becoming queen in a few months, you can officially make Fenshegus's stance fit your ideas."

"Yeah, that was the plan." I shrug my shoulders, feeling slightly defeated. "It just seems like it's not enough. Every day, I'm getting more messages about fae being stripped of power, and I'm worried what will happen between now and then."

"I know, but I'll help. Madok is on our side, as are King Ewan IV and Queen Dia. Really, all of Umbrimina." His hands come to my cheeks, tilting my face up. "I also know Darius and his family are working on what they can do. We'll figure out what's going on and fix it."

Gods, I want him to be right. His determination to help is a pleasant surprise. We look at each other for a heartbeat, and then his mouth is on mine, kissing me hungrily. Damn, this male can work magic with his mouth. He breaks the kiss, rubbing his thumb along my lower lip. I'm on my toes, lifting up to meet him and resume our kiss when hoofbeats sound.

"Moro bless us," Madok says, thanking the God of Jubilation. "There you are." He's riding Conaill's mare and stops just in front of us. Pulling up beside him is Mina riding Mionnan. "We've been looking for you." They must note our curious looks as they explain.

"Mionnan came barging through the town, clearly distressed," Mina says. "He grabbed my shirt and pulled me out of the shop." She motions to her torn sleeve. "His eyes were wide and determined, and I knew something was wrong. I called out to Saori to finish our business and hopped on."

"Sharaf did the same." Madok leans down and pats Conaill's mare, shaking his head as he continues. "Wouldn't even let me finish my ale. We met up on the road into the forest. It was then that we realized something must have happened to the two of you."

"Well, you're about two hours too late," Conaill replies and continues to walk. "Maevery was attacked by vampyrs just up here." Is it me, or did Conaill growl when he said that?

A gasp comes out of Mina as a snarl rips free from Madok. "I was actually going to get you, Mina." As we come to the site of the attack, Conaill removes his glamour, and the grisly scene comes into view. "I promised these vermin retribution for attacking Maevery. One your particular skills could help me with."

"Gods above, I don't know whether to say a prayer to Bas or Polemas," Madok says, looking around. "My first thought would be Bas, but damn, it looks like a war zone here, so maybe Polemas might be a good idea too."

We take turns explaining what happened. When Conaill explains his plan to torture the vampyrs, Mina becomes positively giddy. For as straight-laced and upstanding as she is, Mina excels at her unofficial role with the rebellion. While Tilde might be in charge of spying, Mina is the information extractor.

Madok, it turns out, can move the ground, allowing him to bury the vampyrs. While he does this, we explain the revelation of my power being suppressed and what we plan to do. They're also let in on the fact that we're all fighting on the same side and are in the Order. For the first time in what seems like forever, I don't feel like I'm fighting a losing battle.

Chapter Twenty-Three

Knock, knock, knock.

Turning my head to the door, I sigh at the intrusion on my peace as I go to see who's there. To say today's been a long day would be an understatement. Hopefully, whoever's there will go away quickly. I open the door to a frowning Conaill.

"What took so long?" he demands, storming in. He's got a bag slung over his shoulder, which he throws on the bed.

"Um, excuse me?" I say, hoping my tone portrays the level of incredulity I'm feeling.

"What took you so long to open the door?" He opens his bag and starts to take things out. It's then that I realize he's planning on staying here tonight.

I completely ignore the question and instead ask, "What are you doing? You aren't staying here." I storm over and glare up at him. "This is my room. Go find your own."

"Not a chance, Red." He shakes his head. "Not after what we found out today. There's no way I'm leaving you alone. At least not until your power comes in and you can defend yourself."

Screw that. Looking around, I see a dagger on the table next to me. With little thought, I pick it up and throw it. *Thwack.* His head whips back. The blade passed so closely that his hair moved from the wind. His eyes blaze with heat when they meet mine.

"Fuck, that's hot, Red." He stalks toward me, picking me up and pinning me against the door. "But I guess I should say until your power comes in and you can use *it* to defend yourself even better." His mouth slams to mine, kissing me deep and hard.

I'm not even sure how it happens, but my legs are around him, my fingers running through his hair. Conaill's hand trails up my side, teasing and caressing me with just his fingertips. He palms my breast, and I moan as he breaks from the kiss. I'm about to complain when his mouth lands on my neck. Open-mouthed kisses trail along my neck, turning my body liquid. What is it about my neck being kissed that's such a turn-on?

Nipping behind my ear, he soothes the slight sting with his tongue. "Conaill," I cry, and his mouth finds its home back on mine.

Pound, pound.

"Get off each other. We need to talk." A rough voice cuts through the fog.

"Go the fuck away, Madok," Conaill yells, then his mouth is ravishing mine again.

"You know how I hate cock-blocking, but Darius will leave early in the morning. It's now or never." Madok says through the door. If his tone is anything to go by, I very much doubt he hates cock-blocking.

Conaill loudly growls out a "Fuck" then slides me down his body. As our bodies slide against each other, I have to suppress a moan at the torture.

He throws the door open so hard that the heavy wood bangs off the soft beige wall. Madok strides in confidently, letting out a chuckle, followed closely by Darius and Mina. Only she seems to be embarrassed by the interruption.

"Make yourself at home," I say dryly as Darius plops into a chair by the fire and Mina sits on my bed.

"Don't mind if I do," Madok replies. He throws himself on the bed next to Mina, causing her to bounce slightly and fall into him. "Sorry about that, Lo," he says, clearly not sorry in the least.

"Ugh, can't you ever just grow up? You're how old and still act like a child?" she grumbles, pushing herself off him.

"Three hundred and twenty-one years young, same age as Con." He winks.

I look at Conaill and study him. I didn't realize he was so much older than me. I mean, I knew he was older, obviously, but not that much older. I'm startled out of my thoughts by Darius's deep voice.

"So, not sure what exactly is going on, but this one over here" — he looks pointedly at Madok — "told me I need to come with him and bring my *plant shit.*"

"What?" Madok says innocently when Mina glares at him. "He knew what I meant."

"Thank you, Darius," I say, then sigh. I explain about today's revelation and that Zsofia thought he might help us learn how to identify it. Turns out, Darius met Zsofia when she was an acolyte at the temple to Leighis in Samaith. She tutored him in healing and introduced him to his current passion for medicinal botany.

"So… I'm not really supposed to know about this. It's something very few know, and I'm not even sure how she learned." Darius spends a moment searching through his book, turning it around to show us what he's found.

"So thor thairis is part of this family of plants. They're all used to stop something," he explains.

I don't hear what he says next, as a movement from my bed distracts me. Madok keeps trying to touch Mina, and she's having none of it. Anytime he gets close to touching her, she smacks his hand away. Mina's on a mission and won't be distracted in any way.

I turn my attention back to Darius as a small smile sneaks out. I've missed the background he gave, but luckily not what we need to do. We spend the next hour going over how we can identify what has been tainted by the suppressant.

Gods, this is going to take a while. I try not to be too dejected, but damn, it's hard. The suppressant only needs to be ingested once per week. Meaning that for at least one week, pretty much everything I drink and eat has to be tested. It could be worse, I guess. The suppressant degrades in high heat. This means cooked food is safe to consume. As long as someone doesn't add anything afterward. *Crap, nothing is safe.*

"Okay, I just want to double check," Mina calls out, pausing her pacing. She got tired of fending off Madok a while ago and started pacing. I swear I can see the paths she's worn between the window and the fireplace. "So, we need to find discoperiet salt and sprinkle it on her food and drink. If it has the thor thairis, it will turn green. In liquid, it creates a fine green film on the top." Darius nods, and Mina smiles proudly, as if she just aced a test.

"One question," Madok says, holding his hand up as if he's in school. "What if it's already green? Or like, really dark so you can't see if it's changed colors?"

Shit, I didn't think of that. "Then you scrape the salt off," Darius says, as if it's common sense. "If it's still green, then it's positive."

Mina nods her head, "Got it, then we can deglamour anyone who came in contact with it. If their hands are spotted, they were working with the suppressant specifically, not just the herb."

"Why can't we just start with that?" Madok says. "Cut out the testing part."

"Because," Mina snarls out, "it'll let them know what we're up to. If they aren't one of the first fae we deglamour, then they can hide."

"Besides, we want this to occur in a setting we can control," Conaill adds.

"Got it," Madok acquiesces. "Well, until that time, it will look suspicious if you aren't eating or drinking anything without testing it first. But I think Lo and I can come up with reasons why the two of you eat alone." Madok winks at me as a distinct growl comes from Conaill.

"I can also make sure to bring you things that I've already tested, so no one sees anything," Mina adds. "Also, I don't think it's a good idea for you to sleep alone anymore, so I'll room with you from now on."

"Yeah, that's not happening," Conaill says, his tone brooking no argument. "If she's sharing her room with anyone, it'll be me."

"Excuse me!" I blurt. "I don't recall inviting you to share my room." No way is he just going to demand that.

"Oh yes, you did." Conaill stalks toward me. I vaguely register Madok grabbing Mina's hand and pulling her to the door. "The minute you opened those soft thighs and begged me to fuck you, you did."

"And on that note, we'll be going," Darius says, the three of them escaping out of the room. Mina actually winks as she shuts the door. *Traitor.*

"I most certainly did *not* beg you," I say. I back up a step, but I'm stopped by the mattress hitting the back of those same thighs Conaill just mentioned.

"Oh, you most certainly did. I remember it vividly." Then his lips are on mine, and I forget what I'm arguing with him about. Pulling away, he says against my lips. "Besides, you and I have unfinished business."

Our lips meet, battling for dominance in a kiss that has my thighs clenching. A moan escapes my lips when my back hits the mattress and his hard body presses into mine. Taking control of my senses for a moment, I pull back. His eyes are dilated, and the green flecks in his hazel eyes are brighter. "What do you mean we have unfinished business?" I ask.

"Just that." He dips down, kissing me again as he runs his hand up my body. Stopping at my breast, caressing the flesh, he murmurs, "You didn't honestly think that taking you outside earlier was enough." His hand pulls down my top, pushing my breasts above the fabric.

Moaning loudly, he dips his head, licking my nipple. "Gods, your boobs are amazing." Pressing my hips to his, I wordlessly beg for more, but he stops instead. "Gods, there's so much more I want to do to you. So much more I can show you. When I'm done with you tonight, you won't be able to walk in the morning, let alone ride a horse."

Taking my nipple into his mouth, he sucks on it before delivering a bite that stings in a way I never thought I'd like. "Promises, promises," I say, reaching to undo his shirt.

With a chuckle, he stands up, pulling me to him. As fast as I can, I rip his shirt off. *Astrid, bless me,* his body is a work of art. Before I can do anything else, he spins me around so my back is pressed to his front. His impressive cock is hard and demanding, pressing against my lower back. Large hands gently glide over my stomach and then up my breasts. A low moan escapes my lips when the tips of his fingers whisper over my nipples.

With one hand, he grabs my face, angling it so we can continue our kiss. The other to my thigh, gathering my dressing and nightgown. Lifting my hand, I thread his hair through my fingers. My other hand drifts between us, massaging his thick length.

Without warning, my head's pulled back, my hair wrapped around his fist. "No touching," he demands, tilting his hips away. "I want to play with you, and if you touch me, I'm not sure I'll get to do everything I have planned."

"But I want to play too," I whine, but stop when his fingers reach my bare thigh.

"Oh, you'll get your chance to play." He kisses his way down my neck, sucking and licking. "But not until I'm done."

When his fingers reach the front of my panties, his knees buckle slightly, and he lets out a groan. "Gods Maevery, you're soaked." Rubbing my clit through the fabric, my breath catches at the added friction. Gods, this feels so good. One finger gently traces around the top of my panties before dipping down and into me.

I cry out, and my panties are ripped off me. "Hey, I liked that pair," I say between panting breaths.

"I'll buy you more," is all the response I get before the rest of my clothes are ripped away, leaving me naked against him.

Pulling me back to him, his mouth plunders mine again as two fingers enter me. "Gods, you're so warm and tight." Bringing his fingers to my mouth, he paints my lips with my own arousal. "Open, Maevery. See how good you taste," he demands. When I close my mouth around his fingers and suck, I feel him twitch against me.

His mouth replaces his fingers, and I'm spun again, his hands lifting me by the thighs. My legs wrap around his, and I'm lowered onto my back. We kiss again, his hand working magic between my legs.

"Conaill. Please, I want you in me," I beg.

"Not a chance." He shakes his head. "You'll come twice before I'm inside you again. And then…" He pauses to grind against me. "Then you'll come again."

Fuck, he's going to be the death of me. But gods, what a way to go. He plays my sex as if it were made just for him. His thumb gives just the right amount of pressure on my clit as his fingers find that one spot that makes me liquid. We kiss as I writhe under him, my body so close.

"Come for me, baby," he says, breaking the kiss. "Now."

And I'm undone. Shudders rack through my body, and my legs go limp, my breathing ragged. "That was one," Conaill says roughly in my ear before kissing his way down my body. He pauses when he reaches my core, and I look down.

"What… what are you doing?" I question. "Why did you stop?"

"I just wanted to admire what I'm about to taste." His tongue comes out, swiping through my cleft. My leg trembles of its own accord, and he laughs. The male actually laughs. "Ready for number two?"

Before I can even respond, he feasts on me. His tongue is licking me, seeking every drop of pleasure he dragged from me with the first orgasm. "Godsdamn, you taste so good." My head falls back as my hands go to my breasts.

Using the flat of his tongue, he presses against my clit. I moan in pleasure as he slides two fingers inside me. Tormenting me with tongue and fingers.

"Conaill, please," I cry. "I need more. Please, Con, give me more." My hips lift, trying to get closer to the magic that is his tongue.

He chuckles, his breath tickling my clit, "As you wish, Princess." He nips my clit, and my hips push up. I moan so loud I'm sure the entire inn can hear, but at this moment I don't care.

"Do that again," I say breathily, and he complies. He feasts on me as if he were starving. Alternating between licking and nipping until I'm writhing uncontrollably, just on the edge of completion. "More. Harder," I demand, desperate to come. I feel him smile against me, and then he's worrying my clit between his teeth. Not hard enough to hurt, but just enough to give me the pressure I need.

"Conaill!" I cry out. The orgasm is so intense that I black out for a moment. When I come back to myself, Conaill's still between my thighs. A wicked smirk on his lips and his chin glistening with the evidence of my orgasm.

Standing, he undoes his pants, freeing his rock-hard cock. "My turn now." A predatory gleam shines in his eyes as he comes over me. "I'm going to take you now. Last chance to say no."

"Take me, Conaill. Take me hard and fast." His eyes flare at my words, and his scent intensifies. Warm leather and vanilla fill the air, and I breathe deeply, as my arousal somehow increases.

"Gods, Maevery, you'll be the death of me," he says as his tip nudges my entrance. Slowly, so torturously slowly, he enters me. Inch by glorious inch, until he's seated to the hilt. He kisses me deeply before he says, "Hold on."

He pulls almost all the way out, and I miss him for a moment before he surges forward. I groan with pleasure as he pumps into me. Harder and harder. My legs wrap around his waist, heels digging into his ass, providing me with just the leverage I need to match his thrusts. His large, calloused palm cups my ass, lifting me slightly.

He leans down, kissing me deeply, not breaking his tempo. I cry out, breaking the kiss as he hits just the right spot. When my nails rake down his back, he throws his head back and cries out. His tempo picks up, thrusting faster and faster. My hands push against the headboard, both to hold me in place and to allow me to match his thrusts.

"Yes, Conaill, yes, yes, yes." I practically scream. "Don't stop. Don't stop." My lips seek out his. Kissing him deeply, our tongues mimicking the dance we're doing.

"I'm close, Maevery." His forehead drops to mine. "Please tell me you're close."

"I am," I assure him. "So close. Just need a little more," I say between pants.

Reaching between us, he presses on my clit, and I erupt. Whole body spasms pour through me. I can feel myself clamp down on him, setting off his own orgasm. He groans loudly, head thrown back, tendons stretched. Gods, he's sexy when he comes.

Chapter Twenty-Four

Silence blankets us as night descends. We're lying in bed, my back to his front. Eventually, when I could think again, I left to clean up with Conaill close behind. When we lay down, he pulled me to him like it was the most natural thing in the world. And if I'm honest with myself, it scares me.

His hands trail over my arms and sides. Gently caressing my skin, not in temptation but in exploration. I'm beyond sated, and the intimacy between us is something I've never experienced. Conaill seems to have amassed quite a few of my firsts since I've met him.

I turn my thoughts away from firsts and instead study his strong hands. They're capable of such violence, and yet, right now, they're so gentle and reverent. In fact, as demanding a lover he was, not once did I ever feel anything but worshipped and cherished in his hands. For some unknown reason, I thread a hand through his, hugging it into my body. It's then that I notice small scars covering his hands and arms. None of them are large and they're mostly invisible. For any fae, let alone a high fae, to have that many scars, he must have been severely wounded. Or he was wounded when he was already close to death.

Conaill must have realized my mind is in deep thought. "What has this beautiful head thinking so hard?" Leaning forward, he presses a gentle kiss to my shoulder before rolling onto his back, taking me with him. "While I generally enjoy and appreciate your large brain and intelligence, I feel like I didn't do my job thoroughly if you can still think that intently."

A very undignified snort leaves my mouth. "If you did your job any more thoroughly, I think I would've died from pleasure," I say, adjusting so my leg is thrown over his hips.

For a moment, I'm transfixed by the glorious chest beneath my palm. My fingers run over the sculpted muscles of his chest and abs. Under my fingers, raised lines like those on his hands and arms crisscross his torso. The golden tan of his skin is still unblemished, not marred like it would be with regular scars.

"Just wondering where all these scars came from. And why they blend in?" I say, my fingers dancing along a particularly long band of raised skin.

It cuts along his hip before disappearing under the sheet that's doing very little to cover his growing arousal. Abs tensing, he lets out a low grunt as my fingers follow to the end of the scar low on his other hip. Hand grazing, ever so gently, over the head of his cock. "And how can you be this aroused after everything we did tonight?"

Suddenly, his hand is holding mine in place. When I look up, his eyes bore into mine. "If you keep doing that, you'll see just how aroused I am." He stops, kissing me deeply. "And just how much stamina I have." Raising my hand back to his chest, he gently covers it with his. "So if you don't want answers to your questions, just let me know."

"Ugh, I would love to play more, but... my curiosity is winning out." I press my lips to his nipple, earning me a smack on my bottom.

"Behave," he demands, but I notice he hasn't lifted his hand.

"Fine. Besides, I'm a little sore." I tuck my chin down, burrowing into him more, embarrassed by that for some reason.

"Oh, really." The smirk in his voice comes through loud and clear. "And why is that, Red?"

"Shut it. I'm sure you know how huge you are. And well, none of my other lovers were even close to that big."

"I'm making a rule. No talking of past lovers when we're in bed." His tone is terse, and I obviously struck a nerve. To be fair, I really don't want to hear about his past females either. "That being said, you're more than welcome, encouraged even, to keep telling me just how huge I am."

I sit up quickly and swat his chest, but he just winks at me. "Get back here, Red," he says, pulling me back down to him, this time with my head on his chest. "I'll tell you how I got these scars, but we have to play a game."

Blowing out a breath, I agree. "Fine, but what kind? I don't really want to move."

Holding me tighter, he says, "You're staying right there. A secret for a secret. I'll tell you the secret behind my scars, you tell me one in return."

I think about it, and soon I'm nodding my head in agreement. "But you have to go first."

He kisses the top of my head as his hand trails up and down my back. "Well, as I'm sure you know, I was in the military. So some of the scars are from that. This one." He opens his thighs, tilting the leg I'm not draped over. A thick scar runs from just above his knee to midway up his inner thigh. "This one is courtesy of a nasty son of a bitch named Esdras."

"Did you kill him for it?" I ask.

He lets out a laugh, startling me with its sincerity. "Absolutely not. Next to Madok, he's my best friend." Sensing my confusion, he continues on. "Esdras and I roomed together our first time at Tamrinisk. It's our military academy, like Sabaid."

"I know what Tamrinisk is," I say, exasperated.

"Just checking. Anyway, we were rooming together and became fast friends. In the room next to us was another first-timer, Tarrikos. Or Tarry. Anyway, we got placed in the same squad and bonded in the way only those who've seen battle together can." I nod against his chest because I get it. You don't survive military life by not forming strong bonds.

"So as young males do, we liked to screw with each other. Silly dares and pranks. Harmless, really, but made to embarrass or get even. Anyway, on my third stint at Tamrinisk." He pauses. "You have mandatory service every seventy-five years, too, right?"

"Yup, I've got sixty-nine more to go until I go back." I pause for a bit, realizing something for the first time. "Actually, I don't. In a few months, I'll be queen. Reigning monarchs are the only ones exempt, as our military is formed with them as the head. I mean, I'll have constant training and military advisers, but I won't ever have to go back to Sabaid for academy training." That thought makes me incredibly sad for some reason.

"Same for us. Although, as your husband, I'll be King Consort of Fenshegus, so now I'm wondering how anything military will work with us. I mean, when I'm King of Kystenvar, you'll be its queen. Shit, this is too confusing for bed talk." He takes a drink of water from the nightstand before offering it to me and continues. "So, Esdras made a bet between Tarry and me that whoever could swipe the rival squad leader's *secret* stash of whiskey would get his first weekend pass when we went into the field.

"Esdras loved military life, so he stayed in and is now a lieutenant colonel. Anyway, one week he was checking on something there, and that's when he dared us. I decided to be stealthy and scale the wall in the middle of the night. The squad leader's room was in a tower with the river directly under it. I figured if I slipped, I would just have the water rise and catch me. Turns out I suck at scaling walls. Slipped and when I was caught by the water, a tree branch came with it and impaled my leg. Fucking spring runoff."

I laugh. "Sorry. It isn't funny, but it kind of is."

"Oh, Esdras and Tarry laughed their asses off. I was in the infirmary for two days and lost. The healers were away at a conference, and I had to wait. My body tried to heal itself, but they had to open it back up to get a sliver that didn't come out. Thus, the scar."

"Poor baby," I say, patting his chest. "I take it Tarry won?"

"Yes," he grits out, clearly still sore about losing. "Turns out, he'd been sneaking around with the squad leader, anyway. So he just went straight to her room, and when she fell asleep, he put it in his bag."

I laugh deeply and fully. "I look forward to meeting these friends of yours."

"Your turn, Red," he says. "What's one of your secrets?"

"What about your other scars?" I say, trying to keep him talking. His voice soothes me like nothing else has for a long time.

"You get that secret next. After you tell me this one." His reply comes quickly, as if he knew I would balk.

"You scare me," I say, my voice barely above a whisper. I feel him stiffen under me, and I'm quick to ease him. "Or rather, how you make me feel scares me."

Tentatively, he asks, "In what way?"

Continuing to trace his map of scars, I gather my thoughts. "I know we talked about this earlier, but everything is so much more complicated now."

"That's true."

"I understand you have different facets you present. I do much the same. It's just the strength of the feelings. How fast they came. I've never experienced anything like it. I know I'm young, so maybe that is it, but…"

He cuts me off before I continue, "I haven't either, and I've much more life experience than you."

"That's true. You're practically ancient," I say through a smile he can't see.

"Ha-ha, brat," he deadpans, then says, surprisingly serious, "I am older, but I know what we have is unusual. Whether I've lived twenty-four years or a thousand."

"It still scares me. I don't like feeling out of control, and you make me feel that." Tipping my head up, I realize everything that he's feeling is being shown on his face. It's like, in this moment with just me, he can let down his shields. And that scares me, too.

"I've got you, Maevery." His strong arms pull me in closer. "I'll be your anchor. When you feel lost and out of control, not sure where to go or what to do, I've got you. I'll anchor you so you can always find your way back. You're my anchor, too."

Rising up to meet him, we kiss thoroughly and deeply. It's not enough, though. I roll so he's on top and give myself over to him. I can't explain it. Can't explain any of the feelings that have grown between us. Can't explain why I feel so safe when it's just the two of us. Safe in a way I haven't since my parents died. The only thing I can think of, is that I'm starting to merge Conaill and Walthier in my mind.

It isn't long before Conaill's taking me gently. Our bodies dance together instead of the battle that they waged earlier. With each tender thrust, I feel his hold over me growing tighter. Yet, it isn't one-sided. His eyes show me that I have power over him, too. And just like his, it's growing stronger by the minute. In the end, we come together. Our bodies fused, our breaths combined.

"You know," I say, back in his arms a while later, this time with his chest against my back. "You never did tell me about the other scars. More pranks between you and your boys?"

"Oh gods, how I wish that were the case." He snorts, kissing my temple. "Madok, Esdras, Tarry, and I have been doing the same work the Order is doing long before you were born. Granted, it was way more disorganized before you." Another kiss. "In the beginning, I was way more involved in actually helping the common fae seek sanctuary. These"—he grabs my hand and runs it along his forearms — "are from a crin attack."

I turn my head, my confusion prominent. "But… what?" The tallest crin are only about two and a half feet tall. At six feet four inches, he should be easily able to kick a crin a few hundred feet. My back shaking from his light laughter, I continue. "I mean, crin pretty much only attack children and smaller common fae. When they even do attack. Don't they mostly eat carrion?"

"They do," he confirms. "But instead of the usual two or three crin that travel together, there were eighteen. I was escorting a group of zenko on the last leg of their journey from Samaith. Best guess is that the crin thought they were lost children from afar. Still not sure why they were in such a large group, but anyway, they attacked. The zenko who could shifted into their fox form, carrying the others, and were able to slip past. That left me to take on all the crin."

"That sucks," I say, my jaw popping as I yawn. "What about the others?"

Resting his head by mine, he says, "Nothing special there. Just years of minor fights and protecting the common fae. Before you pass out, what's another secret?"

I think for just a minute before saying, "I hate my boobs."

"What?" he practically shouts, grabbing my hated boobs in his hands. "How can you hate these? I love them." Giving them a squeeze of reassurance, he speaks directly to them. "Don't worry, ladies, I'll never hate you."

My elbow connects with his abs, and he whooshes out a laugh. "Stop it. They're too big. They get in the way at training if I don't bind them tight enough. Fighting without preparation sucks. And they make my back hurt. Without real powers, I can't heal my back when they irritate it. It sucks."

"Okay, okay. I conceded that point to you. But just remember that soon you'll have that power."

"I so look forward to that day. But until then. Tell me one more secret before I fall asleep."

He's silent for a long time, and I'm starting to drift off when I hear him whisper, "I loved it when you called me Con. And Maevery, I knew it was you at the masquerade. I saw you slip into the antechamber before you took the potion."

Chapter Twenty-Five

The next two weeks fly by in a whirlwind. Tilde joined up with our group at Tamrinisk, bringing with her the first of Iskra's letters. Gods, how I miss her, but I've gotten two more since. The first was delivered by a beautiful owl with purple eyes, the second by a pure white eagle.

When we're not actively traveling, we've been inundated with appointments at important sights and meeting the fae of Kystenvar. I'd classify the fae of Kystenvar as friendly and compassionate. At least most of them. They do display a wariness of Conaill, though.

When I asked him about this, he shrugged. "My dad's a dick, and as far as they know, so am I. It lets me help the Order more if no one suspects me." His logic makes sense; I just wish they could see the Conaill I know.

As long and exhausting as the days are, my nights are worth it. Every night, Conaill shows me exactly how much he wants me, and I show him as well. It's not only the sex, though. We talk and debate; we ask questions. I've learned so much about him, and if I'm honest, a lot about myself through all this.

Everything I've eaten or drunk has been tested, much of it containing the thor thairis. Frustratingly, no one in our party has been revealed to have spotted hands. I'm beyond stressed and so close to my limit that I've started to snap. I hate that. I'm not the fae who snaps when something doesn't go her way. If we don't find the culprit soon, I may just have a full breakdown. Despite the fact that I'm no longer taking the thor thairis, none of my powers have awakened. As if my stress levels needed anything else to worry about.

I'm relaxing in the warm water of a bath, eyes closed, when a feather-light caress skims across my shoulders. I smile, knowing it's only Conaill. His intoxicating scent invades my senses, a drug my body is quickly becoming addicted to. "Join me, Con."

Soft lips follow in the wake of the caress. His breath tickles my ear before giving a gentle bite to the lobe. *Damn.* I'm sure it'll be fine if we're late for dinner. Soft laughter echoes off the marble walls, and I know he's scented my arousal. "No," he breathes sharply, moving away.

My eyes fly open to see him holding out a single, long-stemmed, yellow rose. The edges kissed with deep red. With a roll of my eyes, I stand and reach for my towel, but Conaill's too fast. His eyes blaze with passion, but he simply holds the towel open, rose still in hand. As I step out of the bath, my body's encased by both the towel and him.

"You don't like my present?" Through the mirror's reflection, I can see his full lower lip is sticking out in a little pout. For that moment in time, he looks absolutely adorable.

"You know how I feel about roses," I glower, ignoring the offending flower. Conaill's taken it upon himself to leave them around as "surprises" for me. A lavender rose on my pillow. Salmon-colored roses on the carriage seat. A green rose replaces my bookmark. A multitude of red and pink roses seems to be stalking me.

One morning, Mionnan even had white roses braided into his tail and mane. He walked straight over to Conaill and nuzzled him in thanks, the traitor. He then pranced around for the rest of the morning. So proud to show off his flowers. When we stopped for lunch, I asked Lukavo to try to remove the flowers that remained. That didn't go over well, and he nearly took off Lukavo's hand. Needless to say, Mionnan got his way and kept the flowers in until they fell out on their own.

I dry myself and dress quickly. We have to leave soon for our next appointment, and I need to talk with Conaill alone.

"Hey, Con?" I ask as I curl myself into him on the bed where he has been reading a book.

Marking his place with the flower, he sets the book down and wraps his arms around me. "Yes, Red?" he asks, bringing my hand to his mouth, kissing the back gently before wrapping his arm around it and placing it on his chest.

"Can you put up a sound shield? I still can't get one to stay consistently." I mummer.

"Babe, seriously?" I look up; he doesn't need to say anything. I can read the *are you kidding me* look loud and clear. "I constantly want you. I love every sound you make when we're together. I never want you to be quiet. You can bet that phenomenal ass of yours that there's always a sound shield around our room. Or carriage, or really anything I can take you in."

A small laugh bubbles out. "Yeah, that makes sense." I nibble on my bottom lip, nervous to talk to him about this, but knowing I need to.

"Maevery, what's wrong?" he says gently.

With a sigh, I let him know what I've been worrying about. "We'll be in Illus tomorrow." I begin. Illus is the capital of Kystenvar, where Conaill lives. We'll be staying there for two days before heading back into Fenshegus.

"Yeah, what about it?" His hand's drifting up and down my back, easing my tension slightly.

"Well, I don't want to stay in Qalea Castle." I take a deep breath and continue, hoping he won't be insulted that I don't want to stay there. "It's… Tavarik disgusts me. Like, every time he's in my presence, I grow nauseated, and I have to try not to say what I really think. I know he's your dad, but I was hoping to minimize my interactions with him."

Booming laughter fills the room, causing me to jump. Conaill's head is thrown back, his entire body is shaking from the laughter escaping him. "Red, I *loathe* my father. I may be acting in public, but regrettably, he's not. There's no way we're staying there. I've been trying to get my mother to leave him for centuries. But she's old-school. Their marriage was arranged for political gains, and she's paid for it ever since. We only have to endure one dinner with him. After that, you won't have to see him until the wedding. We'll be staying at my place in the city."

Oh, thank the gods. My shoulders relax, and more tension flows away. "Thank you for that."

"Maevery." He gently guides my face up to look at him. Emotion simmers behind his eyes, and I'm utterly captivated. "There's nothing, absolutely nothing, I wouldn't do for you. If something hurts you, I'll destroy it. If something makes you happy, I'll never let it slip away from you. I don't understand the power you have over me, but it has me completely enthralled. And I never want to escape."

His lips brush across mine, the most gentle of caresses. It's not enough, though, and I deepen the kiss. I don't have the words for him. I know I'm falling for him. But I can't say it yet. Instead, I show him with my body. It isn't long before we're both panting, neither of us caring that we'll be late. Clothes are quickly shed, and he pulls me on top of him, sheathing himself inside me. It only takes minutes before we're both tipping over the edge together.

King Tavarik evidently enjoys pageantry and spectacle. The whole of Illus seems to be decked out in banners of black and gold. As we ride closer to the castle, crowds of fae start to gather and cheer. Crowds of mostly high fae, the common fae conspicuously scarce. The decorations increase, and soon the sea of black and gold is interrupted by splashes of emerald green. Banners combining both the colors of Kystenvar and Fenshegus are waving in the light breeze. The combination is a nod to our two countries joining in this marriage.

"Did you know about this?" I say to Conaill, indicating the melding of our colors.

"Nope, and I know my dad would never think to do so." His eyes dart around, constantly at attention. He wanted me to ride in the carriage for safety reasons. I quickly shut that down, and he has been edgy ever since. I remind him we have the guards that've been with us the whole time, in addition to Madok, Mina, and Tilde. He capitulated only after I promised to be fully armed as we rode through town.

Turning the corner, my jaw drops open at the sight that greets me. Exquisite is the only word that comes to mind when I behold Qalea Castle. The castle doubles as a fortress with an outer wall of turrets and crenelated walls, arrow slits, and a drawbridge. But atop each turret sits a tall, open-air structure capped by an elongated dome and a tall, thin spire. The top of each window on the castle proper comes to a delicately pointed arch. Fragile-looking stonework scrolls across the top of the window, each window unique. Arches in a similar style can be glimpsed as well.

Once we've drawn closer, I notice the intricate geometric and floral motifs that cover the entire castle and most of the outer wall. The stonemasons who built this castle must have been masterful. When I say as much to Conaill, he informs me that the fae who built it was, in fact, gifted with the power to shape stone to his will. My eyebrows arch at this. Command of earth isn't uncommon, but the ability to shape stone into something not naturally found is exceedingly rare.

Mionnan and Conaill's mare prance across the drawbridge, stopping once we're in the inner courtyard. I'm instantly surrounded by Tilde and Mina when we dismount.

"Gods, can you believe this place?" Mina exclaims, her eyes darting constantly, trying to take in everything.

"It's such a shame that King Tavarik gets to live in a beautiful place like this when he's such a repugnant ass," Tilde whispers.

"Tilde!" Mina chides. "You can't say things like that."

"What? It's not like anyone here isn't thinking the same thing," Tilde quips.

"I sure as fuck think it," Conaill says, startling all of us.

"You'll get no argument from me," Madok agrees.

The tension eases, and we all relax a little. At least until Tavarik flings open the doors and struts out. His entrance into the courtyard is ostentatious, and it's clear he'll only allow the attention to be on him.

"Conaill, my boy!" he bellows. "I hope your trip's gone smoothly. No one giving you trouble?"

The smile Conaill's giving his father is part of what I like to call ass-hat Conaill. We agreed that while we're here in the capital, it'd be best to keep our masks in place, so to speak.

"None at all," he says, bowing slightly. "There was a spot of trouble with some vampyrs, but we took care of them."

"Ah," Tavarik says, waving off the idea that vampyrs would cause any problem. "No idea why they insist on going after high fae when the common are overrunning the land as it is."

I freeze. *He did not just say what I think he did, did he?* The sooner we get out of here, the better. Mina, Tilde, and Madok have also stiffened. They're able to recover quickly and simply pretend not to have heard.

"Father, common fae are important too." Tavarik stiffens, but Conaill continues. "I mean, who would do all the jobs and tasks that are beneath high fae?"

Tavarik's evil laugh booms out. "Very true, very true. Come, let's go inside and have a drink. You must need one after all the travel." He goes to guide Conaill inside, but is met with resistance.

"I'll join you in just a minute. I need to speak with Maevery about some last-minute changes I made," Conaill quickly says, and I'm so grateful for the extra moment I now have to compose myself.

Waving us off, Tavarik turns to go inside. "Come on, Kalimina," he says, ordering his wife inside. She'd been so quiet I didn't even realize she'd joined us.

Madok gathers up Mina and Tilde, both of whom are reluctant to leave me. "It's okay. Go in." I assure them. Madok shares a pointed look with Conaill before letting out a sigh and clasping him on the shoulder.

As they disappear, my hand is grabbed, and Conaill's dragging me to a small room on the side of the courtyard. The cramped space is being used for storage and doesn't offer much room. As the door shuts, taking with it most of the light, Conaill throws up a silencing shield.

"Gods, Red. Please know that I hated saying that. I don't believe it." The words tumble out, and I'm pulled into his arms like I'm the only thing centering him right now. It takes me a moment to realize he means when he commented about the common fae. My heart is breaking for him. How must he have felt, always having to portray this asshole persona? He has to say horrible and demeaning things that completely go against everything he believes. To have everyone think he's just like the father he despises?

"Con…" I gently pull away, my hands lifting his face from where it rested on my head. Staring into those beautiful eyes of his, I try to display everything I feel but can't say yet. "I know, with every fiber of my being, *exactly* who you are. We've talked and shared so much in the last few weeks that I feel I know you better than myself. There isn't a point in the rest of my life or the next, when I wouldn't know the real you. I'll never judge you for the mask you have to wear, just as you don't judge me when I have to play the vapid princess."

He chuckles, and I can see I'm getting through. I bring his face to mine, kissing him tenderly. Sliding my arms around him, I pull back slightly. "I'm your anchor. And you're mine. Remember?" He's silent for a moment before the truth sets in.

"Anchors. We'll always anchor each other," he says, and I nod. Strong arms wrap around me, lifting me so we're eye level. Foreheads pressed together, he swallows thickly before continuing. "I love you, Maevery."

Before my mind can even process what he just said, he kisses me in the most reverent way ever. The kiss shows me just how much he respects and worships me. I'm lost in the kiss, a mewl escaping my lips when it's broken.

"This is so not how I've been imagining telling you," he says sheepishly while lowering me to my feet.

I'm reeling from his admission. Dragonflies are racing around my stomach, and I feel as if, in this storage room, at this moment, all's right with the world. "What? You didn't plan to confess your undying love in a musty storage room?" I joke, not sure what else to do. "I mean, that's how I always imagined it."

My heart lightens even more when his beautiful laugh fills the room. "Thank fuck I got landed with you." Wrapping me in a hug, his body relaxes against mine, a smile on his lips where they rest against me.

"Con?"

"Yeah, Red?

"I love you too."

Chapter Twenty-Six

Moro must be on our side right now because Tavarik was called away shortly after dinner. As soon as her husband left, Kalimina's mood instantly became lighter, and dinner was much less formal. Even with Tavarik's departure, though, the thought that we're basically in enemy territory never left me. If the king or any of his cronies found out about our roles in the rebellion, our titles wouldn't help us. Keeping that in mind, we head to Conaill's house as soon as dinner's over.

A smile cracks my lips when I see a large black and white bird waiting for us. Walking over to him, he hops to the side, revealing a letter from Iskra. Clasping it in his beak, he holds it out for me, then flies over to a tree as if taking up sentry duty. Iskra must have told him to wait for me.

"I always like it when Isk sends you letters. I love how she always uses different kinds of birds," Mina says, smiling.

Tilde humphs. "You're telling me. She wanted to send one on our way to Sabaid. The bird she wanted to ask to carry your letter was spectacular. Bright red body, green tail with black tips, and the head was covered in these feathers that started as orange and morphed into red as they met the body. It was beautiful." She's wistful as she recalls this, which for her means it was truly amazing. "But it had just had a clutch of babies and couldn't do the journey. Supposedly, it told her it would find her at Sabaid when it could make the trip."

"It must be so cool to speak to animals." Madok cuts in, his face contemplative.

"Tell me about it," I say, a tinge of unfair jealousy in my voice. "Try being the only female in your family who can't. It was rather annoying when they would hold entire conversations, and you had no idea what half the group was saying."

They all laugh, and Conaill throws his arm around my shoulders. "While green does suit you, Red, jealousy really isn't your thing."

I elbow him firmly, but not hard, and motion for him to lead the way. We're given a thorough, but brief, tour of his home. Everyone is exhausted after the day, and we all retreat to our rooms.

"I just need to read this and give Isk my response," I say, sitting at his desk in the office adjoining his room. "I don't want that bird to have to wait too long."

"I'm sure it's totally fine having a little longer rest." Conaill's voice comes from the doorway, and gods is he sexy. His arms and legs are crossed, his shoulder leaning against the door frame.

"Okay, fine." I wrench my focus back to my letter. "I just really miss her."

Conaill's footsteps grow louder as he nears, stopping behind me and placing his hands on my shoulders. "I get it. If it were a letter from one of my siblings, I wouldn't want to wait to read it either." He bends, kissing my cheek, then goes to pour himself a drink of amber liquid from the bar caddy by the fire.

"Where are your siblings? Why didn't we see them today?" Conaill told me he has five siblings: two younger brothers and three younger sisters. Quite large for a fae family, actually.

After a sigh of appreciation for whatever he poured, Conaill says, "Well, Aemir, my brother closest in age, is doing his mandatory military service, as is my youngest sister, Rhaewiya. Zayn, my youngest brother, is gods only know where, trying to bed females." Conaill takes another drink before continuing. "He once told Aemir and me that he wanted to 'bed a different female in every major city in every kingdom.' So… I guess he's trying to accomplish that."

Shaking his head as if to get rid of the image, he says, "Chandra, my oldest sister, is currently an acolyte to Astrid, so she's there."

"Wait," I say. "I thought your father said your sister, who was an acolyte, was named Ahinoam?"

"She is. She just hates that name and goes by her middle name. Only my father calls her by her first name."

"Makes sense." I nod, opening my letter.

"Which leaves Azyia, who is studying medicine in Nuwen." He takes another drink before filling a glass for me. "Now read your letter and let me know if we need to kill anyone for being mean to Iskra."

I laugh, but really, Iskra would have a line of fae ready to kill anyone mean to her.

Mae,

Oh my gods! Why did none of you tell me that Sabaid would be this hard? I mean, I kind of knew from the letters you sent, but nothing prepared me for this. I'm so sore every day. I love the classes, though. Battle planning and tactics may be tied to military law as my favorite.

So far, I've been holding my own in sparring. But really, was there any doubt? I'm worried about when we have to start sparring as a team. What do you do when there is so much fighting around you? How do I avoid getting my head bashed in by someone behind me if I'm focused on my opponent? Wow, I'm going to have to go to the temple of Polemas here a lot more. And Bas. And Sofiya. Better make it all of them, really. Please send me any tips you, Tilde, or Mina have. Or I guess anyone in your crew. I could use it.

We had our first weapons class, and I kicked everyone's butt. It was great! This giant of a male said I wouldn't be able to beat anyone, as I was just a spoiled princess who'd probably never touched a weapon. Oh, did I show him. I had to use one of the practice swords, instead of mine, but I was able to put him on the mat with the sword at his throat in less than five minutes. I don't think anyone will underestimate me now.

Anyway, I need to finish this up. I'm meeting up with a boy in a few minutes. Please thank Tilde for the suggestion for me. Also, the bird's name is Agleusadh, and he'd love it if you could spare him some raspberries. They're his favorite.

Last thing. Please don't get mad at me, but I did a thing and I have to get this off my chest. Remember when you caught me talking with Mionnan before we left? Well, I made him promise me that he'd always look after you and do what he could to protect you. I didn't know what you were heading into, and I was worried. He has a great sense of character, and he loves you as fiercely as you love him.

I have to go now. I love you forever!

Isk

Oh, Iskra, I shake my head and take a piece of paper from a stack on the desk as well as a pen.

"So do we need to head straight to Sabaid?" Conaill says.

"Not quite yet," I tell him about the letter and start my reply.

"Well, maybe not Sabaid, but I think I'll speak with Tilde. What was she thinking, giving advice to Iskra like that?"

"I love how protective you are of her. You knew her for less than two weeks, and yet you treat her as if she were your baby sister," I say, my throat clogging with emotion.

"Well, I love you," he says, giving me a kiss before turning to walk out. "And I care about anyone you love as much as you do her. Besides, as soon as we marry, she will be my sister. Be right back."

"Wait, where are you going?"

"To talk to Tilde, as I told you." A wicked gleam in his eyes. "Besides, you said the bird likes raspberries. I happen to have a raspberry bush in the garden that should be full of ripe fruit."

I smile as he walks out, and I return to writing my reply. I've just finished when I hear Mionnan scream, followed by another bloodcurdling scream from someone else.

Standing so quickly, the chair falls to the floor. I take off sprinting through the house.

Following the screams to the stables, I find Mionnan blocking Lukavo in a stall. Lukavo clutches his arm, blood streaming through his fingers. *Oh gods,* Mionnan must have bitten him. Everyone's gathered around staring at the spectacle in front of us.

"Your Highness," Lukavo pleads. "Please call off your horse. Please."

I'm about to do just that when I remember Iskra's letter. She also told me to trust him when we parted. And I trust her, so instead I say, "No."

Wide eyes look at me in confusion. Lukavo's and the crowd's. Only Conaill doesn't seem shocked; instead, he's absentmindedly stroking Mionnan's neck and murmuring to him.

Lukavo's about to begin pleading again when he's cut off by Conaill. "Why were you skulking around my stables?" he demands.

With blood still streaming down his arm and a quiver in his voice, Lukavo says, "I wasn't skulking. I forgot something in my saddlebag, and I was trying to get it. I must've startled him." He gestures to Mionnan.

"Understandable." Lukavo visibly relaxes at my words. "Except, the horse you were riding isn't in this part of the stables at all. In fact, I distinctly remember seeing you in the house *with* your saddlebag." Every word I speak increases the visible tension in Lukavo's body.

Suddenly, he flings his hand at Mionnan and Conaill. Dirt and wood chips fly in their faces, and he makes a run for it. He barely slips by and runs faster than I could imagine. Madok and Tilde chase after him, but I don't know if they can catch him.

"Stop!" I scream. Without warning, the ground in front of Lukavo rises up like a monolith, and he runs straight into it, falling to the ground. This gives Madok and Tilde enough time to reach his side before he can escape again. Madok strips off his belt and uses it to tie up Lukavo before hauling him back this way.

Try as I might, I can't move. I'm rooted to the spot in shock, questions popping up continuously. What just happened? Who just did that? Did Madok do that? His power's earth, right? Why is my whole body tingling? Why did Lukavo run? Why did Mionnan hurt him? Was he trying to hurt Mionnan? Why was he here?

I'm brought out of my stupor by a velvet-soft nose and warm huffs of air. Mionnan's come over and is nuzzling my face. Absentmindedly, I bring my hand up to his nose and stroke his soft hair. Turning to him, I bury my face in his neck and breathe in his horsey scent. Mionnan's head is now wrapped around my back as if he's giving me a hug. Slowly, the hug brings me back to reality.

"Thank you, Mionnan," I whisper and step back. He must know I'm good now, and he backs up. Most who came out to check on the commotion are on their way back in, but the crew, as Iskra called them, is staring at me. I guess it's up to me what happens next.

A throat clears, and Conaill breaks the silence. "So I guess you have power over earth, Red."

Cocking my head, I look around. Everyone looks as if they're in agreement. "What do you mean? I didn't do that. I *can't* do that. It was Madok, right?"

"No, Maevery. It wasn't me. I wish I had thought of it, but…" Madok trails off.

"Then who else has earth power?" I scan everyone, trying to find the culprit.

"Mae," Mina says gently, her hand taking mine. "That was you. No one else has earth powers. Your power finally awakened." Happiness shines brightly in her face.

"What? I have earth powers…" I stammer.

"You have earth powers," Conaill says proudly.

Madok's chest puffs up. "Guess I'll have to train you. Soon you might even be as good as me." He winks, and the stupid gesture breaks the tension in my body, and I laugh.

"Now," he continues. "Time to see what's going on with this one." He indicates Lukavo, who tries to talk, but Tilde simply punches him in the face. Knocking him out cold. "Thank you, Tilde," Madok says.

"Tildewynn. I told you, you have to earn the right to call me Tilde," she says blank-faced.

"Fine. Thank you, Tildewynn," he corrects, rolling his eyes. "Anyway. Conaill, you still have the room in your basement?"

"Sure do," Conaill replies. "You can get to work in there. Figure out what he was doing and why."

Nodding, Madok throws Lukavo over his shoulder like a sack and makes his way to the house. He's stopped almost instantly by Mina's arm thrown across his chest.

"Yeah, you can move him. But *I'll* be the one going to work," she informs him.

"I don't know what you think *work* might mean. But trust me, the work *I'll* be doing isn't something for a lady like you," Madok says and tries to walk again.

A low whistle comes from Tilde as I shake my head. "Well, this'll be fun," I say, and Tilde nods.

Both Conaill and Madok look at the three of us as if we're crazy.

"Mina," Conaill starts. "Madok is good at what he does, but this isn't going to be pretty or fun." Seriously, he adds, "You know Madok will do whatever it takes to get him to talk. Even torture."

Mina snorts. "Uh, yeah. I know." Turning to Madok, she says, "Now, if you could please be a good boy and take him down to the room for me, I'd greatly appreciate it. If you ask nicely, I'll even let you watch the master work."

Mina simply turns and walks back into the house. Both Conaill and Madok's mouths hang open in absolute shock.

Gathering himself, Madok points to where Mina went, "Did she just?"

"Yes, she did, big boy," Tilde says, walking with me toward the house. "Now get your shit together and do as she says."

Chapter Twenty-Seven

Sniveling echoes off the cold, dank walls of the underground room where Lukavo is being held. The room's subterranean location makes it chilled. The condensation leaving our lips is a telltale sign of just how cold. The fae lights' gentle flickering ominously hints at the room's purpose, as do the chains and manacles hanging from the walls, and the fact that the chair is bolted to the floor.

"Why exactly do you have this room in your home?" I question Conaill, shivering slightly.

"Well, for starters, it came with the house," he says. "But also, unfortunately, sometimes we need to question fae. Given that my father is an unrepentant ass, I can't do it at the castle so…" He shrugs.

"Please, please," Lukavo pleads, his voice quivering. "I didn't do anything. You know me, Your Highness. What could I have done?"

"I honestly don't know." My voice comes out tired and wavering. He's not wrong. In all the years I've known him, he's never given me pause. But I also remember Iskra's warning. "But, clearly, Mionnan was trying to tell us something, and I have to trust in that."

Bang! Everyone jumps at the sound of the door slamming against the stone walls. Tilde stands tall, commanding the doorway, malevolence radiating from her face, something clutched in her hand. Striding straight toward Lukavo, she slaps him so hard in the face with whatever it is in her hand that his head snaps back.

"Ouch," Madok says, even as he nods in approval.

A collective gasp from the females and growls from the males sound as Tilde drops a pair of gloves on Lukavo's lap. Gloves covered in the distinctive spots left behind by suppression potion. Loud, racking sobs come from Lukavo at the sight of those gloves, and my heart stills. Thank the gods for Iskra and Mionnan.

"I found those while searching through your things. They were hidden in a secret compartment in your luggage. Don't even bother denying it." She sneers.

Mina, who's been silently glaring, steps forward, the light dancing in her eyes. "You messed up, Lukavo," she purrs. "You should've been getting rid of the evidence as you made it."

A cry of alarm escapes Lukavo's lips. While she was talking, vines that broke through the cracks in the ground were winding around Lukavo's legs, working their way up and replacing the ropes.

Unsheathing a knife, Mina cuts the now irrelevant ropes. The vines only stop growing when they've secured his entire body, including his head and neck, to the back of the chair. "Now I get to play," she says deviously. "And I don't leave *my* evidence behind, so let me tell you, whatever you think I might be capable of…" Her face is now inches from him, her knife caressing the side of his cheek. "It's nothing compared to what I'll actually do. Get ready for a very, very, long night."

Mina's eyes glance down before grimacing. "Bas and Polemas, spare me, you're not even going to let me play, are you?" A dark stain is spreading on his breeches as tears make tracks in his dirty face. "In case you were wondering. This is just for that," she says, straightening. A thorn growing out of one of the vines wrapped around his leg, pierces his flesh, and he screams. With every jerky movement, it tears his flesh a little more.

"Is it wrong I'm so turned on by her right now?" Madok says to Conaill, his eyes glued to Mina.

"Uh, yeah." Comes Conaill's instant answer.

"What? I'm just saying that skill could be interesting in the bedroom." Madok shrugs. "Minus the thorns, of course."

Mina glares at him, announcing, "You only wish Madok. Now stop the commentary, or I'll kick you out."

"Oh, I do wish," he grumbles out, but says nothing else.

Turning back to Lukavo, Mina says, "Now, where were we?"

Much later, Lukavo's given up pretty much everything. The ability to withstand torture isn't one of Lukavo's strengths. Then again, I'm not really sure I'd be able to withstand what Lukavo's been put through, either.

A steady *drip, drip, drip* is the only sound accompanying Lukavo's whimpers and heavy breathing. But it isn't water. It's the blood dripping out of his fingertips where vines tunneled under and grew, forcing the nails off. His kneecaps were pushed out of place by vines tunneling through his knees and out the other side, only to weave in and out of his legs before doing the same to his hips. I had to leave at that point before I emptied my stomach.

I'm back now, because frankly, how can I let this happen without knowing what's actually happening? I don't agree with torture. I never have, but right now, when so much is at stake, I don't know what else to do. Developing a truth serum needs to be at the top of the research list; of that, I'm sure. Steeling my stomach, I return my focus to Lukavo and what he's told us.

Turns out, he came to the palace with the specific intention of suppressing my powers. He wasn't the first, though. He wasn't sure when it started or who it was before him. He knows only that he was a replacement. That thought alone stirs another wave of nausea. He's also been reporting on the Order activities he knows about. Thankfully, he doesn't actually know who is in the Order. Mina clarified that by tunneling a vine through Lukavo's penis from tip to base with a particularly sinister sneer. Both Conaill and Madok winced in sympathy, their faces turning a particular shade of green.

But while they were trying not to be sick, I was rejoicing. Not only has the Order been breaking the law by smuggling in common fae from other kingdoms seeking sanctuary and protection, but I've also been using the royal coffers to pay for supplies. Technically, until I'm queen, it's stealing. An offense that would be punishable by death for anyone other than Iskra or me.

"One last question, Lukavo, and then the pain stops. Okay?" Mina asks, her sweet voice completely opposite to her activities in this room. Crouching down, she gently strokes Lukavo's face. "I know it hurts. But I have to do this to protect Princess Maevery. To protect Fenshegus. You understand, don't you, Lukavo?"

He nods, but continues to cry. "Please, Lukavo, tell us who ordered you to do this. I know you'd never betray Princess Maevery if someone wasn't threatening you to do so. She's been so kind to you. Helped you out. She even arranged for you to spend some time in Nuwen and Samaith learning with their healers and alchemists when the trip is done."

Lukavo looks up at me and sees the truth in my face. His crying intensifying, he whimpers, "I can't. He'll kill my family if I say anything. Please don't make me."

"Lukavo, we can help you. Tell us who it is, and everything will stop," Mina pleads with him. "We have a healer upstairs who'll fix everything. Another fae is here too. One that has the power to make you forget everything that happened tonight. You never have to remember any of it. You can continue with us for the remainder of the trip. During that time, we'll get your family out and to safety in Baress. Prince Darius will know where they can hide until you can join them. When we get back to the palace, we'll say you drowned in the Cale. Instead, you'll take a boat and meet them. You can stay there or get on a boat and travel wherever you want."

"Really?" he says roughly. His voice is hoarse from screaming. Mina assures him, and my heart clenches. We all know full well he isn't leaving this room alive. For seven years, he drugged me. Preventing my power from awakening. Even if I could move past it, neither my girls nor Conaill would.

"Who ordered you to give Princess Maevery the suppressant?" Conaill asked calmly.

"Please, please, you have to promise to protect my family," Lukavo says, begging. "Please. They didn't know anything, I promise."

"We will," I promise easily. That I can and will do.

With one last pleading look in his eyes, he softly says, "The king regent."

I'm sorry, what? There's no way I heard that. Uncle Emeric has been there for me since my parents died. He helped to raise Iskra and me. *Oh gods, Iskra.* If he's been suppressing me, what has he been doing to her?

I train my focus back on what's going on in the room. It's pandemonium. Everyone's talking over each other. Questions are thrown at Lukavo so quickly that he cannot answer before the next one is asked.

"Please, please. I'll answer everything. Please, just one at a time," he pleads.

Some sense of order, if you can call torture ordered, returns. No, he doesn't know why. He only did it because the king regent threatened to have his younger sisters thrown into the mines in Saetoris. As far as he knows, Iskra was not targeted. Yes, this started before my parents died. He has no idea how the king regent obtained the thor thairis or where he learned of the suppression potion.

Hanging his head, Lukavo says, "That's it. That's all I know. I swear."

From the back of the room, Conaill's voice assures him. "I believe you." Before anyone can react, Conaill slashes a blade across Lukavo's throat.

Blood floods out of his neck as my own tears fall. Tears for the friend I thought I had and for what happened to him. As life drains away from him, he looks at me. Unable to speak, he smiles softly, mouthing "I'm sorry" and "Thank you" before the light drains from his eyes and he's gone. I know that for however long I live, I'll never not be able to see the regret and sorrow that filled his eyes in his last moments.

Conaill comes to my side, wrapping his arms around me in an embrace that I need more than I need my next breath. "I'm sorry, Maevery. I'm so sorry. But he hurt you. Suppressed your powers for seven years. I will not allow anyone to one hurt you and live."

"I know, Con. I know." I assure him. And I do know. I just don't know what to do next.

When we're done processing what we can in the moment, Madok says he'll take care of the body, assuring that no one will know. The rest of us leave the room, and I follow Mina. As soon as she makes it out to the garden, she falls to her knees, purging everything in her system. She continues long past the point of bile, dry heaving even when nothing is left. I knew this was what she'd do. She was trained for this in Sabaid. They made her into this. But no matter what, they couldn't break who she is at her core.

She'll do what's necessary. She always has. But every time, I feel like a little more of her is slipping away. Every time she tortures someone else, it tortures a part of her soul as well. I asked her once why she did this. She said it was a burden she knew she could take on, so someone else didn't need to.

"I have a towel and some water for you when you're ready," Tilde says.

I continue to hold Mina's hair, not caring that stones and wood chips press hard into my legs where I kneel. Reaching for the towel, I hand it to her. This is our routine. I hold her hair and rub her back, staying with her until she's ready to put on a brave face and pretend. Tilde provides the towels and water, ensuring Mina's privacy from onlookers. *Gods, I hate every part of this.* I hate that Mina has been put through this enough that we even have a routine.

She wipes her mouth before holding out a hand for the water. Once she's composed herself, she sits up, then stands shakily. "Thank you."

"Gods above. Stop thanking us for this. There's nothing to thank us for. You would do the same," Tilde replies, her voice shaky, and I know she's holding back tears.

"When I'm queen, I won't let you do this anymore," I say, my tears streaming down my face.

Mina just lets out a soft laugh. "Try to stop me."

"Why do you insist? We know you hate it. Gods, the entire Eighteen knows it," Tilde says of our squad at Sabaid. Every one of us has helped Mina after she's put her training to use.

An ironic smile flits across Mina's ghostly face. "That's exactly why I do it. I hate it. I know that I'll only do what's necessary. I don't enjoy it like others do. Someone who enjoys it will continue when no answers remain, just so they can prolong their pleasure. I won't. I can't."

"We'll be here for you until the day you decide you can't do it anymore," I say. "And then we'll be here to put all the pieces of you back together."

When the sky's the dark gray-blue of early morning, just before the sun rises, Mina lets us know she's ready. As we make our way back to the house, I see Madok coming toward us with Conaill leaning against the doorframe.

Madok stops directly in front of Mina, his eyes transfixed on her. He says to me, "Please see to Conaill. He'd never let you know it, but every time he kills, it fractures him. Please be the glue he needs. Lo, you're coming with me." Without waiting for my response, he puts his arm gently around Mina and guides her away. She doesn't resist, so I make my way to Conaill, Tilde to her room, I assume.

Grabbing his hand, I lead him to our room. Using his water powers, he fills the tub with hot water. In silence, we strip each other, both needing to wash the night away before we can speak. Before we can be us again.

Chapter Twenty-Eight

Conaill and I lay in bed wrapped in each other's arms, the music of the birds chirping outside. We bathed each other earlier, water as hot as possible, in an effort to wash the evening away. Both of us knew it would only wash the surface. No amount of soap will ever remove the stains from this night. With languid strokes, Conaill's hand travels along my back as we lie in bed for what seems like hours. Sheets of the softest silk enfold us, providing warmth and protection, but I can't feel them. The sun's golden rays fill the room with their heat, yet inside I'm as cold as a frozen lake. The only thing I feel, the only thing I know right now, is Conaill. Now more than ever, he's anchoring me.

"Maevery," he says, and I tip my head up from where it was resting on his chest. "Gods help me, but I need you right now. Please let me know if that's okay."

Yes, one thousand times yes. Now that he's said it, I know it's the only thing that will start to make me feel whole again. His love, both physical and emotional, is exactly what I need. "Yes, Con. Please, yes."

Our lips meet in a sweet, tender kiss. A kiss filled not just with love, but with the promise that we have each other. Yet slow and tender isn't what either of us needs right now, and soon the kiss turns feral and demanding. *Gods, he knows how to kiss.* I swear to Astrid, his kiss could bring me back from death just so I would get to experience it again.

Moans fill the air. His? Mine? I'm not really sure, and honestly, I don't care. Rough, calloused hands grip my hips before caressing my butt.

"Gods, Maevery. This ass!" he growls out, and I chuckle as a loud crack sounds and my ass smarts.

Breaking the kiss, I lift up, looking incredulously at him. "Did you just spank me?"

"Damn straight I did, and I loved it. As I've said before, if you misbehave, I'll very much enjoy punishing you," he retorts before bringing my mouth to his for a brief kiss. "Don't even think of pretending you didn't like it."

He's kissing me again before I can even attempt to deny it. I won't tell him, but I loved it. Rolling me over, Con thrusts his hips into mine. His erection glides against my clit. Grabbing my hands, he brings them above my head, placing them on the headboard. "Don't move, or the punishment I give you won't be nearly as enjoyable as a spanking."

My whole body flushes, and I eagerly agree. Clasping both of my hands in one of his, he skims the other down my body. Stopping only to knead one of my breasts. Bending his head, he laves the other, sucking my nipple deep into his mouth.

"Con!" I cry, my back bowing as he bites down on one nipple while pinching the other, sending a bolt of pleasure straight to my core. He licks and soothes both nipples in turn before kissing his way down my stomach.

I try to bring my hands down, eager to run my fingers through his silky soft strands, but he just grips them harder before staring up at me. His face is right there, right above my pussy, and I need him to keep going. Need it with an ache that has moisture escaping from me.

"I told you not to move. Now, be a good girl and keep your hands there. I want to feast on you, and I need both of mine to do it properly."

I nod, gripping the headboard so he knows I'll do my best.

Using his hands to spread my thighs, he lifts them over his shoulders so I'm completely exposed. Running his nose just above my slit, he inhales before growling low in his throat. "Gods, that right there. You leaking for me is my favorite smell in the world."

Darting out his tongue, he licks up my slit before swirling it around my clit. The whole time, never taking his eyes from mine. It feels so good, and I almost let go, but I stop myself just before. A deliciously evil smirk lifts his lips seconds before he growls, "Good girl," and he buries his face in me.

Oh gods. My arousal pours out of me at his words. Arousal he greedily licks up, growling as he does it. Tongue spearing into me, then licking his way up, he stops just short of my clit before doing it again and again.

"Con," I cry out, not caring if I have to beg him. "Please, Con."

One finger enters me, pumping in and out. Each time, stopping to caress my inner walls. His nails aren't long, but I can feel every edge adding another sensation, and gods, it feels so good. Another finger is added, and yet he still hasn't lavished any attention on my clit.

"Con, please. I'm begging you. Please." I still haven't let go of the headboard, and I need to be rewarded for that. "Con, I need more."

He bites my clit, and I feel it all the way to my toes. Heat ignites at my feet as tendrils snake their way up my legs. He isn't biting hard enough to hurt, just enough to put an edge to what I feel. He alternates between biting and sucking my clit, all while his fingers continue to fuck me as if our lives depend on it. The heat has reached my core now, and with one more strong suck of my clit and caress to my walls, I come. I come so hard I'm pretty sure I pass out for a minute.

When I return to consciousness, Con is still licking me. His face glistens with the evidence of my orgasm. "May I let go now?" I ask, not sure I can take any form of *punishment* right now.

When he nods, I quickly bring my hands down, pulling his face to mine. I don't care that I can taste myself on him. I actually like it. He always seems to know exactly what I need. Breaking the kiss, I stare into his eyes before smirking. "My turn now."

Rolling him onto his back, I straddle his hips so my sex is directly over his. He actually has the audacity to fold his hands behind his head before saying, "Do your worst."

Challenge fucking accepted. Kissing my way down his chest, I stop at his nipples. I give each one a quick lick and a bite, earning me a jerk of his cock beneath me. I continue my exploration, kissing the skin around where he so impressively lies on his stomach, never quite touching him. I plant one small kiss on his head, licking up his pre-cum, and he hisses.

I continue down, nudging his thighs further open so I can settle in fully. I look up at him as I kiss the soft skin just to the sides of his base. Still not actually touching him. My nails trace up his thighs, and his dick jerks again. When my finger runs ever so gently over his balls, he says my name, pleading in his voice.

With just the tip of my tongue, I lick him from root to tip. Swirling my tongue around his head, I finally take him in my mouth. He lets out a string of curses before thrusting his hips out.

"Oh no, no, no," I say when he pops out of my mouth. "If I couldn't move my hands, you can't set the pace."

"Mae, please." His eyes are pleading. "I'm begging you, stop teasing me."

I grip his shaft, working him in my hand. Shaking my head, I simply respond, "Now be a good boy and let me control you." Hazel eyes flash a moment before my mouth descends on him.

He's too big for me to take all the way, so I keep one hand wrapped around his base, pumping him while I take what I can to the back of my throat. Working him with my hand and mouth, my tongue massaging his shaft, it isn't long before he's begging me to let him move.

I shake my head around him and then bring my other hand up. When I cup his balls and start to massage them, he loses it. "Please, baby, stop. I'm going to come if you keep going. I want to be inside you when I do."

Gods, I want that too. Not ready to relinquish control just yet, I move up his body and position him. Gripping my hips, he nods and thrusts up into me at the same time I sink down on him.

We move together seamlessly. I refuse to give up all control, though. Entwining our fingers together, I lean forward, positioning his arms just above his head like he did with me. I continue riding him as he continues to drive his cock up. Lifting his face to mine, we kiss hard and thoroughly. In no time, we cum together, both of us crying out.

On my right forearm, just where they meet, a burning pain stings me. Oddly enough, it doesn't hurt, but rather sets off another orgasm in both of us. I collapse on Conaill, and he takes my weight easily. Wrapping his arms around me, he holds me close. We stay there for a while, and I can feel him soften inside me. This was exactly what I needed. He's exactly what I needed.

The crisp, sweet juice of the ripe strawberry Conaill is feeding me, dribbling down my chin. I go to wipe it away, but he gently grabs my hand and shakes his head. Wordlessly, he leans forward and licks the juice off before kissing me.

"Mmm. You make even strawberries taste sweeter," he says before leaning in for another kiss.

I indulge him for a moment before pulling back. I'm sitting on his lap in one of the large black velvet chairs in front of a crackling fire. We're wrapped in black robes of the softest, fluffiest cotton, and I'm so taking this with me when we leave here. Despite the thick layers of cotton between us, I can feel his need firmly pressing into me.

"We can't, and you know it," I say, stalling him when he tries to kiss me again. "This has already cost us a day, and we still have to figure out what's going on. How am I going to prevent Uncle Emeric from drugging me again? Should we still pretend we can't stand each other when we get back to the castle? A million other things. Fuck, ow, ow, ow." I break off crying.

Pain sears my inner forearm, exactly where the bite of pain was earlier. Conaill hisses in pain, grabbing his as well. Scrambling off his lap, I shove the sleeve of my robe up. The skin on my inner arm is raised and rapidly darkening. Eyes flying to Conaill, I see that whatever is going on is affecting both of us.

As the mark continues to darken, a pattern starts to appear. Four lines, each the same width, twist and wrap around each other, forming an intricate design. The pain has lessened, and I run my fingers over the mark, tracing the strands.

"It's a love knot…" Conaill breathes, awe in his voice.

"Wh…What?" I stammer.

"The mark," he says reverently, his face meeting mine. "It's a Kystenvarian Love Knot."

My head whips down, and I realize that the lines do, in fact, form the exact same design that was so intricately beaded onto that green ball gown I loved so much. "Isn't that a mark given to,"

"Mates of Kystenvarian royalty," Conaill finishes.

"Does that mean...?" I trail off.

With our eyes locked, Conaill licks his lips before saying, "We're mates. This means we're mates."

Chapter Twenty-Nine

My fingers scrape over the smooth pattern of the wooden table we're sitting around. I'm not really taking in what's going on around me. At least until I feel a prickling in my head as Conaill takes my hand. With a shake of my head, I take a fortifying drink of wine. The liquid is cool with just a touch of sweetness. I take another, admittedly large, swallow of it and train my focus on what's going on in the room.

Fae lights illuminate the oak-paneled dining room where everyone is sitting. In the center sit piles of our dinner dishes and empty wine bottles. The rich, cream velvet drapes are drawn as an extra precaution. A sound shield was placed around the room first, but neither Conaill nor I wanted anyone to be able to see.

"While I think you two being mates is amazing," wariness creeps into Tilde's voice. "It does present… issues."

"Tilde!" Mina practically shouts. "How could you say such a thing? You know Mae has always wanted to find her mate. Just like her parents did."

Holding her hands up in surrender, Tilde answers, "Yeah, I know. But I also know that as far as the king regent is concerned, these two" — her hand flings out toward us — "despise each other. It's kind of a disaster. Prince Conaill needs to keep up his jerk persona if we want his father and the king regent to trust him. We can't afford to lose that inside perspective."

"No way can we lose that," Madok agrees.

The air in the room feels oppressive and heavy as I sigh. No one says anything for a while, as we all think. Taking another drink, I'm about to suggest we take a break when Tilde snaps her fingers, garnering everyone's attention in the process.

"I have an idea. Prince Conaill, how long can you hold a minor glamour?"

"Please, seriously drop the Prince when we're in private. To everyone in this room, I'm just Conaill, or Con if you prefer." He waves the title away. "But, in answer to your question, I can hold for a few weeks to a month. As long as it isn't too big. Of course, the closer I am, the longer I can hold it."

Tilde pushes back from the table, the chair nearly toppling over as she starts to pace. This usually means she has a plan forming in her head. "Okay, so for now we need both of your arms to be glamoured to hide the mark."

"Or wear long sleeves," Madok adds, not really helping.

Rolling her eyes, Tilde ignores him. "Now that your power has awakened, Mae, I'm assuming your common magic will grow, and we can use the next few weeks to train. You and Conaill" — she bows her head to him in deference, which he just waves off — "will glamour the marks so that they stay hidden. You continue to don the public masks and pretend around your parents and the king regent that you can't stand each other.

"That will hopefully still allow Conaill to glean any information he can about what's going on from the bigoted side. No offense," she says, briefly looking at Conaill.

"None taken. My dad is a bigoted ass," he says, good-naturedly while draining the last of his wine. "I don't know if it's only in Kystenvar, but here, mates are supposed to be able to communicate telepathically. I've been trying, but it doesn't seem we can do so yet."

"My parents could," I say. *Gods, I forgot about that.* They'd have whole conversations without ever speaking a word. "I've been feeling a tingle in my head sometimes. Not sure if that's you, or just my wishful thinking."

"It's probably me." He smiles. "I've been trying every few minutes." Taking my hand in his, he kisses it tenderly.

"With that out of the way," Madok drawls, "let's get to work."

We spend the next few hours furiously planning. Given everything that's going on in Fenshegus and the continent, it won't look too suspicious if we speed up the trip. The remainder of the Kystenvar leg is set to be over soon, anyway. Only smooth roads through the forest remain before crossing the Cale back into Fenshegus.

Once in Fenshegus, we can skip a few stops and reschedule those for a "Honeymoon Journey." We can't skip visiting the Temple of Astrid just outside the Forest of Alm to get our marriage blessed; however, nothing else is mandatory. Tomorrow, we'll enchant the horses and wagons, allowing us to cut the travel time in half. The only reason we haven't done so yet is that there wasn't a need, and it made sense to take the journey slower.

Once everything is figured out, everyone breaks into different tasks. Mina and Madok are in charge of sending out messages and coordinating changes. Tilde is seeing to the supplies and securing the enchantments for the horses. While Conaill and I set about planning the next moves for the Order.

"Con?" I ask softly when we enter our room. He's kneeling in front of the fireplace, a match in his hand, when he turns around. Night is about to fall, and there's a bite to the cold air.

"Yeah, Red," he says, then lights the fire. The warm light flickers off the dark blue of the walls, bringing some much-needed warmth. The soft crackling of the fire provides the background music for the evening.

"Do you think we can do this?" I try to prevent it, but I'm sure he can hear the trepidation in my voice.

Worry crosses his face for a fraction of a second before hiding it behind his beautiful face. "Do what?"

"Hide our bond? Prevent anyone from knowing we're mates until the time is right. Figure out what's causing the common fae to lose their powers and stop it? Discover exactly why Uncle Emeric wants my powers suppressed. And then deal with everything that brings?" The words are tumbling out faster and faster as I speak. My anxiety's flaring, but I've been unable to shake it since learning of Uncle Emeric's betrayal.

Conaill holds his arms out, and I rush to him. My rapid footsteps are completely muted by the plush carpet under my feet. When his strong arms enfold me, I know I'm home.

Resting his cheek on my head, he says, "Maevery, you've got this. You can do anything. For gods' sake, you created and are leading a kingdom-wide Order without anyone the wiser. But, babe," lifting his head, he gently raises my face and looks into my eyes. "When you don't think you can do something, remember, you're not alone. You have *the crew,* as Iskra and Saori like to call us. We can, and want to, take away some of your burden. You can and *will* rely on us. Just as we rely on you. No one can do this alone, but with all of us. I know we can figure everything out."

Kissing my forehead gently, he adds, "I love you, Maevery. Never doubt that. Trust me when I say I'll never lie to you. So, when I say you can do something, please know that you can."

His words and his touch act like a balm, soothing away my worries. Soon, I'm feeling more like myself, and even though I still have trepidations, I'm starting to believe him.

"So," I say, a coy smile on my lips. "You'll never, ever lie to me?"

He pulls back, laughing gently. "Well, more like I'll never lie to you when it comes to matters of the heart or something important. I mean, I might lie and say something doesn't make your butt look big. But I love your ass. So it looking big isn't really a turn-off for me." He winks, squeezing said butt before lifting me up, causing me to giggle. "Now, why don't I show you just how much I love you? And that ass."

We laugh, and still carrying me, he stalks to the bed. Between kisses, I try to divest ourselves of our clothing as best as I can, causing even more laughter. Tumbling onto the soft sheets, we spend the rest of the night showing each other just what we mean to each other.

Chapter Thirty

Before long, another week has flown by. We got back on the road the day after our mating mark showed up. It seems surreal that only one more week remains on the trip. Not being able to truly spend the time needed to show Conaill the beauty of Fenshegus saddens me. But time is of the essence, and I'll have a lifetime to share all my favorite places with him.

Each morning, I practice with Madok as he helps me gain control of my power. It's astounding how much earth power he has. If I didn't like him so much, I'd say it's disgusting how he makes wielding it look so easy. I'm struggling, but I'm getting better each day. The trick, though, is somehow keeping the training secret. While the crew knows, no one else does.

Hiding my training was easy the first few days as we were traveling through dense forests. Huge trees towered over us, blocking out most of the light. Trees so large that eight full-grown males might not be able to surround them, even with their arms stretched out. Green and purple leaves the size of serving plates fill the sky in a patchwork, allowing dappled light to reach the forest floor. Hundreds of birds watch over us, creating a symphony while we train. Mina, being the genius she is, realized she could open up a hollow in a tree that we could escape into for training.

I shake my head, a giggle escaping when I think back to the first time she did this. Training inside an actual tree was very surreal and interesting. A bonus of this was that it allowed me to perfect fae light. Our "training rooms" worked so well that we left some of the hollows open. The entrances hidden with a permanent glamour, Mina could carve into the trees.

After training one day, Mina entered the secret hollow, leading a Dryad. One who happened to be the high priestess for the community of dryads that were to protect this particular forest. Quiet and observant at first, once we explained our idea, she became a very animated talker. Every time she moved, the hollow would be filled with the sound of the air rustling her leaf-like hair. She approved of our idea to use these trees as safe homes for refugees. She and Mina left shortly after to set up many of the largest trees. Getting them ready to welcome the first refugees soon. Mina caught back up with us in time to cross the Cale and told us the high priestess would reach out to the dryads of other forests to do the same.

Currently, we're on our way to the main Temple of Astrid in Senveldy. The temple is about halfway between Otthon and the Forest of Alm, which is in the lower east side of Fenshegus. I absolutely love this part of Fenshegus. For as far as the eye can see, undulating waves of grasses and wildflowers dance with the wind. Patches of purple, blue, yellow, and pink pop up through the green grass. Eager to make their presence known. Bees, butterflies, and countless other bugs buzz in a relaxing melody. Flitting from flower to flower, ardently trying to sample the nectar of every flower in this fragrant meadow. Small copses of short trees break up the grassland sea, but nothing large enough to use like we had in Kystenvar.

So far, Madok's gotten around this issue by having me focus on precision and accuracy. Trying to separate a single speck of dirt and have it follow us is incredibly difficult, but doable out in the open. If I mess up, which admittedly I do quite often, Madok either covers it up or takes the blame.

"I'll be over by that copse of trees," I say to no one in particular. We're stopping for lunch and to water the horses. Might as well get in some practice while everyone is busy.

"Hold up, Red," Conaill calls before running to catch up with me. "I have something for you."

Mischief twinkles in his eyes as a creamy white rose emerges from behind his back. Rolling my eyes, I take it from his outstretched hand.

"Why do you insist on giving me roses?" I ask. "You know how I feel about them."

"I do." He winks, and damn if that doesn't make him a little sexier.

When we reach the copse, he grabs my hand, leading me into the center. It isn't very big, but it affords some privacy. Sitting on the soft grass, Conaill pulls me to him and lies us down. With one arm behind his head, I'm tucked into his body with the other. My head on his chest, the soft, steady beat of his heart bringing me peace from the chaos. Absentmindedly, my hand traces the pattern of dappled sunlight on his body.

I love lying with him like this. When we're like this, he isn't Crown Prince Conaill of Kystenvar. I'm not the Crown Princess, soon-to-be Queen Maevery of Fenshegus. It's just us, Con and Mae. We're free to be who we truly are at our cores, not having to be on guard or censor ourselves. The warmth of the sun settles into me, and my eyes fall closed. The soft scent of wildflowers combined with the warm leather and vanilla scent I've come to associate with Conaill relaxes me more than I've been in a long while. Sighing softly, Conaill kisses my head and squeezes me to him tighter.

"What are you thinking about, Con?" I mummer, pressing a kiss to his sternum.

"You," he says succinctly, before adding, "How lucky I am to get to spend the rest of my life with you. Trying to figure out how I survived over three hundred years without the warmth you bring to my life."

"Oh, is that all?" I giggle.

"Yup. That's all." He smirks. *Well, that, and how much I want to sink into you right now. I wonder if she'd be open to that?*

"Conaill Malik Axel Bharath Yastahiqul!" I practically shout and sit up. "Of course I'm not open to that. Anyone could see."

A confused look crosses his face. "Seriously, the full name? And what are you talking about?"

"You said you were thinking of wanting to have sex with me right now." I rush out, making sure no one is close enough to hear.

"Mae, I always want to have sex with you," he says drolly. "But I didn't say that, I..." He cuts himself off, confusion marring his face. Suddenly, his eyes widen, and he moves to sit directly in front of me. *Red, why wouldn't I think you'd be up for it? The first time we were together was in the woods after the vampyrs.*

"Yeah, *after* surviving a near-death experience. I wasn't exactly thinking clearly," I say, waving off the notion.

So you're thinking clearly now? he says, his eyebrow raised.

"Of course I am." *Wait, he never stopped smiling. His mouth never moved. What? Did I hear his thoughts?*

My eyes widen, and his radiant smile beams back at me.

Damn straight you did, Red. He kisses me, and without breaking the kiss, I hear him say, *Just need to figure out how to block each other. Can't have you realizing how much I think of you. How much power you have over me. Or how much I think of the sounds you make when you come.*

I break the kiss and playfully smack his chest. "Con!"

"What?" He chuckles in response. "You're by far my favorite drug. And you're mine. I'm allowed to think of taking you as much as I want, in any position I want. I won't do anything without your permission, but that doesn't mean I won't be thinking about doing it. But that being said, we should figure out how to speak intentionally with each other. I mean, do you want me to know everything you think of?"

Ugh, he might have a point, I concede.

"Damn straight I do," he says, and I glare. The glare doesn't last when he kisses me, though.

Instead of practicing my earth powers, as originally planned, Conaill and I attempt to figure out this mind-speaking. It's a struggle at first, but after a while, I think I have the basics down.

Focusing, I can picture an open door leading to a room. The room is the calming, deep blue that he loves, with large windows that let in the natural light and warmth, just like the windows in his house in Kystenvar. Rolling forests as far as the eye can see fill the view from the windows, and I recognize them as the same forests we traveled through in Kystenvar. The same forests he told me were his refuge from court life. My mind's clearly made this room just for him. In addition to his favorite color and place, the room somehow encapsulates everything I feel for him. His love, his scent, it's all there. It's everything that makes Conaill who he is. Sending Conaill a thought is easy enough; I just have to speak it to the room. Any thoughts he sends to me sound from that room as well. If I want to block him out, I simply need to close the door.

Well, in theory, I just need to close the door. I've yet to be able to shut it all the way, or even halfway, really. It's much easier to just not send our thoughts to each other. Unfortunately, we've tarried too long and must get back on the road. When I go to stand, I notice Conaill is motionless. Wide eyes stare over my shoulders in utter shock.

"Red," Conaill says breathlessly, and I can almost hear him gulp. "Um, don't freak out, but you need to move really, really slowly."

Well, thanks, now I'm freaked. I project the thought to him, causing an adorably sheepish look to take up residence on his handsome face.

Sorry, I just don't want you to freak and startle it. I've never seen one before. Even in my head, his voice sounds breathless and awed.

Body taut, I glance over my shoulder as smoothly as I can, expecting the worst. When I catch sight of what startled Conaill, I let out a huge laugh. Jumping to my feet in excitement, I shout, "Klaudio!"

He whinnies, hoofing at the ground in happiness before prancing over and throwing his head around me in a hug.

"Maevery, he's a unicorn," Conaill says, clearly stunned. "How are you on a first-name basis with a unicorn? Aren't they really, really reclusive?"

"Well, yes, normally," I say, stroking the milky white hair on his neck. Klaudio is just as stunning as I remember. At about five feet at his shoulders, he's the perfect representation of a unicorn. Pure milk-white hair with a long mane and tail that's a deep, russet red. Strands of gold and silver mix in the red, causing it to glimmer in the sun. Atop his forehead is a golden, intricately curled horn that's easily thirty inches long.

"But this is Klaudio," I explain, planting a kiss on his velvety soft nose before continuing, "he's an official messenger for the unicorns. At least, that's what Iskra said he told her. The first time he came to us was just after our parents died. We're not sure how he found us, or why, but ever since, he visits us now and then."

Klaudio snorts, turning to face Conaill. His head is held high and proud, showing off his strength and his horn. With flared nostrils, he walks over to Conaill, thoroughly inspecting and smelling him. It's only when it's clear that Conaill's been approved that he lowers his head and allows Conaill to pet his neck. It's then that I see a note tied to his mane. My smile instantly widens. There's only one fae I know who Klaudio would carry letters for. Removing the note, I begin to read.

Mae,

Thank you so much for the tips, and please thank the crew. They've saved me a few times, and wow, am I grateful. Anyway, I was hoping you might be able to help. Well, now that I think of it, I'm not sure if you'll know anything about it. But I heard about something some of the fae were doing, and I want to do it too.

My roommate, Cerridwyn, comes from Koosh. It's that small town in the Forest of Alm we visited with Mom and Dad right before they died. Anyway, we've gotten really close, and one night I was talking about how much I hate the laws Uncle Emeric enacted.

Okay, you know I think a lot of his laws are dumb, but it was the one about affected fae having to leave their families and be forced into those horrible camps. Before you freak out, yes, we had a sound shield. And yes, not only have the animals vouched for her, but Klaudio has as well. So I know I can trust her.

Anyway, she was telling me a lot of fae are actually fighting back against this law and others. She's heard that some are providing shelter, and some are giving supplies and money. I really want to help. I know I can't do much from Sabaid, but I was thinking that once my service starts, I can be a liaison with the animals and maybe get them to assist. What do you think? I know we agree the law is horrible and that when you're queen, you'll get rid of the law, but what about in the meantime? What about the common fae in other kingdoms who are still losing their powers and their freedoms?

Let me know if you've heard anything and if you want to help too. I love and miss you!

~Isk

Blood drains from my face. My world narrowing to the neat script on the page in front of me. She can't do this. She can't put herself at risk. She can't. She can't. She can't.

"Maevery!" Conaill shouts and shakes me, pulling me out of my head.

Suddenly, everything I've blocked out comes flooding back. It's all too much. I can't breathe. My mind keeps flying to the worst possible outcome, and suddenly, I'm falling. The ground rises up to meet me. I don't feel Conaill's arms catch me. I don't hear him scream for Madok. I don't see the terror in his eyes. Everything is black, and for a moment, I'm blissfully numb.

Chapter Thirty-One

Maevery! Maevery, wake up."

My eyes flutter to see Mina leaning over me. *What? Why is Mina here?* The ground is hard and uneven under me, yet for some reason, it's comforting. Glancing around, I realize it's not the ground, but Conaill's lap that I'm being cradled in while Mina, Tilde, and Madok surround us. When I see Klaudio is also here and looking worried, everything comes back. My panic sets in again, causing my heart to pound.

Mae, just breathe. You fainted, but you're okay. I have you. We've all got you and Iskra. We have a plan; everything will be okay. Conaill's deep voice comes through our bond. His comforting tone starts to soothe my frayed nerves. "We read the letter and have a plan."

"How long was I out for?" I question no one in particular.

It's Madok that answers. "Only a few minutes. Tildewynn actually thinks pretty quickly on her feet." He nods toward her. The full use of her name indicates he's being completely serious.

"In this case, we don't think it's safe to send a letter back," Tilde says while Klaudio stamps his feet in affront. "Klaudio, it isn't that we don't trust you. We have the utmost faith that you would deliver it safely. The problem is someone might find it after you deliver it, which wouldn't be safe for Iskra."

He snorts in what can only be interpreted as resigned agreement before Tilde bows slightly toward him. "Klaudio has agreed to carry me to Sabaid so I can talk to Iskra in person." Klaudio nods enthusiastically, stamping his feet in agreement. Unicorns have their own special magic, allowing them to travel faster than anything else could. "I'll explain to her why she can't get involved and keep you out of it."

"But you know Isk. Now that she knows about the Order, she won't be okay ignoring it," I butt in.

Mina holds up a hand, forestalling me. "We thought of that. Tilde will say that until you're queen, she can't get involved personally. But we can get her money to the Order if she wants to, so they can buy what's needed."

I nod my head. It isn't the best plan, not by a long shot, but it should work. We go back to the horses and get ready to continue the journey. Tilde gathers what she will need, and then she and Klaudio are on their way.

The small city we're staying in tonight is one that normally brings me joy. Tanulas is famous in Fenshegus, and all of Panellas, really, for art. In fact, the whole city is covered in it. The horses' hooves clack a staccato beat on the patterned cobblestones as we journey through the winding streets.

Galleries and studios dot the streets, interspersed with homes and shops. Neighborhood squares sing with the sounds of laughter and children playing. Older fae gather and talk, their raucous laughter mirroring that of the younger generation. Artists stand on stools and ladders, painting huge murals on the walls of some of the neighborhood squares. Each mural showcases something unique about that neighborhood.

At first, it's hard to notice, but now and then symbols of the Order can be seen. Symbols have been hidden in the graffiti and posters plastered on the walls. An unending knot encased in a circle – the union of wisdom and harmony. Three interlaced arcs formed from one line – everything and everyone is connected, with no end and no beginning. Brightly colored parasols hanging near doorways – shelter can be sought here by those fleeing danger. Window boxes full of anemones – reminders to have hope and to persevere, to trust that a better future can be found. Innocuous to the uninformed, but each has a double meaning. Along one street, a poem has been painted on the walls. Only those versed in the Order would see the meaning behind the word choice.

Each symbol only reminds me of the danger Iskra is now in. Conaill must notice as he leans over the carriage seat, gathering me to him.

"Mae, it'll be okay. Tilde will talk with her. They'll reach her by tomorrow night." His lips brush my head tenderly just as we pull to a stop. Before opening the door, he whispers, "I love you. I'll protect Iskra like she was my own sister."

I squeeze his hand in acknowledgment before he exits the carriage and helps me down. Time to put our masks back in place. On the road and in private, we've relished the opportunity to be ourselves. But here, in public? Masks are essential. So, pasting on a smile that I don't feel, we go about and play our parts.

I show off one of my favorite cities to Conaill, hoping that I can forget about everything else for just a little while. As we walk the streets, I realize the art is helping to center me, my anxiety and stress lowering incrementally each time we stop to admire an artist's work. I'm still worried for Iskra. I won't stop worrying until I know she's safe, but at least it isn't overwhelming me.

After stopping to hear a street musician, Conaill lifts my hand to his mouth and kisses the back gently. *There you are. The real you is finally peeking through. Feeling better?*

Some. I'm still worried, but it's getting better. I let him know, and I have to admit, one good thing from today was unlocking the ability to mind-speak with Conaill.

We continue our stroll until we reach our dinner destination, a small restaurant my parents loved. One of the owners was friends with them from Sabaid, so we always made sure to come here when we were in Tanulas. The restaurant is intimate, not able to hold more than thirty. The walls are painted a soft, buttercup yellow, and dark wooden beams line the ceiling. Fresh flowers are on each table; no two tables holding the same bouquet. Soft music floats in through the windows from the street musicians, creating an ever-changing symphony.

The fae lights here are by far my favorite, though. Sculptures, both tiny and great, are stationed around the room. The sculptures are of the Dochais, the hope-bringers. Each bears a lantern or torch filled with the gentle flicker of fae light. I've always thought they looked like thcy were leading the diners to a better, happier place.

Seeing them, I'm reminded of the bedtime stories my parents would tell, and a pang of longing courses through me. The Dochais were mythical fae creatures. The only living thing that could kill the wraiths without needing tinuvar. On the battlefield, they would bring hope and courage to the just and strength to the righteous. Fear and doubt would be gifted to the wicked and evil. The last time they were seen was during the Great War. They fought until all died off. Their sacrifice allowing all fae, common and high, to prosper and thrive.

The restaurant hasn't changed at all, a fact which fills me with joy and only a tinge of sadness. If I close my eyes, I can imagine my parents here, laughing and enjoying good company. But it's time to make new memories. Memories with those who mean the most to me now. Dinner's over quickly, each of us devouring the delicious food that seems to have only gotten better over time. I needed this meal with these fae. Not only is it the first time I've enjoyed myself, but it's also the first time I've tasted anything since getting Iskra's letter. For this one meal, she wasn't the only thing my mind would land on.

Stepping out of the restaurant door, a gallery across the street instantly catches my attention. I stop abruptly, which causes Conaill to stumble slightly. "I'm going to check out that gallery real quick," I call out, not waiting to see if anyone heard me.

"Maevery, it looks like they're getting ready to close. We can come back in the morning," Conaill says, but I won't be dissuaded.

"It'll only take a minute." I let go of his hand and rush across the street. Conaill and some guards follow behind me, cursing under their breath. I know I shouldn't have done that, but I can't explain it. I have to get in there.

I'm at the door just as the worker is about to flip the sign to closed. His wide eyes are an obvious sign that he recognizes me. Before he's able to say anything, I blurt out, "I know you're about to close, but please. I have to see one of your paintings."

Bowing incredibly low, he murmurs, "Your Highness, of course. For you, anything." Straightening from his bow, he holds the door open wide, motioning me forward. "If you tell me which one, I can let you know all about it."

"It's over there," I say, making my way to it. Stopping directly in front, I take in everything. The painting is medium-sized, about three feet long on all sides. A peony in full bloom fills the center, with four smaller buds taking shelter beneath it in the lower-left corner. It's stunning. The petals are a rich, creamy orange that ranges from soft coral to vibrant deep peach. I've never seen a peony like this. But it isn't simply that it's a peony, or that it's Iskra's favorite shade of orange, which has me enthralled. The longer I look, the more it fills me with emotion.

The swirling colors evoke movement and sensuality. Some remind me of a lively dance between friends, while I see a lover's embrace in others. Taking a step closer, I notice that the background makes it look like the peony is lying on a tapestry. When I lean in, I see the tapestry is of a majestic oak, under which a unicorn proudly stands. All on a field of deep green.

It's the royal crest, my family's crest. Every brush stroke adding to its beauty, the artist is obviously extremely talented. But the beauty isn't what's captivating me. It's the depth of feeling it evokes that has me so enraptured. The emotion that's filling me is continuously growing. I still don't know what it is, I just know, with everything in me, this painting was meant to be mine.

"I'd like to buy this painting, please," I say, never taking my eyes off it.

Clearing his throat and shuffling his feet, the gallery owner says, "I'm sorry, Your Highness, this painting isn't for sale."

I look at him, and he drops his head as if afraid to look at me.

"What do you mean? Is this not a gallery that sells art?" I say, well aware I sound like a brat. Shaking my head, I try again. "I'm sorry, that was rude. I'm just so captivated by this painting. It… speaks to me," I say, turning back to it.

"I'm sorry, Your Highness, this is the only painting here that isn't for sale." I look toward him and see he's looking at the painting as well. Happiness and loss are fighting for dominance in his eyes. "This was the last painting my wife, Nisserra, did before she died."

I suck in a breath. "That was my mother's name," I whisper, a tear escaping me at this additional connection.

He just nods, obviously knowing the name of his queen. We stand in silent appreciation of the painting for only gods knows how long. Soon, Conaill makes himself known, and it's time we leave. I thank the owner, and we make our way to the inn.

It's been a long, emotional day, and as I lie in Conaill's arms, I allow him to center me. He knows exactly what I need, and when he finally enters me, it's tender and thorough. Both of us are seeking the solace and peace only found from each other.

Chapter Thirty-Two

Conaill softly knocks his boots into my hip, startling me. "Red?" He smirks as I shake my head and bring my attention to him. He's sitting across from me in the carriage, legs stretched out with his feet next to me. The silver curtains are drawn for privacy, and the interior has the perfect level of light thanks to two fae lights. Not so much that it's bright as day, but not too little so that it's dim. *Godsdamn, does he look sexy in this lighting.* The smirk on his face a clear indication that he received that thought loud and clear.

Oops, I think to the accompaniment of his deep rumble through the bond.

"Sorry. Just lost in thought," I say. It's been two days since I saw that painting, and I still can't get it out of my head.

"Nervous?" he questions, concern evident in his eyes and tone. "Having second thoughts about marrying me?"

"Maybe…" I say sheepishly. He looks so affronted that I chuckle and reassure him. "Not at all. You?"

"Maevery," he says in complete seriousness. "There's no one else I'd ever want to marry. Even if we weren't being forced to get married," he smirks, reaching out to grab my hand. Not satisfied simply holding a hand, he completely rearranges. He's now on his knees in front of me, and both of his strong, calloused hands hold mine. "I would marry you a thousand times. I'm thrilled my father and Emeric…" He pauses, grimacing in what I can only imagine is revolt for Uncle Emeric. "That they forced our hand."

"What?" I scoff. His finger comes up to my lips, and he shushes me, forestalling my argument. I glare, but he isn't deterred.

"As much as I want to kill him, I'm also grateful. If they hadn't arranged our marriage, I'd never have been forced into this journey. I never would've gotten to know you. To know what makes you tick and what buttons to push. To fall in love with you. To find my mate." An unbidden tear falls at his words. Rising up, he kisses it away before continuing.

"In this life, the last life, or the next, you're the only one I'll ever want to share it with. I love you, Maevery," he says. He's only inches away from me now, somehow having moved closer.

"I love you too, Con," I say. "You're the only one I'd want to share it with, either. I'm so happy I'm forced to marry you." I laugh.

He smiles darkly, and suddenly I'm very aware of his hands on my thighs. Hands that are toying with the bare skin by my garters. *Wait, when did he lift my skirts?*

Mae, he thinks down the bond as he has his hands spread my thighs, fitting himself between them. *As much as I abhor the trappings of formal clothes, I fucking love seeing you in garters and stockings.* His face caresses my leg, the silk of my sheer black stockings skimming his cheek. His hands gently press my legs wider. Leaning in, he kisses the skin of my inner thigh, just above my right garter.

"Con," I say, my breathing increasing. "We're in a carriage; we can't."

He looks up at me through thick, dark lashes and slides his hands to my hips. With a quick tug, my ass is at the edge of the seat, skirts pushed out of the way. Still looking up at me, he licks the skin of my upper thighs, so close to my core I can feel his breath. At the same time, I hear him growl, *Watch me,* through the bond.

"Did you…" I pause; his hands are now at my panties. Slowly, he strokes my folds over the fabric. I lick my suddenly dry lips and try again. "Did you just growl?"

Looking me straight in the eye, he growls, shredding the barrier of fabric between us. Bringing them to his nose, he inhales. "You smell like heaven," he murmurs before shoving them into his pocket. "But you taste even better."

It's all the warning I'm given before he's licking up my seam. "Mine," his growl fills the carriage before he descends again to feast on me.

"Con!" I cry as he moves my legs to his shoulders before his hands cup my ass. His tongue expertly strokes my core before delving deep.

Damn, Mae. I love your taste. I can't get enough; I could feast on you for hours. His words flow across our bond as he licks me from bottom to top, stopping only to swirl his tongue around my clit before sucking on it.

I cry out. *Con, baby, more.* Mewls of pleasure escape my mouth. *Con, do it again.*

As you wish, Mae. He's sucking on my clit again, pausing to flick his tongue back and forth before sucking again. My hands fly to his head. Fingers tangling in his hair. *That's it, baby. Direct me where you want me. Use me. I'm not stopping until you come, and your orgasm is coating my face.*

He slides a finger in, and I groan, pushing his head down. *Shit, Con. Sorry.* I say through the bond. I'm breathing too hard to speak, so damn is this mind-speaking amazing.

He laughs, and his warm breath tickles my sensitive core before he's licking me again and again. *Mae, I love it. I love you taking control of your pleasure. If you could feel how hard I am, you wouldn't worry about being assertive.* He adds another finger, and then another. Pumping them in and out. On each withdrawal, he crooks his fingers, causing them to graze my walls, each time hitting the spot that makes my vision narrow and my body tremble.

"Conaill!" I shriek when he gently bites my clit at the same time he brushes over that spot. His back quakes as he chuckles, and I can't care. One hand leaves his hair, pressing against the wall, giving me better leverage to push into his face.

Gone is his laughter. "Mine!" he growls loudly again before continuing to stroke me, biting down each time he passes that one spot. I come apart, yelling his name as I do. *Gods, Mae, I could drink you every day*. He's lapping up all my moisture from coming, his eyes never leaving mine as he does.

Slowly, my breathing returns to normal as he sits back in his seat. I'm wrecked. Completely and utterly wrecked. My legs are open, falling to the sides. My skirts are around my waist, and there's a distinct wet spot on the underskirts. Meanwhile, he's somehow kept himself relatively in order. The only indication he was just between my thighs is the obvious erection straining his pants and his disheveled hair from my hands.

My eyes narrow at his smirk. *Well, two can play at this game.* I think, making sure I don't share that thought. My look turns wicked, and he must spot the shift in me as I turn from prey to predator.

His head tilts, like an animal trying to figure something out. Narrowing his eyes, he asks, "Red, what are you thinking?"

I mimic him, sinking to my knees, palms trailing lightly over his thighs. His cock twitches, and he grabs my wrists. "Red. Mae. What are you doing? We'll be at the temple soon."

Rearranging my face into innocence, I say, "Well, you got a taste of me." My voice is sweet as he swallows deeply. Pulling my hands from his grip, I reach for his pants. Freeing him, I say, "I figured it's only fair I should get to taste something too."

Glancing down, I see pre-cum already leaking from the tip. "Mae," he pleads. Without taking my eyes off him, I lean forward. One hand encircles his base as best as I can; he's too big to get my hand all the way around. With a feather-light touch, I trail the fingers of my other hand up and down the rest of his shaft.

Stopping when the head of his cock is just in front of my lips. My eyes lock on his as I lick my lips, and he groans my name like he's praying. Closing the distance, I lick the glistening bead of moisture leaking from him.

His head falls back, hitting the wall with an audible thunk as he mutters, "Fuck."

Smiling, I take him into my mouth and begin my torture. Gripping his base with one hand, I pump him up and down. I suck him into my mouth on the upstroke as I swirl my tongue on the underside of his shaft with the downstroke. Continuing to work him, he starts to thrust into my mouth. I trail my other hand up his inner thigh before cupping his balls, giving them a light squeeze before I massage them.

"Mae, gods Mae. Astrid herself must have blessed you. Fuck, it feels so good," he groans.

I squeeze him harder, stopping just before pleasure turns to pain. Without stopping, I say through the bond. *I don't care that she's a god. You will NEVER say another female's name when you're with me.*

"Yes, Mae. I promise. Just please don't stop," he begs.

I return to the pressure and pace he likes, and it isn't long before he's there. "Mae, I'm going to—"

Light floods the carriage, and I jerk back to my seat.

"Fuck!" Conaill roars as the door to the carriage slams shut. "Godsdamn it," he mutters. Laughter bubbles out when I realize he had just enough time to turn to the side, but now his jacket is definitely not wearable anytime soon. *It's not funny*!

Oh, it most assuredly is funny. I say back. We quickly put ourselves back together, realizing that at some point the carriage stopped. Mina is yelling at Madok on the other side of the door, and giggles erupt from me again.

"Seriously?" she yells, and Conaill laughs too. "Seriously, you big oaf?"

"What?" Madok says, false innocence evident in his tone. "We've been stopped for a while, and we didn't hear anything. I figured they had to be done by now."

My cheeks are so hot they must be on fire. A muffled slap rings out, and both Conaill and I laugh harder.

"You stupid, ignorant, immature lout." *Oh shit,* Mina is pissed. "Just because you finish in a minute doesn't mean he does. Undoubtedly, they have a sound shield up. You have a nose on that arrogant face; use it."

Conaill is laughing so hard he might fall over.

"Now that is just a lie 'Lo. You know damn well that I don't finish in a minute." Another slap sounds, and my eyes are as wide as they can go now.

"Did he just say…?" I question.

Conaill looks just as confused. "Did they hook up?" he says.

"Not to my knowledge. I mean, Mina's more reserved, but she would've told me about that.

"You. Ass!" Mina says, carefully enunciating each word. "How. Dare. You! And how dare you to Mae? Yeah, they might have sound shielded, but clearly the scent has been getting stronger. It doesn't get stronger *after*. Gods, how did I get stuck with you?"

Oh shit. I forgot about anyone being able to scent what was going on. My hands cover my face. *Is it possible to die of embarrassment?*

Conaill grabs my hands. Pressing a kiss to each one before tenderly whispering, "Mae, it's okay. Only Madok or Mina would be close enough to smell anything. You know, as soon as they figured out what was going on, they'd have made sure of that."

"Ah, my sweet 'Lo, that would be called luck," Madok rumbles. "And as you so succinctly put it, the smell has lessened. So clearly they *are* done now." Madok pounds on the door. "Hey. Thought you'd want a heads-up. We're only a half hour out from the temple. You know, just in case you wanted to… freshen up."

Another smack sounds, this one muffled as if it's on cloth. "Madok! That is entirely inappropriate."

"Yeah, well, so is getting busy in a carriage. Poor Henrae up there had to keep driving; it's not like he could give them privacy like the others did. And stop hitting me." Madok's voice trails off as if he's walking away.

Oh gods. Bas take me. I forgot about the driver.

The remainder of the ride passes quickly as we rush to set ourselves to rights. In only a few moments, we'll be pulling up to the Temple of Astrid. She's the Goddess of Passion, but it isn't just love and sex she oversees. Any passion someone has in their life falls under her rule. Be that for their pursuits, work, friendships, or really anything one might be passionate about. She also happens to be Fenshegus's patron god. I've been here many times before, but never for this ceremony.

Today, Conaill and I will ask for a blessing from the goddess for our marriage. Anyone looking to marry in Fenshegus must ask for the blessing before they can be allowed to marry. Temples of all sizes can be found in almost all cities and towns. In fact, the furthest any fae might be from a temple is only a day's journey. However, for Fenshegus royalty, only the high priest or priestess at the main temple will do. Or so we're told.

The carriage wheels crunch on the gravel ground as it rolls to a stop, and Conaill reaches for the door. Before opening it, though, he looks at me. His love reflects in his beautiful eyes, and I nod in assurance that I'm ready. With efficient movements, the door is opened, and I'm standing in front of a beautifully imposing temple.

The temple resides in the heart of Senveldy, a bustling city just on the outskirts of the Forest of Alm. The towering trees that Alm is known for are more sporadic, and instead, short trees and shrubs are more common. When the temple was first built, the high priestess insisted that nature be allowed to flourish and be part of the city. Wide and accommodating roads wind around the large trees scattered here and there. While shorter trees line the roads, patches of wilderness are left alone as parks.

Each of the trees here flowers in different seasons. No matter when you visit, you're always greeted by a riot of colors. Today is no different, and yellow blooms dance on the trees as the wind flits lightly through the branches. As we walk up the pathway, those same yellow petals crush beneath our shoes, softening our footsteps.

Made of white stone and marble streaked through with a deep green, the temple stands out among a sea of trees. A veritable beacon for those seeking Astrid's favor. Columns as tall as five males encase a main building large enough to house five hundred fae. Centered in the facade of the main temple is the largest door I've ever seen, allowing fae of all types to enter the temple. Those doors are currently flung open, flanked by the priests, priestesses, and all the acolytes.

The high priestess stands tall in the center, a general ready to command her troops. Each is dressed in deep wine-red robes over a soft caramel tunic. Only their sleeves differ, an indication of their rank. The longer and more ornate the sleeve, the higher the rank. A garnet, the invoking stone of Astrid, is their only form of decoration or individuality. Some choose to wear garnets in the form of necklaces, rings, or hair clips. Others have used it as buckles for their robes.

The grounds to either side of the main temple are dotted with little buildings that are built in the same style as the main temple, just without the columns. The size varies for each depending on their needs. Some are large and hold either the dormitory or the dining hall. Somc scrve as storage, while some serve as meeting rooms for small matters. Nature envelopes the entire complex, providing a symphony of birdsong. An oasis of wild in a bustling city.

Nearing the doors, I realize for the first time that an acolyte is out of place. Rather than at the ends with the other acolytes, she's standing proud, only a few feet to the right of the high priestess. Waist-length brown hair cascades in glorious waves around a tall, beautiful, high fae female. Her sun-kissed skin is a perfect complement to the robes. Her angular face is gorgeous, but it's her eyes that captivate me. The same hazel eyes I've looked into what seems like a million times now.

She looks to the high priestess, seeking permission for something. When a nod is given, she lifts her robes and runs straight for Conaill. With open arms, he scoops her up, spinning around until she giggles at him to stop.

When her feet touch back down, and she's righted herself, I say, "I take it you're Chandra?"

Chapter Thirty-Three

Chandra is exactly how Conaill described, and their love for each other is evident. A thought hits me that she and Iskra would get along great. As we walk toward the high priestess, Chandra talks non-stop with Conaill, pestering him for information as only a tenacious little sister could.

As we approach the high priestess, Chandra bows and resumes her previous position. Short straight hair curtains the strikingly handsome square face of the high priestess. Conventional standards might not consider her beautiful, but her presence is captivating and enthralling. Her deep chocolate eyes command the attention of anyone caught in her gaze. When she speaks, her voice is light and beautiful, like a bird calling the day to start.

"Your Royal Highnesses," she says, bowing.

"Your Grace," Conaill and I say, giving a small curtsy and bow in respect of her position.

"Please join us, and we shall get started." Turning slightly, she holds her hand out to the interior of the temple, indicating we should walk ahead.

The interior of the temple is a riot of color compared to the austere exterior, and yet just as striking. Huge fae lights line the interior and reflect off the gleaming walls, the effect warm and welcoming. Small rooms line the walls of the temple, each sitting empty for today. No two rooms are alike, and they often change depending on the needs of the room's occupants. Worshippers coming here often want to perform certain acts for Astrid, and the rooms allow privacy. Whether that is ensuring conception, deciding between two paths in life, or even in marriage counseling.

Tapestries hang along the walls in a seemingly chaotic array. However, each tapestry has been deliberately placed, allowing the viewer a glimpse into the storied life of Astrid. Mom taught me how to read the tapestries the first time she brought me here. Near the door, they share the story of Magic's First Awakening. The place where magic first entered our world, and from which all fae, high and common, were first born. Seven bright lights burst forth from the cliffs of Tenega on the kingdom of Nuwen's northern shore. Each light represents one of the seven gods. The creation of all the fae and our lands, both this continent and the others, is the next tale told by an assortment of tapestries. The ancient fae species each have their own tapestries, all harmoniously hung with care. As you move on, the tapestries shift to showing the life of Astrid. The closer you get to the altar, the closer you are to today.

At first, the story of Astrid's love and subsequent marriage to Bas is told. The God of Life and Death, hand in hand with the Goddess of Passion, as they look out on the world. A little further down, a weeping Astrid is revealed, devastated over the loss of the humans from our world.

Her grief is palpable as, unlike fae, humans were the children of Astrid and Bas. Created in love from their union. History doesn't mention what happened to them, only that one day, thousands of years ago, all humans disappeared. Fae of all kinds surround Astrid, offering her love and support during her time of grief.

I'm sorry for your loss, Goddess, I say in prayer, just as my mom taught me. Letting her know that her loss and pain will never be forgotten. Finally, as you approach the altar, she's healed and has found her joy and passion again. I'm probably biased, given that she's my kingdom's goddess, but I've always loved the story of Astrid. Her story is one that fae can relate to; it makes me feel closer to her than any other of the gods.

I've been so lost in the tapestries that I'm a little startled to realize we've reached the main altar. The high priestess smiles at me, aware that the goddess has captivated me and that I haven't heard what she's said. With a delicate hand, she indicates we should kneel on the cushions placed in front of the altar. I pause for a moment, captivated by the beautiful altar before kneeling. It's carved from what looks like a single piece of myrtle, one of the many trees in this area. Intricate carvings of flora and fauna, made from birch and cherry wood, adorn the altar. Each detail is so perfect it feels alive.

After we kneel, Chandra and Madok stand to the side of Conaill, Mina to mine. Now standing before us at the altar, the high priestess smiles as running footsteps echo off the walls.

"I was wondering if you could make it in time," the high priestess says as we turn to see Tilde running toward us.

I jump up and run to her. Mina reaches Tilde simultaneously, and we all hug.

"I'm so happy I made it in time," Tilde says, breathing hard. "I'd never forgive myself if I missed this."

A tear rolls down my cheek, and it isn't until this moment that I realize how much I needed her. Mina and I hastily wipe away our tears before turning back to the altar. We head to our spots, and just as I'm about to kneel again, the priestess stops me. I look at her questioningly, but she just laughs softly, her hand open to Tilde.

Taking my hand, Tilde places a bracelet on my wrist. As the cool metal brushes my skin, I realize it's one of Iskra's fire opal bracelets she loves so much. Her favorite one, in fact.

"Your sister wrote to me," the high priestess explains. "She asked permission to send something in her stead. That bracelet represents both her and her love for you." Tears of joy and heartache fall down my cheeks, but she wipes them away with her sleeve. "Stop crying and let us ask the goddess to bless this union."

When I've composed myself, Conaill grabs my hand, mouthing *I love you.* With a smirk, the high priestess raises her arms and turns to face the altar. Behind the altar, a towering statue of Astrid holds court. Made of the purest white marble, she radiates warmth, and I can feel her love for us.

"Astrid," the confident voice of the high priestess booms out. "Goddess of Passion, giver of love and friendship, beacon of hope and trust. We ask for your blessing upon this union." I squeeze Conaill's hand gently and look into his eyes. Eyes that radiate love for me. I want those eyes, with all his love shining forth, to be the first thing I see every morning and the last thing I see each night.

The priestess reaches down and dips her hand into a bowl on the altar before turning to us. "Her Royal Highness, Crown Princess Maevery Saoirse Croia Nikolette Roighail." She steps down and swipes her fingers across my brow. The sweet almond scent of the anointing oil fills the air as a sense of peace washes over me. "Is joining in union to His Royal Highness, Crown Prince Conaill Malik Axel Bharath Yastahiqu." She anoints Conaill as she finishes saying his name, then returns to the altar.

"They ask you to bless their union. Look into their hearts and souls. Use your wisdom and grace, and please let your wishes on this blessing be known." She falls silent, and everyone waits.

As the oil on Conaill emits a soft glow, the oil on my head grows warmer. An ethereal voice rings out, and I realize it's Chandra singing. Goosebumps prick my skin at the beauty of her voice. The hauntingly lovely voice fills the temple, echoing off its walls and calms my racing heart.

"We thank you for your blessing, Astrid," she says, her hands now held in prayer in front of her. Stepping forward, she holds out her hands, palms up. "Now, if your representatives could please hand me the rings."

Madok and Mina step forward, each placing a simple golden band in her hands. The high priestess brings the rings to her lips, kissing each before gently dipping them in the anointing oil. Turning to Conaill, she places his ring on his right ring finger, then does the same with mine. A golden ring to indicate Astrid's blessing of our union. Should she have decided not to bless the union, silver rings would've been used instead. Once we marry, this ring will be moved to the left hand, nestled next to the wedding ring.

"Rise and face your future," the high priestess says.

We do so, holding each other's hands, and neither of us can contain our smiles. Conaill rubs his thumb across my ring, and I can't help but think it's this moment when our lives together truly start. Not when we marry in two months' time, but right now. With the blessing of Astrid, and this simple golden ring declaring that a goddess has deemed our love worthy.

"Your union is blessed. May you be the fertile soil beneath each other's feet, growing in your love and respect for each other each day. May you be the air that fills each other's lungs, speaking to each other with kindness and understanding. May you be the water that rains down, washing away the sorrow that life may bring your way. May you be the fire in each other's souls, keeping passion aflame in your hearts and in your bed. Until the day Bas sees fit to separate you, may your love for each other never wane. And when you join the other in the Land of the Blessed, may your love for each other continue on," she finishes, and once again, a tear streaks down my face.

Conaill swipes the tear away with his thumb and kisses me soundly. Pulling back, his voice thick with emotion, he says, "Thank you, Your Grace. Madok and Mina have some gifts of tribute and offerings we would like to give the goddess. If you would please let us know where we can best distribute them, we will be thankful."

"Of course," she says, and leads them out, presumably to show them where the gifts can go. Soon, it's just Conaill and me in the temple. We're wrapped in each other's embrace, and it's the happiest I've ever felt.

A short time later, I'm standing by the carriage as Conaill leans against it, when Mina and Madok return from distributing our gifts. Chandra and the high priestess just behind them.

"Is it me, or does Mina look very ticked off?" Tilde says, walking up from readying her horse.

"Yeah, she looks pissed," I respond.

Conaill snorts, "That's her perpetual state when she's around him without a buffer."

"True," I say, and Tilde nods.

Removing his foot from where it was resting on the carriage step, Conaill straightens. My eyebrow quirks when he alternates stretching his arms across his chest. His sexy wink is all the response I get.

"Time to get this over with," he mutters and strides toward Madok without another word.

The wide smile Madok has been showcasing is dimming the closer Conaill gets. In a flash, his jovial face morphs to one of confusion. Faster than I could imagine, Conaill throws a perfect right hook, landing squarely into Madok's face. In quick succession, a jab plows into Madok's stomach.

"Conaill!" I screech, running toward them. When I've reached their side, Mina is doubled over in laughter, and the high priestess's lips are tilted in a definite, if somewhat subdued, smile.

Bending low to Madok's ear, Conaill says very clearly. "That was for earlier today. Madok, I love you like a brother. But if you *ever* purposely try to catch Maevery in a compromising situation again…" He pauses, making sure Madok can see how serious he is. "I will end you. Now, you'll apologize to her, and you'll treat her with all due deference and respect she deserves."

Madok twists toward me, his eye already starting to swell. *Con, you didn't need to do that. But I'll admit it was very sexy seeing you all possessive,* I mind-speak to him.

Red, it was very necessary. He sends right back. *No male will ever see you when you're like that again except for me.* He's glaring at Madok as he says, "Well?"

"I'm sorry, Your Highness." Madok bows. He actually bows. He hasn't done that since our last official event. "It was immature, and I shouldn't have done it."

Mina is still laughing at Madok while he does his best to ignore her. Tilde, who has no idea what happened earlier, is clearly confused but chuckling softly.

"Madok," I say. "I forgive you, but don't do anything like that again. Not just with us, no one deserves that happening to them." I lean in close, my face only inches from his, and speak so low that my voice only carries a few feet. "Besides, I fully believe in payback. And let me tell you, she's a real bitch."

Madok blanches, and now Mina's laughing so hard that Tilde has to hold her up. Turning to the high priestess, I say, "Please forgive the violence. My mate is a little protective." Conaill shrugs, clearly not offended or sorry.

Holding up her thumb and forefinger so only the smallest of spaces lies between them, she says, "Just a smidge." A smile graces my lips, and she continues. "And while I don't condone violence in general, especially not so close to the temple," her gaze shifts to Conaill. "I can't help but think Astrid would approve of your passion to protect your mate."

With the tension now cut and a general sense of happiness in our group, apart from Mądok, we say our goodbyes. Conaill and Chandra move off to stand under a large tree for privacy while I head into the carriage. Tonight is my last guaranteed night with Conaill until he's back in Otthon for our wedding. We've talked about trying to sneak away to Keneven, but nothing has been promised. Especially as we have to keep up our charade.

The inn we're staying at tonight is small, but beautiful. The interior is a mix of dark wood and bright stone. Fae lights of all sizes twinkle, and I can't help but be enchanted. The aroma of fresh-baked bread fills the air, along with a mouthwatering scent that I hope is our dinner. If the smell is any indication of how it will taste, it will no doubt be delicious.

Our party has booked up all the rooms in the intimate inn, and as such, it's only us in the dining hall tonight. The grooms, maids, and guards decided to throw us a little celebration of their own. Tonight is the last night we'll all be together, and my heart is full from this little family we have created. They still refuse to call Conaill or me by anything other than Your Highness, but at least they are no longer constantly bowing to us, as we made our dislike of it known. At least when we're not in public.

Gerelle found a violin somewhere and decided the evening called for music. I had no idea he was as skilled as he was. If he ever retired from being a guard, he could make a career as a musician. Another guard, Tomaz, found a drum and another a tambourine. Together, the three of them kept the music going long into the night.

We spent the evening dancing and laughing, and I saw pure joy everywhere. At one point, the innkeeper and his wife came in, arms laden with baskets full of wine bottles. Refusing to let them leave, Tilde pulled them into the fray and had them dancing in no time. Turns out, the wife used to be in a traveling show and joined the makeshift band, singing both traditional songs and bawdy tavern ditties.

Late into the night, Conaill and I snuck away. Once behind the privacy of our door, I pounced. His lips meet mine in a duel for possession. We kiss as passionately as possible while divesting each other of clothing. Naked, he topples me onto the soft, plush bed, settling himself between my legs. Tenderly, he brushes my hair out of my face before leaning down to kiss me sweetly. Our bodies remaining entwined in some manner for the remainder of the night.

As the soft morning light filters in, we finally fall asleep. Conaill holds me tightly, my back against his chest. Feeling safe and loved, I fall asleep, a smile on my lips.

Chapter Thirty-Four

Conaill and I took an exorbitant amount of time saying goodbye to each other this morning, neither of us caring that it caused us to start later than planned. Given the revelations about Uncle Emeric, we can't trust that my letters will be private. Considering Conaill and I successfully, albeit unknowingly, corresponded for over a year for the Order, we decided to use that method for personal letters as well. The letters won't simply be personal, though. The weeks on the road solidified the need for the Order. The number of drained and affected common fae in both Fenshegus and Kystenvar is staggering. To know that other kingdoms have it worse is unfathomable.

We've been riding for a few hours, and now my ass is killing me. Shifting in my saddle is a futile exercise in finding comfort. Mionnan is the smoothest horse I've ever ridden, but spending the last week in a carriage is taking its toll. Trying to ignore my discomfort, I study the surrounding beauty.

After four hours of riding at an enchanted speed, we're about a third of the way home. Towering pines stand sentinel along the road, the sea of green periodically interrupted by blurs of motion. The soft gray of a rabbit or squirrel. A coppery streak, I think, is a fox. Blues, yellows, blacks, and reds flit from here to there, clearly industrious birds, too busy to bother with us.

"When we crest this hill, we'll break for lunch," Gerelle calls out. Carriages and wagons left at first light, so they should have set everything up for us.

"Thank the gods," Tilde groans.

"Is your backside hurting too much?" Mina quips. "I would've figured with all the *riding* you like to do, this would be nothing."

I laugh, but end up choking on nothing. Meanwhile, Gerelle's ears seem to be awfully red, and his cheeks have pinked.

"Why, you little wench!" Tilde scoffs, but she's laughing, too.

Letting go of her reins and somehow not managing to lose control, Mina outlines her body. "Who are you calling little?" Damn, I love how Mina embraces her lush curves.

"Not your ass, that's for sure." Tilde smirks. "But, if you must know, I'm freaking starving! Although I'll admit, my butt does ache a little."

Smiling, Mina declares, "Well, maybe if you had a bigger butt, say like mine" — she winks — "you'd have some extra padding, and it wouldn't be sore."

Tilde and I laugh, and soon we're slowing our horses and cresting the hill. Lunch is out and ready, and even if it's simple, it looks and smells amazing.

Red, can you hear me? Conaill's voice comes from that room I've designated as his, and I smile. His voice is muffled, but clear.

I can! We just stopped for lunch about a third of the way back. Grabbing a plate, head toward a tree nearby where Mionnan is munching grass. *How far are you?*

Well, Madok and I have a smaller entourage, if you recall. I nod even though I know he can't see me. *We sent everyone else the normal route. Madok and I wanted to stop in Koosh, that village your sister mentioned, and check in with the Order.*

Makes sense. But won't that add time to your journey? I pat the ground next to me as Mina and Tilde saunter up.

Not really, we'll go to the southern coast and then catch a ship to Illus.

We continue to mind-speak throughout lunch, but have to stop when we get back on the road. There are a little over seven hours left today, and I have to concentrate on keeping my mating mark covered, as well as practice my earth power and shielding.

Goodbye, my love, I say, unsure if it'll work. I send him thoughts of an embrace.

No. His voice is soft. *No goodbyes. Just until we see each other soon. I love you, Maevery.*

Arms stretched high above my head, I press into my headboard. *Gods, that feels good.* The late morning light is peeking around the edges of the curtains. I know I need to get up, but I can't seem to care all that much. There's something so restorative about the first night's sleep in your bed after a journey. Having got in late last night, I was luckily able to avoid Uncle Emeric. Ugh, there's no way I'll be able to avoid him today.

Tap, tap, tap.

Saori pops her head in, her smile bright and welcoming. "Your Highness, I've brought you my *special tea* to help get you going." She winks and sets the overflowing tray on a table.

Saori's *special tea is* really just regular tea with a healthy dollop of whiskey. "Are you sure you weren't sent to me by the gods?" I ask, shrugging into my robe. As I head over to the table, Saori sprinkles the discoperiet salt over everything.

"Well, shit." Muttering under her breath, she swipes up the pot of clotted cream, now a bright green, dumping its contents into the toilet. I insisted that Saori be told what was going on once we had proof she was innocent. Out of everyone who could have potentially given me the suppressant, at no point did I even entertain the idea that it might have been her.

"Well…" I sigh, pissed off about not being able to top my favorite cranberry orange scone with it. "So much for Uncle Emeric not having a backup in place." The rest of breakfast seems safe, so I'll count that as a win.

I eat quickly and then get ready while Saori fills me in on what needs to be done today. This morning, I have training with the weapons master, followed by hand-to-hand, and then an appointment with Porvi to go over the basics for my wedding dress.

"Unfortunately, after that, you have lunch with the king regent." Saori meets my eyes in the mirror, sympathy emanating from her warm brown eyes. Wrangling my hair into a complicated braid for training this morning, she lets slip a mischievous look. "Now, I took it upon myself to place some… discrete inquiries to certain science-minded individuals."

Confusion clearly written on my face, she laughs and produces a small purple box from only gods know where. Inside, on a bed of ivory velvet, sits a small, yet elegant brooch and a matching ring. Woven from platinum and gold threads, each is enameled with the Roighail crest. They're beautifully detailed and something I could wear at royal functions.

"Saori." I pause, grateful, but unsure what these have to do with science. "They're exquisite, but I still don't know what you mean."

Sitting next to me, she takes both in her capable hands. "When you let me know what was going on, I figured that even if you found who was responsible, you'd have to continue to test your food at court. My brother-in-law works for Dr. Tudos." She waves off that little fact and turns over the brooch.

"I wrote him a letter and asked him to pass it along to Dr. Tudos. I wanted to know if he knew of a way for a person to detect poisons discreetly. One that would allow them to keep the detectant powder on them." She stops abruptly as if just realizing something, her eyes wide. "Princess Maevery, I never mentioned the suppressant. Please believe me. I just said that with all the unrest, I was worried for you."

The next words tumble out of her mouth faster than I've ever heard. "Please believe me, I would never put you at risk. I have told no one about the suppressant; I promise. I..."

Holding up a hand in the universal sign to stop, I reassure her. "Saori. Please stop. I know you wouldn't, and I think it'd be reasonable for you to say you're worried about me. Plus," I lean in conspiratorially. "Dr. Tudos is in the Order. He's helped me out many times, in fact."

Relief floods her face, and her shoulders relax. "Oh, thank the gods." With a deep breath, Saori explains. "You fill the brooch with the discoperiet salt like this." With a quick flick, she opens the back, revealing a latch that's invisible unless you know exactly where to look. Flipping it to the front, she holds it straight.

"Notice the unicorn's horn? In this position, the salt is stored. But you can gently move the horn into a more upright position." She shows me, and it's as simple as pretending to play with the brooch. "Now it's primed. You just have to lean forward at a slight angle and..." She does, and an almost imperceptible amount of discoperiet salt falls from the bottom. Just enough to test whatever I'm leaning over. But not enough to be seen unless you watch for it.

"What in Sofiya's name? Saori, that's brilliant. Thank you!" I exclaim.

She waves me off. "Don't thank me. I didn't design it."

"Maybe not, but you thought of it for me. Now tell me about the ring," I demand, and I can't help the smile I'm giving her.

"Well, that one didn't come from Dr. Tudos." There it is again, that mischievous expression. "This was actually your grandmother's."

I cock my head, uncertain I heard her correctly. "Grandma Ja?" I ask, even though I know there's no way it's from Grandma Willadrud, my mom's mom. Only a member of the direct Roighail royal line, Dad's side, can wear the crest. Mom could only wear it after she married Dad.

Nodding, she explains. "Well, you know that your grandfather, King Oren the Second, loved your grandmother, Queen Ja, very much. Mates, they were." She smiles, clasping my hands in her soft, warm grip. "Mates for three generations on each side. Astrid has really blessed your family. Anyway, during the Great War, King Oren had to leave Queen Ja here to keep order in the kingdom. The fae loved her and knew she'd take care of them at any cost." I smile, remembering the stories of how fiercely she protected Fenshegus, even though she was originally a princess of Samaith.

"Well, they both had many enemies and could never be sure who to trust." Saori shakes her head. "King Oren had this ring made and presented it to her before he left to lead the Great War. It's similar to the brooch. All you need to do is press your finger here." She indicates a spot hidden on the band. "That releases a poison detector. Discoperiet salt in your case, but same thing."

Suddenly, I'm struck with the most amazing thought. This ring, my mother's necklace. The females in my family have never been content to sit back and let things happen to them. They did what was necessary to protect themselves and others. A poison-detecting ring. A hidden throwing star. My family sure has some fierce females.

"Wait," I say as a thought strikes me. "If this were Grandma Ja's, wouldn't Uncle Emeric know about this ring? I mean, she was his mother."

Saori shakes her head. "Not at all. You know, I came to the palace ages ago in service to your mother. Well, she and your Aunt Isalyth became fast friends after your parents married. Before Princess Isalyth became a priestess for Leighis, your grandmother gave her this ring. I was there getting your mother ready for something when she showed her how to use it. We were all sworn to secrecy. No one but the females in that room knew about it. I wrote to Her Highness asking if she knew of where I might get a ring like hers for you."

Saori stands, my cue to get dressed for the morning. "She said she no longer needed the ring, and she'd modify it for the discoperiet salt. I guess being a priestess for the Goddess of Healing comes with a good deal of herbal knowledge."

Dressed, I throw my arms around her. I don't know what god is watching over me, only that they clearly put her in my life for a reason. *I really should spend more time at temple.* Now if only I could figure out which one.

Chapter Thirty-Five

Beads of sweat tickle down my lower back, between my breasts, and drip from my elbows. *Damn, I didn't realize I'd gotten this out of shape.* Quickly, I squat, dodging to the left and barely getting hit by a giant fist. Twisting, I jab with my right. But I'm not fast enough, and my target bounces back laughing.

"What did you do the whole time you were touring the kingdoms?" Errol, my combat instructor, laughs. "Obviously not training. Being pampered, were you, Princess?"

Oh, hell no. Feinting to the right, I let a left hook fly. He goes to block it, and I drop. My leg sweeps out, and I take his feet out from under him.

Wham! His back slams onto the gray mat, the sound reverberating off the walls of the gym. He freezes for a fraction of a second, and it's all I need to get the upper hand. Wrapping my legs around his arm, I pull while leveraging my hips up. The perfect armbar, and he damn well knows it. Then again, he did teach it to me.

A quick tap of submission later, and I free him, collapsing to the mat. He pops up as if the last hour was a light walk around the park.

"You're disgusting, you know that?" I huff, completely spent. "You're so lucky no one was in here to hear you talk to me like that. I know I gave you the freedom to say whatever on the mat, but…" I trail off.

"I knew we were alone." He holds out his hand to help me up, but I swat it away. "But if you really want to point fingers, you're the disgusting one who's lying in the sweat puddles. One that isn't all yours." As if you prove his point, sweat drips off his face, landing on me.

"Ew! Errol, gross!" Getting up so fast my vision wavers, I grab his sweat-slicked arm. Once I'm steadied, he heads to the bench. Grabbing two fluffy white towels, Errol throws me one.

Tall and trim, Errol's body is tightly packed with lean muscle. Dark, golden hair tumbles in close-cropped curls, and his amber eyes sparkle with mischief. Errol's only about five years older and is like a brother to me. His dad is the head of the royal guard, and we grew up together. It also explains why he's so damn good at fighting.

"Seriously, Maeve, did you not practice at all?" Genuine concern laces his voice, and I take pity on him.

"Let's sit." I gesture to the bench at the side of the mat. Once seated, I gulp the water greedily. The refreshing liquid revives my flagging energy. A fortifying breath later, I explain the last month, leaving out as much as I can. At one point, he's so enraged he paces.

"Well…" Errol inhales deeply. "You've got me. You know that. I'll make sure I'm stationed with you more until your wedding. Then, your mate can better protect you."

"Errol!" I shush him. "What part of 'we can't let anyone at court know we're mates' is confusing? You have to get used to not saying it."

"You let me know," he says.

"You don't count, Errol," I say, laughing when he grabs his chest, stumbling back like I shot him with a crossbow.

A thunderous crash sounds, and we both jump. "Oops," Tilde says, clearly not sorry she scared us. Or, that by flinging the doors open, she knocked over a rack of stretching bars.

Sauntering over, her eyes devour Errol. "Hey, Errol," she purrs. "You're looking awfully good today."

Errol slowly peruses Tilde's body, clearly taking a very, very thorough inventory of anything that might have changed since she last saw him. "I could say the same, Tilde." He licks his bottom lip, and the scent of lust floods from both of them. *Yuck*. "Any chance you want to have a private session tonight?" His voice is deeper now.

"Why, you know what? I do think I could use a private session tonight. My room or yours for this… session." She's directly in front of him, trailing her fingers along his bare chest.

"Gods, will you two get a room?" I exclaim. "I'm right here, and you're acting like animals in heat."

Neither even bothers to look at me as Tilde says, "My room, it is." Errol winks and then heads toward the doors. Stopping to briefly pick up Tilde's mess.

When I have her attention, I give my best, *what the fuck* face. She just shrugs. "What? We have an arrangement. It's easy and mess-free."

"You know damn well that isn't what I mean, Tilde," I retort.

"Ugh, fine. I won't arrange my conquests in front of you anymore. Is that better, *Your Highness?*" She half-heartedly curtsies.

"Why yes, it is, Lady Tildewynn." My eyes roll. "Now, what's up?"

She sighs. "Well, there's good news, and… there's bad news."

"When isn't there bad news?" I groan, and we head out, taking the back way to my chambers.

"Well, the good news is, you don't have to have lunch with the king regent today." I perk up at her words, my footsteps lighter on the stone steps.

"But the bad news is, you have to meet with him in, like, thirty minutes instead." Before I can even complain, she holds up a hand to me. "The reason your lunch is canceled is that news reached the king regent of a group of common fae that entered the kingdom somewhere to the north. Not only were they helped by someone, but the garrison stationed nearby had its detention centers destroyed."

We've reached my hall, and I stop. Turning on the plush carpet, I quickly throw up a silencing shield. "Why didn't you say you had more than just one piece of good news?"

"It was a good news sandwich." Her shoulders shrug. "I wanted to surprise you." We both smile at the thought of the detention center's destruction.

"Was anyone injured?" I question.

She shakes her head. "So far, the news we've received says only one high fae was injured when he threw a rock at a guard and slipped in the mud, breaking his arm in the process. Otherwise, no guards or common fae."

"Well, that is good at least," I continue toward my room, pulling Tilde with me. "Now come on, I'm going to need help if I'm going to meet that treacherous snake on time."

We giggle and take off running. Not caring if my behavior isn't exactly queenly at the moment.

Chapter Thirty-Six

Come on, Mae, you can do this. My feet travel along the same repeating path, trying to build my courage. *This is ridiculous.* Hiding in the servants' stairs won't help me.

Red? Conaill's voice fills my head. *Why am I getting a sense of distress from you?*

Wait? You can sense what I'm feeling? I look at his room in my mind, trying to puzzle out how he can do this. *Why can't I sense yours?*

Mae, stay on topic, Conaill demands. While I can't sense his feelings, I can imagine him rolling his eyes right now. *We'll work on that later. Why the distress?*

Because I have to meet with Uncle Emeric now, and I'm freaking out. Leaning my head against the cool stone wall, my hair flutters around my face as I let go of a resigned breath.

Conaill's growl fills my head. *You will not be alone with him.*

Unfortunately, I have no choice. Before he snaps, I add, *Tilde will be just outside the door. She's fully armed and back in her role as a guard for me.*

I don't like it. He rumbles. *But… I can't really do anything from here.* He pauses for a moment. *You have this, Maevery. You've been working on shielding, and you're strong. Remember the plan. As soon as you're crowned, we'll fuck him up.*

Laughing, I steel myself, preparing to female up and meet this head-on. *Thank you, Con. I love you.*

Love you too, Red. And then he's gone. Only the sounds of my thoughts and pounding heart fill my mind.

Projecting confidence I don't feel, I stride through the door. For a moment, I'm overwhelmed. The bright light and colors are a stark contrast to the dull gray stones of the corridor that was my temporary refuge. Purposeful strides take me to the room that Uncle Emeric's been using as an office.

Knock, knock. I gently rap on the door. A brusque "Enter" is called out, and I boldly open the doors, stepping over the threshold.

Uncle Emeric doesn't look up as I enter. Head trained down, he is writing furiously. His desk, my dad's desk, looks nothing like it used to. It's still the same imposing chunk of oak. It still has the same intricate carvings that I would spend hours studying as a child. I loved listening to Dad tell me the stories behind the carvings. The beautifully carved Roighail crest takes pride of place. The left side tells the story of the founding of Fenshegus thousands of years ago, when Astrid bestowed this kingdom on its first king. To the right, a depiction of the creation of the Treaty of Panellas after the Great War.

Once King Harrend of Saetoris was defeated at the Battle of Chast in Baress, the seven kingdoms came together to create a better life for all in Panellas. I'm particularly proud of two parts of the treaty that Grandpa helped to draft. First, slavery was outlawed in all kingdoms; although at the time, only Saetoris and Baress kept slaves.

Baress's were criminals who regained freedom once their time had been served. Saetoris enslaved any common fae they decided didn't have *enough* magic, as well as those they conquered. The treaty also demanded reparations for those who were enslaved.

Second, child labor was also banned. While most of the kingdoms didn't practice child labor, either by law or social norms, three did. Saetoris, Baress, and Samaith. Now, the only way children were allowed to work was during harvest time on family farms. They also had a set amount of hours they could work, and it couldn't interfere with school or sleep. How either of these disgusting practices was only outlawed six hundred years ago is beyond me.

It's the top of the desk that's changed the most. Dad used to spread everything out. The entire desk would be covered in a sea of papers, not one inch of wood showing through. It was complete - but organized - chaos. Mom told me the maids tried to clean it up once, and Dad lost his mind, not at them, but rather because he couldn't *find* anything. He made the maids swear they would never clean the desk again. Now… now everything is organized and perfectly placed. The pens are lined up precisely. The papers are stacked in neat, organized piles, in, out, and working on. It's clinical, devoid of the chaos that is life.

Finally finished, Uncle Emeric looks up. "Ah, my dear!" He gets up, coming to me with arms open for a hug. Suppressing a shudder, I give him a hug as if nothing's wrong, and I don't know he's been betraying me for years.

"I'm so happy you're back. I've missed you and, I'll admit, I'm glad your tour ended early. The palace isn't the same without you." I'm guided to the large, dark green chairs by the windows, and we sit. "I wanted to talk with you about the upcoming plans we need to make and hear about your trip. Would you like me to ring for tea?"

Thank the gods he asked instead of forcing it. "No, thank you," I rush out. "I have plans to catch up with some friends for lunch and to go speak with my seamstress for details regarding my… wedding dress." I wrinkle my nose, hoping he'll buy my reluctance.

He eyes me quizzically for a second before saying, "Are you still apprehensive of the marriage? The reports I received indicated you two were getting along well."

Sighing, I sink down into my chair, relaxing as if I'm lifting a weight off my chest. "Then you probably were only getting reports of what was going on in public. Behind closed doors, however, was an entirely different story. You told everyone it was a love match; we had to pretend." Looking out the window, I'm struck by just how much I missed this city. Beyond the palace gates, the tangled warren of streets sings with life.

"But…" Uncle Emeric hesitates. "I heard you were sharing a room?"

Umm, yeah. How to explain that? "Well, you've met him," I say, stalling for time before realizing how it sounds. "He's a lecher. He pretended to be sleeping in my room, but would sneak out and find a different female's bed to warm. Then, he'd sneak back in the morning." I sigh and look at my lap. My glamour abilities have gotten better, but I still want to make sure that my long sleeves are covering the area, just in case.

"Hmm…" Uncle Emeric scrutinizes me, and I force myself not to squirm under it. "That doesn't seem like you. Maevery." He leans over, his cold hand grabbing my own. His hands are smooth and manicured, unlike Conaill's rough, calloused ones. Softening after years of not training with a sword. Or any weapon, really. "You've never been the type to allow that. I mean, he could have easily been caught. I'll talk to him about being more discreet."

It's a struggle not to roll my eyes. Of course he doesn't care if my future husband is sleeping around, only that he should be more discreet. "What am I supposed to do? It isn't as if I can prevent him from doing it. It's not like I actually want him in my bed."

With a condescending pat, he releases my hand. "I'll take care of it. Don't worry your head about it. Now, before you go, we need to talk about a few things."

"Okay, about what?" I ask.

"Well, the first is about your marriage ceremony and then your coronation." He heads over to his desk and grabs his planner. "I know you're busy, so I won't take up too much time. Can you meet with me in two days for lunch?"

I pretend that I'm thinking about it when, really, what choice do I have? "Yes, I believe I don't have any plans that day." I go to stand, but I'm stopped immediately.

"There is one other thing." My heart beats faster at his ominous tone. "What exactly happened to Lukavo?"

Shit, shit, shit. It's okay, I remind myself. We planned for this; I just need to follow the plan. Looking away, I attempt to portray that I'm trying to hold in tears, when really I'm trying to slow my pounding heart. Gods, I hope Uncle Emeric buys this.

With a steadying breath, I turn to him. "Did you not get the letter? He died when we were crossing the Cale. I sent the letter as soon as we landed in Keneven."

His shrewd gaze assesses me. "I did. It says he drowned."

"But… but then, I'm sorry." I'm trying to look as innocent as possible. Imagining what Iskra would do and look like in this scenario. "I don't really know what you mean. He did drown."

He clearly isn't fully convinced of my innocent routine. Then again, he isn't fully immune to it either. "What I mean is, how did he drown? Lukavo was an extremely good swimmer. And he was smart. What was he doing in the Cale and not on the boat?"

"I don't know. Honestly." Taking a breath, I run the heel of my shoe against my shin. My court dress covers the movement as the heels that go with it are sharp enough to hurt. My eyes well with tears easily now, just as I hoped. "Everyone was playing cards. He got up. Said he needed some fresh air, I think. Next thing I know…" I break off, gulping down a large breath.

I risk a look, and relief floods me. He's buying it. Well, at least more than he was. "Next thing I know, the crew is running around shouting. We went to see what was going on, but were stopped. They told us to stay out of the way. We didn't find out what happened until everything was over."

Uncle Emeric takes my hand. Holding it gently, like he used to do when I was upset or overwhelmed. "I see. I'm sorry to have brought it up… I just didn't understand. I had hopes for him, and I was saddened by his loss."

An uncomfortable silence echoes through the room as we sit, each seemingly lost in thought. I'm trying to figure out a way to extract myself when a loud knock sounds. The door eases open soundlessly, and Tilde pops her head in. *Thank the gods.*

She steps in and curtseys briefly, but respectfully. "Your Grace, Your Highness." Her head bobs to each of us in turn, and I try not to laugh. Her being formal with me will never seem right. "I'm afraid that if we don't leave now, we will be late. Are you ready to go? Or do we need to reschedule your afternoon?"

Glancing at the clock, Uncle Emeric jumps up. "I had no idea that so much time had passed. Please don't be late on my account. I'll see you at dinner." As I'm shooed out of the room, I feel lighter than I have in a while. The huge weight of this first meeting has been lifted, and I can move on from this.

Chapter Thirty-Seven

A quick lunch later, Tilde and I set out. The warm sun of the spring day demands we walk to my appointment, guards following like puppies. I've spent so much time wandering the cobblestone streets around the palace that they feel like an extension of my home. Shops, cafés, and homes line the ribboning streets, each with their own unique character. As a child, I loved playing hide and seek here, neighborhood and palace children alike joining in. It was so much simpler then. No one cared about rank. No one cared what type of fae their playmate was.

At once, I'm struck by what I see. The streets don't sound the same. The adults are still here, greeting us and calling out, but the children are all gone. There's no joy, no laughter. The last time I walked these streets, they were filled to bursting with fae from all kingdoms, here for the Council. It masked the absence of little feet running, inquisitive minds imagining, and the camaraderie that these streets evoked. I try discussing this with Tilde, but as she only came here after we met at Sabaid, the change doesn't seem as drastic.

The bright turquoise door of Porvi's shop opens as we approach it. Another customer steps out, and after a quick goodbye to Porvi, she slams to a halt.

"Your Highness," she squeaks out and sinks into an incredibly low curtsy. She's lovely; dark mahogany curls frame a round face, anchored with deep brown eyes. Her clothes are well-made and cared for, but obviously old.

"Hello, I hope your meeting with Porvi went well." I gesture inside. "She's the best seamstress ever, and I know you'll be pleased with her work."

Her eyes meet mine before rapidly dropping her head. "I'm sure I will, Your Highness. I'm to be married soon. I've saved and saved for this dress," she rushes out, clearly more comfortable now that she remembers the reason for being here. "My Riko and I haven't had the easiest of times in the last few years. What with having to take care of my father after he got hurt and couldn't work anymore. And then my Riko lost his job when the factory owner found out his best friend wasn't high fae. But he did find a job at a grocer's and we finally managed to save up enough to get married.

"I was going to make my own dress, but he insisted that we use some of the money to buy me a dress. I make all our own clothes, you see, and I couldn't justify spending the money." She breaks off. If the smile on her face and the faraway look in her eyes are any indication, she's remembering that conversation. "But he said that he insisted, and that I deserved it." The color from her face suddenly drains. "Oh, Your Highness." She curtsies even lower now. "You didn't want to hear all that. I'm so sorry. Please forgive me."

She hustles out of the way, trying to flee. Placing my hand on her arm, she stills instantly. "Please don't apologize. I always love meeting new fae. I wish you all the happiness in your marriage. Your Riko sounds like a great male. May Astrid bless you." She curtsies once more, then takes off running, her curls bouncing with every step.

"That woman is very much in love with her male," Porvi exclaims, closing the door behind us.

"For the love of all the gods, please send me the bill for her dress. There's no way I can let her pay for it," I insist.

"And some lingerie for her as well," Tilde says with a wink. "Help her and Riko keep that spark alive."

"Done," Porvi says and gestures to the sitting area. "Although if she did make that dress, I may also have to give her a job. The needlework on it was exquisite. Now, about your wedding dress. Tell me your ideas, and I'll tell you no, then make you something even better."

Laughing, I do just that. No matter what Porvi designs, it will be absolutely amazing. She always seems to know me better than I know myself.

The soft crackling from the fire has provided my background music for tonight, only occasionally broken up by the popping of sap. I've been trying to read all night, but my thoughts keep straying. Setting my book on the table next to my bed, I rub my eyes. The day's been long and very enlightening. Porvi told us that more and more fae have been pushed out of the area. Some are due to being common, some fleeing to what they deem safer.

Things have gotten much worse than I'd ever imagined. In addition to Uncle Emeric making it illegal for common fae to come into the kingdom without his prior approval, he's also been pushing for segregation. Anyone having contact with fae who've lost their powers must be quarantined and pay a large fine. It's made many of the high fae shun their neighbors. Parents are even refusing to let their children play with others for fear of this.

I also discovered that common fae have started to go missing at an alarming rate. Those who have sought help to find their loved ones have met dead ends and apathetic authorities unwilling to look into the matter. I have to fix this, but I don't know how until I'm crowned. I'm worried how much worse things will get before then. It's not like I can talk with Uncle Emeric about it. He's the reason it's gotten so bad.

I need a distraction. I'm about to reach for my book again, but decide against it. I know of a better distraction. I open the door to Conaill's room in my mind. Softly, in case he's sleeping, I whisper, *Con?*

Instantly, I relax, and my heart lifts when I sense his presence. *Hey, Red. I missed you. How did your meeting go?*

I let it all out, divulging not only how the meeting went, but also what I found out. It's like once I start, I can't stop. Words tumble out until none are left. *I don't know what to do, Con.*

I know, Red, I know. But don't worry. We'll fix this. We'll make it right. In a few short months, we'll be married, and you'll be officially crowned. Make it one of your first official acts. Get rid of Emeric's shitty laws and rules. Punish those who are abusing power and reward those who are trying to help.

Snuggling deeper into my bed, as if that's the solution to my problems, I think about what Conaill said and how I might go about doing it. *It's easier said than done. I've known some of these fae for years, for my whole life. What do I do with Uncle Emeric?*

His growl floods the bond, and my lips tip up at his protectiveness. *Well, if it were up to me, I'd let Mina take care of him like she did Lukavo. Then, I'd chop him into little pieces and leave him to rot. But… that's me. He isn't my uncle. I didn't use to trust him or count on him. I know it isn't easy, Red, but he does need to be punished.*

I know. I sigh. *I really do. It's just hard to reconcile the Uncle Emeric I knew with what I've found out about him. It's like they're two different males.*

Even though Conaill is far away, I feel his comforting presence. It feels like he's pulling me in and holding me safe in his strong arms. *Maevery, I'll support you. No matter what. You want to forgive and forget? I've got you. Gods, I really hope you don't want that option though. You want him dead? I'll sharpen your happy daggers for you. Want to lock him up forever? I'll build him a jail and throw away the key. Whatever you want, I'm here to support you.*

Con. I say, hoping he can feel me right now. *I fucking love you.*

I fucking love you too. His laughter ripples down the bond. *Now, let's distract you. Tell me about your wedding dress.*

Absolutely not, I reply. *You have to wait. Plus… I have no idea.*

What? he asks. *Didn't you meet with your seamstress to tell her what you wanted?*

Yes, but Porvi always does whatever she wants. It always turns out better than what I thought I wanted, I admit.

He laughs again. *Fine, ask me anything.*

Anything?

Well, anything I can give you an answer to, he amends.

I think for a moment. There's so much I want to know, but I'm not really sure what I want to ask right now. I for sure want to avoid anything that could be heavy. Neither of us need that right now. Finally, I settle with asking something I've been wondering about for a while. *How did you and Madok become friends? Seeing how you're from two different kingdoms and all.*

Ah, that. Well, to tell you the truth, it took a while. He's upbeat, so I know I chose wisely. *His parents were used to be Umbrimina's ambassadors in Kystenvar. We were born in the same year, so we were always thrown together. Grew up together, in fact, and hated each other the whole time.*

What? I interrupt. In no world would I imagine those two as anything other than the best of friends.

He laughs. *Yeah, he was such an annoying shit. Plus, his parents actually loved him. I mean, I know Mom loves me, but Dad? He only loves what I can do for him. Anyway, they doted on him. Let him actually have fun and be a kid. As the crown prince, I never got any of that. I'm sure you know what it's like being raised to be the next ruler.*

I do, actually. *Yeah, Iskra had some of the same lessons as me, but I always had way more. She also gets so much leniency.*

Exactly! He pauses briefly. *It made me resent him. Plus, Madok is crazy smart. He may not seem like it, but he loves learning. We shared a private tutor, and he never had to study. I was always compared to him. Always made to feel stupid. I know I'm not stupid, but I did struggle in science and math. I had to study and work my ass off. Beyond that, he was always playing pranks.*

I see that hasn't changed. I laugh, extinguishing my fae lights.

Not in the least. He chuckles. *I seemed to be the brunt of them, too. Even if they were mostly harmless. Anyway, when the time came for mandatory service, I was ecstatic. He'd go back to Umbrimina for good, and I wouldn't be stuck with him. Cut to my first service station, and who should walk in? Madok. In an annoying twist of fate he was also stationed there. About a month in, we were in the field when wraiths attacked.*

I gasp. I've never actually seen a wraith, but you don't grow up in Panellas without being scared of them. They're death-bringers. Skeletal and tall, a haggard black cloak covers their withering flesh and sinew. Shrunken faces are dominated by fully black eyes devoid of life. Only the Dochais and Tinuvar can kill a wraith; they're able to heal from everything else. It's part of the reason other kingdoms put up with Saetoris's horribleness. So far, Tinuvar has only been found there. If they stop supplying the other kingdoms, we'll have no defense against them, especially not with the Dochais gone. A shudder rolls through my body. *Are they like what we're taught?*

Worse. He confirms. *I had just stabbed one in the heart with my Tinuvar blade when it got stuck. It lodged in the ribs, and I couldn't free it. Another one chose that moment to attack me. I had nothing; only a dagger of steel remained. He had me flat on my back. His gnarled, bony hands encircled my throat, and he was about to take my magic. I tried to cut him with my dagger, but it was like he couldn't feel it. My vision started to flicker out when a loud battle cry rang across the field. It was unlike anything I'd ever heard. Suddenly, beautiful air filled my lungs. Relief coursed through me, even if I was drenched in wraith blood.*

Madok's parents had given him a sword with a Tinuvar core before he left. He'd cut its head clean off. Then he simply reached out a hand and helped me up. Laughing floods the bond, and I'm so confused.

How is any of that funny? I question him.

It isn't. It's what he said to me, that is, he says. *I remember him saying, "Welp, fuck. Let's get a pint and make up a better story for how you got yourself covered in wraith blood. Can't have the future king not be the hero." Ended up doing just that. Insisted I take the glory. I guess he was always such a brat because he felt bad for me and wanted to draw attention away from me. He even rolled around in the wraith blood, so he looked just as bad.*

I laugh, totally imagining Madok doing something like that. We continue talking late into the night. So late, the fire is down to embers. I'm drifting in and out when Conaill sends me an image of our last night together. I'm falling asleep, just as I am now, and he's bending down to kiss my head, muttering that he loves me.

Chapter Thirty-Eight

The speed at which my routine falls back into place is astonishing. Each morning, Mionnan and I ride on whatever path he has decided we will take. Sometimes he wants to run and be free, so we head to the nature parks surrounding the palace, or one of those interspersed through the capital. Sometimes, he chooses to amble leisurely through the city streets. How he picks where we go is a mystery to me. Somehow, every city walk he chooses sheds light on fae needing the Order's help, or a problem that I can actually do something about now.

After our walk, it's a quick breakfast followed by some sort of training. Usually, I rotate through hand-to-hand, weapon, or boring but necessary future queen lessons. It's these lessons I dread the most. Since I was little, I always knew I would be queen one day, although I never imagined it would happen so soon. My schooling was tailored for my future role, making the majority of these lessons redundant.

Sometimes we go over geopolitics, sometimes we delve into Fenshegus's economics and its imports/exports. Law and history lessons are my least favorite. Not that I don't enjoy history; it's my family's history, after all. I just can't help but notice how far we've strayed from what our original lawmakers and kings intended. At the end of each of these lessons, I find myself repeating the same mantra. *Soon. Soon I can right the wrongs; soon I can help the helpless. Soon, I can truly make a difference.*

Lunch is next in the city and one of the more enjoyable parts of my day. Each day, I try to pick a different establishment owned by hard-working, everyday fae, be they common or high. I relish finding unknown spots. Where the food is made with love by those who want to share it. I want my status as a princess to mean something, to help those I can. Even if that simply means increased traffic for the proprietors from having a princess give her stamp of approval.

I fill my afternoons with social obligations, charity work, and sneaking in as much Order work as I can. A spiderweb of connections throughout the city holds everything in place for the Order, allowing me to fill the pockets of those who can get supplies. I've found that I can help ease the burden of the fines and lost wages during quarantine from the asinine new law Uncle Emeric enacted. I'm fast running out of easily disposable money, though. It won't be long until the male in charge of organizing and keeping track of the royal purse strings will notice and inform Uncle Emeric. But until the day comes, I refuse to think too hard about it. When I'm able to sneak away, I practice my powers in the nearest hidden spot before returning for the evening obligations.

Evenings have been the least routine, with no two evenings alike in a row. When I'm able, I try to eat dinner with friends in the palace. Many times, though, I've been forced to eat with Uncle Emeric, and I don't know if I've ever been so grateful for Saori. Both the ring and the brooch have saved me many times from consuming the suppression potion. It seems every other night is another formal dinner where they have also come in handy.

Regardless of what's going on, each day ends with mind-speaking with Conaill. Sometimes our talks are heavy and deep. Sometimes, silly banter and simple conversations fill our minds. Other times, we share our pasts. These talks have allowed us to grow closer, even when we're so far away.

A few times after dinner, Uncle Emeric has met with me to discuss and plan my upcoming wedding and subsequent coronation. I'm honestly astounded by how open he is with planning these. Especially in light of his reluctance prior to the Council of Pan, and the fact that he's been responsible for my suppressed magic for years. Yet, each meeting has gone surprisingly well. While Conaill and I were on our official engagement journey, it seems Uncle Emeric started planning everything.

My birthday is June twenty-fourth, three days after the summer solstice. As the summer solstice is one of the five major holidays that all of Panellas celebrate, Uncle Emeric decided to use this as the midway point between the wedding and the coronation. The wedding will take place one week before the solstice. The coronation will be four days after the solstice. Allowing me to celebrate my birthday as its own day, according to him.

It's considerations like that which have me so confused. Why be so kind in so many different ways, and yet still have me suppressed? It's a question I've asked myself ad nauseam. As well as discussing it with Mina, Tilde, and Conaill. None of us can figure it out, but we know he must be up to something.

Uncle Emeric planned everything except for some details and personal touches he'd like me to make. The color of the decorations. What kind of flowers do I want? Peonies, obviously. Who I want as my attendants. What are my food and dessert choices? The questions are basic, but they do allow me to make the ceremonies my own. Especially as the coronation is extremely structured, with the actual wedding only slightly less so.

Personal interpretation is not welcome at the coronation. It's a ceremony that dates back thousands and thousands of years. Meticulously structured, and most is dictated by law. Fenshegus weddings are very small and personal, with only immediate family and two attendants on each side. Only the reception after the wedding allows any personalization. The wedding dinner is where true extravagance can occur.

Conaill and I have talked extensively about what choices to make. It isn't only my wedding reception, but his as well. Lately, when I want Conaill to have a say in something, I tell Uncle Emeric I need to think about it. This gives me enough time to mind-speak with Conaill so he can be part of the planning. Of course, I can't let Uncle Emeric know what I've been doing, so creative phrasing has been very important. So far, everything's gone smoother than I expected, so I make sure to squeeze out a little time each week and make an extra offering at whichever god's temple I think is helping out at the time.

With how full my days are, it doesn't surprise me that over a month has passed since I returned to Otthon. The wedding is only three weeks away, and my nerves are as frayed as a dog's tug rope. I haven't seen Conaill since the day after the blessing, and I won't see him again until the day before the wedding. Our constant mind-speaking is the only thing that has helped me get through the days.

The nerves aren't just for the wedding or coronation, though. Each day, I see more and more injustice. News is constantly reaching us of more and more common fae losing their power. How can we just sit here and do nothing? How can any of the kingdoms?

Red, Conaill's smooth voice floods my mind. *Are you stressing again? Everything will be fine. You'll always look beautiful. Go ahead and stress eat whatever you want right now.*

Oh, shut it, Con! My reply comes automatically. Once, just once, I let it slip that I was worried I'd look fat the next time he saw me due to all my stress eating. He promised me I wouldn't, and even if I gained weight, he'd still find me sexy. He then sent me image after image of exactly what he wanted to do to me when we were together next. Even now, my core's damp just thinking of it.

Seriously, Red, what are you stressing about? Concern is evident in his soothing voice.

Just how fucked everything is. Walking into the Lousy Lord, I pause for a moment. Pressing my back against the gray stone wall, I scan the interior, hoping to ground myself. The fae lights are bright and welcoming. Perfect for the lunchtime crowd scattered throughout, congregating in twos, threes, and fours. Each table is an isolated island; its inhabitants are only worried about their immediate island's concerns. Most seem to be joyful, with only a few serious islands. The rich aroma of meaty stew reaches me, and my stomach grumbles, adding its own contribution to the low hum of talking fae.

Navigating to the dark wooden bar, I smile and portray my worry-free princess facade. *Like, how can we really make a difference when so many are affected? When the kingdoms aren't even doing anything, how can we as individuals?* Turning from pulling a pint, Merl spots me and gestures to the room he reserves for us, and I trudge toward it.

Red, first of all, we are making a difference. His voice is commanding and firm. Making sure I know that even though he isn't physically here, he means what he says. *For every single fae we help, we're making a difference. I also just finished meeting with Darius. His dad just officially declared that Baress will take refugees from any kingdom, regardless of what type of fae they are. Emperor Callen* is *doing something.*

One kingdom? That isn't enough. I lament, accepting the proffered glass from Mina. Taking a long swig, I welcome the sweet, crisp flavor invading my mouth. *I know it's better than nothing, and in three weeks Fenshegus will join them, but two out of seven kingdoms?*

Maevery, do you honestly think Darius and Emperor Callen are the only ones who have the same thoughts and beliefs in their family? He asks.

"Thank you, Mina," I say, tipping my glass. "Just give me a minute, please. I'm talking with Con."

She waves me off. "No worries, Mae. Take your time. I've got Daire to keep me company." It's only then that I spot Teachdaire purring contentedly on her lap.

"You're going to be covered in hair." I laugh, but reach out to pet him, too.

"Eh, who cares?" she continues to stroke him with one hand, refilling our glasses from the pitcher with the other.

Sorry, I just got to the Lousy Lord, I apologize unnecessarily. We both understand that we can't ignore everything around us just to speak. *To answer your question, no, I don't think they're the only kind ones in their family. But what does that have to do with anything?*

Seriously, Red? Who is Darius's sister? He asks, clearly flabbergasted at my response.

It takes me a moment to understand his implication. *Oh my gods. Con, I'm so stupid.* Darius's sister is Queen Aydana of Nuwen.

Conaill's rich laughter fills my head, and gods, do I miss him. *You aren't stupid, just stressed. Darius told me Nuwen has also opened its borders for refugees. They're offering free medical evaluations and testing to those who've lost their powers. They're looking for a cause and a cure.*

My shoulders drop, a small measure of relaxation running through me. *That does make me feel better. I mean, they have the best medical university in Panellas, and Leighis is their patron goddess.*

I agree, Conaill says. *It isn't enough. Not by any means. But the Order isn't alone. Madok can't say much, but his parents told him Umbrimina is also going to be doing something about it in the next few days.*

Wait, I thought they weren't ambassadors anymore? How do they know? I ask in confusion.

Conaill's response is immediate. *According to Madok, they're super close with King Ewan and Queen Dia. I think that his dad and Queen Dia grew up together. I haven't heard anything about Samaith, but given what I heard during the Council of Pan, I'm sure they're on our side.*

So it's only Fenshegus, Kystenvar, and Saetoris that aren't doing anything. I say, feeling slightly better. In less than a month, Fenshegus will be off that list, leaving only two kingdoms.

Conaill snorts. *I'd actually say they're reaping the benefits of it. I can't fucking stand it. Each day, it's harder and harder to keep my mask on.*

I know, Con. I'm so sorry you have to do it. I break off as Merl enters with two huge steaming bread bowls full of savory stew. "This smells amazing. Thank you so much, Merl."

"Seriously, Merl," Mina agrees. "Daire, go to your dad. I'm about to devour this and don't want to drip on you." Teachdaire hops off and stretches before prancing to Merl.

"You're more than welcome, Your Highness, milady." Merl bows low, even though I've told him it's unnecessary in private. "Let me know when you're done, and I'll tell you about the new… wine shipment I just got in. I think you'll like some of the vintages."

"Absolutely," I say, understanding Merl's code. *Con, I'm so glad I have you to help me make Fenshegus everything I know it can be. That being said, I have to go now, Con. I'm sorry.*

No worries, Red. I need to focus on this boring meeting, anyway. I love you, Maevery. He sends me an image of himself winking while holding out a rose.

Snorting, I send one of me giving him my favorite, yet very improper, one-finger salute. Through his laughter, I say, *all kidding aside. I love you, Con. Remember, I'll be your anchor. Please reach out to me when you need it. Despite how it seems today, I can take it.*

His laughter dies as he replies, *I know, Red. I'll always be your anchor, too. I love you. See you soon!*

Dipping into my stew, I turn my focus back on Mina. "Sorry about that."

"You should be," she says, affronted. "You two are so in love it's disgusting. But I'm just saying that because I'm jealous." She digs her spoon into her stew, pulling out a steaming chunk of meat and vegetables. She pauses to blow on it, then says, "Seriously, if you find a worthy male like Conaill, send him my way. I could use a male like that in my life. And my bed."

"What about Madok? He seems to have a thing for you," I say around a mouthful of potato perfection.

Mina chokes on her stew, glaring at me. "How dare you say anything so vile? He's everything I'm not. I couldn't be with a graceless lout like that. He never takes anything seriously. It'd drive me to an early grave." She shudders, and I laugh.

"Come on, he isn't so bad. And he's not a lout," I implore.

"Okay, that was bad of me. He isn't a lout, but he drives me crazy. He's just… not right for me." Tearing off a chunk of the bread bowl, she dips it in the stew, soaking up some before popping it in her mouth.

"Okay, I'll concede that," I admit. "I can't actually see you two together long term. But… you could always take him for a ride?" I waggle my eyebrows at her, eliciting a laugh.

"Please. That male wouldn't know what to do with a female as awesome as me." She winks and drains her wine.

We finish lunch, gossiping like old times. Afterward, Merl joins us and throws up a silencing shield. I let them know what Conaill shared with me, and their relief is palpable. Merl informs us that he just took in a group of fifteen kinnara. Five of whom have lost their powers.

Mina's visibly upset at this, and I understand why. The kinnara are a completely harmless race. A beautiful, high fae-like appearance graces their upper bodies, while their lower bodies resemble those of a bird. They even have wings along their backs. They have a magical affinity for music and can make the most beautiful songs. Overall, the kinnara are a peaceful race and have never been known to hurt another.

Merl's struggling to find housing until they can be moved out of the city. Without music, Kinnara struggle and weaken. He's had to move them every other day as they can't go long without making some sort of music and long-term sound shields aren't possible. Putting all our heads together, we're able to come up with an acceptable solution that will hopefully keep them safe. At least until we can get them to a boat bound for one of the safe kingdoms.

As Mina and I make our way back to the palace, I realize I'm feeling a bit better. Earlier, I could only focus on what was going wrong. How hopeless everything felt. But with the help of Conaill, Mina, and Merl, I'm finally starting to see some light.

Chapter Thirty-Nine

The longer we've been apart, the more we seek each other out.

Hey, you. A loud voice booms from Conaill's room in my mind.

Startling, I spill the stain I was using. *Damn it, Con.* I laugh lightly. *You made me spill my stain. Now I have to make up more before I can finish these slides.*

Finally able to carve out a little time, I've spent the greater portion of the afternoon in the best laboratory in Otthon, Lorg Laboratories. Given my title, I always knew I couldn't become a scientist. Well, at least not as a career. I had amazing tutors and professors, though, and when I was old enough, they introduced me to Dr. Eszez. Seeing my passion, she made sure there was always a spot for me in her lab to help.

Sorry, Red. His tone suggests he isn't really all that sorry. *What are you working on for Dr. Eszez?*

Well, I was about to stain cells from fae who've lost their power. Tossing the cleaning rag back, I make more stain and go back to work. *We're trying to see if there are any changes on a cellular level. We know it's a stretch, but we're not sure where else to go.*

You'll get it, Red. Your amazing brain is only second to that sensational ass of yours on my list of your top attributes. His seriousness is ruined when his laugh bursts forth.

Uh-huh. Sure. Setting the samples down, I head to the sink to wash up. *I have to focus now, go away. Love you.*

Yes, Your Highness, he says, sarcasm dripping from every word. *Love you, Red.*

Two days later, I'm winding through bustling streets on my way to an appointment with Porvi when I decide to reach out. *Boo!*

Seriously, Maevery! I can't help but smile when he responds, somehow sounding both happy and pissed simultaneously. *You just made me jump in the middle of a Council meeting.*

Laughter tumbles out of my mouth, and I ignore the curious stares of those I pass. My guards are so used to my seemingly random outbursts of laughter that they aren't phased anymore. *Poor baby. I'll make it up to you when I see you.*

You'd better, he growls.

What's being discussed? I ask, genuinely.

He sighs before answering. *How Dad can funnel money earmarked for underprivileged fae into building a new summer house for his latest mistress. I'm trying to figure out how to prevent it.*

Doing my best not to physically shudder in revulsion, I say, *I'll let you focus on that then, so you figure it out.*

Thanks, Red, he says gratefully. *I really need to stop this.*

Con, it's okay. And truthfully, it is, but that doesn't stop me from teasing. *I mean, I was going to ask you to help me pick out lingerie. I'm not really sure what looks best on me. I was thinking of sending you images when I tried them on. Get your opinion on what looks best.* I say as seductively as possible. *But I agree, you do need to focus.*

Wait. What? Maevery, it isn't that important. I'll just pull the money out of my accounts. He rushes out. *Please, Mae. For the love of all the gods, please.*

You know, I kind of like it when you beg. I giggle. *But, no. You're the crown prince. Your subjects must come before lingerie. I'll just buy it all. Lace. Leather. Bows. Silk. I'll get some of everything. Love you!* Then I very firmly shut the door to his room in my mind.

Payback comes calling a few days later. Daggers flying from my fingertips, a practice target showing just how precise I can be when Conaill's deep voice fills my head. *I have a present for you.*

Really? I squeal excitedly. I mean, who doesn't like presents?

I do. It's in your bedroom. I have to go now, but let me know what you think. His caress flutters along our bond, and then he's gone. It's so tempting to end my training session early, but I can't. When it's finished, twenty minutes later, I rush up to my room.

You've got to be kidding me. I shove this thought at him when I see my room. Laughter is the only response I get.

Roses fill my room. Thousands of roses, all in different colors. No surface is safe. Even my bathroom wasn't safe. Throwing open the window, I toss them out, completely not caring about raining roses on any unsuspecting fae that walks by. That night, any lingering annoyance vanishes when I find a perfect peony resting gently on my pillow.

I'm eating lunch a few days later when Conaill asks, *If you could change one thing about you, what would it be?*

Easy, my height, I respond, then think better of it. *Wait, no. I'd make my boobs smaller. You?*

Blasphemy! Conaill gasps. *Your boobs are perfect. In fact, I'm missing your perfect tits right now.* It makes me laugh, and I almost miss his answer. *My hair. It's too wavy. Unless I have it super short, it gets in my eyes. I don't like how I have to get it cut constantly.*

His hair is always flopping into his eyes, but damn if it doesn't make him sexier. *I happen to like it when it does that.*

Please, Red, help me. Conaill sends two days later.

What now? I respond, rolling my eyes.

My dad is insisting that I find myself a stable mistress. Dad even wants to put forth a bunch of candidates, he says.

Multiple pairs of eyes fly to me as I choke on my wine. *Conaill, you can't drop something like that on me. I'm in the middle of dinner with a bunch of courtiers and ambassadors.*

And I was supposed to know that how? I picture Conaill rolling his eyes as he says that. *And seriously, help. I've tried everything, and he won't relent.*

I sip some wine, thankfully not choking this time, and apologize to those around me. *Well, then you can tell your father that, should he ever introduce a female to you with that intention, I'll happily make it so that he's never able to play with his favorite toy again. And I won't even clean the castration clamps first.*

Gods, Maevery. A shudder is evident in Conaill's voice. *Polemas must love how bloodthirsty you are.*

I shrug, even though I know he can't see it. *You're mine, and I don't share. Not going to apologize for that. And if it helps, just tell your pig of a father that I said I would do that to you if you were ever as indiscreet as he is. He'll never buy it if you say I won't let you have a mistress. At least not as long as we still have to pretend not to like each other.*

He's much more relaxed when we mind-speak later that night. Even if, according to his father, he needs to let me know who's really in charge, and installing an official mistress is the perfect way to do that. I make a mental note to visit the temples of Leighis and Sofiya. Surely one of their many acolytes, priests, or priestesses will know of something I can put in Tavarik's wine to make him impotent. At worst for a while, at best for the rest of his life.

Con? I all but scream into his room in my mind. It's early, but I've been up for hours. The rug beneath my feet silences each of the steps in what feels like miles of pacing. But, for all that the plush fabric has cradled my feet on this journey of dread, I can't feel it. I can't feel the damp fabric of my nightgown clinging to my clammy, sweat-soaked skin. Or the tendrils of hair that have escaped my braid and are now glued to the nape of my neck. Do I need to add wood to the fire? Or maybe I should smother it? Gods, I can't even tell what the temperature in my room is. I'm completely numb.

Dread dances along each of my senses. It's all I can feel. All I can taste and smell. Each breath pulls it further into me. Rooting it so deep, I don't know if I'll ever be able to rid myself of it completely. Tendrils of dread snake along my body, firing each nerve they pass. Each brush of my nightgown, each time my foot connects with this stupid rug, it isn't fabric that I feel caressing my skin. It's dread, clamping down on my skin and successfully finding a new spot to bury itself deep within me.

Con? Please. Can you hear me? Panic fills the words as rivulets of escaped tears flow freely down my cheeks. I try to see the time, but my eyes are too watery to make anything out. I've just finished swiping at my eyes when I hear the only sound capable of exercising any of the dread from my body.

Maevery, baby, what's wrong? His words are sharp, and he's definitely alert, even if they still contain the gravel of sleep.

Con! I collapse in relief, a puddle unable to move. *I don't know. I don't know.*

His caress comes through the bond, but it isn't comforting like it normally is. I know it's there. My mind recognizes the concept, but I can't feel the warmth that comes from it. As if that was the final raindrop falling into a too-full lake, all the cracks give way, breaking the dam, and sending utter carnage into the unsuspecting forest on the other side. I'm caught in the rushing water. Each time I break the surface, I'm thrown into more debris and pulled back under.

Sobs rack my body so hard that there's no way my muscles won't be sore later. Wrapping my arms around my body, I try to hold myself together. I refuse to let this dread drag me down and drown me.

Time passes, the light in my room increasing in a gentle cascade. The black of night transitions to a deep blue, casting the room in an eerie glow. It isn't long before the glow mutates; my room is now filled with the fiery red of early dawn. Through it all, I'm aware of Conaill's presence in my mind. Constantly reaching out to me, knowing there's nothing he can do but be here for me.

Just as the light in my room is reaching the blush that signals the arrival of the golden warmth of day, I notice a rope in my mind. With all my might, I swim against the current, desperate to reach the lifeline. When I'm close enough, I see a huge silver and gold anchor attached. As my hand makes contact, the water slows, and I register the hauntingly beautiful song for the first time. I've never heard the rich baritone, but I know without a doubt that Conaill is singing for me.

I let the unfamiliar words wash over me. The rise and fall seeking out the dread, cauterizing its hold, and chasing it away. When the voice has liberated me from all but the smallest scrap of dread, I push my aching body up and slump against the foot of the bed. Conaill's voice wavers, his tension easing, when I mentally reach out for him, but he doesn't stop. He sings the song through once more before falling silent.

Chapter Forty

I'm so sorry, Con. I have no idea what that was about. My voice is small and meek, even though no actual words escape my lips.

His reply is instant and firm. *Don't you dare apologize. I never want to hear you apologize for anything like this again. Do you understand?*

But, Con… I start, but I'm cut off almost instantly.

Maevery, listen very carefully. There are no buts. You will NEVER apologize to me for something like this again. Dominance and authority emanate from his tone. *I am your mate. You're mine. Mine to cherish. Mine to love. Mine to take care of. It's my privilege to do, to be, whatever you need me to be. Just as you would do for me. Got it?*

I nod, murmuring my assent.

Gods, Maevery. I was so scared. I know it must have been nothing compared to what you were going through. I could feel your panic and terror. I didn't know how to reach you. He pauses, silent for a second before continuing. *Are you okay, Red? Can you, or rather, do you want to tell me what happened?*

I let my head fall back against the intricately carved plum wood, pulling my knees to my chest. I'm reminded that my nightgown is drenched in sweat when I try to hug my knees closer. Groaning in disgust, I turn and try to find a handhold to pull myself up. When I finally stand up, I head to the bathroom to clean up.

I'm okay now, I assure him. *And honestly? I have no idea what that was. Nothing like that has ever happened to me before.*

I've made it, albeit slowly, to the sink in my bathroom and reach to turn the water on. Right now, I'm so thankful for the fae responsible for indoor plumbing. My nightgown falls to the floor, and using the cloth hanging next to the sink, I attack the drying sweat.

I don't really know how it started. I just woke up, dread taking over my whole body. My heart was beating so hard I thought it would beat out of my chest. I felt like I couldn't get a lungful of air, even though I was able to breathe. I couldn't, still can't, figure out what was wrong.

Padding naked to the hook next to the bath, I encase myself in my robe. Using it like armor against the memory of the night. I do my best to explain what I felt, but I know I'm failing. I've just returned to my bedroom when Saori knocks and enters. She halts, still as a statue, taking in the disarray of my bed and the obviously worn path my feet trod over the night. Nose flaring slightly, she must register the stale sweat that's permeated the room. Sitting in the high-backed chair near the fireplace, I shake my head, running my fingers over the celadon velvet that covers the arm.

Do you have any idea what caused this? Conaill asks softly. *Did something happen yesterday, or last night, that might have triggered a nightmare you don't remember?*

I think hard for a minute. *Nothing. I can't honestly think of anything. I just feel… I know something is wrong. I can't explain it. I have this feeling deep in my gut.*

I thought you said the dread went away? Conaill asks, confusion evident.

It did. It's gone. But… I break off, trying to figure out how to phrase what I'm feeling. *I just have this feeling, the sense. No, that isn't right. I have this… knowing inside me that something horrible happened. It must have been what woke me up. But as soon as I woke up, dread hooked its claws in me and took control.*

It wasn't until I saw the rope you must have thrown me that I was able to get even a semblance of control. And when I touched the anchor, your voice broke through. I just held on and let the song wash everything away. I sit, staring at nothing, when a gentle weight settles on my shoulders. Jumping, I realize it's Saori's hand and place mine on top, holding her in place. Sympathy and compassion fill her eyes.

She gestures to the tea tray I've only now noticed is on the table next to me. "Let me know if you should need anything, Your Highness. I just tested everything, but I can do it again if you didn't see me." She says, using the same voice one might use when trying to calm a skittish foal.

"No," I croak. Clearing my throat, I try again. "No, I trust you implicitly, Saori. Thank you. And please, no need to call me Your Highness. Not when it's just the two of us."

She squeezes my shoulder gently. "Okay. Please let me know if you need anything, Maevery. For now, I'll go make sure you aren't disturbed by anyone else until you let me know otherwise." I smile my thanks and nod before she turns and walks out.

As the rim of the porcelain teacup touches my lip, a thought strikes me. I reach out, hoping he's still there. *Con?*

Relief flows through me at his instantaneous reply. *I'm right here, Red.*

You were singing in a different language. What was it? I ask softly, trying to recall the words.

A moment passes before he replies, and when he does, it's almost shyly. *It's… It's ancient Umbriminian. Mom's from there. Another reason Madok and I were always put together. It's a tradition in her family to keep the language alive. So, when I was little, she taught it to me. Madok and his parents also speak it. I think that helped Mom out a lot, especially when they were assigned as ambassadors. She finally had friends around who she could talk to about my asshole of a dad.* He scoffs, his building anger filling his room in my mind.

Real friends who wouldn't run off to tell Dad. No one else understood it, so even if they spoke out in the open, nothing they said would be reported. Gods forbid it did. That would've for sure resulted in another beating for her. I gasp, which causes Conaill to pause.

Did… did you just say another beating? Conaill, does your dad beat her? I ask, even though I know I shouldn't.

It takes a minute, and when he answers, sadness is now woven with his anger. *Yeah. Has for as long as I've been alive, at least. He's always careful to do it where it won't leave marks. I told you I've tried to get her to leave him countless times. This is why. I was eight the first time I saw him hit her. I ran to her and threw my body in front of her like a shield. Guess I was trying to protect her.*

Anyway, he continues as if what he said isn't mind-blowing and heartbreaking. *Dad kicked me out of the way. Said he wouldn't have a soft-hearted son, and I needed to learn how to make sure I was always obeyed as a future king. Then, he had a guard hold me while he beat her. I fought to get free, to go protect her the whole time. My arms and legs were whirling and kicking, doing their best to fight and break free. Little as I was at the time, I was useless against a fully grown royal guard. I cried and screamed the whole time. Only stopping when he said he'd keep going until I could shut up and act like a "real male."*

I spent the next four days with her. Trying to take care of her. Doing everything the healer said to do. That was the first time I asked her, begged her, to leave him. I told her we could flee to Grammy and Grampy's. That they would take us in. She just shook her head and told me that as the future king, there was no way I'd be able to leave. Said she'd never leave me alone with that monster, and she'd happily take a million beatings if it meant I was safe from him.

Once again today, tears are streaming down my face. Only this time, they fall for the horror that a little boy and his mother had to endure. *Conaill, I'm so sorry.* I start.

Please don't apologize. He cuts me off. *It was a long time ago, and it's in the past. We got through it.* He's silent again, and I let it go.

Pushing a feeling of comfort toward him, I attempt to change the subject. *Your voice is beautiful, by the way.* He huffs out a laugh, and I can't help but ask, *What was the song you were singing? It sounded beautiful.*

He's silent for so long that, if it wasn't for the fact that I can feel his presence through our bond, I would've thought he'd left. When his answer comes, my heart fractures all over again. *It's a traditional Umbriminian lullaby. My mom used to sing it to me when I was a baby and then later when I was sick. I used to sing it to her when… Well, whenever she was hurt. It always seemed to help her, and I… I didn't know what else to do.*

Chapter Forty-One

Glares bore into me from every direction. The brightly lit room does nothing to hide my fidgeting. With only a few remaining Council sessions before I'm crowned, I can't blame them for the annoyance they must be feeling. I haven't been able to sit still all day. I've been struggling to focus on what's being discussed, and they've had to repeat themselves many times. Uncle Emeric trains a soft look on me. I'm sure he's interpreting my anxiousness as nerves about my wedding to Conaill tomorrow.

I have zero reservations about marrying Conaill, but I can't let him know that. I can't sit still because my body is alive with too much energy. Conaill let me know he was entering the palace right as the meeting started an hour ago. I wanted to rush out and into his arms. But I can't. I can't trust anyone here to know what I actually feel for him. At least I've perfected glamouring and no longer worry about anyone seeing the mating mark.

The rest of the meeting, I make a conscious effort to stop fidgeting and pay attention. The meeting is about the budget for next year, and given what they're discussing, I really should've been paying more attention. I'll never allow this budget to continue when I'm in charge.

As it stands now, it strips away too much from projects and charities aimed at helping citizens and the environment. I do not need another vacation house or monument to me. Only the plans to expand some universities sound good to me.

Three interminable hours, Uncle Emeric finally says, "I think that is all for now. We shall meet again in three days. Your Highness" — Uncle Emeric looks at me — "if you could please stay back for a moment?"

I nod as he sets everyone else free. Heavy chairs scrape against the wood floor as the advisers stand and bow to each of us in turn before filing out of the room.

As the door clicks shut, leaving us alone, Uncle Emeric begins, "I just wanted to say that I understand today and tomorrow will be hard. I've tried to arrange everything to minimize how much time you will need to interact with the prince. You've done a great job of hiding your real feelings, and I know the next two days will be especially hard."

Gods, he doesn't even know the half of it. Training my eyes over his shoulder, I study a painting of a meadow filled with picnicking courtiers. It's soft and lovely. Such a contradiction to what goes on in this room. Clearing my throat, I say as demurely as I can, "Yes, it will. I thank you for your consideration, Uncle." *Please be the end of this conversation.*

"It does help that we're honoring the Kystenvarian custom prohibiting you two from being alone together the day before the wedding." He chuckles, completely unaware that this is the exact opposite of what I actually want. Slightly awkwardly, he continues, "I… I also wanted to confirm that you want to walk down the aisle alone? I know I'm not your father… but I'd like to think my brother would want me to walk with you in his place."

Bas will take me before I ever let this male take what should rightfully be my father's place. He betrayed me. My father would be appalled at his brother's actions, both to me and this kingdom. But I can't say that. I can't say anything I'm feeling. So instead, I settle with, "Thank you. I really appreciate the offer. This is something I just need to do myself."

With a curt nod, he holds open the door, clearly dismissing me. "Well, if you change your mind, I'm here for you."

I plaster a saccharine smile onto my face before making my escape and dropping the farce of a smile as soon as I can. There's so much to complete before tomorrow, and no time to do it. I change course for the kitchen when my stomach reminds me that I haven't eaten today. When I find a servant on the way, I ask if she'd be able to let Mina and Tilde know to meet me in the kitchens instead of the pink sitting room. She runs off, and I continue.

Con? Where are you? I send the thought through our bond, and his response is strong and immediate.

I'm in the game room with Madok, Darius, and Calian. Getting my ass handed to me in cards. Give me a second. The frantic energy of the kitchen assaults my senses when I push the kitchen door open. My ears are greeted with a symphony full of the sounds of banging pots and pans, the chopping of meat and vegetables, and orders being shouted. I almost miss it when he asks, *What can I do for you, my love?*

Waving off the curtseys and bows, I ask for a simple lunch. They rush off, and I enter a small, attached dining chamber. When I respond, I'm very much aware I sound whiny.

Are you sure we can't sneak off anywhere? Please, I need you. I beg, sending him an image of me wearing a new set of lingerie that reveals more than it hides. His groan fills my mind. Quickly, I morph the image to one of me on my knees, my mouth worshipping him.

Fuck! Maevery, that isn't fair. Laughter bubbles out at the frustration in his voice. *Now, not only am I losing at cards, I'm doing so with a fucking hard on, as my friends call me pussy whipped.*

So, is that a no? I question.

When he answers me, his voice is soft. *It is. I actually like this tradition. Makes it more special when I finally get to have you alone.*

Fine. I huff, but get it. *Don't let them kick your butt too badly. I'll see you at dinner, I guess.*

He says goodbye as I'm presented with a simple but delicious lunch. I'm about to take a bite when the door swings open, Tilde and Mina bounding in.

"Hiding? Huh, never took you for a coward," Tilde chides.

"Seriously. We should kick her out of the Eighteen," Mina adds, her arms crossed. "Pretty sure 'No Cowards Allowed' was one of the rules."

Ripping my roll in half, I launch the pieces across the room. Ridiculously fast reflexes save both of them from a roll to the face. "Listen, here wenches." Throwing up a sound shield, I continue, "I just sat through a three-hour meeting where the only thing that was accomplished was the stroking of male egos. If I have to put on my simpering princess mask again before I eat, I'm liable to kill someone."

Taking their seats, Mina steals some of my fruit. "Fair point. You turn into a bitch when you're hungry," she says before popping a grape in her mouth.

Tilde quirks a brow. "So, she's always hungry?"

"Shut it wench." I laugh, sticking out my tongue.

The door opens, and a maid holding two plates enters. She curtsies and says, "Sorry to interrupt, Your Highness. I thought Lady Aphilomina and Lady Tildewynn would care for lunch as well."

Both Mina and Tilde thank her profusely before taking the plates, and then she's gone. We attack our lunches with a fervor that would disgust those fancy wedding guests I'm most definitely avoiding.

Chapter Forty-Two

Tap. Tap. Tap. Saori's hands still, the laces of my corset hanging limply from her fingers. We both look around, trying to find the source of the sound. The tapping comes again, and with it some of the tension I've been living with for days. Ever since the night I woke in complete panic, I've worried about Iskra. But the hawk tapping on the window can only be from her.

Saori rushes over, and the hawk holds out its leg, a tiny rolled missive attached. Iskra is the only one I haven't been able to reach since that night. Saori takes the missive, thanking the hawk before it flies off. My hands tear the parchment from her hands as she spins me back to the mirror.

"Now, can you finally relax some?" she asks. She's trying to be serious, but the huge grin on her face ruins the effect. Finishing my laces, she adds, "No fussing. I'm well aware you don't like corsets, but court dress demands it."

Huffing, I declare, "Well, I'll just have to make that one of the first things I fix." Ripping off the seal, I read Iskra's letter.

Mae,

I'm so sorry it took so long to write to you. I got your message just as we had to leave for a weekend navigation course, and I wasn't able to read it until we got back.

Thanks for sharing the tip about where to get study files. I'm doing great, and there's no need to worry. I'm doing well in all my classes. Well, all but one. But I'm not failing, so I won't worry you about it.

I wanted to let you know that I met someone. It isn't serious, well, at least not yet, but I think it could be. I really like him. His name is Fionn, and he's from Orom. When he gets out, he wants to go to university to become a science professor. It's his first time through Sabaid as well, so we have a lot of classes together. I was hoping I could introduce you to him when you come to graduation. I really, really like him.

I hate that I can't be there for your wedding. I hope you have the best day ever, and I know you'll be the most beautiful bride. Please tell Prince Conaill that if he hurts you, I'll hurt him. I need to go now. I have another survival course that starts tonight, and I need to pack for it. I'm actually excited for this one. I get to be paired with Fionn! I love you so much, Mae.

~Isk

My posture turns to complete crap as tension melts from my body. A sharp tug of the corset laces and a stern look from Saori force me to straighten again. With quick efficiency, she has me dressed and sparkling. My ears and throat drip with jewels perfectly matched to my pale blue gown. Iskra's fire opal bracelet adds a splash of her personality to my right wrist. The final touch is a stunning tiara. Diamonds peek from seven strands of gold, delicately woven together. Every movement causes them to wink at the viewer.

With confident hands, Saori places it on my head. The delicate weight somehow makes the next day and a half feel more real than it ever has.

"You look just like your mother," Saori murmurs, doing her best not to let her voice crack. Tears threaten to fall from her eyes, and I fight back my own as well.

"Don't you start that," I admonish. "If you cry, then I will. And it'll ruin my makeup."

With one hand, she wipes the unshed tears while waving me off with the other. "You'd better head out, Your Highness. Can't have you late tonight."

Just then, a knock sounds at the door. Quickly, I thank Saori and open the door. A monumental arrangement of roses fills the doorway. My jaw actually drops open, and I glare at the innocent flowers. *Seriously, Con? You know I hate roses,* I direct down our bond.

As laughter fills my mind, the roses start walking toward me. "This was waiting outside your door." Tilde strides in, Mina right behind her.

I love you. And I don't care how old we are or how long we've been together, Conaill's deep voice sends delightful shivers down my spine. *I'll always mess around with you and tease you. I think it'll keep us young. Don't throw them away, though. You're liable to kill some poor unsuspecting fae if you just chuck them out a window again.*

Shaking my head, I gesture for Tilde to place the flowers wherever. I insisted Tilde had today and tomorrow off from working as my royal guard. I need her with me as my friend, not as my watchdog. She refuses to actually relax, though, and I know she'll be constantly assessing and checking in.

Both she and Mina look stunning. They each wear gowns similar to mine, if less ornate. Tilde's gown is pale pink, with silver lace accents and embellished with thousands of seed pearls. Mina's pale jade gown doesn't have any embellishments apart from the jade and opal-encrusted cuffs, which connect the sheer cream sleeves to the bodice. I'm about to tell them how beautiful they look when I hear Conaill's voice through the bond again.

Do try to hurry up. I miss you and can't wait to see my devastatingly beautiful bride. A smile tilts my lips as my head tips down. I feel inexplicably shy at his words. *Just know, whatever I say, whatever I do, I'm beyond happy that I get the privilege of spending the rest of my life with you. I love you.*

"Ahh. I see Conaill has distracted Mae again." Mina's voice startles me, causing my head to pop up. Laughter fills the room, and my cheeks flush. Pulling my arm through hers, Mina leads me to the door and down the hall. "Come on, Mae. Let's put our bitch faces on and be mean to Conaill."

I can't help it. I throw my head back and laugh deeply, causing Tilde and Mina to do so as well. Stares of bewildered fae follow us as we make our way to the grand staircase, where Conaill and I will be greeting guests. Regrettably, so will Uncle Emeric and King Tavarik. *I love you too. And I apologize in advance.* I push the thought to Conaill.

We've barely managed to compose ourselves when the grand staircase comes into view. I falter, my heart skipping a beat as I catch sight of Conaill. He's even more handsome than the last time I saw him.

His thick, dark brown hair has grown out, making its waves more pronounced. It's meticulously styled, but that one section, just in the front, has fallen. I have to force myself not to go to him and brush that stubborn lock of hair back into place. Spotting me, he takes a quick look around, ensuring no one is watching, then winks. Knowing exactly what I want to do right now.

Con. You look so handsome. And sexy. Gods, do you look sexy. He chokes and then coughs slightly when my thoughts reach him.

I think you're just biased. I'm not nearly as sexy as you. Blush once again stains my cheeks at his words.

I'm not being biased, though. Everything he's wearing has been perfectly tailored to his body. The formal black jacket and pants accentuate his golden tan and muscular body. Braided black appliqués encircle the wrists of the jacket and climb up his forearms. His broad chest fills the jacket, his shoulders stretching the fabric taut. Did he get even more muscular during our time apart? The only color comes from a sash of gold, secured at his waist with an ornate onyx and diamond brooch. Onyx and diamonds also adorn a golden chain, stretching from shoulder to shoulder.

A slightly smaller onyx and diamond brooch attaches a short cape of black brocade over his left shoulder. A thin, braided, jet black cord drapes across his chest, stretching from the brooch at his shoulder to under his right arm, holding the cape in place and leaving his right arm free. As I walk closer, I realize the braided appliqués on his sleeves are actually Kystenvarian love knots. The largest love knot lies exactly over his mating mark. My heart swells even more when I notice that the pattern on the brocade is also love knots.

I may be biased, but you're still sexy. I take my spot next to Uncle Emeric before continuing. *I may just have to find a certain little alcove tonight.* He coughs, glaring when I send him my memory of our first interlude.

"Ah, Maevery," Uncle Emeric booms. "You look beautiful." Taking my hands, he gives me a light hug and kisses my cheek.

That's just mean. A quick glance shows me Conaill's glare is firmly in place. *These pants don't exactly hide anything. I can't be greeting guests when I'm at half-mast.*

Now I'm the one choking.

"I say, Princess Maevery, is everything all right?" King Tavarik asks, and I wave him away.

"Of course, Your Majesty. Just swallowed wrong," I say, bowing my head slightly, remembering Queen Kalimina telling me to never subjugate myself to him. "I hope your journey was pleasant. Where is Queen Kalimina? I was looking forward to getting to know my future mother-in-law better."

"Ah, yes," he grumbles. "Running late. Some female thing or other." He deflects before turning to Conaill. "You really are a lucky male. She cleaned up quite well. At least getting her with an heir won't be an issue." Bile rises at his lascivious laugh.

Mask in place, Conaill sneers while looking me up and down. "As long as she doesn't talk." With that one sentence, he goes to walk over to take his place in the receiving line.

Mae, I didn't—

I cut him off. *I know. I love you, and I won't hold anything you say around them against you.*

With a chuckle, King Tavarik dismisses Conaill. "Eh. I know how he feels. Shackling yourself to a female isn't something any male really wants. Am I right, Emeric?"

"There's a reason I'm still unmarried." Uncle Emeric snickers.

My mouth drops open, and I have to remind myself to close it. "It isn't as if I'm thrilled to marry that sorry excuse for a male either." I stalk off to take my place, ignoring their responses.

I wasn't lying. Conaill stiffens next to me. *I'm not* just *thrilled to marry you. I'm ecstatic to be marrying you. Fucking ecstatic.*

He laughs softly under his breath. *Me too.*

Before long, Uncle Emeric and King Tavarik join us. Just before the doors open, Queen Kalimina takes her place. Her golden gown is beautiful and reserved. She looks exquisite, if a little sad.

Well-wishers descend as the doors are thrown open. The next hour is spent thanking fae and engaging in meaningless small talk. Faces and names fly by and by the end, I can't remember most of the names or what was said. When the receiving line is finally over, my face hurts from holding a smile for so long.

Taking my hand, Conaill places it on his to lead me into dinner. *Red?*

Yeah, Con? I say through the bond as we enter the banqueting hall.

This time tomorrow, I get to call you my wife. I can't fucking wait.

This time, the huge smile that graces my face isn't forced as we take our seats. *Me either.*

Chapter Forty-Three

Only the barest sliver of light illuminates my room before Saori throws open the curtains and orders me up. I'm exhausted. After the ten-course dinner, I was forced to mingle with guests and answer the same well-meaning, if nosey, questions repeatedly. When I crawled into bed, it was well past midnight. Anticipation keeping me awake even longer.

Even my excitement for today can't stop me from grumbling at her. I've just finished using the bathroom when a veritable platoon of maids march into my room, each saluting with a perfect curtsey. My rooms are now their command center as they busy themselves following unknown orders. A newer maid rushes over, a glass in her hand. Excitement radiates from her young face.

"As you ordered, ma'am." She hands the glass to Saori before curtseying to me and joining the maids in the bathroom.

After quickly testing the contents, Saori holds out the glass. "Drink every last drop, Your Highness. It's an energy and restorative draft. Not only will it make you feel amazingly well-rested, but it'll take care of those bags under your eyes." She leans in, examining said bags. "Hmm, maybe I should get another one. Gods know you could use those things to pack for your honeymoon."

"Hey." I playfully swat at her as she backs away, smiling. The light-yellow draft is surprisingly tasty, and within moments, I'm feeling much better.

An hour later, I've eaten, and my entire body's been scrubbed and moisturized. Every unwanted hair is gone, and my nails have all been perfectly shaped. I'm in front of my mirror, about to have my hair and makeup done, when my door is flung open.

Mina and Tilde whirl in, both sporting wet hair and fresh faces. Maids follow behind, using common magic to hold their dress bags aloft and hang them next to mine. Soon, we're all sitting in chairs as a swarm of maids buzz around us.

With sure hands, a maid with water power dries my hair, leaving it soft and silky. Once finished, she moves on to Tilde. A short time later, my hairstylist has worked wonders with my hair. She's arranged it in an artful coil low at the back of my head, leaving only a few curling tendrils to cascade down. With a curtsey, she collects her things before another maid attacks my face with what I can only describe as brutal efficiency. Powders and creams appear as if from nowhere. Brushes apply what seems like layer after layer, but somehow still manage to be weightless.

Finally, I'm allowed to look in the mirror, and I love it. I look elegant and sexy, all while still somehow managing to look natural and like myself.

"Oh, Mae," Mina exclaims, tears pooling in her eyes. "You're gorgeous!" She's lost the battle, and tears flee down her face.

"NO!" her maid reprimands, and we all jump. Clearly able to control water, the maid removes the fallen tears and any that are threatening to come. "You will not ruin your makeup. I've spent too much time making you even more perfect than you already are."

She whirls, pointing a makeup brush at each of us in turn. "Absolutely none of you are to even think of crying. I don't care how happy you are. We've all worked too hard. Should you even think you might cry, you raise your hand, and I'll take care of it." She levels us with a glare worthy of the most hardened battle general. With a curtsey, she adds, "Forgive me, Your Highness. I wish you all the happiness and blessings of the gods on this day."

With stunning efficiency, she gathers her things, heading out with the maids who've finished their jobs. As soon as the door shuts, a cacophony of laughs bounces off the walls. I have no idea who that maid is, but she's getting a bonus for helping to lighten the mood of the morning.

"Shit," Tilde says, studying the door. "I hope she didn't go far. I'm about to cry laughing."

She must've only put her things away as she is back an instant later. With a decidedly disgusted sigh, she sets about removing unshed tears and sets us to rights again. Saori gently touches my shoulder, and I turn to her.

"It's time, Your Highness." Taking my place on a dressing dais, Saori slides a screen into place, allowing me to get all my undergarments in place. I've just finished when Porvi and two of her assistants stride in. I assume it's them at least. Each is hidden behind a massive garment bag floating just above the floor, common magic allowing them not to drag.

"Your Highness." They curtsy in unison. The two assistants take their bags to Mina and Tilde to help them get dressed. Each will wear the traditional A-line, cap-sleeve dress. Their dresses are a soft lilac and fit each beautifully, last I saw them.

Porvi's smile is radiant as she brings the largest bag to stand tall in front of me. "Are you ready to see your wedding dress?" she asks, my heart skipping a beat.

"Are you kidding me?" I laugh. "I've been begging to see it. You're the sadistic one who wouldn't let me."

She waves me off. "That's because I know best. Besides, if you had seen it before, you wouldn't be able to contain your excitement, and you couldn't keep your mask in place."

She's right. She's one of only a handful of fae who know Conaill and me are mates. I didn't really have a choice when she saw the mark by accident. But I'm not thinking about that. Right now, all of my focus is drawn to the absolute work of art Porvi has revealed.

"Porvi," I whisper. "Porvi, this is the most amazing gown I've ever seen. I can't thank you enough."

"I'd do anything for you, Your Highness." She's on her knees right now, fluffing out the hem. "But, as happy as this day is, I do have some sad news. Would you be able to soundproof?"

Okay, this is weird. Quirking an eyebrow, I nod and do as she asks. Grabbing her soft hands, I help her to stand. "What's wrong?"

Looking away, she takes several deep breaths. *Wait, is she about to cry?* "I'm so sorry, Your Highness. But I fear this will be the last dress I'm able to make for you."

"What? What's wrong?" *Gods, something must be really wrong.* I'm racking my brain for answers when it hits me. "Porvi, are you afflicted? Did you lose your magic?" It has to be this. She uses magic to make her creations so amazing. She loves what she does. What will she do now if that joy is taken from her?

A single tear falls from her eyes. With a simple shake of her head, I take a deep breath and relax slightly. "No. Not yet, at least. But… it isn't safe here anymore for common fae. I'll be leaving today with my sister's family to find somewhere more sympathetic, at least until after you're crowned and can put everything to rights. We just fear that so much prejudice has infiltrated and taken root that it'll take a while to exorcise it all and make Otthon safe again. Once it happens, I'll be back here as fast as I can."

Pulling her into my arms, I hug her, putting all my affection into it. "I will, Porvi. I'll make Fenshegus safe again for everyone. I promise."

She pulls back. "I know, Your Highness. I've always known you were meant for great things." She smiles and collects herself. "Now, let's get you dressed so I can show off my finest work."

Message received. We won't talk about this anymore. It takes some time to get into the dress. At one point, Porvi actually has to sew me in. Now, as I stand on the dais, I can't help but beam.

"Mae!" Mina says breathlessly, her arm raised high. "You look like a princess!"

The maid rushes over, wiping Mina's tears as Tilde scoffs at her.

"She is a princess, Mina. Sheesh, did you start celebrating early?" Tilde sighs.

"Oh, shut it," she snaps back. "You know what I mean."

I raise my hand as well, and the maid rushes to my side now. "I really do feel like one today, Mina." I laugh.

The dress fits my figure perfectly. A delicate cream lace collar extends down my chest and arms. A plunging keyhole neckline, showing off a hint of my ample breasts. The bodice cinches my waist before flaring out into a generous bell shape. The lace overlay continues, covering the entire dress. Some parts are sheer, some are covered in exquisitely embroidered appliqués. Thousands of seed pearls and clear glass beads are hand-sewn onto the lace, enhancing the embroidery.

Graceful appliqués of peonies extend from my shoulder down the outside of my arm. They end in pointed cuffs, which extend to just past my wrists. The satin under the lace is magnificent as well. While the lace is cream, the satin is ombre. White satin covers my breasts before transitioning through a light champagne and ending in the pink of a perfectly bloomed peony. Appliqués adorn the bottom of the dress as well. The cream lace is now enhanced by pale pink peonies with soft green stems and leaves.

Porvi tells me to move, and when I do, I'm shocked. By all rights, this dress should weigh a ton. But every step I take is effortless. It's as if the pearls and beads aren't there. As if the many layers of the skirt are made from air. She's also made it so that the dress flows perfectly with me for each step.

"Porvi, this is amazing. It's so light. How?" I ask.

"Magic, my dear." She winks. "Now let's get your train on." Her eyes widen in excitement.

"There's more?" I say.

"Of course! You have to have a train." She waves me off, rolling her eyes.

"Yeah, Mae." Tilde joins in. "Every princess needs a train for her wedding."

"But it's pointless. I mean, I can't wear it at the banquet. And the ceremony itself is small," I counter.

"Mae, it's Porvi. You know she'll have figured everything out." Tilde tilts her head in question. "Besides. When is the next time you get to wear a train? You have to take every opportunity."

Did she really just say that? My face must clearly give her pause, because she tilts her head again in question. "I'll be wearing a train in a few days. You know, for my coronation."

"Yeah, but those are ceremonial robes." Mina shrugs. "Nothing exquisite like Porvi will have made. Just go with it." I roll my eyes but smile, anyway.

"You know, Mina, I always thought you were incredibly intelligent," Porvi says, smiling as she unravels a roll of fabric with a flourish, and everyone in the room gasps. The motif from the lace overlay continues on the lace of the flowing train. Only, instead of pearls or beads, tiny crystals twinkle as they catch the light. She attaches it to a hidden spot on my waist and fluffs it out. The overall effect is breathtaking.

As we admire my dress, a knock sounds on the door. Tilde goes to open it and takes a package from a maid. She hands me the note on the box first.

Maevery,

Every Roighail female has worn this tiara on their wedding day. It isn't much, but it's said to have been given to the first female of our family to be married by Astrid herself. I'm sure you have something else, but I want you to have it. In case you want to continue the family tradition.

Uncle Emeric

Opening the box, I pull out a simple but elegant golden tiara. *Oh my gods. It's real; it wasn't lost.* No one has seen it for hundreds of years. A solid plate of gold forms three mountainous points in the front, with the middle one being the tallest. The sides slope down gradually, forming the band. A cabochon emerald the size of a pearl onion anoints each of the outer points. The central emerald is almost twice as large. It's simple; there are many tiaras, much more elaborate, in the family vault. But how can I not honor tradition? While not Roighail by birth, my mother and grandmother were allowed to wear this on their wedding day.

Raising my hand, I hand Tilde the tiara, kneeling down. With tear-filled eyes, she places the tiara on my head. It fits perfectly, and I can't help but hold back a sob. The last time this was worn was when Mom married Dad. Wearing this tiara feels as if she's with me here today.

The maid with water powers has her hands full. Now everyone is crying, including her. Soon, all tears are wrestled away and conquered. After thanking everyone profusely, I grab Mina and Tilde's hands, striding confidently out of the room. A few months ago, I was dreading this day. Now, I'm walking toward the first day of the rest of my life with my mate.

Chapter Forty-Four

The grand banquet hall of the Maise Palace has been completely transformed. I've lived in this palace my whole life and have never seen it so resplendent. Garlands of flowers cascade from the ceiling and in swaths around the room. Centerpieces made up of slender golden vines shoot up from the tables before exploding out into a golden bush filled with flowers. The vines themselves are thin and tall enough not to obstruct anyone's view, while the golden bushes are thick enough to kiss the bush next to them.

Specially made drapes cover the floor-to-ceiling windows, which normally look out onto the palace square and the city. The hand-painted drapes alternate between two designs. The first is a specially made crest created by combining the royal crests of Fenshegus and Kystenvar. An ornate, intertwined M and C form a monogram on the other.

Hundreds of fae lights twinkle like stars in the sky. An effect made even more radiant by the new drapery blocking out the afternoon sun. It's these fae lights that have kept me entranced during the unending dinner. Instead of being stationary, as they normally are, they float along in the sky, moving with careless abandon.

What are you thinking about, Red? Conaill says through the bond as he brings my hand to his lips for a kiss.

How these lights remind me of the ceremony. I respond, a small smile on my lips.

In Fenshegus, wedding ceremonies are private. Only the immediate family and attendants participate. Ours was no different. It was small and intimate, just how I would want it. For me, that was only Uncle Emeric, Mina, and Tilde. In addition to his parents, Conaill had all of his siblings, as well as Madok and Prince Calian representing him.

When it was my turn to walk into the temple and meet you at the altar, all I could see was you, I explain. *You, Con. Only you held my attention. I couldn't tell you the words we recited or what prayers were said. I didn't feel the blade that cut our palms, or the silk ribbon that tied our hands and arms together. Only you and how you made me feel.*

It was the same for me. Conaill says. *When I saw you for the first time, my heart stopped. You were, and are, the most beautiful, ethereal being. Everything else just faded, and all I could see was you. I could feel your blood mix with mine, the soft skin of your arms. But honestly, I don't even know who cut us or who tied the ribbon.*

I try to hide the giggle that escapes me. *I have no idea either. The only other thing I recall is seeing the fae lights through my periphery. It felt like they were dancing around us. Like they are now.*

He smiles, but then his attention is snared by King Tavarik before he can respond. A gentle squeeze of my hand confirms his understanding. Servants hustle about the room like bees around a hive. A non-stop flurry of action. A perfectly orchestrated dance that, to the casual observer, appears as nothing more than chaos. When a server comes to remove the last of the courses, an audible sigh leaves my lips.

"Here. You looked as if you needed another glass of wine. Especially if we have to endure any more speeches." Darius winks, handing me this life-saving glass. "You look absolutely stunning, might I say, Princess Maevery."

"Why, thank you, for both the kind words and the wine," I say before taking a hearty drink. "Although, one of these days you'll have to teach me how you sneak around ever so quietly."

Done with his conversation, Conaill leans over. "I must say, Darius, I thought we were friends. Yet here you are." His tone is icy and threatening. "Bringing wine to my wife, clearly trying to get her drunk, handing her compliments, and teaching her how to sneak around? And on my wedding day, no less."

I almost laugh at Darius's confused face. Winking, Conaill laughs. "I'm so glad you could make it. Although, seeing as you didn't bring me a glass of wine…" Conaill trails off, and Darius chuckles.

"I just didn't want you to drink too much. Too much wine can make the wedding night, shall we say… problematic?" he says. "Or would uncooperative be more fitting? Poor Mae doesn't want anything drooping on her wedding night."

I laugh freely, not caring whose attention I've gained. Conaill offers me a hand, and we stand up, coming around the table to join him.

"You may have that problem, but that isn't something I've ever had to worry about," Conaill responds. "With all the single fae here tonight, maybe you should be the one watching how much you drink?"

"True, very true," Darius says, stroking his chin as if he's in deep contemplation. "But with so many options, how will I choose?"

I laugh again, happy and carefree for the first time in months. Everyone I love is safe; I'm married to my mate, and in a few days, I'll finally have the power to set my kingdom to rights. I can't even get myself to worry about Uncle Emeric and why he was suppressing my powers. I'm about to offer my opinion when Tilde joins us.

"Well, just because you have options doesn't mean they'll choose you," Tilde says before swiping Darius's glass, draining it in one long swallow. "I just got confirmation that there'll be one more speech."

A collective groan escapes us, but Tilde holds up a hand. "It's just the king regent's speech. He won't give it for a while, I'm told."

"Tilde," Darius begins. "Are you not single? Perhaps we can find some way to kill time?" His eyebrows waggle suggestively, and I try and fail not to snort at his suggestion.

Tilde eyes him up and down, licking her lips, and Darius's smile widens, turning seductive. "Yeah, that's a no." He sighs, and she pats him on his chest. "Don't feel bad, Darius. It's for your own good. You could never handle me. I'd eat you alive."

Snatching two glasses off a passing tray, she hands Darius one. "But I'm down to help you find a playmate tonight." And just like that, Darius is smiling again.

"To finding playmates," Darius says, holding his drink aloft. Calian, Madok, and Mina have joined us, and all five toast enthusiastically.

Are you seeing what I'm seeing? I ask Conaill through the bond.

Well, that would depend, he replies. *Are you seeking Madok glare daggers at Mina?*

Nodding my head, I slide my hand into his.

Well, that would be because he's too much of a chickenshit to admit he wants her. I choke on my wine as his response hits me.

Holding up my hand, I shake my head. "I'm okay." I scratch out. "Just went down the wrong pipe."

Sheesh, Red. Keep it together. The rich timber of Conaill's laugh fills my head.

I squeeze his hand before turning to Calian, ignoring his laugh.

The next hour is spent dancing and laughing. When we dance together, we hold each other as close as propriety will allow. When we aren't dancing, we mingle with those we haven't seen for a while, talking just a little longer when it is someone we like. Soon, Uncle Emeric is standing on a dais, gently tapping what looks like a dessert spoon against his crystal glass.

A hush falls through the crowd like a wave retreating from the shore. His pompous smile grows larger as all eyes land on him. *This is it,* I remind myself. After this, we can just enjoy time with those we care about and slip out whenever. Pulling me to him, his arm around my waist, Conaill must have had the same thought.

"As the king regent, at least for a few more days…" Uncle Emeric pauses to chuckle along with his usual cronies. "I'd like to thank you all for coming out to celebrate the union of Her Highness, Princess Maevery, to His Highness, Prince Conaill."

Applause breaks out, eyes turning to us. We raise our glasses in silent salute before Uncle Emeric begins again. "Not only am I happy to gain a nephew-in-law, but I feel like every citizen of Fenshegus benefits from today as well. With their joining, the kingdom of Fenshegus is also symbolically joined with that of Kystenvar." Another round of applause breaks out, prompting Uncle Emeric to bow his head slightly.

"Yes, it's a partnership that I think will be as fruitful as I hope the union of Princess Maevery and Prince Conaill will be. With that thought in mind, I wanted to share with everyone my wedding present for the happy couple. Princess Maevery, Prince Conaill, if you too could be so kind as to go stand by the windows." With an open hand, he gestures to a small, raised dais standing before the drapes. Someone must have brought that in during his speech, as it was not there before.

As we make our way there, I finally know what it must be like for a salmon swimming upstream. Our journey is fraught with obstacles in the form of over eager wedding guests. Most want to make sure they not only fawn over us, but are seen doing so. Conaill steps up first, then helps me. It takes a moment to arrange my skirts, but when they are, I look at Uncle Emeric. I expect him to continue, but instead, he stoops, talking to a guard. *Why is there a guard in here?*

A sickening smile spreads across his face as the guard speaks. It's then that I hear something. *Tap. Tap. Tap.*

Do you hear that?

His whole body is rigid. Senses on high alert. His nod is almost imperceptible as he looks for his boys. They're all next to us, standing just below the dais. Mina and Tilde, among them, are also on high alert.

I have no idea what that was. Even through the bond, he sounds uneasy. *Emeric is fucking up to something. I can feel it.*

But what can he do here? My breathing's increased, and that sense of dread has returned.

Gods, Maevery, I can feel your dread. He takes a fortifying breath before quietly calling to Darius. When Darius nods, Conaill speaks through the bond again. *Mae, do you trust me to take care of you, no matter what happens?*

I answer without hesitation. *Of course. You have my heart. I trust you with everything. You're my anchor.*

Is your blade on you? Just in case. He asks as another wave of dread rolls through me, so strong I almost buckle.

No, I almost cry. *I wasn't expecting to have to shed blood at my wedding.*

Fuck. Conaill's growl fills my mind as he draws my arm around his waist. Right to one of his ceremonial daggers. *Neither was I, but the boys, Tilde, and I put a plan in place on the off chance something happened. I have complete faith in your ability to protect yourself and anyone you want. Please know that.*

I nod again and realize Madok has moved next to Tilde and Mina, whispering to them frantically.

I've been practicing. Conaill assures me *I'm now able to glamour not only myself but also others, to look like we're doing something else entirely.* My eyes fly to his. That would take an incredible amount of power. *Do you know what Darius's power is?*

No, he refuses to say. Despite the pounding in my heart, I mentally take in the room and every potential ally or enemy. What I can use to my advantage and what I need to avoid.

Darius is able to change what someone is feeling. What their emotions are, he shares.

I'm sorry, what? He can manipulate emotions? My eyes fly to him, and as he nods, the sense of dread in me starts to retreat. *Holy shit. He can manipulate emotions.*

Yes. He's too noble to do it to anyone without their consent though. Conaill squeezes my side. *If needed, would you give him consent to alter your emotions so that we can escape if we're unable to hold a glamour? He's able to make it so you can still react and think as you would; you just won't feel them, won't show them.*

I look at Darius's soulful, deep brown eyes. They shine with care and a hint of worry. I don't even need to think. I trust that Darius wouldn't truly do anything that might hurt me. When I nod, his eyes close, and he gives me a slight bow.

"As we all know," Uncle Emeric's voice booms across the room, using common magic to magnify it. "All of our kingdoms have been dealing with the scourge of common fae losing their powers. In Fenshegus, laws were made to help reduce the spread of the blight. To prevent it from spreading to high fae. To prevent resources from being taken away from us, from the citizens of this kingdom."

Cheers sound from around the room. Bile rises at the outward display of hatred that's being accepted. Conaill grips my hand as his thoughts reach me. *Soon, Maevery. Soon you will make it right.* The tapping's gotten louder. Now sounding as if more tiny hammers have joined the fray.

"But some fae have been thinking they're above the law. Groups of fae have been coming together across all the kingdoms. Illegally smuggling in common fae affected by this mysterious scourge. Stealing resources from you. Stealing resources from the royal coffers. Resources meant for the fae of the kingdom. This is treason."

Shouts of death to traitors sound among the cheers in the room. *Con?* I cry. *Is my glamour holding?*

Yes, Mae. Our knuckles are white from how hard we cling to each other.

This has to be about me. I checked in with everyone I'm in contact with in the Order yesterday. My lungs start to constrict, and if it wasn't for my corset, I wouldn't be able to hold myself straight right now.

Mine as well. Fuck. I almost flinch at how loud Conaill's growl is in my mind. *I'll fucking kill him. I'll see him crying and begging at your feet for mercy if he so much as harms a hair on your head.*

"Yes, I'm just as mad as you," Uncle Emeric's voice has risen, almost shouting now. He pauses a moment before lowering his voice back to normal. "As you all know, Princess Maevery will be crowned in less than two weeks. I can think of no better present than helping to rid Fenshegus of those that seek to do harm to our great kingdom."

"I've spent months pursuing the leader of this so-called Order of Auxilium. Every time I thought I had them, they slipped through my fingers. But earlier this week, my fingers closed around the head traitor. And now they can't escape."

My heart is pounding so fast it must be audible to everyone around us. With what he just said, it can't be me, but who? What poor, innocent soul is taking the blame for my actions? Not only am I terrified of what's going on, but I'm also now pissed.

Maevery, I've got you. Conaill's voice is soothing, like one you'd use on a scared horse. *Anchor yourself to me. Use me as the base of your power. Your glamour is holding; I've got mine ready as backup.*

"After countless hours of… questioning," Malevolence glows in his eyes as he says this, and I know he means torture. "This traitor confessed to everything. So, to you, Princess Maevery and Prince Conaill, I give you the gift of a kingdom that has had the head cut off the treacherous snake trying to bring it down."

Applause and cheers break out, the sound almost deafening. But not loud enough to drown out the *TAP, TAP, TAP* that's risen to a crescendo.

"Now, before I reveal the traitor, I want to warn you it may be difficult for some. I never would have suspected the traitor's identity to be so. Unmistakably, why they went undetected for so long. But I want to remind you, they confessed to it all." Uncle Emeric pulls out a sheaf of parchment, dripping with official seals. "I have it here. Her written and signed confession. So, without further ado, I present you with the destruction of a traitor." Uncle Emeric bows to the bloodthirsty crowd. When he stands, light floods the banquet hall while little shadows dance around.

Maevery, Conaill practically shouts in my mind. *I'm controlling your glamour now. You don't have to look. I've got a sound shield in place. Baby, I have you.*

Turning, the first thing I notice is the birds throwing themselves at the window. All tapping with their beaks, feet, wings, whatever they can. Clearly, the source of the sound. With a deep breath, I look into the courtyard. When my brain finally processes what I'm seeing, the only thing keeping me off the floor is Conaill's strong arms caging me to his body.

Chapter Forty-Five

A bloodcurdling scream rends the air. Only when my throat starts to burn do I realize I'm the source of the scream. My worst nightmare fills my vision. In the center of the courtyard, a pyre is set, as guards stand around holding torches. Tied to the pyre, her uniform stained and bloody, Iskra is crying and screaming.

"ISKRA!" I shout, not caring that she can't hear me. "Iskra. Please, Bas, please don't take her from me, too. She's all I have left." Rivers of tears flood down my face. My arms go around Conaill; the fabric of his jacket fills my numb hands.

As one, the guards lower the torches to the pyre, and flames erupt. Orange engulfs her. Bright and searing, orange flames cover her as if it's the last clothing she'll ever wear. Once the initial flare is over, the flames lower, and I can see her battered but beautiful face. Her delicate face is screaming and crying. Her pain is clearly visible. And there's nothing I can fucking do about it.

Screaming, I collapse on the dais. "ISKRA!" I shout again. My fists pummel the glass. If I can just hit it enough, I can break it and escape to save her. I vaguely register Conaill's warmth wrapped around me. His voice murmurs something in my ear.

"Bas, please don't take her," I whimper, trying to plead with the God of Life and Death. "Please. It isn't her time yet. Please don't leave me alone. She's all I have left of them."

Suddenly, Iskra stops screaming in pain. She's crying, but she doesn't look like she's in pain anymore. I look around, frantic to find her rescuer. But there isn't one. All I see is Madok, hand stretched out touching the glass, while sweat pours down his face.

As the bright orange blaze lazily climbs up her tattered uniform, she stops crying. Her face looks serene, actually. Her head tips up and somehow, despite the glamour, finds me in the window. Her eyes lock with mine, and she smiles.

"I'm so sorry, Isk. I'm so sorry. This is all my fault," I cry, not caring that she can't hear me. "I love you, Isk. You are the best sister ever, and I'm so, so sorry."

As the flames climb higher, my vision blurs from the tears. I roughly wipe them away. I refuse to be unable to see her when I say goodbye. My hand splays on the glass, the tears they wiped away trapped. "I love you, Isk. You'll be with Mom and Dad soon. It'll be okay. I'll fix everything. I'll build a temple to Sofiya in your name. I promise Isk. I promise. I love you."

Her smile is bright as she looks at me and nods, as if she can hear me. She speaks, and I realize she's mouthing, "I love you. Don't blame yourself. I love you."

Suddenly, she stops. Her body sags, the life fading from her eyes.

"ISKRA! ISKRA!" Blood coats the glass where my skin has split from impacting repeatedly. "Iskra, I love you. I love you," I sob. I sob like I haven't since I got the news that Mom and Dad died.

"Maevery, Maevery?" I finally hear Conaill's worried voice.

I can't tear my eyes from her. I can't leave her alone. With a cracked voice, I say, "Con."

"I'm going to get you out of here. I love you. I know you're hurting. I've still got the glamour going, so do whatever you need to."

I nod against him, tears staining his jacket. Suddenly, a large warm hand presses on my shoulder.

"Maevery…" Madok's deep voice shudders. "Maevery, she wasn't in pain. Not in the end. One of my powers is to take away or enhance what someone physically feels. As soon as I could, I took the pain from her." He's silent for a second, and when he speaks again, I can tell he's been crying. "I know it isn't much, and it really changes nothing, but… she wasn't in pain. She wasn't able to feel anything."

"Thank…" I start but have to clear my throat to get it to work. "Thank you. She always liked you." Finally looking at him, I see the sweat tracks on his face. His skin has a green tint, and he looks seconds away from being sick. "Thank you for helping her."

"Hold on to me, Maevery. I'm getting you out of here. Ignore what I'm about to say. I have to remove the sound shield, but I've got you glamoured." He lifts me up into his arms and stands. I cling to him as if he's the only thing keeping all the shattered pieces of me together.

"King Regent Emeric…" Conaill somehow says clearly and boldly. "Princess Maevery and I would like to thank you for helping to stomp out this treachery." I tremble at his words. "You've done a great service to this kingdom."

"Of course," Emeric says. "As hard as this was, I had to put the good of the kingdom first."

"That you did. You've done well as regent." Conaill bows slightly, and I cling tighter. "If you may, please excuse us. I'm afraid the shock of finding out about Princess Iskra's treachery was too much for Princess Maevery, and she fainted. I'd like to get her some fresh air." Iron coats my tongue. I've bitten my fist hard enough to draw blood to keep from crying out.

"Of course, Your Highness," Emeric replies.

Immediately, we're moving. As soon as we leave the banquet hall behind. Conaill is sprinting. Running so fast that the paintings and tapestries blur. Soon, we're in my room. Safe behind closed doors.

He tries to help me out of my dress, but he can't get it. Tears are falling freely from his eyes, blurring his vision.

The dress that started as a dream this morning has morphed into my nightmare. "Just cut it," I say. "I never want to see this dress again. It'll only remind me of her."

The sound of his dagger being drawn is startling. The fabric cuts as if it were butter and suddenly, I'm free. Without pausing, Conaill slices the laces of my corset. He strips me, removes my shoes and stockings, and finds a nightdress to cover me. He then lowers me into the bed, tucking me under the covers. He's just as efficient at removing his own wedding regalia. When he's in a simple shirt and underwear, he joins me in bed.

We lay there wrapped in each other's arms, seeking warmth and solace from each other. I'm not sure how much time has passed when a knock at the door sounds. Conaill goes to check who it is before joining me back in bed.

Tilde leans down and puts herself in my sight. Black tracks trace down her cheeks, creating easy paths for the tears that are still flowing. "I'm so sorry… Madok couldn't keep taking her pain. He was going to burn out. I'm…" Her voice breaks, and she swallows. "When I realized that, I ran out, and I ended it."

I can't speak, but I don't need to. The question lingering in my mind is written clearly enough on my face.

"When I got down, I looked for anything I could find that was metal, but there was nothing. At least nothing near enough. Nothing except her necklace." I suck in a breath. Isk always wears… wore a necklace with a fire opal of some sort. "It was the only. I… I reshaped the metal. I had it pierce her heart." Tears cascade faster over her sharp cheekbones. The grip she has on my hand is so strong that I should be in pain from it. But I can't feel any more pain right now. "I'm so sorry. I didn't want her in pain. I only had a few moments before Madok would be forced to stop and… I didn't want her to be in pain again." She's sobbing now, just as hard as I am.

When I finally get my sobs under control, I lift her face to mine. "Thank you. Thank you for helping her along without pain." Tilde throws herself into me, and we hold each other as we cry.

Chapter Forty-Six

Tilde and I lay wrapped together. Conaill moved over and is at my back. At some point, Mina comes in and joins us. I only realize when Conaill gets up, giving Mina his space. I don't know how long I lay there, barely being held together by them. I only vaguely tell the time by the passing of sunlight in my room. Someone, Saori maybe, tried to get me to eat, but I couldn't. Conaill managed to get some water in me, but that's it.

Fae come in and out; some speak, but I don't process what they say. Maids and footmen come in, make a lot of noise, and then leave again. Later, Conaill and Saori bathe and dress me in simple pants and a shirt. Calian comes in saying something, and then I'm in Conaill's arms as he carries me through the palace.

He's taking me out of this nightmare. At least he thinks he is. But the nightmare is in me now. My hours have been spent cycling through a catatonic trance or reliving Iskra's last moments. Every time I close my eyes, I see hers, scared and in pain.

Mae? Conaill's gentle voice comes out as a whisper from his room in my mind. It's the first time in gods know how long he's been able to pierce my awareness. I don't have the will to speak, either verbally or through our bond, so I simply nod against his shoulder.

Maevery, I'm getting you out of here. I canceled the birthday celebration, and we won't have to come back until the coronation. It will take a while to get out of the city. There was an earthquake, and most of the roads around the palace were destroyed. It burst some of the pipes, flooding others too. Without setting me down, he climbs into a carriage and holds me close as we travel all through the night.

When the carriage rolls to a stop, I vaguely recognize the manor we're in front of. A simple but elegant four-story manor towers over us. A tickle in the back of my brain says I know this place, but I don't care enough to search for it. When an older female marches down the cream marble steps, it finally clicks into place.

This is the home Mom grew up in. It's the seat of power for the Duchy of Tearmann, and that's my grandmother striding toward me with purpose.

I wince when light floods the carriage interior. Grandma Willi stands at the open door, looking like a general about to command an army.

"Your Grace," Conaill says when we're out of the carriage. "Thank you for your hospitality. I felt it'd be best for Maevery if I could get her out of the palace. And Otthon in general."

"There's absolutely no thanks necessary." Grandma Willi's voice is sharp and clear. "I should be thanking you. I should've been there, but these old bones don't travel like they used to. And please, just call me Willi." She turns around, leading us into the manor.

"Now, I have all your rooms ready, but I need you in the study first." Conaill's still carrying me, and I only vaguely register my surroundings.

I stare, unseeing, at a slightly off-center tile on the fireplace when suddenly I'm covered in freezing water. I gasp, fully noting my surroundings for the first time since the wedding dinner. Streams of cold water fall off me, soaking the floor below.

I'm sitting in a hard wooden chair, in what used to be my grandfather's study before he died. I look around wildly. It looks the same, if smaller, because of the huge males taking up all the space. Conaill, Madok, Darius, Calian, Tilde, and Mina are here. Another male stands with them, but it's one I don't recognize. When my eyes fall on my grandma, taking her truly in for the first time, I start crying all over again.

In seconds, Grandma Willi has me in her arms, head pressed into the ample bosom she passed down to me. Tears hit my face, and I realize she's crying as well. She allows us to cry for only a moment before setting me back.

"Now, Maevery, I know you're grieving. I know what it's like losing someone too early." Her voice cracks momentarily before she trudges on. "But you can't check out. You're a strong female. You have a kingdom counting on you. You've whole races of fae counting on you to make it right. It's okay to grieve. But you have to keep living, too. Iskra would want you to live your life."

I nod, knowing she's right. She hugs me one more time before shocking me. "Now that everyone is here, like I asked, what are we going to do to kill that bastard?"

Con? What's going on? I mind-speak to him. *Why are we here? How long has it been?*

Mina got in contact with your grandmother. She told us to get you and your most trusted here with all haste. It's been three days.

"No sense glamouring your mating mark," Grandma Willi says, and our heads snap to hers. "Don't even try hiding it. I know mind-speaking when I see it. Don't forget your grandfather and I were mates, and I saw it with your parents too."

Once Conaill has removed all the glamours, she speaks again, "Now, like I said. How are we going to kill that bastard who murdered your sister?"

The next week is spent plotting and planning and then revising. I've found out the other male is Esdras, one of Conaill's best friends, the same Esdras partially responsible for the scar on his thigh. We'll be leaving this afternoon in order to get back in time for my coronation and to put our plan in motion. Conaill and I are almost finished packing when we're called to join Grandma Willi in the study.

Fury emanates from every pore as Grandma Willi paces the study like a caged predator. Bodies line the walls and it seems like everyone else was called here, too. When her steps take her to a large decanter of whiskey, she grabs a glass and fills it. Drinking it down in one go, she holds out a paper to me. A paper filled with royal seals and marks.

"That fucking, murderous bastard," Grandma Willi says, before slamming another glass of whiskey. "Read it. And then we need to do some serious planning."

As I start to read, my hands shake so badly I can't continue, collapsing into a chair. Conaill takes the paper from me and reads aloud.

Royal Proclamation of Fenshegus,

Due to the recent discovery of treachery by her sister, the former Princess Iskra, Princess Maevery has severely deteriorated. Princess Maevery was unable to remain at court due to this deterioration and fled in the middle of the night. After much consideration and deliberation, a tough decision was made. In the unanimous opinion of the Royal Council and His Majesty, the King Regent Emeric, Princess Maevery Roighail is no longer considered to be of sound mind, and therefore not fit to rule. As such, she has been stripped of her rank and removed from the line of succession. The title of King will be transferred to His Majesty, the former King Regent Emeric.

Long live, King Emeric.

The entire room erupts. A rage hotter than anything in this world burns in me. There's a lot that I'm unsure of. But I do know some things. I will not allow this to happen. I will not allow Emeric to steal my throne. I will avenge Iskra. And I will make Emeric rue the day he was born.

Epilogue

Arafa cursed as she sat in the shade of the only tree she could find in a sea of grass. Taking off her shoes, she cheered happily when she found the offending people that had snuck in. She had just completed the Great Rite. A week straight of meditation and trials in the Plains of Hope. Only one more task remained, and then she'd finally be a full citizen of Baress.

She just had to make it to the oracle first. Standing, she took a long drink from her water skin and continued. It took her two more days to reach the oracle. When she finally got to the door, she took a cleansing breath and confidently stepped over the threshold. What she didn't know was that this would merely be one step out of millions on her journey.

The oracle sat in a simple, but well-cared-for, room. Next to the oracle sat the official recorder. She'd record the oracle's words, as well as Arafa's completion of the Great Rite. Once this was done, citizenship would be bestowed.

"Come in and sit." The recorder gestured to a mustard-yellow pillow. "When the oracle holds out her hands, simply place yours in hers. Palms down, please."

Arafa did as she was told. When she placed her hands in the shockingly warm ones of the oracle, she gasped. The oracle's eyes had turned milky white, and when she spoke, it was as if the voice of hundreds was speaking in unison.

"The time is almost here. The Dochais will return when one of pure heart has risen. One willing to put aside their heart and breath for the good of all. For only with the help of the Dochais will this evil be defeated."

That was the last thing Arafa heard before unconsciousness overtook her.

Acknowledgements

We know that it takes a village to raise a child. I can now confirm it takes a village to write a book as well. There are so many people who helped me on this journey and I cannot express how much their help and support means to me.

Carly, thank you for making me get off my ass and write this story. I honestly don't know what I would have done without your initial organization of my chaotic thoughts. You never complained when I would randomly text you some of the oddest questions, especially on "those" scenes. Thank you for always giving me your honest feedback, even when I didn't want to hear it. I'm so glad I told them to shove it when they said I should be careful about having you for a friend.

Allison, Sharleen, Mya, Angela, and Nathen, thank you so much for reading my initial manuscript and giving me your honest feedback. You helped me reshape and rework to make this book what it is today. Without you, I know I would have struggled to really tell this story.

To my son. You are the reason for everything. You push me every day to be the best mom I can be and to give you an amazing life. Thank you for understanding and being patient whenever mommy needed to write. I promised you and now it is time to get you that kitty cat.

Hannah and Manolis, thank you so much for the beautiful artwork that helped my world come to life. I know it wasn't easy working with someone who didn't really know what they wanted. Somehow you figured out what I wanted before I knew myself.

To you, thank you. Thank you as a reader for coming on this journey with me. I hope this book was everything you needed it to be.

www.ingramcontent.com/pod-product-compliance
Lightning Source LLC
LaVergne TN
LVHW040214110826
845146LV00005B/1284